ORANGE
KAREN
TRIBUTE TO A WARRIOR

COMPILED BY: CHRISTINA EDSON
EDITED BY: SUSAN ETHRIDGE, JENNIFER GRACEN, STEVEN LUNA, AND K.D. MCCRITE

Visit: http://orangekaren.wordpress.com

ISBN-13: 978-1483925844
ISBN-10: 1483925846
LCCN: 2013905983

CreateSpace, North Charleston, SC
PRINTED IN THE UNITED STATES OF AMERICA

Acknowledgements

This anthology started out as a small idea. A desire to help a friend in need. With the help of a phenomenal team of people, it became so much more.

Thank you to the Orange Karen Anthology Committee: R.B. Wood, Janelle Jensen, Jesse James Freeman, K.D. McCrite, Steven Luna, Jennifer Gracen, Glenn Skinner, and Susan Ethridge. This project couldn't have got off the ground without you.

Susan Ethridge, Steven Luna, K.D. McCrite and Jennifer Gracen donated their time and editing expertise to shine and polish the amazing stories in this collection.

Glenn Skinner donated his time to format the anthology for both ebook and paperback. This book couldn't have been created without him. Well, I guess I could have used a three-hole punch and orange string, but Glenn's way is much better.

R.B. Wood has helped immensely with logistics, marketing, and researching the ins and outs of putting together a charitable endeavor.

The committee and I also owe a special, heartfelt thank you to Kip Ayers, who donated his time and costs to create a stunning cover. You captured Karen's spirit right from the start.

Finally, I'd like to offer my eternal gratitude to all the authors who submitted stories for this anthology. We received an overwhelming response, and it brought tears of joy to my eyes to know that so many people were willing to share their efforts and their talents in order to help Karen and her family.

Thank you.

Christina Esdon

Dedication

To our Orange Warrior, Karen DeLabar. Your unshakable courage, effervescent spirit, and zest for life are awe-inspiring.

Foreword

by Jennifer Gracen

If you're lucky in life, you have a best friend. (Aside from your spouse, for those of you who were about to say it's your spouse.) Your best friend is the first person you call when something goes right, because you want to share it with them more than anyone else. No one else will be happier for you than they will. And when something goes wrong, you need to hear your best friend's voice to ground you and help you feel better. That voice isn't even the voice of reason, necessarily, but the voice of your safe place. In your darkest moments, only talking to your best friend will comfort you. He or she is your emotional lifeline amid the swirling tides of life. And knowing that your best friend loves you no matter what, and accepts and appreciates you for who you are, unconditionally and completely, is a gift you never take for granted if you've got any sense.

Karen DeLabar is my best friend.

That's why I was asked to write the Foreword for this book, and I'm honored and privileged to do so.

Try to imagine how upset I was when her husband, Eric, texted me from the hospital on June 5, 2012 to tell me he'd had to bring her back to the emergency room for the second time in two days. *What?* She'd had a fever, been sick over the weekend, but what the hell? Then, as hours passed, more horrific texts streamed in from Eric. They had no idea what was wrong with her, but they were running tests. It was like a bad episode of *House*, only without the practical jokes and the cutting, irreverent sarcasm. Within hours of being admitted, Karen was transferred to ICU, intubated, and placed in something akin to a medically induced coma. She wasn't technically in a coma, but she wasn't really there, either. (Think of staring at the ceiling, no life behind the eyes, not really in a state of consciousness.) She was fighting for her life, and the doctors didn't know if she would make it.

It was three weeks shy of her thirtieth birthday.

For the ten days that she was in a coma, I walked around in a daze, devastated, my insides churning with terror. I had just seen her... she had been *fine*. Less than two weeks before, Karen, Janelle, and I had enjoyed the most wonderful weekend together. I couldn't wrap my head around it. Karen couldn't *die*. She was young, she'd been extremely healthy and fit prior to this mystery illness, she was beloved by many... and, most poignantly, a mother to two beautiful little girls, ages two and four. She couldn't *die*.

Strangely enough, in the grand scheme of things, I actually haven't known Karen for that long. She and I met on Twitter, of all places, in April 2011. We chatted a few times, and I liked her immediately. You hear the phrase "zest for life" thrown around, but Karen obviously really had that. She was vibrant, smart, funny, positive, and open. The kind of person it's really hard not to like, because you can just tell it's all sincere, authentic, not an act. But one day in early May, she sent out a tweet that was unlike her usual sunny tweets; she was sad, upset. Something in her tone, even though it was just a tweet, struck me. Made me want to *talk* to her, to reach out to her. (I can't help it: I'm a nurturer. It's in my DNA.)

So, I messaged her privately and asked her to call me, which she did within a few minutes. We were on the phone for over an hour —

BOOM. An instant and genuine connection. And that was it. From then on, we spoke on the phone every other day, and chatted online or sent texts every day. In each other, we found the truest kind of friendship: genuine understanding, appreciation, and acceptance. I am fortunate to say that I have many friends, and always have. But rarely had I ever made a connection like I did with Karen. Serendipity. And, luckily, we live only 2 ½ hours away from each other, so we were able to meet in person by July. When I saw her across the hotel lobby and she rushed over to hug me, it was like hugging a long-lost sister.

Karen and I feel things passionately; we love big and bold, and the main objects of our passion are the same. Family, especially our children (she has 2 girls, I have 2 boys). Friends, both "in real life" and online. The arts, particularly books and music. And, of course, writing. We have so much in common. So what if she's twelve years younger than me. Soul connections don't pay attention to calendars.

Karen wasn't just a wife, daughter, and stay-at-home mother before Toxic Shock Syndrome tried to take her life. She was an active member of her community. She spent time with her family and friends. She went to Gold's Gym almost every day for workouts and classes, sometimes going twice a day. She was a longtime member of the Catasauqua Area Showcase Theater Company, having participated in several shows. She sang in her church choir. And, in early 2011, she became an active presence on Twitter. There, she met other like-minded people, writers from all over. She began interacting with them just because she's friendly. She likes to talk to people. She was genuine, and that showed. To some in the Twitterverse, she was a smiling, adorkable (her word, and it describes her perfectly) friend to chat with; more than that, in time she became a prolific book reviewer and a vocal supporter of indie authors/publishing. And did I already mention her devotion to her high school sweetheart and husband, Eric — he with the golden heart and moral code of a Boy Scout — and her two tiny, precious daughters, Lily (aka Peanut) and Joss (aka Trouble)? Okay, just making sure.

So perhaps you have a fuller picture now: Karen was a well-rounded force of nature when Toxic Shock Syndrome tried to take her away from the life she'd lived so passionately and all of the people who loved her and valued her so fiercely. A sudden, awful illness is horrible for anyone; the fact that it was happening to someone like Karen — not even 30! a mother to two young kids! friend to so many! a freaking gym rat! adorkable! — made it all the more devastating.

Eric would send texts with updates on Karen to me and our other sister of the heart, Janelle Jensen; then Janelle and I would post on Twitter and Facebook to everyone else. The news of Karen's sudden illness and frightening fight for life brought an outpouring of love and concern on the Internet, the likes of which I had never seen before. These "online people" — people who'd never even met Karen — responded with overwhelming compassion and worry. *Hundreds* of them.

They tweeted back, kept an online grapevine going to let others know what was going on, asked people in their "real" lives to pray for Karen... one man, a Twitter friend all the way out in Washington State, contacted me one night to ask how he could send a pizza to the hospital. He wanted to make sure Eric would eat something. (Case, you *mensch*. You restored my faith in mankind that day, with your small but amazingly heartfelt gesture.) Eric sent out a link to the hospital so people could send Karen e-cards and get well wishes... and the number of incoming cards shut down the hospital's printers for a day. The staff said they'd never seen that kind of response for a patient before. The walls of her room in ICU were covered with messages of encouragement and compassion; Eric made it a point to put them all up so she'd see them when she woke up from her coma. We all waited, hoped, and prayed, collectively holding our breath.

Thankfully, Karen *did* wake up from her coma. She did survive. After all, she is the Orange Warrior — just ask any of her friends. In the months that followed, she fought her way back to a normal life, despite constant pain and uncertainty — weeks after she regained consciousness, doctors were still unsure whether amputations would be necessary. For two months, she spent two hours a day, five days a week in a hyperbaric chamber, in the hope that she'd be able to keep her fingers and feet — tissue death is almost inevitable with TSS, and the extremities are usually hardest hit. She became addicted to the powerful pain meds that were initially necessary to manage her condition, and then suffered through withdrawal from them. Finally, she endured the amputation of her left pinky toe and several reconstructive surgeries on her left thumb. And as I write this in February, eight months after her hospitalization, she still goes to hand therapy twice a week, and will for some time to come. They still don't know if she'll ever have full movement in her thumb and index finger again.

But she's back at the gym now. She participated in a three hour spin-a-thon in mid-February, a benefit for pediatric cancer. Yes, you read that right. She'd done it last year, and she was determined to do it again this year. It is that fighting spirit, that determination and grit, that unwillingness to give up or give in, that saw Karen through her illness. It is that heart, filled with generosity and goodness in spite of everything she has endured, which inspires others to love and admire her so.

Karen honestly has no idea why her story has affected so many people. (Duh. Because she's adorable.) But as her best friend, someone in her inner circle, someone who knows, I can tell you how overwhelmed and grateful, how simply mindblown she has been by it all. She was humbled by and grateful for every card, every tweet and post, every prayer, every wish she received for her return to good health and her return to her family and friends. She still is. Always will be.

The Anthology is almost complete, and as I thought about what I wanted to say in this foreword, something occurred to me. This collection of stories was created by a group of writers who simply wanted to help Karen, our friend in need, with her massive medical bills. But it has become so much more than that. This book has become a testament to the truth and power of friendship —

specifically, the validity of friendships originally forged online. The Internet has pervaded every aspect of our lives in recent years, and yet there are still some who espouse the notion that friendships made online somehow aren't "real". As though the fact that a handful or even a bucketful of dishonest people who misrepresent themselves in the digital world automatically devalue every truthful intention of every other honest person on the Net. Can you say "fallacy?"

Karen and I had *many* talks about this before she got sick, and certainly have after. We didn't, and still don't, understand the naysayers and their need to disparage, belittle, or even vilify friendships formed by people who met online. Well, guess what? This unique, amazing collection of stories proves them, and that whole notion, wrong — spells it out in neon orange letters, as a matter of fact. Everyone involved did so purely because they had met Karen online, liked her, and wanted to do something to help. That was their only motive. That goes for every author who contributed a story to this anthology — as well as the fifteen or so authors who didn't make it in, but sent a story. The same can be said of the main OKA group who oversaw the whole project, the editors, the proofreaders, the guy who handled the manuscript formatting (thanks, Glenn!) and the guy who designed the cover (thanks, Kip!). If those aren't "real" friendships, "real" feelings, then I don't know what "real" is.

So there you have it. This book is for Karen, but it's also so much more. I am unspeakably proud to be a part of this unique project. If you bought a copy of this Anthology, I thank you from the bottom of my big, goopy heart. I know I can speak for my best friend on this one and say that Karen does too.

Table of Contents

Introduction

by Karen DeLabar

When I look back over the events of the summer of 2012, one thought comes to my mind: dying would have been easier.

On Saturday, June 2, 2012, I was getting my four-year-old daughter ready for her very first dance recital. I've always had my foot on the stage, so this was a big day for me as well. Unfortunately, I felt like I was hit by a bus. My hands shook while I braided her hair and twisted it into a cute little ballerina bun, and I wiped sweat from my brow when I loaded her into the car. I kept telling myself to get through the night, that I was a stage mom and I wasn't going to let a stupid summer cold keep me from this.

As the night went on I became weaker, often swaying in the wings while little ballerinas flittered around me. Other moms offered to watch my daughter so I could leave, but I was adamant: I would sooner die than miss her dance. I should have known God had a sense of humor. I fell asleep that night with a 102 degree fever, not yet high enough for a trip to the ER. I compared my symptoms to a stomach bug that was going around. I tossed and turned that night

hoping the next day would be better. The fever continued through to the next day and finally reached over 103 that night. Off to the ER I went. After a round of blood tests and some fluids, my fever lowered. I was diagnosed with "something viral" and was sent home. I was told it could take up to two weeks to feel better. Lovely.

On Monday, my fever broke; unfortunately, it also felt like my body broke, as well. I couldn't move. Pain worse than labor pain pounded through my body, centering around my neck and shoulders. By Monday night I was laying in front of our bedroom's air conditioner, sweating and shaking. Tuesday morning, my husband, Eric, and I wondered if I should go back to the ER, but the doctor's voice telling us it was viral was still echoing in our minds. Not to mention the $100 copay for the ER visit that we just didn't have.

Hoping a shower would loosen up my body, I somehow made it to the bathroom — only to get sick several times. I'd finally had enough. I thought, "Let them send me home again, I'm going back to the hospital."

Later, I was told numerous times that had I not gone back, I would have died at home later that day.

We arrived at the ER around 7 AM, and by 7 PM, I was admitted into the ICU. My heart was pumping at a mere 25%; a normal range is between 55-60%. The doctors and nurses wondered how I'd even managed to walk in on my own accord. They intubated me and told my husband to go home for the night. With the doctors' word that they'd call if anything changed, he left. And I started to crash.

When he walked back into the ICU the next morning, instead of seeing a conscious and healing wife, Eric was greeted by a kidney doctor throwing out ways to prevent kidney failure. I was hooked up to an additional thirteen machines, including an IV that provided hypnotics. These drugs allowed me to move my body when needed for tests, but would bless me with no memory of the events. The unknown infection was taking over my body, causing it to throw out random clots. Rushing against the clocks, the doctors hooked me up to IV machines pumping lopressors, medicines designed to pull blood in to my core to protect the vital organs. This quick thinking saved my life, but doomed my extremities that had already lost blood flow. The toxins pooled where there was decreased blood flow, causing an intense rash. The rash later turned to blisters, which popped, leaving open wounds — disgusting, angry, limb losing wounds.

The doctors were stumped. They tested me for almost every disease known to man, but nothing was coming back with answers. They interrogated Eric about what I ate and where I'd gone.

They inspected every cut, scrape, and black and blue mark on my body — and with two young, energetic kids, I had a lot of places to check.

When the four different antibiotics they placed me on took care of the infection, and they weaned me off of the more invasive medicines and machines, they took me off the ventilator. I was in the ICU for ten days; I remember none of it. Although the hypnotics didn't put me in a coma, some referred to my time out as such because of the state of my consciousness. Most of the time, my family was met with what my dad called the "thousand mile stare". I would just stare at the ceiling, at some far off place no one but me could see. There would be no sign of life in there, just eyes. However, other times I'd be alert and flipping off my brothers, or trying to rip the tube out of my throat. My parents told me that seeing me fight off the nurses brought them more hope than when I laid there nicely taking my medicines like a good girl. It meant I was still in there, fighting.

Just before consciously waking, I had several dreams that will stay with me for the rest of my life. Some, thanks to the high doses of narcotics, were just plain crazy and lovely at the same time. But there is one in particular that I think helped define not only my recovery, but me. The specifics of the dream are long and detailed, but what only really matters is the last portion of it. I'm lying in what appears to be a 1950s hospital room, with a shiny black and white checkered tile floor. The nurse struggling to keep my arms down has her dark hair pulled up in a high bouffant hair-do with a nurse's cap stuck on top of it. Her ruby red lips are drawn up in a snarl as she throws her weight on top of me to stop my struggling.

My body is thrashing from side to side, and I can hear myself sobbing silently, "It's too late, I'm gone." Fear coursed through me and I turned my head towards an open window. The scene outside was breathtaking. A white picket fence stood just outside the window, with the greenest pasture outside of Ireland stretching out for miles. The colors were so vibrant against the drab hospital room that it took my already labored breath away.

Just then I heard my husband's soothing voice. "Don't fight, Karen. It's going to be okay." Misunderstanding his message, rage bubbled up inside of me, and I thought of my two precious daughters. At just two and four years old, I could not imagine not being there to kiss their booboos away. I refused to believe I wouldn't be there for catching fireflies on a summer night, doing their hair for school dances, or consoling them through their first heartbreak. I made myself fight harder. I bucked and swung and tried my hardest to scream to the doctors, to my husband, to God, that I was not ready to die. The harder I pushed against their confining arms, the louder they tried to console me, until everything went white. That's when I woke to my brother and husband.

It turns out that while I was finding my courage, they were trying to take my tube out. I was fighting them because in my confused state, I thought they were telling me it was over and to let go. In reality, they were telling me to calm down so they could take the tube out properly. My first few days awake were difficult for me. I couldn't understand what had happened. I saw the wounds on my feet, my thumb was hard, black, and deflated, yet I asked the doctor if I'd be out in time for the Warrior Dash that was taking place in three days. Looking back, I believe ignorance was the bliss that helped save my sanity.

I had no idea that I would have to learn how to swallow again, or that my dad wouldn't be able to watch my weak attempt of feeding myself and would have to leave the room. I was completely unaware that being in a bed for just two weeks would rob me of all the muscle and strength I worked for over three years in the gym to get. I'll always remember my mom's tear rimmed eyes as I made those three hobbled steps towards her that stole my breath and left me shaky for hours afterward. Pain would ravage my body for months, leaving me screaming into pillows at night so I wouldn't wake my children. If I would have realized that then and there, my story might have gone differently.

Nurses and doctors tried to make me understand that my road to recovery was going to be a long and rocky one, but their words always fell on deaf ears. "Yeah, yeah, I get it, Doc, long road, whatever. I'm not going anywhere, I've got time."

Giving up has never been an option for me. Even when the podiatrist told me that there was a possibility of double amputation up to the knees, I just knew deep down that I would make it work. I spent two hours every day for fifty five days in a hyperbaric chamber, praying that the elevated circulation of pure oxygen at twice the atmospheric pressure the chamber provided would save my feet. I now have two feet and nine toes. I like to think my left pinky toe gave the ultimate sacrifice to save my feet.

I worked with several hand specialists before I found a wonderful microsurgeon in Philadelphia, who reconstructed my dead left thumb using tissue from my arm. It's a long process with multiple surgeries, and by the end I'll have a working thumb again.

I always thought of myself as a strong person, but it wasn't until I heard the stories of my time while I was under hypnotics that I fully understood my strength. I was on enough meds to down a 300 pound man for a week, and yet I fought to take my own tube out. I even tried to take out a nurse when she tried to restrain me.

Simply put, I don't quit.

On days when my feet don't work, or the pain is too much for me, I remember my dream. My subconscious mind was reminding me that I'm a fighter. I truly believed my time was up… and yet I pushed harder. I didn't let anyone, not even my perceived death, stand in my way. If I can do that subconsciously, I can think that way consciously. Some days, it takes everything I have to put a smile on my face, but I remember to do it at least once. After all, what's the point of living if you can't smile? I would have fought for nothing if that was the case.

Life is truly a blessed and beautiful thing. I have many mementos — by way of scars, pain, and overall way of life — that remind me what I went through to ensure that I have a life to live. Whenever pettiness and pride creep in to ruin my day, all I have to do is look down to my hands or feet to remember how precious life is.

Life can be so chaotic that we forget to slow down and appreciate this gift that was given to us. Because no matter what your beliefs are, whether it was given to you by your parents or from God, life is a gift.

It's true that I do look back and sometimes think it could have been easier, but then, I never do anything the easy way. I'm a fighter. I fight.

In Collusion With Trees

by Jesse James Freeman

Y ou can knock until your knuckles bleed." She couldn't get far enough away from the door to make her feel safe. Thankfully, there was a bolt she was able to latch. She crouched under a window. The panes had been patch-worked over with newsprint. "I'm never opening that door." She was sure of this and she repeated the sentiment, as much for her own benefit as for what was on the other side of it. "Never."

A farm house. Why was she in a farm house? She'd never even seen a farm. She'd barely ever left the city. How was there a farm? Grandma wallpaper pattern and paint peeling wood chipped trim. This place was abandoned, forgotten, off the map.

Well, not entirely abandoned.

"You're not the first to lock themselves in that room." The knocking had stopped and was replaced by the voice on the other side of the door.

"How many times have you done this before?"

"Many times."

Her elbow was pressed into an ancient toilet, the kind she'd only seen in books. The tank was mounted high on the wall and had a pull-chain. The smashed porcelain pieces at her feet had once been a sink. Water hadn't flowed into this place in a long time. There was barely light. There were no smells. There was no...

"Why can't I see colors?"

Light traveling to her eyes registered all wrong. Most things were a dull grey. Light was too white. Shadow was too deep.

"Why would you need to?" That's what the voice asked her.

Why would she need to?
She rubbed her eyes until they formed tears. Maybe she rubbed them until they bled. She had no way of knowing the difference between blood and tears. She watched the droplets that clung to her hands and slowly ran across the lines of her palm.

Sad, fortune-telling rivers.

"How long are you going to stand on the other side of that door?" She pushed her back more firmly into the cracked wallpaper under the window. She stared up, trying to find the yellow in the sunshine that broke through the cracks in the paper covering the glass panes. "What do you want with me?"

She had nothing. There was no rectangle of glass and plastic pressing its shape into the denim pocket of her grey jeans as she pulled her knees into her chest. The glowing screen had kept her entire life stored within it, and was the spider-web that held close to her all that she had loved. She smiled just a little when she was able to remember her own name — it seemed odd that was possible.

It struck her as funny, all those pieces of plastic that made us who we were in the world.

"I'm not going anywhere," said the voice. *"I have to stay until you unlatch the door."*

"The floor'll rot out from under your feet before that happens."

"I have to lead you down the hallway."

Her hand reached for a triangular shard of porcelain. Even white didn't look right to her eyes. She let her hair fall into her face, the strands were colorless.

There was no yellow in the linear pattern of light cast from the window to the wall before her. Her hand tightened on the shard from the broken sink.

"Why do you want to lead me down the hall? What's down the hall?"

"Something."

"There are already somethings where I am now." She looked away from the door. "I have an old-timey poop-throne."

"There is nothing in that room."

She closed her eyes — because maybe when she opened them again...?

"I'm in this room."

"That's what I said. There is nothing in that room."

She hadn't made the decision to jump from the floor and make a run at the door. It just happened. She slammed her shoulder hard into the wood and the door shook but the latch held. Then she was banging her palm into wood.

"Go away, asshole. Before I break this door down myself."

The door shook and the echo was heavy in the room, but the hinges were strong. She only stopped when it didn't make sense to keep going any longer.

"You can simply unlatch the door and turn the knob."

"Yeah! I know that." She put her back to the door and crossed her arms. Her hand stung, but only for an instant. "I just want you to go away."

"Why?"

"Because..."

"Because why?"

"There are a lot of becauses! One-because is that I don't know who you are or why I'm locked in here. Two-because is that I don't even know where this is..."

"So, two becauses?"

"Fuck you, asshole. There's a three-because."

"What is three-because?"

"I'm not telling you three-because."

"W..."

"Don't say why!"

"I was not going to."

"You're a liar."

"Why?"

She pushed herself from the door and crossed the room. Her fingers realized they were still holding a porcelain shard and she let it drop to the floor. She wasn't opening the door and there was no need for a weapon. She wasn't even sure if that was why she had picked it up in the first place.

She needed a weapon against the voice. Right?

"Three-because is that you hurt my feelings."

"That's impossible."

She let her fingers run across the newspaper that covered the window. It was so old she couldn't read the words printed on it.

"Why is that impossible?"

"It's illogical that you consider yourself possessing such."

"Arguing with you is worse than any boyfriend ever."

She pressed her finger into a hole in the newspaper. The sunlight wasn't warm on her fingertip.

"I wouldn't speak to you at all. If you would just unlatch the door."

"Four-because isn't going to let me open that door."

"How did I hurt your feelings?"

"Forget it, weirdo. We're not bonding any more than we already have."

"It's because I told you there's nothing in the room, isn't it?"

She spun on her heel and was yelling again. "Oh, you think? How can there be nothing in the room when I'm in here? I'm definitely a something. Who do you think you're talking to?"

"What makes you a something?"

She realized her arm was raised and finger was pointing squarely at the door. She'd always hated how she couldn't help using her hands to emphasize her words when she got angry. That she was pointing to a voice on the other side of a door in a forgotten bathroom made the act seem even more irrational.

"That's the stupidest thing anyone has ever said to me."

"So tell me."

She put her hands in her pockets and turned away from the door. "I don't know."

"Open the door."

"No."

"Then tell me."

She pushed her fingers into the newspaper on the window and liked the sound it made as it ripped and tore. "Tell me where I am! What is this place?"

"There's nothing out there, either."

"I don't believe you."

She shoved her hands apart and the paper tore and crumbled. The dirty light was blinding. She kept pulling until the window was cleared of obstructions.

Until she could press her fingertips to the glass.

Her eyes adjusted to a black and white world. A planet overcast in haze and fog that she stared through from the second floor window. There was a sloping roof of old shingles that made a perilous descent toward a field of tall grass.

"Why did you take all the color away from the world?" She blamed the voice. "Isn't it enough that I'm trapped in here?"

"There is nothing in there. You are not trapped."

"I've never even seen a farm. A real farm. Is that what this is?" She tried to make out the grass swaying in the wind through the fog. There were trees beyond.

"There is nothing..."

"'...out there.' Yeah, you told me that already."

"Come unlatch the door. Come walk down the hall. It is the only direction in which you will find somethings."

"There are trees."

"What if there are?"

"You admit to trees?"

"They are not for you."

"You're hoarding trees?"

"Disregard trees."

"You're in collusion with trees?"

She gripped the top of the window and pushed a little. There was a splintered gasp.

"Haven't you had enough?"

"Enough what?" She grunted. "Lies?"

"I am not the one who has told lies."

"I'm lying to myself, then?"

"You are prolonging."

"If you've got somewhere to be..." She pushed up and strained her legs. "...don't let me keep you."

"I cannot go down the hallway without you."

"I'm not going down the fucking hallway."

"I'm sorry."

"I don't want your damn apology."

"No. I'm sorry for all the pain."

She stepped back from the window. She had cracked it just a sliver. "You're responsible for all the pain? Because there was a lot of it."

"I mean the pain that is to come."

There was a quiver in the muscles of her hand. The voice was right — there had been a lot of pain.

"How could it be any worse than what it was?"

"So you do remember?"

"Of course I remember. There's no way I could forget." She watched her fingers flex.

"This is why you won't unlatch the door."

"Shut up." She pressed her shoulder into the window and pushed up hard. "Isn't that what..." She heard the wood crack. "...what it's all about?"

"It does not have to be."

The window barely moved. "That's part of being alive." Her eyes strained and she groaned as she pushed. She could make out the grey grass swaying over a colorless landscape. There were trees beyond the fog.

"There is nothing in that room. Do you not understand?"

She took a step back. "But there is something if I go with you?"

"If you unlatch the door, there will be no more pain."

She ran her fingers into her hair. The window hadn't moved another inch. Her shoulder ached. She remembered how unbearable everything had been before. She rubbed it and looked over her shoulder at the door. "Life?"

"Is pain."

"It hurt." There was no confusion regarding tears then.

"The hallway awaits."

"The something. What is it?"

"It is what it is not. There is no pain."

She could barely make out the tops of the tall grass dancing with the wind. "I never believed in a place with no constant ache."

"Ten steps. No more and no less, once you've crossed the threshold."

"So many holes in my heart… no matter how much I poured into it…"

"…it could never be filled."

She considered the latch — she couldn't stand much more of the emptiness that had stolen all the colors. Ten steps beyond. No more and no less. She could feel the wind seeping in from the crack in the window she'd pushed up with all she had in her. The cool brought her gaze back to the window glass.

There was nothing in the room. There was nothing out that window. Just a world that had turned grey and black — barely lit by a colorless sun.

"No more?"

"No less."

It was the wind that pressed it against the window. After the start that shook her, she almost turned from it to walk to the latch. She tried to make herself turn away from it, but she could not. She was already walking back to the glass before she even realized why. How was it that something so ordinary that she had disregarded every day of a life — a life she could scarcely remember — had become so fascinating suddenly?

She pressed her hand to the glass. The wind held the leaf tight against it and she cursed the fact that there was anything between it and her hand. She traced her fingernail against the glass, painting an invisible outline around the pattern of what the storm had brought to her.

It was the most beautiful thing she had ever seen.

"It's past time." The voice was sure of itself. *"It is time to walk to the latch."*

She pressed her lips to the cold glass and kissed the pane. The leaf held in place as the grass tilted this way and that, and the fog pushed off the field just enough so that she could see beyond. She had not been wrong.

The leaf against the glass was bright orange.

"There is only pain."

She began backing towards the door. "But there are trees."

She didn't take her eyes from the color that burned off the leaf on the window — and she had never run faster or jumped higher. She laughed when the glass cut her skin. Never had she felt so alive as when she tumbled down the slanted roof through broken shards so she might crash to the ground.

She had a field to run through and a forest of orange-leafed trees to explore.

The voice on the other side of the door smiled before walking down the hallway alone.

Jesse James Freeman is the author of *Billy Purgatory: I am the Devil Bird* and *Billy Purgatory and the Curse of the Satanic Five*. He was a contributor to *Write for the Fight: A Collection of Seasonal Essays* and *Nightfalls: Notes from the end of the world*. When not writing, he is at war with cobras, lasers, yetis, goats, and people who understand proper comma placement. He lives in a double-wide trailer in an undisclosed remote area of Texas.

Henley's Scars

by February Grace

Henley is old now, and so am I.

At least, that's the way I feel sometimes, when I look at him and remember all that we have been through together.

He was a gift from my grandmother to me when I was four; every stitch in his little body knitted with loving care. It didn't matter that he wasn't fancy like the teddy bears at the toy store; that his arms and legs didn't bend, but were always curiously splayed out as if he was surprised by something, and had jumped in shock and frozen that way.

It never mattered to me that his left eye was a little bit bigger and lower set than the right, or that his fur was a curious shade of bright orange not naturally found on bears in the wild. All that mattered to me was that Grandma had made him, just for me, and told me that he was always going to be there.

He was always there, through many adventures and washing machine cycles and dryer tumbles, to clean him all up after I had a cold or tonsillitis or some other manner of childhood illness. I attributed super-hero powers to him in my small mind, imagining that only someone made of extraordinary material could survive the trip through such hot and violent machinery. I never seemed to notice that every time, he came out of the process a little older; that his stitches would be looser, his stuffing just a little flatter. Sometimes a stitch would pull and I would tearfully take him to my grandmother, who would lovingly find the closest-matching yarn she had in her stash at the time, get out a needle, and begin to sew over it.

That is how Henley got his scars, and to me, each one made him more perfect.

Each line was a little victory over unraveling; and I always marveled that she left no visible knots, even though knotting the yarn would have been a much faster way of finishing off the repair work.

No, she never took short cuts where he was concerned. She took great care with him, as she always did with me. And the older I get, the more I appreciate not only the craftsmanship that went into designing my little sunshine-colored companion, but the love and affection that went into maintaining him as a stable presence in my life.

No matter what went wrong, Henley was always there. I soaked his 'fur', worn and threadbare in spots even where there were no 'scars', with my tears on more occasions than I can count. He never seemed to mind.

When I went away from home, he was always my link back to it, to safety, to warmth and love in my grandmother's arms; a magical place unequaled anywhere else, even in the embrace of my own mother.

Henley went on airplane rides with me and took long, hot summer vacations. He rode in the car, always seat-belted in securely beside me. He was my first thought in the morning, and my last at night, as I snuggled him close under my arm and never let him go.

Once or twice there was a real scare concerning his condition. The day I turned six, a large hole appeared and his stuffing began to leak out. Later that year his eyes began to fray, and I was terrified he would go blind.

Over the years those eyes were sewn back on many times, changing his expression slightly every so often, in ways that only I was aware of. Each new configuration of his features seemed to add to his wisdom, and so too, mine as I grew. Our imaginary conversations became more involved and complicated.

I hated it whenever anyone tried to tell me what Henley was thinking, or worse, saying. No one should ever put words in a teddy bear's mouth, I declared; only they know what they're really thinking and only their specific child can interpret it to the world.

My mother never liked it when Henley was interpreted as saying that he hated raisins in his oatmeal, and so did I.

Many times over the years, my friends tried to talk me out of carrying Henley around with me, or, when I got older, from displaying him on my bed. He was to be replaced, they said, first by dolls, then by electronics, and finally by a boy's gifts — gaudy bears with rough synthetic coats and lifeless plastic eyes, won for me at carnival games and school Spring Flings.

I'd always end up giving such trophies away to younger siblings and their friends, feeling that to keep them would somehow be disloyal to my best friend, my one and only bright orange Henley, with his precious, artful scars.

I'm not ashamed to admit that Henley came with me on my honeymoon. Instead of making fun of me, the man I married understood that Henley was a member of the family and treated him as such. Henley has been photographed with landmarks and monuments alike, each picture lovingly arranged and appropriately captioned in his own special scrapbook.

Every trip he'd come back a little more worn, a little more frail. I never dreamed of attempting to repair him myself, though, no matter how old I got. That was a job that only one pair of skilled and loving hands could do.

So I would pack him up carefully and take him to see Grandma, and she would strain to see with aging eyes where the old stitches left off and begin to stitch in new thread, to give an old friend life again.

"We all have our scars, don't we little guy?" she would say so gently, as she tucked in a little fresh stuffing to add to the old, sewed over the hole or weak spot, and always finished by giving him a little kiss on top of the head.

Every time she handed that bear back to me, I would feel the same love that I'd felt for him, and for her, when I was four.

Never did I imagine this day would come.

Henley has a little hole in his leg, and it really needs repairing, but I cannot take him to see Grandma now.

I never accepted that the day would inevitably come when he would outlive his creator, but it has.

She is gone, and I don't know how to fix him, or where I'll find the strength to try. Even though when I close my eyes, I can hear her voice as clear as day, telling me just where to begin a row of stitches over the original knitting and when to finish it off, it is something that I just can't imagine doing myself. Henley has a hole in him, but it is nowhere near the size of the hole in my heart.

Henley is getting old, and so am I.

His fur has faded from bright orange to a muted, pumpkin color that I can't quite find the correct shade to match.

It doesn't matter, though.

Today I will get out a needle and yarn, and I will do my best to repair him, standing instead of the woman who cannot be replaced.

If Henley could talk to you right now, the way he talks to me, he'd tell you that it's our scars that make us beautiful. They prove that we're alive, that we're survivors.

Henley and I will somehow learn to survive without the presence of the one who made him.

He will endure my clumsy repair work, and I will remember how loved I have always been.

I will learn to accept the changes and loss that come with aging as we grow old together; beautiful, flawed little Henley, and me.

∽o∾

February Grace is a published artist, writer, and poet. Her work has appeared in *The Rusty Nail, Vine Leaves Literary Journal, Rose & Thorn Journal,* and *Poetry Pact Volume One, 2011*. She released her debut novel, GODSPEED, in 2012.

Change Finds You

by Cara Michaels

T he date of record is October thirtieth, two-thousand-twelve. This is Special Agent Everett Benjamin."

The voice drew my attention from the digital voice recorder resting on the table. The red recording light assured everyone observing that my words would be captured for all time, with "all time" defined as "until the Gemini Group buried the story". At best, anything I said today would end up in a heavily redacted report buried in some government archive. Hadn't stopped me from trying to get the word out, though. No, the FBI could take credit there. Getting nabbed at a convenience store just proved I'd never been intended for the undercover life. I'd only lasted two months on the official run.

"For the record, please state your name." The special agent sitting across from me held an air of comfortable superiority. As homegrown investigative organizations rated, he still believed his FBI sat at the top of the food chain.

How sweet.

"Dr. Savannah Welborn."

"Thank you, Doctor." For a tough FBI guy, he had a nice voice. Kind of deep, kind of mellow.

The pen held between his index and middle fingers drummed an uneven, impatient beat. The air conditioning kicked on, a background hum of recycled air smelling faintly of paper and dust. Like the room needed to be colder. What brainless desk jockey thought hypothermia contributed to productivity? The beds of my fingernails had turned blue some fifteen minutes of waiting ago. My body had already forgotten how it felt to be warm. Inside, outside, and everywhere in between. I ground my teeth to hold in a shiver.

"Not a problem, Agent Benjamin," I said. I even flashed my gritted teeth as I smiled. Just call me Doctor Cooperative.

His gaze slid over my Celldweller concert tee. Beneath the table, worn blue jeans allowed refrigerated air to sneak in at the torn knees. Like I needed his visual disdain to tell me I was way underdressed for a federal interrogation. They didn't do anything without a tie or stockings.

At least my feet stayed warm in socks and sneakers.

"Sorry," I said. "I didn't get apprehended in my Sunday best. I'll try harder next time."

His lips pinched, biting down on whatever he wanted to say and emphasizing his stern features. Add a sense of humor and strip away the premature aging of his job, and I put him in his early thirties, maybe. Salt dashed his black pepper hair, the cut military short.

"You understand why you're here, yes?" he asked.

"I can play stupid if you'd prefer to explain it for the viewers at home." I gestured to the large mirror dominating the end of the room on my left.

Benjamin clenched his teeth, let out a slow breath.

"You've been charged with obstruction of an ongoing investigation, as well as aiding and abetting the vigilante organization known as the Paladins."

He made a good show of flipping through a manila folder stuffed with evidence. Of my so-called crimes, no doubt. My actions over the last several years tied me to the Paladins and — if one knew where to look — to the Gemini Group who had unintentionally created them. I'd built the Gemini Group, created the experiments, written the procedures. I'd documented its transition into a monster as the sons and daughters of my trial groups grew and revealed the changes in their genetic codes.

The cells made to save their parents had resulted in unexpected, even terrifying mutations. A woman with Ehler Danlos Syndrome gave birth to a daughter who could dislocate and reshape her bones and body at will. A man with early-onset Alzheimer's fathered a child with eidetic memory. A treatment for severe hypothermia resulted in a son with extreme cold tolerance, who could manipulate the temperature around him, and even generate ice from the water in the air.

In short, my efforts to cure disease created superhumans.

But Karen Gemini, the reason any of my work had been possible, accused me of using her to play God.

She had it right, maybe. At least in the beginning.

Like a proud parent, I'd been thrilled by these gifted children. But like regular humans, they came in all shades of good, bad, and indifferent. Some made an effort to use their unique abilities to help the world around them. The public had taken to calling them the Paladins, and it suited them. Honorable, fierce, and steadfast in the face of a world turning on them.

On the opposite end of the spectrum, Karen Gemini gathered the blackest souls to her bosom, a nightmare brood poised to unleash hell on earth.

The FBI and Agent Benjamin might not yet realize it, but the Paladins stood in the way of gathering darkness. And as the woman whose research had started all of this, I stood to shield the Paladins.

If Benjamin meant to intimidate me, he needed a new strategy.

Go ahead, Agent Benjamin. Take me down. This is so much bigger than you know.

"Dr. Welborn?" Benjamin's gaze, his eyes an eerie amber-orange, fixed on me.

"I'm sorry," I said. "Did you want me to deny the allegations? For dramatic effect?"

He turned away, but not before I saw him grimace. Aw, did my attitude hurt his career advancement opportunities? Tough shit.

He needed to toughen up his poker face for this job.

I'd stepped into sharky waters with open eyes. I'd known the risks of siding with the Paladins. Of siding *against* Gemini.

I smiled.

He rolled his eyes, tension visible along his jaw. "Belligerent charm. Does that work for you often?"

"What do you want from me here, Agent?"

"Names. Aliases. Addresses. We want the Paladin operation."

I laughed. Not a polite titter, but a snort of disbelief. "Sorry to say, but you're doomed to disappointment."

"Doctor—"

"No."

"Doctor—"

"Should I say it again? Spell it, maybe?"

His pupils flared, the black emphasizing the unusual iris color. What kind of recessive gene had won the DNA lottery to create orange eyes? The color belonged on a cat, maybe. Or an owl. As a human, he looked freakish enough to know all about being different.

"Do we lock all men up because a handful of them are rapists or murderers or pedophiles? Do we lock up every mother because some killed their kids?"

"Apples and oranges, Dr. Welborn," he said. "There are *billions of* humans, and only a small percentage commits such crimes. These aberrations to the genetic code of humans are dangerous, Doctor."

I stiffened at *aberrations*.

"Guess it's a good thing we're the majority, or maybe someone would decide we should be wiped out, too."

Damn it, but he was supposed to be one of the good guys. He should get it. He should understand why I protected them.

Why I would always protect them.

"Doctor," he said, his voice more cajoling now. "These are serious charges. You could go away for a long time. The rest of your life, even."

I smiled at the black finish of the table, toying with a fallen strand of my hair lying there. I brushed the butter yellow filament to the floor. "The rest of my life won't be long, Agent Benjamin," I said. "I'm too much of a threat. They won't allow me to jeopardize their plans."

"What plans?" He verbally pounced. "You think the Paladins will kill you? I can offer protection, Dr. Welborn. I have the backing of the United States government."

"Expand your thinking, Agent." My back ached from sitting straight and pretending I didn't care about any of this. "This goes far beyond the Paladins. They aren't the problem. They're the solution."

"They are dangerous freaks, Doctor, with abilities that do not have a place in human nature."

"They didn't go looking for change, Agent," I said. "Change found them."

"How very Zen. You should send it to the fortune cookie makers. 'Change finds you. Your lucky numbers are…'"

"Pissing me off is not the path to my cooperation," I said.

His right eyebrow rose.

"In case you were wondering."

"I'd need a GPS to find *that* path." He rubbed his temples. "However the Paladins came to exist—"

"No one has told you?" I let out a short laugh. "My hands aren't clean there, Benjamin. Nor are those of your precious government."

He stilled, the frozen stance of the prey catching the scent of the predator.

"You expect me to believe the Paladins are — what? A government sanctioned project?"

"No."

"No, what?"

"No, I don't expect you to believe."

His momentary shock shifted to indignation, his brainwashing — excuse me, his *training* — overriding instinct. "Maybe come up with something more original than a super-soldier program gone wrong."

"The program was meant to save people," I said. "Superhumans were just a happy byproduct."

He chuckled. "Seems you missed your calling, Doc. You should have been a comic book writer. They love that crap."

I shrugged. "Probably wouldn't still be paying student loans."

And just maybe the Paladins never would have happened. Most of them never would have been born, for sure. Or maybe the project would have found some other hot shot geneticist who saw in Karen

Gemini the same breakthrough in cellular cloning I'd seen. Only this doctor would maybe have no qualms about exterminating the second generation *mutants*.

"This isn't a joke, Doctor," Benjamin said.

"I'm not laughing."

A knock sounded on the door. Benjamin tilted his face down, hiding his expression.

"Excuse me a moment."

My heart begun to thud harder and faster as he rose and exited the room, leaving me alone with the voice recorder. And its little red light. *I'll get you, my pretty. And your little light, too.* I contemplated picking it up and throwing it at the mirror. Beyond satisfying a momentary need for gratuitous violence, I didn't see it helping.

I almost did it anyway.

I sighed and stared up at the ceiling, wondering if I'd make it out of this interview alive. Doubtful. Gemini had to know I'd been brought in. Without the Paladins to protect me, she had the perfect opportunity to take out her enemy number one.

"Doctor?" Benjamin peered around the door. His expression foretold bad things in my near future. "We're done here. Please come with me."

The tension in his tone, in his body, set me on edge. Just because I accepted my imminent death didn't mean I wanted to throw it a welcome party. As I stood, the agent looked away and I snagged the recorder off the table and tucked it in my jacket pocket, taking a big chance my observers weren't paying attention.

Benjamin kept close as I walked into the hall, more like a bodyguard than a prison escort. With the bland walls, bland carpet — everything bland, bland, bland — this place could *be* a prison. They needed one of those Extreme Makeover teams to swoop in here and make the place more "where I work" than "where I'm sentenced".

And I needed to get my head in the game.

Gemini didn't play around. Whomever Benjamin had been talking with had beaten a hasty retreat, leaving us quite alone in the hallway. His edgy pace and constantly scanning eyes told me he expected trouble, and I had no reason to believe otherwise.

"This must be one mean hallway," I said. Twin PhD's did not stop me from making jokes at inappropriate moments.

"Funny, Doc," Benjamin muttered.

"What's going on, Benjamin?" I pitched my voice low, though there didn't seem to be anyone around to hear me.

His hand hard at the small of my back, he kept us moving down the empty hall.

"Transfer of custody. Quantico. Straight to the top," he said. "You're on some nasty radar screens, Doc."

"What can I say?" My ears did some involuntary twitching thing, listening for anything out of the ordinary. But what constituted ordinary in an office building filled with the legally armed and dangerous? "Everybody wants me."

The hallway opened up to a bank of elevators. The primary source of my uneasiness multiplied. Empty hallway turned into empty cubicles and offices.

"Benjamin?"

"Yeah, Doc?"

"Did everyone pop off for lunch at the same time?" The hair on the back of my neck rose.

"Seems unlikely."

"Just a bit." I swallowed, trying to ease the desert in my mouth. "This is the part where I die, Benjamin. You should find somewhere else to be. Make sure you get home to the wife and kids."

"No wife. No kids," he said. "And I will take it with great personal offense if you die on my watch." So saying, he slid his standard-issue 9mm hole-puncher from beneath his suit coat with his free hand. The click of the safety at once reassured me and scared the shit out of me.

"Oh."

He pressed the down button on the elevator.

"Me, either," I said. Guns seemed so much bigger in real life. "Um, no family, I mean."

"I know. Your file is pretty interesting reading." His hand flexed on my back. "On second thought, let's take the stairs."

He hauled me into a run. We hit the stairs, our thudding steps echoing through the ten-story well stinking of wet concrete and old socks. The humid air — no air conditioning here — brought a sheen of perspiration swimming to the surface of my skin. My armpits itched, a combination of sweat and anxiety. Each landing sported a giant number in clean, white paint, marking our progress. We skidded around the corner of the third floor landing.

The handful of men sporting big, black guns registered maybe half a second before Benjamin spun and pinned me against the wall. The stairwell exploded. Light. Sound. Something burning. Benjamin's body, shielding me, jerked again and again. Pain erupted in my chest as he fell away. I collapsed half on top of him, his orange eyes open and glowing under the fluorescent lights. Such strange eyes.

"Benjamin." I couldn't hear a damn thing, even my own voice. My hand rested over his chest, finding the absence of his heartbeat. I laid my head on his shoulder, too tired to move. "You should have run, damn it."

A smoky scent burned my nose, blurred my vision. A mouth pressed against my ear, mumbling. Some meaningful and pithy farewell, I bet. Another flash of light turned the world to black.

❧—o—❧

"Wake up. Savannah? Come on, Doc. Wake up."

Crack. Flesh-on-flesh pain ignited along my cheek, and I drew in a huge breath, my whole body bowing up, stretching to the point of breaking. Air, wet but fresh and earthy, filled my lungs. Electricity crackled along my nerves, every part of me alive with pin-and-needle prickles.

I exhaled and my body relaxed into trembling mass. My hands clenched, digging into damp earth.

"Wh—what?" My voice didn't want to work properly. I coughed and tried again. "Why am I not dead?" Above me, autumn trees, bright with reds and golds, danced against a cloudless blue sky.

"You tell me." Benjamin leaned over me, eyes sparkling like orange fireworks. "What the fuck is this, Doc? What did you do to me?"

"Holy— you're dead. You are one hundred percent dead. I landed on you and saw your brand of dead up close and personal."

"You're one of them," he said. "Aren't you? A Paladin. A genetic freak. How else do you survive dying?"

"You don't," I said. I struggled to pull myself upright, muscles complaining bitterly. My tee shirt had turned purple-black with bloodstains. "But, Benjamin... I'm not a Paladin."

"You have to be," he said. "There's no other explanation."

"Uh, yeah there is," I said. "I just don't know what it is yet. But the genetic changes are directly tied to the children of the first generation patients."

I rolled to my knees, making it to my feet through will alone. Thankfully I had plenty because, fuck me, it hurt to move. Like a body shot of lightning mixed with fire and maybe a splash of acid for fun. We squared off against each other, dueling dagger gazes and all. He topped me by half a foot, but I had a mean stare. Meaner than I realized, even. A flash of surprise darted across Benjamin's face, then his whole body just... deflated.

"I didn't know," he said.

"Know what?"

He didn't answer, but walked a few steps away. Bending, he fished my purse out of leaves and dirt. "You got a mirror in this thing?" He opened it without permission and rummaged, finding my compact and handing it over.

I flipped it open and studied myself in the tiny mirror.

"You look good in orange," he said.

My eyes, some shade between mandarin and amber, looked back at me, clashing with my red and on the way to bruising cheek. I touched the mark, catching Benjamin's wince in my peripheral vision.

"Yeah, sorry about the slap." He dug his hands into his slacks pockets. "I was more or less freaking out at the time."

"I'd say more, not less," I said, tucking the compact back into my bag.

"I'm apologizing," he said.

"And I'm being surly about accepting." I sighed. "Seems resurrection brings out the less appealing qualities of my character."

He smiled, a scant turn of his lips softening his hard face.

"Well, Special Agent Everett Benjamin," I said, "Either you're a spontaneous mutant, or one of your parents was part of the Gemini trials."

"I was adopted."

"Naturally." Something nagged at the back of my mind. Something… I dug the mirror back out and looked at myself again. My blue eyes were history, I knew. The orange color weirded me out. But more than that, "Do I look younger?"

"I don't know," he said. His right shoulder rose and fell in a half-committed shrug. "Maybe. Yeah."

I stared at my smoother face and cried out inside. I'd earned every line, every crease. Only me and a plastic surgeon of my choosing had the right to take them away.

And I didn't know any plastic surgeons, damn it.

I dropped the mirror and stepped right up to Benjamin. The gray in his hair had vanished and he looked younger by the second. "Who the hell were your biological parents?"

"I told you—"

"That doesn't mean you don't know." I paced away, dragging a hand through my hair.

"But I don't. I swear." Resentment made his words brittle. "I never found out more than what my folks told me. My mom— she had AIDS. And no money for treatment. The docs called me a miracle. She signed me away before giving birth."

If I concentrated, I knew I'd keep breathing.

"AIDS, you say."

"You knew her."

"Yes."

"And?"

"She was one of the first," I said. "The cells created to repair your mother's immune system response… well, your body is obviously capable of self-healing to an extreme."

"And what? You took a bath in my blood and get to share the benefits?"

"There isn't a handbook on how the second gen abilities work," I said, "but I've never seen one transferred to another person."

"So is it permanent?" he asked.

"How should I know?"

"Because you have 'Ph.D.' after your name." He crossed his arms over his chest. "Sorta makes you an expert."

"Well, assuming your cells know when to stop and don't Benjamin Button us back to diapers—"

"Oh, hell no. Puberty in reverse?" His orange eyes popped wide with genuine terror. "Cracking voices, random hormonal insanity, and social maladjustment? That's like the forty-second ring of Hell, right? Reserved for the popular kids who never grew out of mocking those they found lacking?"

"Will you quit?" I held my hand over his mouth. "Shut up for a minute."

He inhaled, slow and deep, then nodded. I let my hand drop to my side.

"Your cells regenerate, even from death. Ideally, they'll keep your body at its optimum condition indefinitely."

"Meaning?"

"You'll never grow old." I lifted my hands, smoother now, like the years had just rolled backward. "You'll never die."

He grabbed my left hand, studying it.

"Hell no," he said, all but shoving me away. "I don't want this deal."

"Yeah, me either." I stared at anything but him. His rejection stung. None of the second gens I knew had the same flavor of strangeness. It made them alone in ways Benjamin didn't understand. He didn't know how lucky we were to share our difference. "But no one asked us."

"No one asked the Paladins." He rocked back on his heels. "'Change finds you.' That's why you stand up for them."

He didn't need a confirmation of what he already knew. "Benjamin, we're here — wherever here is — so there are no bodies for the FBI to find."

"Do you really think there need to be? I doubt anyone is coming looking for us anytime soon."

I thought about the emptiness of the building as we'd tried to leave. "Yeah, probably not."

I patted the inner pocket of my jacket, finding the voice recorder. I drew it out, the small device still intact, the red light still shining.

"Unreal." I laughed and pressed stop. The file size showed a recording over four hours long. I'd only been with Benjamin about two hours before the shooting. "If this still works, our missing time is right here."

"Very sneaky, Doctor," he said. "I didn't see you take that."

His admiring tone flattered me. I'd pulled one over on the feds.

"You had other concerns at the moment."

Internally I wondered about our two hours of death. No white light, no heaven or hell. Just nothing. Because there was nothing after life ended? Or because of Benjamin's cells, had we never truly died? I could admit I'd hoped for something more.

No white light, but the red one might have recorded what happened.

I fast forwarded to the shooting, the noise mainly blasts of static. The gunshots ended, and the only sound came from me. My last gasps.

"Gemini sends her regards, Dr. Welborn," a man's voice said. "Enjoy the afterlife."

I jumped, dropping the recorder as another boom wiped out any other sound. My breath came quick and unsteady. I'd just died. Again. Twice. All over. *Fuck, fuck, fuck.*

Benjamin swept me down to a sitting position and shoved my head between my knees.

"Slow and easy, Doc," he said. He massaged the back of my neck with strong fingers, both relaxing and hurting, and bringing me back to myself. I drew his warmth in, taking comfort in the small measure of contact. His touch didn't make the world better or any sunshine and butterflies bullshit, but it grounded me enough to bear it.

"I'm okay," I said. "I got this." The fat tears streaming down my face blew my cover.

Benjamin didn't call me out, and I added gentleman points to my opinion of him. The recording went on and we made out enough to know we'd been dumped in Nowhereville for the express purposes of never being found.

"Nice." He put his hands on his hips. "We got dumped here for critter chow."

I shivered to think of some animal dining on geneticist tartar. A heap of animals and me sprawled out as an entrails buffet. My breakfast threatened to make an encore appearance. Every scent magnified as I sucked in deep breaths, determined not to vomit like Linda Blair from *The Exorcist.*

"So." Deep breath. Swallow down anything trying to escape. Repeat. "For those keeping score, we're dead. Right?"

"Yep."

"Was your office in on it?" I asked.

"They had to be, didn't they?" He turned off the recording. "How high does this Gemini thing go?"

"Higher than the sky," I said.

"God, then? Or maybe the giants at the end of the beanstalk?"

He startled a laugh out of me, and I started to think I might survive this. Ah, the irony.

"Once the mutations became apparent, funding and directives came from very dark and secretive places. The nature of the project took a nasty turn, so I began to disconnect from it."

"They don't seem to like your leaving."

"I may have destroyed a bunch of my research before I bailed."

Benjamin whistled long and low.

"Are you impressed? Or appalled?"

"Could go either way, Doc," he said with a rueful smile. "You have one hell of a way of making friends."

"With friends like these…" I sighed. "So, is there FBI training on life after death?"

"Yeah, not so much." He seemed torn between laughing… and laughing a lot. "Wilderness survival, though — that's a different story."

"Excellent. So we won't starve or freeze before Gemini can kill us again." I needed a distraction from the rapidly receding pain, from the reminder of my changing body. Being an advocate for the Paladins had proven dangerous enough. Becoming one of them? Would I have to embrace this new version of me permanently? I found my phone in my purse and held it up, checking for signal.

He snatched it out of my hand.

"Hey," I protested. "I have GPS."

He popped the back and tossed the battery. "Which tells anyone watching where you are. Best to keep the details of our survival a secret as long as possible."

I grumbled as he took my hand and started walking. The heightened world assailed me with microscopic sensations. The distant call of a bird. The crunch of leaves beneath my feet. The scent of Benjamin's cologne magnified by the heat of his body. The humid press of his palm against mine. I clung to the last more than I should, needing the simple humanity of skin to skin. Our fingers laced together and I promised myself one day I would thank him for this moment.

One day when I didn't feel so raw.

"I'll get you back to the Paladins, Doc," he said. He scanned the sky. "But I want something in return."

"What?"

He glanced back, uncertainty in his eyes. "My mother."

"Oh. Yeah." Why had she given up her child? She hadn't been pregnant when she'd come to Gemini, so she had to have known she'd been cured and her baby would be fine. "You may not like what you find."

"I know," he said. "What is Gemini, anyway?"

"Who," I corrected.

"Right. I picked up on that." He gripped my waist and lifted me over a fallen tree.

"There *is* a what, too," I said. "The remnants of the project I headed. But at the center was Karen Gemini. The project never would have existed without her."

"What made her so special?"

"She'd been brought to me for DNA testing. Her parents signed her away because she was different." I shuffled the leaves at my feet as I walked. "She'd survived leukemia without treatment."

"And the powers that be wanted to know how."

"Of course. The project grant tasked me with figuring out a way to bottle her body's curative abilities for the benefit of all."

"Not much of a life for a kid."

"She felt used and she grew up to be bitter. Angry. Intent on destroying everything and everyone associated with the project."

He stopped and I thumped into him.

"And 'everyone associated' includes second gens, right?" He paused, eyes on his feet. "Includes me."

"She only kills the ones who don't join her." I wondered if things with Gemini had started to go bad before his birth, and maybe his mother had given him up to protect him from the brewing hell storm.

"You were prepared to die to protect the Paladins." His eyes searched my face, asking questions I didn't dare interpret.

"Yes." My voice came out raspier this time.

"You really are trying to do good, aren't you? You and the Paladins."

"Yes."

"Will they welcome me, do you think?"

Tears stung my eyes. The lives we'd known had ended in a grubby FBI stairwell.

"I know they will," I said.

He nodded, though his face said he wasn't convinced. "I fully intend to keep us alive. Or at least not coming back from the dead again."

Relief made me giddy. Goofy. Amazing how a "let's not die" statement made the world easier to bear. "I like this plan."

"By the way, where are we headed?" He shot me a sly smile, his orange eyes sparkling with resigned humor. I understood completely.

"Reliant City," I said.

"Well, good thing you've got walking shoes on, Doc. We've got ground to cover and people to save."

My inner hero liked his attitude. "With you all the way, Benjamin."

※※※

Cara Michaels is a dreamer of legendary proportions (just ask her about the alien pirate spaceship invasion). Her imagination is her playground, and nothing is quite so much fun for her as building new characters and new worlds with at least an edge of the fantastic. She's writing whenever the opportunity presents itself, and can typically be found tinkering with half a dozen projects, occasionally all at once..

Killing The Fantasy

by Jennifer Gracen

Wyatt's avatar picture was of a tree. It was a lovely maple tree in autumn, brilliant orange leaves dappled with golden sunlight against a bright blue sky. But there were no pictures of him. He'd started following Catherine on Twitter when she'd quoted one of his favorite '80s movies. The banter between them flowed easily. It wasn't long before she teased him about his lack of self-portraits, and he joked back, brushing it off.

Seriously, why no picture? Catherine asked one night, after the first few weeks of chatting.

I just don't like pictures of myself, he wrote back. *No big deal.*

Can you send me one sometime anyway? I'm only curious...

Wyatt responded with a lyric from an old song they'd discussed only minutes before: *Sorry... I can't go for that. No can do. Your picture's great though. Enjoying it right now.*

He lived in Detroit, she in the suburbs of Connecticut. He worked in the fast-paced world of advertising; she was a research librarian at a local university. Different worlds, but they had things in common. They loved to read, loved to travel, and enjoyed the guilty pleasure of '80s movies. Over the winter, after weeks of sporadic, playful banter, Catherine and Wyatt discovered they had even more in common: both were in their early forties, both were divorced, with two kids each and a marital unraveling that had reshaped them. That was powerful shared ground. And once they realized it, with daily contact, a deeper friendship evolved.

Late that winter, Catherine tried again to get Wyatt to share his picture.

You're an advertising executive, she admonished lightly. *Surely you know the power of the visual.*

I do indeed, he responded. *Which is why I KNOW it's best not to have a photo of me out in public.*

Why, do you look like Attila the Hun?

Not that bad, sheesh, he wrote back. *But I'm no young Adonis. Trust me.*

Wyatt's use of the word "young" set off warning bells. He had told her the sordid tale — how his wife had left him for a handsome guy twelve years younger than him. Wyatt had been divorced for three years and only saw his kids on the weekends. Sensing she should drop it, Catherine wrote, *Hey, I enjoy chatting with you. I like your personality. For the record, I don't care what you look like.*

Thank you. For the record, I don't care what you look like either. But you have your picture up, so I know. I just lucked out that you're intelligent *and* gorgeous. #rawwwr

Catherine actually felt her cheeks warm. It made her feel silly; she was in her forties and blushing like a schoolgirl. But Wyatt's compliments often had that effect on her. He never came across as sleazy or lecherous; he seemed plain and sincere in his sentiments.

By early spring, they were chatting twice a day, texting a quick hello in the mornings before work and sharing longer chats online at night, after her young daughters had gone to sleep. She would sip white wine, he would relax with a gin and tonic, and they'd sit at their computers and talk. Gradually, real flirting began. Catherine threw the first sassy softball one night, after two glasses of wine had emboldened her. Wyatt batted it right back to her and upped the ante with brazen quips. The chemistry was strong and undeniable. By late spring, their chats lost most of the neutral tones and heated up.

Sometimes, their words set off sparks that kindled slowly. Other times, their powerful words aimed to set each other on fire, and did.

The more their online friendship intensified, the more Catherine's curiosity about what Wyatt looked like increased. She had pictures of herself on her Twitter account. But he didn't, and he wasn't on Facebook, Flickr, or Google Plus. It almost seemed as if, in a way, he didn't exist. A huge part of his reticence was fed by his concern that his employees and clients should not see him in an unprofessional light. Catherine knew this, and understood. Yet between liking him as a friend and being attracted to his incendiary sexy talk, the need to know what he looked like burned to the point of distraction.

She tried to cajole him into sending her a picture, teased him mercilessly, asked to the point of almost pleading. He wouldn't budge.

You don't need to see what I look like, he would tell her.

It's not about need, she would type back. *It's about want. I'm just curious. Curiosity is natural in this situation. We've talked almost every day for months now.*

Curiosity killed the cat, he wrote. But before she could respond, he added, *Oh God... your name is Cat. I didn't mean that how it must have sounded! I was KIDDING. I'm an idiot!*

Catherine let out a chuckle as she typed, *I know you didn't. It's an old saying. No worries. You don't scare me, sweets.*

Well you scare me, lady, he wrote. *Smart as a whip, strong single mom, & drop dead gorgeous. Talking to you is gonna get me in trouble.* He immediately followed up with his own creative hashtags: *#thebestkindoftrouble #viletemptress*

By May — admitting to herself, but not to him, that she was quite smitten — they began talking on the phone, late into the night. Hearing his voice added a thrilling new dimension to their relationship. Still, she persisted with her one nagging desire.

One night, Wyatt sighed and said, "Fine, okay... I have light brown hair that's going gray around the ears, light green eyes that are probably my only attractive feature, I wear glasses, and I'm six feet tall. Not fat, not thin. Not anything remarkable. Completely and boringly average."

"What's wrong with average? Hey, I don't care if you don't look like George Clooney."

"Clooney? Ha! Catherine, I don't even look like his gardener's sickly cousin."

She dissolved into laughter.

"Come ooooon," she wheedled again the next week. "Please?"

"Maybe I'm horribly ugly. Have you thought of that? Like, pathetically so."

"I don't care," she said in a firm tone. "Have you thought of *that*?"

"You say that now."

"I say it because it's the truth." She sighed. "Wyatt. Do you think I'm that shallow, that I really *care* what you look like? That it would alter how I feel about you?"

"No," he stammered. "Of course not. I don't think you're shallow at all. But I just don't... I don't understand why this is so important. Why do you need to see my picture?"

"I just want to put a face to the words onscreen, to the voice on the phone." She grunted with exasperation. "I just want... a connection. Why don't you get that?"

"I do get that," he conceded quietly. "But I just... maybe I don't want to... kill the fantasy."

She switched the phone from one ear to the other. "The fantasy of a tree?" she teased, trying to lighten the weight in his words.

He responded instantly. "Hey, it's a damn handsome tree. More handsome than I am, that's for sure."

"You're impossible," she groaned.

"Catherine..." His voice trailed off. He cleared his throat after a few seconds. "I could never hope to be as handsome as you are beautiful."

Her mouth went dry at his soft, intense words. No one had ever used the word "beautiful" in reference to her, much less in the way he just had. She'd heard "pretty", sure. Wyatt often called her "gorgeous". But to her, the word *beautiful* had always had a magical quality. One she didn't associate with herself. "Wyatt. That's… that may be the most exquisite thing anyone's ever said to me. Really."

"It's the truth."

"Well, I don't believe that. But thank you all the same."

"You're welcome." The line between them crackled with electricity. He cleared his throat again; she swallowed hard. His voice was thicker when he spoke again. "I think you're alluring and beautiful. I'm hopelessly addicted to looking at your picture. But I'm merely average looking, no great shakes. You don't need to see a picture. It's better this way. Trust me."

"What are you going to do if we ever get to meet in person?" she demanded. "Show up with a paper bag on your head?"

He gave a low, wry chuckle. "We'll cross that bridge when we come to it." And then he changed the subject.

That was, more or less, how the conversations between them would go whenever it came up. She lost every time. The more intimate and sultry their conversations got, the stronger their connection grew, the more that one point of contention frustrated her. But she stamped it down. It wasn't worth blowing up their relationship. His attention delighted her, made her feel better than she had in a long time. Yet the picture thing ate at her. It wasn't only the curiosity factor. She eventually grasped that she trusted him, but it felt as if he didn't trust her. It gnawed at her insides with insidious stealth.

One night in late July, Catherine tossed a grenade into Wyatt's lap. Knowing it was potentially explosive, she did it online, through Twitter Direct Messages, instead of telling him over the phone and possibly putting him on the spot. After her daughters were asleep, she poured a glass of wine, got comfy in her computer chair, and logged on to TweetDeck.

Found out I'm going to a conference in mid-Sept., she wrote, trying to ignore the way her heart rate accelerated as she typed the DM. *Library stuff, online research stuff.*

Sounds as if that could be either kind of interesting or boring as hell, Wyatt typed back. *Which is it, do you think? Are they paying for the entire trip?*

I actually think it'll be interesting, Catherine wrote. *And yes, they're sending me; it was their idea, so they're footing the bill.*

Fantastic, Wyatt wrote. *Good for you then. Where's the conference?*

Well, that's where it gets a little more interesting. Catherine took a gulp of the Pinot Grigio she'd poured to buoy herself. *I'm going to Chicago. Not too far from Detroit...*

Wow, Wyatt typed back. *Um... wow. No, that's not far from here at all.*

Catherine took another sip of wine, swallowed her nerves and her pride along with the golden liquid, and typed, *Well... I was thinking... maybe you could meet me there. Have dinner with me. Or... well...*

...whatever else comes to mind. I WILL have my own hotel room... (wink wink)

Wyatt didn't respond right away.

Catherine's insides churned with anxiety. "Crap," she whispered aloud.

Catherine, came Wyatt's response. *That sounds great. I'd love to meet you in person. I know we've talked about it... ...but I don't know if it's a good idea. I don't know if we should.*

Hot tears sprang to her eyes, making them sting, as her heart dropped to her stomach. All she wrote was, *Why?*

I just... it would... wow. You caught me by surprise.

By surprise? she thought. *We've been friends for six months... flirted, discussed, revealed... some of the things we've said to each other...* She faintly tasted bile. Her hands trembled as she wrote, *Forget it, Wyatt. Forget I brought it up. Sorry. Forget the whole thing.*

His response was immediate. *Catherine, no, wait. Please don't be upset. Let me explain what I mean.*

Nothing to explain, she typed as fast as she could. A tear rolled down the side of her nose and hit the keyboard. *I have to go. Sorry, but I do. Good night, Wyatt.*

Catherine, wait! he wrote back instantly. *Don't sign off! Damn. Please don't go.*

She sat back in her chair and stared at the screen. Her shaking hands remained in her lap.

Are you still there? he wrote.

Fuck! he wrote. *Please still be there, talk to me.*

She didn't move. She closed her eyes, trying to breathe slowly enough to steady her racing heart and will the tears that had welled up to dissipate. Humiliation seared through her. In silence, giving in, she opened her eyes to let the tears roll down her cheeks.

You have to hear me out, Wyatt's words exploded on the screen. *I did that all wrong. Dammit, you have to hear me out.*

After a few more seconds, he wrote, *Damn. You're really gone, aren't you?*

She logged off, turned off the computer, and left her home office. Her insides throbbing with wounded pride and something else she didn't want to name, she walked stiffly down the hall to the bedroom her daughters shared. As she entered, the landline phone rang. She ignored it. Bending down to kiss each of her girls' soft cheeks, she heard the phone ring four times, heard the answering machine pick it up, and heard the low murmur of a man's deep voice. Wyatt's voice. The voice that had murmured sweet nothings, sultry and erotic innuendos, secrets and revelations into her ear late at night… he'd made her stomach flip, her blood race, and her loins burn. His voice made her blood race this time, but with anxiety; her cheeks burned with embarrassment, and her stomach churned with faint nausea. She slowly, deliberately re-tucked the blankets around both of her daughters, not exiting their room until the house was quiet.

Sniffing back the unwanted tears, filled with apprehension, Catherine went to the answering machine in the living room and pressed play.

"Catherine." Wyatt's familiar baritone bowed with something she'd never heard: desperation. "You left before you let me finish. You ran away. And dammit, that's not fair. You sprung this on me, surprised me, and I just… I was going to send you a long email, but you can't always get across in text what you can with actual conversation, and this is important, so now I'm calling you. And you won't pick up the phone. Shit…

"Listen to me. I'm so, so sorry I hurt your feelings, and please know that it was completely unintentional. I'd *love* to see you in person. But when you suggested… the 'or whatever' part… you… shocked me. I mean, yes, we've been flirting for months, and of course something's there. Something… well… real. I know it has been for *me*. I just wasn't completely sure if it was for you too… we've kind of danced around that. And now you're inviting me to… well, frankly, I'm not sure what, and I don't want to assume. But everything I've ever said I wanted to do to you, with you, that we could… God… it all flew through my mind and just knocked the wind out of me, you know? You caught me off guard. Jesus, Catherine… I go to sleep every night thinking of you. That's the truth. I *do* want to see you, more than you know… I just don't think that… ah, hell.

"You know what? I'm talking to air here. When you're ready to talk, please call me. I hope that's tonight. As soon as possible. I don't care what time it is, how late. Just please let's talk, clear this all up, okay? Um…" His voice caught as he added, "Catherine. Please call me."

She stood over the machine and cried. She wasn't sure why. She wasn't sure why she felt rejected, or stunned, or stupid, or hurt. She knew she shouldn't. But she did.

"So you called him back, right?"

Catherine flopped down on her bed and switched the phone to her other ear. "Of course I did. After I stopped crying and pulled myself together. I was cool as a cucumber when I called him back."

"Good. And you talked it all out, and you guys are fine. Right?" Molly chuckled. "Sorry, I'm just trying to make this easier. You sound tired."

"I *am* tired. I talked to him past midnight and had to wake up early to get the girls to school and go to work. We did homework; now they're watching a TV show, and this is the first chance I've had to call you. And I wanted to talk to you all day."

"And I waited for you to call!" Molly retorted. "You can't send me a text like you did and not follow up all day. Bad Cat. Bad kitty!"

Catherine laughed. "Ahhh, real laughter. Thanks, BFF."

"That's what I do. Mission accomplished. So... did he change his mind? Is he going to meet you at the conference?"

"No," Catherine said, her voice lowering with disappointment. "That didn't change. I wasn't going to beg, for Pete's sake. God! I have no idea why he's being like this. It doesn't make sense. Nothing he said was remotely plausible, not after the other things we've said to each other all these months."

"Men are stupid," Molly quipped on a sigh. "The conference is what, six weeks away?"

"Seven."

"Even better. You can convince him. He *wants* to meet you. I know it."

"So what the hell's holding him back?" Catherine cried. "I mean, come on! I'm going to be less than an hour's drive away. All this time he's said he'd love to meet me one day, he wants me, he thinks about being with me. Here's that day! It's here! So what's the freakin' problem?"

"Um, Cat?" Molly addressed her with halting sarcasm. "Isn't it obvious?"

"He's scared," Catherine spat. "No kidding. But *why*?"

"Because he's crazy about you," Molly replied simply. "All the months of your friendship aside, it's gone way past that. He's into you as much as you're into him."

"We're in our forties, for Christ sake," Catherine half snarled. "This high school bullshit is supposed to be long gone."

"Having feelings for someone isn't high school bullshit, and it can be just as scary now as it was back then," Molly said. "His wife leaving him for another man — a hotter, younger man, to boot — probably did a real number on his fragile male ego. Which you've likely done a good job of revitalizing, but still. If he... well... hasn't he joked several times that if you saw him, if you met him, it'd be 'killing the fantasy'?"

Catherine huffed a hollow laugh. "Yes."

"Right. Listen to him. He's telling you exactly why he's scared."

The words sank in, but Catherine expelled a frustrated breath. "Come on."

"No, *you* come on. Look. Here's the truth: if a grown adult, in this narcissistic media age, doesn't put up a picture of him or herself as their avatar? Much less show any pictures at all? There are two reasons. They're either ugly, or married and they don't want to be found out."

"He's not married," Catherine said automatically.

"Right," Molly agreed. "So... well..."

"Jesus," Catherine groaned. "Molly, he's my friend. I don't *care* what he looks like."

"Honey. Get real. He's more than just your friend," Molly pointed out. "He's talked about all the dirty, crazy hot things he wants to do to you, and you've told him things too, right? You two have had some very... intimate conversations. But no matter how many times you've asked, he won't show you a picture of himself. Which means he's either truly unattractive, or he really *believes* he is. Either way, he's got a serious hang up. And you may not get him past it, no matter what you say to him, no matter how sincere you are. The fact is you're only words on a screen, a voice on a phone. He can keep you at bay. You know what I mean?"

Molly paused before adding, "It's been easy for him to have this friendship, this... fling with you, online. Not face to face. He feels free to say anything to you. You can both be completely open. That anonymity has suited him. But you're asking him to change the rules. You're trying to make it real now. If he doesn't want to, you have to wonder why."

Catherine was silent for a long minute as she considered Molly's words.

"This happens to people all the time," Molly said gently. "You hear about this kind of stuff... ohhh, honey. Are you okay?"

"Yeah," Catherine murmured. "And unfortunately, I think you're probably right. On all of it."

"It's not about you, Cat. It's about him."

"Yup. But it doesn't make it sting any less." Her eyes filled with tears. When had she started wanting more, much more? And why was it so seemingly one-sided?

Man, was she in trouble. This was more than a mere infatuation, which was what she'd told herself repeatedly. She was in much deeper than she'd realized. And she'd have to let it go.

∽∘∽

Catherine stared out the window of her hotel room, letting her eyes caress the impressive Chicago skyline.

He's out there somewhere. He could be here right now.

She sighed.

In the glass, she could make out her reflection against the night. She looked at her long, dark hair, her pale skin, her eyes... she looked at what Wyatt had been able to see. He'd told her she was beautiful. Told her many times that she was alluring, sexy, irresistible. But apparently not irresistible enough, since he wasn't even willing to make an easy one-hour drive to meet her in person.

They didn't have to sleep together, for Pete's sake. But was having dinner too much to ask? Meeting for a drink?

Catherine turned on her heel, grabbed her bag, and decided to find the hotel bar.

Ten minutes later, she was sitting on a leather-bound stool, taking a deep swallow of a blood orange martini. It hit her that it was the same shade of orange as the leaves of Wyatt's avatar.

Damn you, Wyatt. Get out of my head. At that thought, the pain of missing him seared through her yet again, and she took a bigger gulp of her martini. She took out her phone and set it down next to her glass. Glancing at it, she took another sip, then brought her elbows up to rest on the bar and pressed the heels of her hands into her forehead. Annoyed, she took a deep breath in and released a long, slow exhale to steady herself. Another few sips of the citrusy martini. She refused to give in to the melancholy, the yearning. She was at the conference to learn, to meet people, and to do her job.

Another sip. It was a beautifully ornate hotel, and the bar was lively. She'd have a drink or two and just stop thinking about him, dammit.

She snorted in derision at herself. If pushing Wyatt out of her mind were that easy, she'd be able to do it all the time. Hadn't happened yet. He was often in her head... hell, he'd been in her head, and the soft ache had been in her heart, for weeks. She just wanted to *see* him. More than she should. And it hurt more than it should. Because it wasn't mutual.

He could have met me here. He didn't come because he didn't want to.

Ugh. You're pathetic. Get over it, Catherine.

With a heavy sigh, she dropped her head into her hands. Her long hair flowed down around her face and forearms, creating a curtain between her and the world. She savored the temporary illusion of solitude. She'd been fine all day, all week, but something had snapped in her when she'd walked into the bar alone. The sudden, unexpected wave of heartache immobilized her.

"Are you okay, Miss?"

Catherine's head snapped up. The bartender was there, eyeing her with mild concern.

"I'm fine, thanks," she said. She realized she'd been sitting like that for a few minutes. "Just... have things on my mind."

A quick, empathetic grin flashed across the bartender's face as he nodded. "You need anything, let me know."

"Thank you," she murmured, warmed by his kindness. As he walked back to the other end of the bar, her phone dinged with a text message.

How's the conference going, beautiful?

Catherine snorted and muttered, "Perfect." She glared at the phone for a long minute before picking it up. This was how it'd gone for weeks now. The pang she got when he messaged her. She couldn't *not* talk to him. Then he'd know just how upset she was, and she didn't want that. He didn't need to know she was hurting, that she still felt... well, rejected. That was her problem. She wanted more; he didn't. She had to suck it up if she wanted to remain friends. And she did, that was the bottom line.

Going fine, she texted back. *Had dinner, now the evening is mine.*

"To sit and wallow over you, like an idiot," she mumbled under her breath.

He wrote back, *Sounds good. Are you at the bar by now, I hope? Anyone to hang with?*

Yes, I'm at the bar, but no, I'm alone. Which is fine. She picked up her glass and took a hearty gulp of her drink. It wasn't fine. She wanted to be there with *him*. The thought clenched at her heart, which made her sad, then angry, and then even angrier at herself. *Stop it already!* she yelled in her head. She took another gulp of her drink and set the almost empty glass down. Her head buzzed slightly. A glance at her watch told her it was only a quarter past seven. Early enough to get drunk. Why not? The first seminar wasn't until nine-thirty the following morning; she could get her drink on and be in bed early enough to make it there without a problem.

You're alone? Wyatt's response read. *Careful. I bet half the men in the place are eyeing you, waiting to make a move. You're likely the hottest woman there.*

Catherine laughed aloud and wrote back, *I'm sure they're not, but thanks.*

Au contraire, mon chère, came Wyatt's answering text. *I bet they are. I'd be staring at you, trying to hide the want in my eyes... you'd probably be able to feel my gaze from across the room.*

Unable to stop herself, in a flare of temper, she pounded out on the keys: *Then it's too bad you didn't come & meet me here. You could've done a lot more than look at me from across a room. But that's what I wanted, not you. Right? Right.*

Her heart rate took off as she hit "Send", and her hands trembled a little as she put the phone down on the bar. She gripped her glass and knocked off what was left of her martini.

Wyatt didn't answer immediately. The two minutes that passed seemed like the longest two minutes she could remember enduring. Then his text came back.

Wow. You ARE angry at me. I was hoping I've been imagining it all these weeks, but I wasn't. I'm sorry, Catherine. I'm really sorry I've upset you.

The words made her stomach flip, and her eyes brimmed with tears. That made her downright furious — with him, but even more with herself.

She texted back, *No worries. I'm in a lovely hotel bar, so I'm going to get a little drunk and then go to bed. You have a good night.* She sniffed back the hot tears.

Catherine... don't go like this, came Wyatt's text.

Before he could go any further, she texted quickly, *You know what? We've had this discussion already. Just forget it. I'm sorry. Good night, Wyatt.* She put the phone in her bag and let her head fall into her hands again. As before, her hair cascaded down and around her as she closed her eyes. She liked the barrier that the long, thick waves provided between her and the world, and intended to sit like that for a while, not caring how it looked.

The upbeat dance song playing over the speakers seemed to taunt her with its happy, lovestruck lyrics. The buzz of conversation and tinkling laughter floated over her shoulders like a cold breeze. Catherine just sat still and silently reprimanded herself. Wyatt had put her off. She had to accept the limits, that this would always be their relationship. That it was just an online fling that had gotten out of control, and she was nothing but a pathetic walking cliché.

She sniffled. Over the months, she'd come to care about him, have genuine feelings that he'd said were mutual, but obviously weren't. She had to accept that he meant more to her than she did to him. She had to accept that they'd never meet in person, that she'd never know what he looked like, that she'd never get to look into his eyes as he said something that made her laugh, that they'd never touch, that she'd never get to…

With a grunt of frustration and self-loathing, her head dropped a bit lower, and she squelched her eyes shut.

Over the music and quiet buzz of conversation, a barstool scraped along the floor. Not the stool next to her, but one on the other side of it; whoever had taken a seat had left that space between them, so she didn't bother to look up. She could feel a presence there and knew whoever had sat down must have been looking at her and thinking she was sick, or crazy, or…

She didn't care. Her head stayed in her hands, her hair shielding her from the world.

"Hi." She heard the bartender speak to the other patron. "What can I get you?"

"Gin and tonic, please," said a male voice.

Something in Catherine's chest flamed. That was Wyatt's drink of choice. Ironic.

"And for the lady, another glass of whatever she's having," the man continued. "Looks like she could use it."

Catherine's breath stopped and stuck in her throat. Her blood raced throughout her body like liquid mercury. That voice… she knew that voice.

Slowly, her head lifted, and she turned her face to look. Sitting there was a broad shouldered, stocky man. He had a kind, round face, already turned to her. His light brown, receding hair had hints of gray by the ears, and behind silver-rimmed glasses, his pale green eyes focused on her, watching her with a combination of nervous ambivalence and riveting intensity.

The corner of his mouth lifted.

Her eyes widened as it hit her. "Wyatt?" she whispered on a stunned breath.

The cautious half-grin widened into a guarded smile. "Hi, Catherine," he said softly.

For a moment, she felt as if there was no air in the room; she couldn't breathe. She couldn't make sense of it, couldn't process it immediately. Wyatt was *here*, sitting inches away. She stared at him in a daze.

Without conscious thought she leaned toward him, where his forearm rested on the bar, and covered his large hand with her own. At her touch, his eyes flickered shut for a moment, and he interlaced her fingers with his.

"It's you," she murmured. "You're really here."

"Yup." He cleared his throat and looked into her eyes, anxiety and yearning clear in his gaze. "Be careful what you wish for. Here I am. Killing the fantasy."

"Are you kidding?" she sputtered, her voice catching. "You just made my fantasy come true."

His eyes rounded and his mouth fell open. She couldn't help but laugh at his reaction. Her other hand came up so she could touch his face, just to feel his skin, have contact. He leaned into it and nuzzled her palm. The sweetness of his action sent electricity skittering through her.

She tilted her head, her brows furrowing. "How did you know where to find me?"

"You told me," he said plainly. "I pay attention."

"But… but I don't…"

Wyatt took both of her hands and lifted them to his lips. His eyes held hers as he kissed the tops of her hands with utmost tenderness, then flipped them gently and kissed her palms. He laced his fingers through hers again. "I had to come. I was losing you." His voice was thick with emotion. "You were distancing yourself, because I hurt your feelings and disappointed you with this, and I didn't want… you've come to mean too much to me. I didn't want to lose you."

Her breath caught as her heart stuttered in her chest.

"The thing is… I thought you'd see me and… that'd be it. You wouldn't equate this," he gestured to himself, "with that faceless but sexy guy who'd seduced you with words." He shrugged. "But I was making your choice for you. Because I was scared. I'm sorry about that. I am so sorry. But ultimately, I guess what I mostly am… is selfish. Because no matter what you thought when you saw me, I had to see *you*. I wanted to look right at you. And if you were let down, if you got up and walked away, I'd have to live with that."

"Wyatt," Catherine said softly. "I'm not your stupid ex-wife."

He swallowed hard and nodded. "That's right. You're not." His brow arched. "And thank God. That'd just be creepy."

A bark of laughter ripped from her throat, and he chuckled at her spontaneous response.

"Ah, Catherine. I've thought about this. About *you*. I had to come. I've wanted to spend time with you…" His eyes flamed as he added, "I wanted to be with you... in all the ways we talked about. All of them."

She shivered at the delicious promise in his tone, the hungry look in his eyes.

"So... here I am." He squeezed her hands, gave a wry grin. "Surprise."

Slowly, Catherine slid off her barstool and moved to him. Still as stone, he watched her. She smiled, put her hands on his broad shoulders, and lightly pressed herself against him. "You have no idea how happy I am to see you." Her gaze was direct. "I'm not running away. I happen to think you're adorable. Surprise."

His arms encircled her and drew her close. He expelled a breath of obvious relief. "I'm glad you're happy to see me. I wasn't sure... I took the chance."

"Gold star for you." Her smile widened.

"I, um..." He reached into his blazer and pulled out a small box, wrapped in orange and gold paper. "I got this for you. I hope it's not too presumptuous..."

Catherine tore open the wrapping and opened the box. Inside lay a slender gold bracelet with one charm hanging from it: a single orange maple leaf, just like ones on the tree of Wyatt's avatar. "Oh my goodness," she murmured, fingering the delicate charm. Her wide eyes flew back up to his face. "It's beautiful. I love it. I just... wow. Thank you, Wyatt."

He watched as she put the bracelet on her wrist, then admired it for another moment. "You were really pissed off at me," he said with a hint of a smirk. "Damn, woman. For weeks you've been on edge. Like a warrior, you don't let things go."

"And don't forget that."

"Believe me, I won't."

She edged closer. "Yes, I was pissed," she said. "I'm not anymore, though. I'm too happy."

He stared at her, ran his fingers along her cheek reverently. "My God, you are so beautiful," he murmured.

She felt her cheeks heat as she whispered, "Thank you." She traced his ear with a gentle fingertip, trailed it down the side of his neck, and he shuddered.

"Christ," he choked out, shifting in his seat.

Adrenaline and confidence rushed through her, and she smiled. "I'm crazy about you. Do you get that yet?"

"Yeah, I get that. And that's good, because the feeling is mutual." His eyes darkened. "You crashed my life. You made me fall for you with words on a screen, your voice on the phone... with the sheer force of your personality. Do you know how incredible I think you are?"

She lowered her mouth onto his for a sweet, tentative kiss. A soft moan escaped his throat as he kissed her back. His lips took hers tenderly at first. Then a nip at her lower lip made her breath catch; she quivered in his arms. His arms tightened around her waist, pulling her in as he deepened the kiss. She responded instantly, ravenously. She wrapped her arms around his neck and let herself lean into him. Their mouths gave and took, hot and hungry, as his hand reached up and tangled in her hair to hold her even closer.

They stood at the bar and kissed, and the world fell away... until Wyatt managed to rasp in the bartender's direction, "Check, please."

Jennifer Gracen wears several hats: contemporary romance writer, copy editor, social media addict, friend, wife, and (most important hat) mother of two young boys. If it wasn't for the advent of Twitter, Jennifer would have never met her Favorite Redhead, Karen DeLabar, for which she will be forever grateful.

Warrior

by Anna Meade

The warrior bowed her head. Her armor was heavy, and she baked in the late day sun. She had been trudging through these woods for hours, searching, searching for him. Where was the cool of the approaching autumn? Her journey, like the summer, seemed endless. He would heal her, or she would die as he tried.

If only she could lie down for a moment, beside that rushing stream, then she'd surely be refreshed.

She trudged on. All illusions of rest were temptations, sent to divert her from her true cause. If she succumbed now, she would never rise again.

Sweat trickled down her nose. Her body felt like an old, worn glove, two sizes too small. She took one step and then another, with her gaze fixed on the far horizon. Her copper hair waved like a banner in the faint breeze, tiny gusts mocking her with the promise of refreshment and cooling.

The clearing where they were to meet was deserted. The warrior rested her hand on the pommel of her sword and waited. Shadows moved across the grass in their unhurried procession.

He came, as she knew he would, in late afternoon when the sun laid its heavy hand upon her head.

His robes made a soft susurrus as they dragged through the sun-scorched grass. He didn't speak until he was a few feet away. "Girl, you know the enchantment will worsen. The pain will increase. But it needn't. I have the power to make it all go away. Just accept your fate." He took a step forward.

She watched his eyes and her heart sank. There was no easy cure. "You needn't lie," she said, drawing her sword. "This is my path, and I'll take it to the end."

He twisted a signet ring on his left pinky finger, marked with an arcane glyph. Summoning all that remained of her inner strength, she swung her sword at his shoulder. He didn't move. It bounced off of him, jarring her arm painfully. She dropped her sword in a pile of damp moss, clutching at her elbow.

"You have a fiery heart," he mocked, "yet you persist in your belief in these archaic myths, that you can vanquish what ails you. I'm no dragon to slay, girl. You cannot hope to win by steel."

The armor was too heavy, her body too tired. She dropped to her knees. "And I am no hero."

While he taunted her, she was thinking of two little girls, all sunshine and teeth of pearl. Perhaps they were trouble, but they were hers. For them, she would fight. For them she would live, even if giving up was easier.

"Mommy," her youngest had said solemnly that morning, "this is for you." She carefully threaded a slim orange ribbon under her mother's right pauldron and tied it in a lopsided bow.

It was her own favor, her talisman, and she guarded it as if it were bestowed by a princess.

"Sad to see girls so young become orphaned. Ah, the cruelty of the world." He stepped towards her, laying his heavy hand on her head, speaking the words of the spell that would end her life.

Death was close. As she knelt in his shadow, a veil of glaringly bright orange-red slipped over her sight. A vein throbbed in her head, her skin growing hot and tight. Overflowing with energy, she tilted her head back and shrieked, her voice echoing through the forest. Pain, searing pain, shot through her. She had never felt such pain. The fine hairs on her arm stood on end.

She was on fire.

It thrummed through her, singing its song in her blood. Her hair burned like a waving torch. She lifted her arms like the wings of a bird, and trails of flame followed.

She succumbed to the flame.

Into the sky she rose, shrieking. She thought her voice sounded transformed, like the cry of a mighty bird. It did not sound pained. It sounded triumphant.

The forest was silent when she opened her eyes. She lay in a shallow crater, at the epicenter of what looked to be a blast of dragon's breath. The trees were blackened, leaves shriveled. Above her, the sky was streaked red and gold, edged with the softest orange tendrils. To the north, a star was burning.

Wobbling on legs too weak to hold her weight, she stood carefully. At her feet was a lump of molten grey. She tapped it, then jerked her hand away immediately and sucked her scorched fingertip. It was her armor, melted into a shapeless mass. Her underclothes had been incinerated as well. She touched her head gingerly. Most of her hair had burnt away, but there were still short orange wisps the width of a paintbrush.

As for the Enchanter, all that remained of him was a wink of gold in the grass, and faint markings indicating the glyph nestled in steaming folds of enchanted fabric.

Wandering back to the stream, she stared wide-eyed at her rippled reflection. From toe to top, she was covered in a fine layer of powdery soot. She wiped a long streak from her face. Then she carefully waded into the deepest part of the stream. It barely reached her knees, but she sat down on the stream bed, letting the chill water push its way around her.

She sluiced all the ash from her skin, and she frowned. What had happened? Had she won? Was this the beginning or the end?

As she wiped her arm, she noticed that the now-faded orange ribbon remained, knotted about her upper arm. She laughed, until her laughter turned into deep, shuddering sobs that left grey tracks on her cheeks. She re-tied the bow more firmly and kissed it, her luckiest charm. She emerged from the stream, and pulled the robes that had been his over her head.

Once she was clean, she turned her face towards the west, and the setting sun.

The phoenix headed for home.

Anna Meade is a writer, singer, & actor, aesthete, geek, and unrepentant Luddite, sprinkled with a touch of whimsy. And snark. Creator of *Yearning for Wonderland* literary blog, *Super Secret Spy Girl*, *Annasongs* and all manner of things wondrous.

Walkin' Blues

by Jeff Tsuruoka

They came for me early in the morning.

It was almost a relief.

Two soldiers, disheveled and grim, like all of us were by then, entered the cell and hauled me out. They marched me down the hall while other prisoners stood at the front of their cells, clutching the bars as I passed by.

By the time we reached the end of the hallway I'd made peace with myself and whichever deity was up early that morning. I was ready to face that the left turn out of the brig and into the yard meant I was to be put up against a brick wall and shot as a deserter.

My body, of its own volition, leaned to the left.

The two soldiers steered me to the right.

"The prisoner, General," said one of my escorts.

A large man with short black hair and a complexion that matched his olive drab uniform looked up from a wooden table when we entered the room.

The deep crags and the lines worn into his face said all that needed to be said about the state of the war for our side.

The General's quarters were only slightly less spartan than mine. He rated a field cot, a table, and a latrine someone dug for him. I got the floor and a bucket.

He stepped in front of me and looked me in the eyes.

"Leave us," he said to the two soldiers.

When they were gone he went back to his map on the table.

"Tell me," he said, "in as few words as possible, why you are here."

I gave him the whole sad story.

He listened, and when I was done, he nodded at me.

"You are the right man for this assignment."

I didn't ask. The man had a reputation for toughness and suicidal bravery. He'd tell me what it was about when he was ready.

"You know of my daughter, Katya," he said. "The one still here with me."

"Of course."

Everyone knew of the general's daughters. Three of them — the Triumverate — possessors of the most potent magic remaining in our war-blasted territory. Katya's two sisters managed to get out before the enemy surrounded us and laid siege to the city. No one had gotten in or out since.

"You want me to get her out," I said.

"The Triumverate must be reunited. They are our best hope of survival."

"And you picked me for this? A condemned deserter?"

We regarded each other for a moment. I saw the pain in his face, the terrible effects of the strain of manning the last outpost — the last hope. I also saw the strength, the resolve, and understood why a battered and bloodied regiment would follow him into a defended breach after a full day of fighting and dying.

"Show me on the map, General."

He did.

"Could you wave in the general direction of the enemy, sir?"

He moved his forefinger in a neat circle around the city. All around it.

I considered it for about a second.

"It's a suicide mission, sir."

"If Katya remains here, she will die. We cannot hold out much longer. We are surrounded and nearly starved out. The enemy's grip tightens every day. But we must hold here as long as possible. Which is more of a suicide mission? Yours or mine?"

He didn't wait for an answer. He'd have waited a long time.

"She must get out. Her sisters need her. Her people need her."

"What does Katya think of the idea?"

"She doesn't want to leave but she knows she must."

"And you're trusting a deserter with this?"

"What you did was... remarkable. This is a job for a remarkable man. When you reach our partisan allies on the outside and reunite her with her sisters, your crime will be forgiven. You will not be permitted to rejoin the military, but you won't be executed either. Not by me."

He consulted his map again and then looked at me out of the corners of his eyes.

"I'm sure a man of your talents will find a place among the partisans."

We eyeballed each other for an overlong, tense moment, but the matter had been decided.

Katya and I armed up in silence; three handguns apiece and a fine assortment of blades. She handled them all like a veteran. I watched her settle her weapons about her person as I shucked the grimy remnants of my uniform and pulled on the rough peasant's clothing the general had provided for me. Once dressed, she and I were a matched set in denim breeches, canvas shirts, and good boots. Her long red hair was pulled up and tucked into a brown knit hat.

The general's aide furnished us with a week's provisions — hard bread and some cheese — and also gave me a pass card, a small square of shiny, bright orange paper. No words. No symbols. Just orange.

"Our allies will know you by this pass," declared the general.

"When do we leave?" I asked.

Katya took a long sip from the canteen and passed it to me.

We'd been hiking for six hours and had four more ahead of us before we reached the city proper.

Her pale skin was reddened by the sun. Small scrapes adorned the backs of her hands but she didn't seem to notice them as she rummaged around in her rucksack for our dinner. The meal break represented our first rest of the mission.

"Deserter, eh?" she said.

Those two words tripled the number she'd spoken since we left the compound that morning.

When the general had introduced us she walked right up to me and put one cool, white hand on my cheek. She'd looked me dead in the eyes and said, "Yes."

"Depends," I said. "Are we talking letter of the law or spirit of the law?"

"Letter of the law," said Katya.

"Then the answer is yes. By the letter of the law, I'm a deserter. I left my unit under hostile fire."

"Spirit of the law, then."

She opened a small cloth package and broke a piece of hard bread in two. She did the same with a hunk of cheese.

"Buddy of mine got his leg shot off. He wasn't dead but he couldn't move. Our captain told me to leave him. The rest of my unit moved out. I went back and got him."

"And for that they charged you with desertion and sentenced you to death."

"That they did."

She didn't look at me as she passed me my portion. The air was thick with things she wanted to say. But we ate in silence and got back on the road.

We reached the city that evening.

The place was quiet, despite the large number of people moving about. There was no bustle, no commerce. Nobody had anything to sell.

Nervous energy drove people into the streets. Ragged and gaunt, they gave us the once-over as they walked by us, but that was all. No one had the time or energy to hassle a couple of simple travelers when everyone knew the city was about to be taken. Fatalism ran rampant. They'd been frightened and hungry for so long it had become their natural state.

We stayed in the city just long enough to pick up some necessities for overland travel. The orange pass gained us entry into an underground market where we bartered two good knives and some of our cheese for a warm coat for Katya. The toothless vagabond running the market threw in a couple of smelly blankets in the name of cause and country.

The closer we got to the city outskirts, the more it began to look like a war zone. What buildings still stood were abandoned and burnt out. Work animals lay dead all around. The last hardy holdouts sent furtive glances our way and then ducked back into whatever hiding place they'd found for themselves.

Explosions sounded in the distance. The enemy liked to remind us they were there by blowing something up every now and again.

We paused at the edge of the last street.

I could feel eyes on us but didn't see anyone on the street.

"Now it gets difficult," I said.

"Doesn't seem right," said Katya. "Leaving all of these people to their fate."

"Best thing you can do for them, maybe the only thing, is to get out of here and connect with your sisters. Concentrate your power and then come back and retake your city. These people'll just have to hang on. They're tough. Like you."

She looked at me. I tried to smile in return.

"Your father's a good man. If anyone can stiffen their spines, it's him."

She looked at me again, eyes ablaze with rage and sadness, and then nodded.

Five minutes later we were in the woods.

❧〜o〜☙

We reached a small town just before sunset.

The place was more of a hamlet than a proper town — nothing more than a collection of shacks and several low-built common buildings — but its position near the wooded road made it important enough for the enemy to take and hold.

From our perch in the woods, we could see townspeople shuffling along in slow imitations of daily life. We also got our first look at the enemy. They were uniformed in olive drab fatigues, armed with rifles, and moved around the little town with precision and calm.

I counted a larger force present than the position seemed to call for.

"I guess we're taking the long way around," whispered Katya.

Her eyes went stony as she watched enemy soldiers patrol the town.

"I know, Katya," I said. "I know."

She turned those eyes on me.

"Yes, I believe you do."

We edged around the town to the east, losing an entire day in the process. The woods thickened, providing maximum cover as we moved. Both of us were cut and scraped raw by branches and thorns.

It was nearing sundown again when we emerged into a rocky, overgrown field. The high grass was brown and dry and the ground strewn with boulders.

"Do you have any idea where we are?" asked Katya.

We hurried across the field and knelt down behind one of the biggest rocks.

I unfolded the map.

"We're off course," I said. "Had to veer way out of the way around that town."

"It'll take us a month to cut through these woods."

"Maybe. But we haven't been spotted and attacked yet either. It's as good a line to follow as any. They're banking on those woods being impenetrable."

"They're not far off in that assessment."

The caw of a big black bird startled both of us.

We looked to the sky.

The bird was as big as I thought it'd be, but was unlike any crow I'd ever seen. A second bird appeared as we watched. They continued their slow circuit around the perimeter of the field for another minute and then bolted off in the same direction.

"Shit," hissed Katya. "Come on. We must hurry."

"What?" I demanded. "Why?"

"Are you blind? Those birds are not what they seem."

She grabbed my hand and pulled me toward the woods in front of us. We rushed in as fast as we could without killing ourselves on tree trunks or exposed roots, and didn't stop until we reached a thicket lush enough to keep even the daylight out.

"You know that my sisters and I can use magic," she said between gasps.

I nodded and coughed.

"We're not the only ones."

"The birds?"

"Eyes in the sky. They know we're out here."

"They can control animals? Can you do that?"

"Not my line."

"What can you do?"

She smiled at me and put her hand against my sweaty face but said nothing.

I tabled the conversation.

We caught our breath, drank some water, and got moving again.

Over the next three days, we made slow but steady progress in an easterly direction. On the third day, the woods gave out very near another small town. A dirt lane ran between the woods and the town. Katya and I had to crouch down low and hold still to avoid being spotted by the mounted enemy patrol that moved up and down the lane.

These men on sturdy battle-trained horses wore fancier uniforms than the soldiers we'd seen in the other town. Their jackets were black and close-fitting, and each man had his gray breeches tucked into high, spit-polished riding boots.

Each rider was armed with a pistol and a heavy cavalry sabre.

My infantry unit had had several run-ins with enemy cavalry, and none of them ended well.

Most cavalry squadrons won't engage infantry if they can avoid it, but these guys weren't most cavalry squadrons. They were the enemy's shock troops, brutal and efficient, and they left bodies and fire in their wake.

There were two troopers visible and they had the lane well-covered.

There was no getting around them.

A group of townsmen, farmers by the looks of their weather beaten clothing, watched them ride by with open disdain. They had the look of whipped men, but they weren't yet defeated.

"I have a crazy idea," I whispered after the cavalrymen had passed by.

Katya looked at me for a few seconds and then grinned.

I drew the biggest of the knives I had on me, stepped to the very edge of the woods, and waited.

At least one of the townsmen spotted me.

I put a finger to my lips for silence and nodded my head towards the cavalrymen.

He did not react. All of the townsmen stood still, looking down the lane as the cavalrymen approached.

Katya sprang out of the woods first. She drove a knife deep into a very surprised trooper's thigh and yanked him out of his saddle.

His partner drew his sabre.

I was on him before he could swing it. I jumped up while he was off-balance and pulled him down to the ground. He didn't lose the sabre though and slashed my left arm open from shoulder to elbow.

I grunted and lunged under his backswing and drove the knife up under his ribcage. His eyes opened wide with surprise and then went still. I pulled out the knife and let him fall.

Katya came to stand beside me. Her entire body shook and her face was flushed, but she was uninjured. Her right hand was covered in blood.

The farmers started hollering at us at about the same time we heard the hoofbeats coming from both directions.

The first shots whizzed by us as we drew pistols and made for the woods.

Katya fell first, shot in the thigh.

She returned fire from the ground and unhorsed a charging cavalryman, but two more followed close behind him. A second bullet ripped into her hand.

I opened up on the troopers riding in from the opposite direction but didn't even slow them down.

I dropped one empty pistol and was drawing another when I felt a violent blow in my abdomen and then a sharp pain. My hand came away bloody when I touched the spot.

A second and then a third bullet thudded home, very close to the first.

Katya was still firing away.

More bullets hit the ground and the trees near us as the enemy closed in.

It was the townsmen who saved us.

They charged into the road en masse, and took fire long enough to get a hold of the dead cavalrymen's pistols and return fire. Three of them were cut down in the short, vicious fight that followed. But when it was over, five of them were still standing and all of the cavalrymen lay dead in the lane. All but one horse were badly wounded.

Moments later, most of the townsfolk were in the lane, taking anything of value from the dead cavalrymen's bodies and tending to their own fallen friends.

A group of children helped Katya to her feet and led her across the lane to the town.

A great bear of a man tended to me. He was bearded and sunburned and was the man others seemed to take direction from.

"Let's have a look," he said as he lifted my bloody shirt.

He looked for a long time. When he let my shirt down and took my arm to lead me to the town, he wouldn't look me in the face.

He didn't have to say anything. I was gutshot and I knew it. He held up more of my weight than I did as we walked.

"Thanks," I murmured.

"Don't thank me, boy," he said. "Damn, we've been waiting for a chance like that for... I don't know how long."

The town was much like the first one we observed. A few dozen huts lay strewn about a large patch of cleared land. A well and a fire pit occupied the middle of the patch.

Two more cavalrymen lay dead close by the fire.

"That's the entire squad," said the bearded man. "But there will be more here soon enough."

The man led me into a log structure and got me to lie down on a bedroll on the floor.

Katya's leg and hand were being treated at the other end of the room. When she saw me, she pushed the woman cleaning her leg away and limped over to the bedroll.

She allowed the bearded man to help her kneel by my side.

His face was grim.

"That bad?" she asked him.

He nodded and looked away from us.

She pulled my shirt away from the wound and placed her unwounded hand down on my abdomen.

The site of the wound glowed a soft orange and got warm beneath her hand.

The room went silent.

Seconds later the glow flickered and then went out.

She did the same to the gash in my arm.

When she was done she slumped down next to me, breathing but unconscious.

"My God," whispered the bearded man. "It is she."

He knelt and clasped my shoulder.

"We heard the bastards talking when they came here, talking about how one of the three sisters might be headed this way."

"What did she do to me?" I asked.

"She did what she could. She's Katya, isn't she? Katya the healer. Katya the seer."

I allowed myself ten seconds to marvel at it.

"We have to get out of here," I said. "Got to get her to her sisters."

"You're not going to get her anywhere in that condition, boy. You know it and I know it."

I tried to sit up but the pain in my abdomen forced me back down.

"I don't have much left," said Katya. She was awake now and sitting up next to the bedroll. "And I won't until I'm reunited with my sisters."

The bearded man wanted to object. Katya wouldn't have it.

"If we stay here, we put your people in danger."

"We're already in danger."

"If we stay here, the Triumverate remains broken and we can do nothing. We must get through. And we will."

I braced myself and sat up.

"She's right," I said.

The bearded man growled something about foolhardy kids, but helped me up and walked us to the edge of the town.

Two young townsmen — twin brothers — accompanied us. They each had short brown hair and prominent chins. They introduced themselves as Rollie and Max, and refused to accept our refusal of their services.

The big bearded man seemed about to give us some kind of benediction but thought better of it and returned to town.

Katya and I limped out to the lane and continued east. Rollie and Max followed at a short distance. Each man was armed with the weapons of an enemy cavalryman.

"Healer, eh?" I said as we walked. Every step was a new experience in agony, but Katya's determination kept me moving forward.

"Such as it is," she said. "I wasn't kidding. I have very little power left. It's all I can do to keep us alive."

"Where'd you learn to fight like that?"

"Father taught his daughters everything he taught his sons."

"Smart man."

"Very."

"What if they send more birds after us? We've got no cover now."

"We can't worry about that. We can only deal with what comes. If we must fight, we fight."

"I'm not afraid of fighting," I said. "I just hope I'm half as good as you when the time comes."

The four of us traveled over wide open country, stopping only to eat and sleep.

Rollie and Max proved invaluable.

They held Katya and me up when our wounds threatened to stop us and used their considerable skills as hunters to keep our stomachs full.

They fought like tigers beside us when enemy cavalry caught up with us on the third day out of town. Both men sold their lives dearly in a short, nasty fight that left Katya with another leg wound.

We took one of the enemy's horses for her to ride for a while. I continued to walk. It hurt less than riding.

Six days later, we found ourselves back in the woods, more dead than alive.

We were well within the sector the general's map indicated we'd find allies, but we'd yet to find anything but pain and disorientation.

Katya used her remaining power to keep us moving, and when that failed her, she used sheer force of will.

Late in that sixth day, we smelled fire.

It rained all of that day but the smell was real.

We followed it down a faint trail I just managed to make out beneath dead leaves and underbrush.

The sound of a rifle being cocked stopped us about half a mile in.

A woman and a boy stood before us in the woods.

Each was armed with a rifle and an assortment of knives, dressed in mismatched uniform parts common to partisan fighters everywhere.

"Who are you? What are you doing out here?" demanded the kid.

He might have been thirteen. Might. The fatigue jacket he had on was at least four sizes too big.

I felt dizzy and lightheaded. The forest floor beckoned me to come and lie down on it.

"You got about five seconds, mister," said the woman. "Identify yourselves."

She was tall — half a head taller than me — and had long black hair tied in a ponytail. She wore pants taken from an enemy soldier and a rough canvas shirt like the ones Katya and I had on. The skin beneath her right eye was puckered and red.

I kept one grimy, bloodstained hand open in front of me and gestured toward my chest with the other.

The kid didn't move but the woman gave me a little nod.

Their rifles did not waver.

I nodded back and slipped my fingers inside my shirt. I couldn't feel my fingertips as I poked around in a pocket heavy with blood and rain.

The rain started to fall harder. The steady drumbeat of big drops crashing into the leaves and branches overhead drowned out everything but the pounding of my heart.

I glanced at Katya standing beside me with her hands in the air. Her eyes were closed and she chanted something under her breath. The rain had washed most of the blood and dirt from her face, leaving her ghostly white against the dark backdrop of the woods.

The pass card was stained red with blood, dark and thick, as I held it out for them to see.

Their grips on their guns tightened. The kid began to shake. I locked my eyes on his and prayed his nerve would hold for just a few more seconds.

Katya put her hand on my shoulder.

I felt her strength in her touch, her heart. Waning, but enough.

One way or another we were almost home.

After a few agonizing seconds, the rain rinsed enough of my blood off the card to let its true color shine through.

It shone bright orange.

Orange.

Katya pulled her hood back.

We all stared at the orange glow for a minute, and then a big smile broke out over the kid's face. I never saw a person so happy to not have to shoot someone in my life. He slung his rifle and stepped right up to Katya.

The woman held her gun on me for a few more seconds and lowered it. Her facial expression remained frosty.

"This way," she said. "Come quickly."

I shook my head.

"She's wounded. Gonna need help getting anywhere."

Katya spun around and grabbed my bloody hand.

"What about you?"

"I'll manage," I said. "Let's get out of the rain."

She didn't answer me but did allow the woman and the kid to lend her their shoulders.

The three of them headed up the rise.

I let them get well ahead of me and then started after them.

I took two steps and fell.

There was nothing left.

The front of my jacket was soaked in seconds. I couldn't tell if it was blood or rainwater.

I heard a yelp out of Katya and then the sound of running feet splashing toward me.

"You bastard," growled Katya.

She dropped to her knees and turned me onto my back.

I felt fresh rain on my belly as she hiked my shirt up to check the wounds.

She didn't quite suppress the gasp.

"You will not die," she said.

I would have loved to answer her, but speaking required more energy than I had left.

"You will not."

She placed her right hand down over the worst of the wounds. There was immediate warmth under her touch and then the tingle, weak and thready, but there.

The woman tugged at her elbow.

"We have to get moving! He's dead already. He's just too stubborn to admit it."

Katya shrugged her hand away but otherwise ignored her.

"You will not die," she repeated. "We've come this far together, gotten through so much. You will not die on me now. You will not."

I used the little bit of strength I had in reserve to grab her wrist and move her hand away from my body.

"Don't waste that on me," I said. I might even have said it out loud.

Katya stood and turned to the woman.

"Help him," she ordered.

"We'll never make it back," argued the woman. "We'll have to carry him all the way."

She staggered back under the force of the glare Katya turned on her.

"Then we carry him."

∽o∾

Sunshine on my face woke me up.

The rain was gone, and for the first time in recent memory I was warm and dry.

Katya was asleep in a camp chair next to my cot.

She looked good, healthy and strong. She'd changed into a clean version of her traveling outfit. I saw no blood on her legs.

I tried to sit up, and though there was some pain I was able to do so.

Katya awoke at once.

"Hey there," she said. "I thought you were gonna sleep the week away."

"How long?"

"Three days. We almost lost you twice."

"Your sisters?"

"They're here in camp and they want to meet you."

I nodded.

"I've been wondering," I said. "Back in your father's tent, you looked at me and said, 'Yes'. What exactly did you mean by that?"

She smiled and put her hand against my cheek, just as she had before.

"I meant I believed we would end up here, sharing a moment like this."

"You believed in a deserter you'd never met?"

She got out of the chair and turned as her two sisters entered the tent. The power radiated off all three of them.

"You are no deserter," said Katya. "And yes, I believe in you."

Jeff Tsuruoka is an author in search of a writing career.

His life as a writer began at the age of six. He wrote stories based on the monster movies he watched on the 4:30 Movie after school.

Thirty-six years later, he still writes monster stories, though the monsters that populate his current work have a little more on the ball — at least in terms of conversation skills and the ability to drive cars — than Godzilla and his pals did.

He is hard at work on his first novel.

Murder is a Job Best Left to Professionals

by Patty Blount

I skirt the edge of the small crowd, snappin' cell phone pictures of the number 20 stock car — parked in front of a local do-it-yourself warehouse store on Staten Island, of all places. I scratch my head and adjust my cap and reckon NASCAR must know what it's doin', buildin' a racetrack this far north of the Mason-Dixon line, but damn if this don't beat all. Most of these folks are here for a can of paint for little Cindy's bedroom or a sheet of drywall for the man cave and don't spare the race car, painted orange and decaled to match the store, more than a glance. The people who do stop, well now, they're some real NASCAR fans, dressed in T-shirts and ball caps bearin' the colors of their favorite drivers, talkin' in that hard gangster way New Yorkers always do and then laugh at the way good ol' boys like me talk.

I've been sweatin' under an August sun that's hot enough to fry spit for a couple hours now, even though I'm no longer the number 20 car driver. The crowd, such as it is, ain't happy. Few of 'em care *I'm* here, the guy who drove this same car into victory lane a total of seventeen times. Seems the show's waitin' on the star attraction, the new driver of the number 20 Renovate-It stock car, Beau Givens. I brang Beau onto the team, taught that little knee baby everything he knows. Eight seasons. Top ten in the points year after year, wins at Talladega, at Martinsville, and at Homestead but does that matter? No, sir. One little throw-down with the championship winner and I'm back doing the show car trips with the Hammerhead Tools Nationwide car, while that pissant little rookie slides into my ride. I'm a has-been and I'm barely thirty-three years old.

I shove my hands in my pockets and slowly push closer to the car, wishin' they'd stop callin' the kid's name. But Beau's not here, and Dwayne Rydell, the show car coordinator, is gettin' all hot under the collar.

"What are you doin' there, Harlan?"

I shrug. "Oh, nuthin'. Just found this phone. Thought I'd try sendin' Beau a text message, let him think it's one of his adorin' fans." I roll my eyes.

"Thanks for that." He slaps me on the back just as someone jostles my arm and I drop the phone. The fan's wearin' a Lance Leeder T-shirt and his eyes go round and white.

"Hey! Hey, you're Hot Shoe! Jesus Christ, it's Hot Shoe Anderson." He takes out his phone, snaps a picture. I try to retrieve the phone I dropped, but I don't see it. "Hey, that sure was funny that time Lance spun you just as the white flag came out."

A ripple goes through the crowd when that man calls me by my name. Suddenly, heads swivel my way and cell phones click. The crowd pushes in and I ride that ripple of excitement, stand a little taller, pin on a plastic smile, tryin' not to remember the two cracked ribs that spin got me. "It's just racin,'" I shrug.

"Hey, you gonna be at Sunday's race?" the fan asks, and I wince. The Nationwide series race is on Saturday. I got no reason to be track side for Sunday's race — except one. Watchin' Beau wreck. It ain't much, but it does make me smile.

"Good Lord willin' and the creek don't rise, I'll be there," I promise, and the fan grins.

"I love the way you tawk." He laughs. Some other fans applaud, a few even curse. Then I hear a female voice shout out an offer to do her. The crowd hoots and my blood goes cold.

Dwayne shoots me a look and hurries closer. "Relax, Harlan. It ain't her."

"Dwayne, we got no real idea what she even looks like, so how are you so sure that ain't her?"

"'Cause I got eyes, Harlan, and extra security all over the damn place." He throws an arm over my shoulders, points at a trio of teenagers near the show car's rear end. "It was that one with the blond hair and big hooters that just shouted at you." I follow his finger, see the girl. Jail bait. Sweet Jesus. "You wanna light up the Internet? Flash her a grin and a wink, but for chrissakes, keep it in your pants. I'm runnin' all over hell's half acre just wranglin' Beau."

I bite my tongue but meet the girl's eyes, smile wide, and wink. Her eyes go round and her friends bounce and squeal. I do my best not to laugh or roll my eyes. I'm flattered, hand to God, but I like my women old enough to vote.

Dwayne laughs. "Here come the cell phones. You'll be all over that Twitter thing in no time." He glances at his watch and swears. "Where the hell is that egg sucker?" He turns to the dark-haired girl who shadows his every step. She shakes her head, presses a few buttons on her phone. "Probably makin' time with some young fan behind the stacks of lumber. Darlin', just go check inside the store, will ya?" The assistant jogs away. "Horney little weasel." Rydell shakes his head with a smirk. "Harlan, you may need to run the show for a bit while I take care of some business."

I nod. "Can do."

Dwayne hands me a Sharpie, and cups his hands over his mouth. "Hey, y'all. This here's the one and only Harlan 'Hot Shoe' Anderson, the driver who took the Renovate-It number 20 car to victory lane at seventeen races." He thumps the roof of the stock car and then steps back while the folks applaud, pressin' his phone to his face. A few of the locals clap — some raise a finger — and some even say that "Fuggedaboudit" thing. I laugh 'cause I always thought that was made up.

"Yo. Harlan Hot Shoe Anderson. I'm a 'uge fan. 'uge! The name's Tony." The man sticks his cigarette between his lips and holds his hands three feet apart to prove it.

I nod politely and he whips out a cell phone, slings his arm around my other shoulder, and clicks a photo without even askin' first.

"Hey, yo, Bobby! Check it out, it's freakin' Hot Shoe himself. Don't piss him off now, don't want him throwin' a helmet at ya!" the man called Tony shouts into the crowd.

"Come on, Tony, back off. Let the man breathe." A smaller guy I'm guessin' to be Bobby steps out of the crowd, slaps a hand on Tony's chest, pushes him back a foot. I nod my thanks.

"Yo. We came here to see Beau Givens. Is he comin' or what?" Another ornery voice shouts.

Before I can reply, Dwayne shifts and adjusts his NASCAR cap. "Well, ol' Beau — he's around here someplace. Here now, how 'bout a nice T-shirt?" He reaches into the show car, pulls out a box. "Here, Harlan. Start tossin' shirts to the crowd."

"He's here? Oh, shit!" The man callin' himself Tony lights up like a swarm of lightnin' bugs and turns to me. "You ain't scared, are you, Hot Shoe? Heard you two mixed it up last week after the Nationwide race."

"No, sir." I shake my head. "Beau just needs to be reminded to act like he's got some raisin' up to be done still, and I reminded him is all."

Big Tony blinks down at me like I'd spoken in tongues. That's when Dwayne's assistant come runnin' out of the store, eyes buggin' and pale as a ghost.

Dwayne takes her elbow, leads her away from the crowd. I follow. "What is it, sugar?"

"He's dead, Dwayne," she whispers in a shaky tone. "Oh, Lord, he's dead. They found him in the restroom at the back of the store."

Dwayne curses and loses his slick grin. "Jee-zus. Okay, honey, I want you to call the hauler, have them load up the car. Then I want you to call JG Racing, get the bosses down here. I'm going inside to take care of Beau." Dwayne's eyes snap to mine, and they're as shocked as the girl's. "Harlan, you take care of this crowd, will you?"

Can do. I'd done the show car gig for close to eight years before Beau Givens stuck his boot up my butt. Takes me no time before I'm scrawlin' my name on the bits of paper and promo cards stuck in my face, posin' for pictures, and answerin' technical questions for the fans. Big Tony and his sidekick, Bobby, they're watchin' me with hard looks. When the sirens scream into the parking lot, I figure I could maybe slip into the background before things get weird.

I take a step and Tony's sausage-fingered hand clamps down on my shoulder. "Where ya goin', Hot Shoe?"

I grin and shrug. "Places to go, people to see. You know how it is."

Bobby and Tony exchange a glance and then Bobby pulls a chain out from under his shirt. At the bottom of it is an NYPD badge. "Detective Bobby Jensen, Mr. Anderson. My partner, Detective Anthony LaDona. We're gonna need to ask ya some questions."

I stare at Bobby and then shift my gaze to Big Tony. Beau's dead and NASCAR fans turn into big city detectives? What the hell is going on? The questions echo to the beat of my own pulse. I hear it thumpin'. What is this? This can't be happening. A few minutes, or maybe it's hours later — I got no clear idea — I'm settin' at a sticky table in the center of a cinderblock room that smells like sweat, smoke, and old coffee. I'm alone and my head hurts. A door opens and Bobby comes in. The NASCAR cap is gone but he still wears the number 20 T-shirt.

"Hey, Mr. Anderson. Can I get you some coffee or something?"

I shake my head. "No, thanks. I — Lord, I just don't understand. What happened? Is Beau really dead?"

Detective Bobby's eyebrows climb up and then he tosses a sheet of paper on the table in front of me. I glance down and nearly vomit. It wasn't paper. It was a picture. Beau. Sweet Jesus, Beau. He'd been stabbed. Someone hated him as much as I do.

"Right t'ru the heart," Detective Bobby says.

I tear my gaze from the picture and look at Detective Bobby.

He tosses a screwdriver on the table. "That's what killed him. Left it right in him."

I say nothing and just stare at the orange handled screwdriver, the kind that's sold in damn near every aisle in the store.

"You're not under arrest. Fact is, this isn't even our case. Tony and me, we were there because the store got a bomb threat a few weeks back. You know, extra precautions for you celebrity types." He smirks. "We talked to Dwayne Rydell and a few other people already. We figured we should talk to you, since you know Beau, you know who might hate him this much."

I don't know what to say. I can't believe it. He's dead. Beau is really dead—

"Mr. Anderson. Harlan. Tony and me, we're big fans. The detectives who caught this case? They're letting us talk to you because of that. We know all this has gotta be hard on you, showing up at these half-assed events, while Beau Givens wears your colors. It damn near broke Tony's heart when you got fired."

I manage half a laugh.

"And you had such a great record. That fight — it was only the one time. Big frickin' deal. But they let you go and let Beau take over. If you ask us, he don't do such a great job."

I'm flattered, of course. But I can't say anything, so I just nod.

"What can ya tell me about Mr. Givens?"

I take off my cap, scratch my head a couple times. "Beau's smart and got a lot of skill—" I shake my head.

"But?"

"But he's got a hot temper and big mouth and thinks he's immortal."

Detective Bobby angles his head and stares at me. "Immortal, huh? Guess the joke's on him. So, what makes him so smart?"

I think on that for a minute. "Well, I guess it's 'cause he knows how to work people, knows how to play the game."

"And that pissed you off."

"Sometimes." I nod. "Hell, pissed damn near everybody off."

"Everybody?"

"Hell, yeah. Ol' Dwayne? He was damn near beside himself that Beau wasn't here with the car an hour before show time. And Beau knows that. We all know that. But Beau comes along when he gets around to it. One of the sponsors flipped his lid a few weeks back 'cause Beau covered their logo on camera. Nearly had the entire crew quit on him after the Darlington race 'cause he kept ignorin' their warnings to save the tires."

"That's not what you'd have done." Detective Bobby grins.

I sit up a little straighter. "No, sir. My crew, well those boys know that car better than they know their girls' Promised Land, if you know what I mean. When they tell me to save tires, I save the damn tires."

"Who do you think would want to kill Beau Givens?"

I think about that long and hard. "Best guess? Jealous husband. Beau probably got caught dippin' his peter in the wrong punkin'."

Detective Bobby makes a 'hmmm' sound. "Tell me about Darla Bixby."

My jaw drops. "What?"

"Darla Bixby. Who is she?"

"I don't know."

"Ya sure about that?"

"Well, I know of only one girl named Darla. Never met her, though, and sure do want to keep it that way."

"Why's that?"

"She scares the tar outta me, sir. She's been sending me messages, gifts, even following me around the circuit. She keeps offering me, ah, you know, favors and what-not, but I don't go dippin' in wells I don't know how deep they go."

"You saying she's a stalker?"

"Yes, sir."

"Has she threatened you or anybody you know?"

"Yes, sir. That's why I got the willies when you said that name."

"Who'd she threaten?"

I adjust my cap and think on that. "Well, she said she'd kill herself if I didn't win a race back in June. I didn't win that race but the messages still kept comin'. She threatened to blow up a Renovate-It store every race day until they took me back. I think she sent Dwayne a message, too, so he talked to the security guys about keeping extra eyes on us."

Detective Bobby scrawls notes on a pad. "Did she ever show up to any of your events, scare you in person?"

I stare at him and gulp. "I surely hope not."

Detective Bobby slides another photograph across the table. It's a picture of me, beside the show car, taken just a little while ago. I look at it, and my head spins.

"We pulled this off a cell phone found in the men's room beside Beau Givens's body."

I blink and relax a bit. "Beau took a picture of me?"

Detective Bobby's eyes widen and he looks like he's tryin' not to laugh. "No, Mr. Anderson. We believe that's Darla's phone and that she killed Beau."

I blow out a loud breath and pull my cap over my face. How the hell did she get that close to me?

"Why do you think she'd want to kill Beau Givens?" he asks.

I fling up my hands and shake my head. "Well, she's a hot mess, that's probably all the reason she'd need."

Detective Bobby blinks. "Huh?"

"Oh, uh, she ain't right, you know?"

"Yeah, right. So what set her on that particular path?"

"I got no idea."

"Me and Tony figure it was you." He says and I jerk in my chair. "She may have done this to impress you."

"Me? I never told her to kill nobody!"

Bobby raises his eyebrows. "So you *have* talked to her?"

"What? No!"

"Huh. That's funny 'cause there's a bunch of calls to you stored in this phone's Sent Calls log."

"I told you, she's been harassin' me."

Bobby nods. "Yeah. You did. We got all units looking for her. And there's a good solid finger print on the screwdriver."

My eyes slide over to the one on the table in front of me.

"Not that one. The one that's in Evidence."

I nod, like I knew that, but of course, I don't. I'm no cop. I drive cars.

"Where's your cell phone, Mr. Anderson?"

I pat my pockets, pull it from the one on my left hip.

"iPhone. Cool." Bobby grins. "Is that the newest one?" He pulls a bag out of an envelope. "What about this phone?"

I stare at the phone in the bag and swallow. "That one's not mine. This one's mine."

"Well, we know this ain't Beau Givens' phone. We found his in his pocket." He says in that tone that suggests I'm a liar. "And we know it's not the killer's phone. We found that one beside Beau's body. This phone, well — this one's a mystery. It's what we cops call a burner phone — a disposable with a bunch of pre-paid minutes. And you know what's weird about this phone?"

I wait for him to finish it out.

"A few things. First, we found it inside your race car."

I take off my cap and scrub a hand over my hair a few times. "Not my car anymore."

"Yeah. That sucks, man."

I laugh once because it does. It really does. "Anybody could have tossed it inside."

"Anybody? Or you? 'Cause me and Tony? We saw ya usin' this phone."

"No, sir. I found it. Wondered who it belonged to is all."

Bobby smirks. "Well, we'll pull the surveillance tapes from the stores outside cameras to confirm that." He leans closer. "But that's not the weird part. The weird part is this phone's logs show calls and texts to just two numbers." He frowns and angles his head to stare hard at me and my stomach drops to my boots. "One of those numbers goes to the cell we found in Beau's pocket. But the other? It's not yours — we already checked. It goes to the killer's phone, so that means, we got ourselves a hit."

I blink. "A hit what?"

"A hit — a murder for hire. Someone hired or conned Darla to kill Beau Givens for you."

"Hired Darla — for me?" I laugh weakly. "My God. She's more dangerous than I figured."

"Yeah, ya got that right. Come on. I'll take you back to the hotel. Thanks for coming down and helping us get this mess cleaned up."

"Oh, yeah. Not a problem."

Twenty minutes later, Detective Bobby pulls up in front of my Marriott. "I'll walk you up — make sure Darla's not hiding under your bed."

"Uh, thanks." I shiver.

We walk through the lobby and onto an elevator. I unlock the door and Detective Bobby scans the room. "Looks fine to me. Well, good night. Sorry about your pal."

"Yeah. Damn shame." I look properly forlorn and head for the mini-bar, where the sponsors left a nice goody bag full of prizes.

"Jesus Christ!" he shouts. "Cut the hick hayseed crap. We all know you did it, Harlan."

I blink at him, shocked, and that ain't no act.

Detective Bobby laughs. "I can't prove it in court, but I know it was you. I told ya, me and Tony? We're 'uge fans. We been watching you for a long time. You play any cards, Harlan?"

I don't reply. My heart's stuck in my throat.

"Card players would call it a *tell* — but cops like me? We know how to read faces, expressions, body language. When that girl told Dwayne Rydell that Beau was dead, you know what your face told me and Tony?" He leans in, grinnin' like a damn fool. "It said I WON."

Panic clogs my lungs. I'm so close — all those weeks of plannin' and I can't, I just can't lose it now. I close my hand around the first thing in the goody bag I feel. It's one of those little orange screwdrivers and I plunge it straight into Detective Bobby's heart. When the smile falls off his damn face and the light goes out of his eyes, I step inside the closet and bust back through the door to make it look like Darla was hidin' inside. I wipe my prints off the screwdriver, fling open the door and start screamin' about the crazy fan in my room. By the time people come runnin', I'm doing CPR on Detective Bobby, my hands understandably covered in his blood.

Hick hayseed? Fuggedaboudit.

Patty spends her days writing facts and her nights writing contemporary romantic fiction. A coworker once said if Patty were a super-villain, she'd be called *The Quibbler*. Her costume would be covered in exclamation points. Fueled by a *serious* chocolate obsession, a love of *bad* science-fiction movies, and a weird attraction to exclamation points, Patty looks for ways to mix business with pleasure, mining her day job for ideas to use in her fiction.

Protogenesis

by Steve & Zack Umstead

Space was cold, a vast empty void crossed with deadly radiation and invisible particles, interspersed with sporadic and rare chunks of rock and gas orbiting fiery balls of plasma. Space was barren, but not lifeless. The rarest of rare chunks could sustain life — sometimes intelligent life, sometimes not, but life nonetheless. Every life-bearing rock was different, unique, except for one common thread: they were lifeless until visited.

The meteoroid tumbled slowly as it traveled through the vacuum. Weak starlight reflected from smooth sides, absorbed by the rough sides. It wasn't large, not as interstellar bodies went, but it was far from unimportant. Its nickel-iron core was protected by a layer of accumulated rock and carbon dioxide ice, the latter of which began to sublimate as the meteoroid approached the yellow-orange star at the center of the small solar system. The thrust generated by the ice burn-off nudged it slightly from its original path and it fell into the gravity well of a planet covered in a thick layer of white.

As it entered the planet's atmosphere, the outer layer of rock began to ablate, leaving a fiery trail above the surface. It shrank as heat consumed its mass. Three miles above the planet's surface, the meteor broke into three pieces, two of which were small rocky chunks that crumbled bit by bit and burned up, providing a spectacular show to whatever creature looked skyward. The third and largest piece, composed of nearly solid nickel-iron, journeyed unimpeded. The outer surface flowed like water, but the heat didn't penetrate. It trailed flaming droplets of molten metal and smoke as it neared its end. The sonic boom it caused would have turned heads below if anything had been listening.

The meteor impacted a wide mass of white and bore hundreds of feet deep, throwing up a massive geyser of sooty ice, finally coming to a rest within the confines of a massive glacier.

A visitor had arrived.

Australian Research Station Casey, Vincennes Bay, Antarctica
March 9, 2036

"You have something, Doctor?"

Peter Higgins looked up from the scope his face was pressed into. "I think I do," he said. "Come here." He motioned his favorite intern, Laurie Rolph, over to the microscope. "Tell me what you see."

The intern peered into the microscope and adjusted the dials. "What am I looking for, Doctor?" She moved the slide slightly. "Oh, now I see. Hmmm." She frowned and turned to Dr. Higgins. "What is that?"

"I was hoping you could help me with that," he replied. "That slide contains a slice of the meteorite the drillers came across yesterday. Iron-nickel, a very standard composition. But what interests me — well, you saw it. What do you think of it?"

"Hmmm," she murmured again. "Bright orange in color. Diaphanous, just a few molecules in thickness. It appears to be some kind of membrane."

"That's the same conclusion I came to."

"But that's extremely anomalous of a meteorite. Not to mention the damage the membrane would have sustained during entry. But this one seems miraculously *undamaged*. That leaves two options."

"And what might those be?" Dr. Higgins asked.

"Either this membrane made it through unharmed, which is highly unlikely, or it underwent repairs after entry."

Dr. Higgins admired the ingenuity of students who hadn't yet been confined by the way society thought, which is why he had asked for Laurie's opinion. But this?

"Repairs? Miss Rolph, are you implying that this thing can repair itself?"

"Well, the meteorite certainly didn't repair it."

"Self-repair. And a membrane." Dr. Higgins shook his head. "It can't possibly be, but all this makes it appear to be..."

"Alive?" Laurie finished.

"But you must know that is even more unlikely than it making it through unharmed?"

"As unlikely as life beginning on our little rock? Dr. Higgins, if life happened once, why can't it happen twice?"

*Australian Research Station Casey, Vincennes Bay, Antarctica
March 19, 2036*

"Doctor, we've done everything we can to study this thing without harming it, and we've found almost nothing."

"We have determined its probable composition," Dr. Higgins replied.

"But Doctor, to prove it is in fact alive, we have to dissect it. We need to know what's inside." Laurie was becoming impatient. After two days, the orange membrane had done nothing but sit inside its little sliver of meteorite. Residue from the nearby surface revealed high amounts of amino acids and a few lipids, and a visible light microscope had revealed what appeared to be simple structures inside the membrane. But the only way they could learn more was with an SEM. That would require coating the object with a metal, most likely killing it if it was indeed organic.

"Well, Miss Rolph, if it is as you say it is, then this membrane should be able to reproduce. Have you considered placing a sample of it in a Petri dish?"

Laurie reprimanded herself for forgetting something so obvious. "I'll fetch a dish," she said, and hurried out of the room.

"And I will prepare our guest for his new home." Dr. Higgins picked up a micropipette and peered into the microscope. He maneuvered it with the ease of a veteran and soon had the membrane intact and ready for the transfer. Laurie returned with a Petri dish and placed it under the scope. Dr. Higgins maneuvered the pipettes into position and transferred the membrane sample to the dish.

"And now we wait," Laurie said.

"I don't think we have to," Dr. Higgins said, his face still pressed into the microscope.

After millions of years crossing the galaxy in cold vacuum, and millions of years more buried in ice, the orange matrix lay dormant. It was designed to perform a specific function, one that would only occur under precise, optimum conditions.

Conditions improved. The temperature rose, light was detected, and trace evidence of oxygen pointed towards several requirements being met. Only one precursor was needed for the matrix to shift into its next phase: a pre-organic growth medium. Fuel. Food.

Higgins stepped back from the microscope, one hand held over his chest. With his other hand, he reached for a digital imaging device sitting on the lab table.

"This is... remarkable," he breathed as he fumbled with the imager's settings.

Laurie took a hesitant step forward and looked at the Petri dish. Her eyes widened and she turned to Higgins.

"Doctor, what's happening?" Her voice shook with what Higgins took as excitement, but tinged with nervousness. The same nervousness he was starting to feel. What he saw before him, and what the imager now recorded, was unprecedented, both in speed and scope. Never in his thirty-plus years of molecular research had he seen something move so quickly, or grow so visibly to the naked eye.

Higgins held the imager at arm's length and moved closer to the table. Laurie stepped sideways to allow him to record the activity.

The agar the Petri dish held was normally a deep red color, having been derived for almost 150 years from boiling a polysaccharide contained in red algae. Within seconds of Higgins placing a section of the membrane into the dish, the agar turned a bright orange, matching the color of the membrane itself. The dish, ordinarily filled to one-half its depth with the red agar, overflowed with an orange substance. Tendrils of orange reached out from the dish, touching the lab table, and continued to extend outwards.

"Remarkable," Higgins whispered again, pressing the imager up to his face.

Laurie took a step back and bumped into another lab table, rattling a rack of test tubes. "Doctor, should we be, ah, concerned with this?"

Silent, Higgins watched the membrane expand. The science behind it was impressive, but the discovery behind it was world-changing. An organic substance had fallen from the heavens. Life, from another place. He imagined the papers he would write, the accolades he'd receive. An image of standing at a podium accepting the Nobel Prize for Physiology or Medicine flashed across his mind.

"Remarkable." He let the imager fall to one side and reached out with his other hand. The membrane looked so beautiful, so full of life. So... important.

Tendrils seemed to stretch to meet his extended finger.

The matrix grew exponentially after coming into contact with basic organic compounds, exactly as it was designed to do. It fed, it expanded, it developed new cell structures, and began shifting into its next phase. Cilia grew on the tips of its new sensor threads, which sampled the atmosphere around it. It used the organic fuel to divide cells at a rapid pace. And it pushed outwards.

Laurie gasped as the tendrils reached up from the growing mass on the table and came into contact with Higgins' fingertips.

"Don't worry," Higgins said. He handed the imager to her. "Keep recording. This is a landmark moment in human history." He watched tendrils spread up his fingers and across the back of his hand. "History," he whispered.

Laurie held the imager up and stepped back against the far wall. Higgins smiled at her anxiety. He knew this membrane, this life, meant no harm. Quite the contrary, he thought as the orange mass crept up his wrist. It was the most incredible, most important discovery since fire. And he, Doctor Peter Higgins, had made it.

"Doctor, are you sure..."

"Yes, Laurie, I'm sure," Higgins replied. He tore his gaze from the orange mass to look at her. She stood, pressed up against the lab wall, holding the imager in one hand, clutching a pendant she wore around her neck with the other. "This membrane might be..."

He stopped. Slight heat came from the tip of the first finger touched by the orange membrane. The heat grew and he felt a burning sensation.

"Ah, Laurie, can you..." He shook his head, tried to clench his fist, but couldn't. Fire seemed to spread through his hand and moved up his arm, following the orange membrane's path.

Higgins opened his mouth to warn Laurie, but without warning the membrane shot up his arm and spread across his face. His arm felt like a white-hot torch. He tried to scream, but gagged as the orange substance flooded into his open mouth and down his throat. The last thing Peter Higgins saw was a hazy orange outline of Laurie Rolph sprinting from the lab.

The second phase, expansion, progressed well. The simple organic compounds the orange matrix used as food were expected. Countless others seeds had been sent across the endless void millions of years ago, and the target planets for those seeds always possessed them. Otherwise the third phase could never take place. The designers of the matrix had taken every possible variable into consideration. Including the rare presence of complex organic compounds. Life.

The seeds were designed to spread life where there was no life, and had been doing so since the beginning of time. But the designers were ruthless in their creation. The matrix had a design for a specific type of life at a specific time in a planet's development cycle. If that cycle was further along than what was expected, so be it. The matrix had one goal: spreading its own life. At the peril of whatever existed.

But something had gone wrong, hundreds of millions of years prior. The meteorite that carried this particular matrix was caught in an unexpected gravity well after passing too close to a collapsed star. Its path was changed and it drifted aimlessly through space for eons until nudged by a wandering asteroid, which put it on course for a little blue and white ball third out from its star. A little blue and white ball that had previously been visited by another seed.

Life had already taken root on Earth, life that was designed by the seeds' creators. But the second matrix didn't know that, nor did it care. It had a goal, and if complex life was found on its target planet, so be it.

Only one life could exist at a time.

*Australian Research Station Casey, Vincennes Bay, Antarctica
March 21, 2036*

Two days. Two days without food and only one water bottle she had scrounged from another tech's desk. *Lord only knows what happened to that tech,* Laurie thought. *Maybe the same thing that happened to Dr. Higgins.* Laurie hadn't seen anyone since she had put the east wing of Casey Station into emergency lockdown. But she knew someone was watching her; the closed-circuit video cameras were broadcasting to the Station Monitoring Center, where Laurie knew that someone had to be watching the entire situation. Or at least recording. She looked at the camera watching the lab she had chosen to hide in and shrugged as if to say, *I'm out of options.*

And Laurie knew it was true; there was no way she was going to get out of here. She'd be lucky if her body wasn't consumed by that orange monster. "I'm as good as dead," she said to the camera, knowing there was no microphone and no one would hear her. *Who knows,* she thought. *Someone might be able to read lips.* "I can't do anything but sit here and die. But I'm glad that thing is going to be stuck in here as well. If you can understand me, you need to come in here and physically kill it. We don't know if it will die of starvation, or asphyxiation, or if it will die at all! We don't know anything!"

Laurie stopped herself. *We do know something.* When they had first observed the original cell, it had appeared dormant. Was it possible to put it back into this dormant state? Why would it be dormant?

The cold, she realized. The original cell had been cryogenically frozen by the mere chance of landing in Antarctica. And Laurie knew she could make the station cold; it was as easy as opening a door.

Laurie emerged from the lab and started towards the east wing's external entrance. As her footsteps echoed down the corridors, she said a silent prayer that she wouldn't run into the orange beast. But it seemed that whatever god was up there wasn't looking her way, because when she rounded the corner, a mass of orange goo sat in front of the outside door.

The matrix was developing nicely. After gaining enough biomass from various encounters throughout the closed area it was in, cells began to differentiate, and it turned into something resembling an animal. Cells on the exterior were dedicated to tracking more biomass using airborne particulates, while interior cells were dedicated to energy production. A group near the center had specialized and become a network of cells sharing information using protein-based endorphins, creating what could be called a neural net. This neural net controlled the rest of the matrix's functions and interpreted data from the epithelial cells, which were currently sending a most curious signal. The neural net found that a large concentration of airborne phospholipids was drifting from one direction. It accessed its limited memory and discovered that the same concentrations of phospholipids were found on the exterior of each of the large biomasses it had consumed earlier. The matrix extended a long orange pseudopod in the direction the phospholipids were coming from and began the process of moving towards the biomass.

Laurie was surprised when the thing began to crawl towards her. She was even more surprised by the agility it moved with; it was far faster than any slime mold could possibly move. But she could see that it was no longer a simple mold or membrane.

She needed to move the thing away from the door, so its movement was fortunate, and she thought for a moment that God was on her side. She ducked into a lab to let the thing pass down the hallway.

But for the second time that day she realized that God wasn't going to be of any service. The creature's lead pseudopod slid into the lab and started extending in multiple directions. Laurie panicked and threw a binder full of lab notes at it. The binder squished into the beast, but strangely enough, only the papers were drawn into the gel. *It's hungry,* Laurie realized. *It wants more food.* She continued to throw papers from nearby tables at it, but the pseudopod continued to advance. Soon, the entirety of the creature was in the lab. The door was still blocked. Laurie frantically searched for more food for the creature.

Inside a low cabinet, she found a brown paper bag with a chicken salad sandwich and bottle of soda. Her stomach growled, but she growled right back at it, and hastily unwrapped the sandwich. She ripped off a piece of it and threw it to the creature. The slime quickly engulfed the tiny piece of sandwich. Laurie began working on a trail of sandwich pieces to the back of the room. Hopefully, the creature would follow it to the back and give her enough time to escape.

But as she placed the remaining sandwich at the back of the room, it dawned on Laurie that she had trapped herself at the back of the room with a trail of breadcrumbs leading right to her. The slime had spread to the full width of the room, and even though the doorway was open and slime-free, Laurie had no intentions of taking her chances and sprinting across this thing. She remembered how fast it had consumed Dr. Higgins. *Not this way,* she thought. *It can't end this way.* She desperately searched for an escape route.

Her only option was less than ideal. The slime had crawled across the floor to reach her, so the tabletops were orange-goo free. Laurie carefully climbed onto the nearest table and sized up the jump. She took her chances and leaped, bridging the gap, and the table held. She was safe — for the moment. She had one more table to reach, and she needed to get there fast. The slime had stopped moving towards the sandwich and was drawing in its pseudopod.

As Laurie crouched to launch herself one last time, the table shifted slightly. Papers fell off, and the slime sucked them into its body. Laurie hesitated and tried to regain her balance, but time was running out. The slime was extending a pseudopod up the table in search of more food: in search of Laurie.

She finally regained her balance, and took the jump. She landed it perfectly, and a short hop put her in the doorway. She ran to the external entrance across the hall and smashed the glass on the emergency release. A yank of the lever caused the door to swing open and subzero Antarctic air rushed in.

As if in protest, the slime shrunk away from the lab doorway and began curling itself into a ball. It lay under a table, and the paper that had been drawn into its body was rapidly disappearing. *It's trying to stay warm*, Laurie thought as she put on one of the parkas hanging besides the door release. *But it won't be able to keep that up for long.*

After a few minutes, the slime began to shake rapidly, reminding Laurie of a cup of Jello wiggling as someone played with it. But the vibrating soon subsided as more and more icy air spread through the lab, and the slime became motionless. Laurie huddled against the wall, trying to bury herself in the parka. Seconds dragged into minutes as she waited, staring at it, until she was sure it was completely dormant.

She stood up and walked hesitantly to the orange mass. She reached out and poked it with her finger. It was firm to the touch, like a hardened piece of rubber.

I killed it, she thought. A huge feeling of relief washed over her. Memories of her co-workers and of Dr. Higgins crossed her mind and she burst out in tears.

She knew she stopped it from spreading, and maybe saved lives. But she knew she'd never see her friends, or her mentor again.

She sniffled and wiped a cold hand across her nose. She knew she needed to lock down the facility and somehow call for help. And she'd have to try to stay warm until help arrived. She didn't want to take any chances of that monster warming back up.

But I killed it, she thought again. *And it would never harm anyone else.*

With one last look at the frozen orange mass, she walked from the lab. She remembered that Dr. Higgins' lab was isolated from the rest of the complex. Maybe she could hide there and stay warm.

Back in Higgins' lab, the silent Station Monitoring Center camera continued to record as a tiny slice of orange membrane crept slowly across a table towards an open Petri dish.

Steve Umstead is the author of the *Evan Gabriel* military science fiction trilogy, and currently has ten different works published. **Zack Umstead** is an honors high school student and the author of the published young adult science fiction stories *Shifter* and *Entanglement*.

"Orange You Glad the Doctor's In"

by R. B. Wood

D octor Singh, Mr. Schnittman is on the phone for you again, sir. He says it's urgent."

Doctor Jatin Singh sighed. He put down the patient notes he'd been reviewing. Pressing the button on his intercom, he said, "Okay, Jackie. Put him through."

"Line two, sir."

Singh punched the speaker phone button a little harder than usual. "Dr. Singh," he grunted.

"Doc, I have to see you, right now!" squeaked the voice from the other end of the line. "It's a matter of life and death!"

"Marty, I'm about to head home. Can't this wait until morning?"

"No! Please. You can't go home! Isn't there some sort of Hippocratic oath for psychologists? I'm in distress here!" The panic was palpable.

Singh sighed. "All right, Marty. Calm down. How soon can you get here?"

Sounding relieved, Schnittman said, "I'm here now. In the parking lot. I can be right up!"

"Okay, Marty, you can..." But the phone on the other line had already gone dead.

Doctor Singh put away his notes and pulled out Marty Schnittman's file. The man had come to him about six months ago. Marty had written a best selling book, but hadn't been able to write a word since. The short, balding, lumpy man had a long nose and watery eyes. He'd reminded Singh of a hopeless rodent the first time they'd met.

For half a year, Singh had tried to get to the root cause of his patient's writer's block. Six long months hearing about issues. Growing up with a single mother, how Marty's wife degraded him and his children ignored him — even after his novel, *Small Man in a Big Bad World,* had hit the *New York Times* Bestsellers list. They were even making a movie now, starring Danny DeVito.

But none of Marty's many neuroses seemed to cause his writer's block. Thinking that maybe his non-existent ego needed a bit of CPR, Singh had tried something he had learned about back in his youth in Bangalore. The stimulation of certain points in the body — chakras — could be done via varoius crystals. He'd recently obtained a small fire opal that, according to legend, would achieve the results the doctor was looking for.

But Marty Schnittman was a pathetic specimen to test his theory? ...No. He couldn't think like that about one of his patients. Yes, the writer was a wreck of a man, but he deserved help. And he was perfect for the new program the doctor was working on.

A muffled shout, a loud thump, and what sounded like the squeal of a wounded animal interrupted Singh's musings. Singh rushed to the door and wrenched it open. He stared in horror at the scene unfolding like a nightmare before his eyes.

Marty Schnittman was lying on the floor next to his secretary's desk. Jackie — Singh's tall, curvy, raven-haired assistant — was straddling Marty, holding him down with her legs while attempting to pull off her own clothes.

Marty flailed at her with his umbrella.

It was a good ten seconds, watching his secretary struggle to get naked while the small man feebly tried to extract himself from between her legs, before the doctor rushed across the room and pulled his secretary off his patient.

"What in the name of God is happening here!"

Marty and Jackie stopped struggling at once, both turning to look at Singh. The trapped animal expression on Marty's face turned to relief while Jackie blinked a few times in confusion.

"Wha...?" she asked, sounding a little drunk. Then she looked down at Marty. The blood drained from her face and her eyes went wide with horror as she noticed her half undone bra and the state of her clothes. The comely secretary jumped up at once.

"He! I... oh God, what's happening?" she moaned.

Marty scrambled to his feet.

"See, Doc? See? You saw it with your own eyes, didn't you?" He ran to Singh and grabbed the front his white jacket. Tears filled the man's eyes and he looked up into the doctor's face with a desperate, pleading expression. He pointed to Jackie. "They won't leave me alone!"

"What did you do to me, Mr. Schnittman?!" Jackie shouted, unsuccessfully trying to button her blouse while grabbing for her skirt and shoes.

Singh's brain finally engaged. "Marty," he said. "Inside my office. Now. Jackie, get dressed and go home. Just go."

The doctor turned his back and slammed the door to shut out the insults his secretary hurled at Schnittman.

"Marty, what happened?" asked Singh.

"It started when you gave me this," Marty held out his hand to show the small, orange stone Singh had presented to him only yesterday.

"It's been a nightmare," Marty continued. "I got home from the office and within thirty minutes my wife was all over me."

The doctor had seen pictures of Mrs. Schnittman, who looked a bit like a baboon in a mumu. Both Marty and Singh shuddered.

"She wouldn't stop!" Marty paced like a madman. "I barely got out of the house with my life. Then I went to the bar up the street, and got hit on by every woman there."

"Well, we seemed to have resolved your self-esteem issue," said Singh wryly.

"I got this," said Marty, ignoring the doctor and pointing to his left eye. Singh noticed for the first time his patient's bruised eye. "When a sailor got mad at me. His girlfriend had started to grind on me..."

"But what about the writing?" Singh interrupted.

"Oh, I wrote a short story in about thirty minutes... a good one, too. Once I finally escaped from all the women." Marty stopped pacing and put the orange stone on the large mahogany desk. "What *is* this thing?"

"I explained it all to you yesterday, Marty. Remember? Orange is a powerful color. And an orange stone, like this fire opal, enhances the second Chakra, which is connected to creativity. We walked through all the Chakras. I thought..."

"No!" Marty shouted. He reached into his pocket and pulled out a smart phone. "No. Creativity is not all it represents! I looked it up. I have the Internet on this thing. The second Chakra is all about sexuality! That's why all these women won't leave me alone. You've done some sort of voodoo thing to me!"

"It's also about creativity and self-esteem." Singh felt as though he was trying to explain one plus one to a young child. "In my country..."

"It's voodoo magic! I don't want it anymore."

"But Marty, you are out of your writing slump! That's why you came to me in the first place. And the side effect isn't completely horrible, is it?"

"I have no idea what to do with women. We've talked about that in our sessions. No idea. They terrify me. First, it was my mother and now my wife. All I want to do is write."

"Well, perhaps if we work together a bit more on this, we can figure out a way to keep the creativity portion the most dominant effect. You did, after all write something — the first thing you've written in months."

Marty shook his head. "I've written one story... I'm sure more will come now. The writer's block has passed. And I want to go back to being invisible to women."

"Marty, that may be true. But I'd like to try something else..."

"No," said Marty flatly. "I'm done with you, too. You and your freakin' voodoo."

"I'm Indian, Marty. Voodoo is practiced in Haiti, Louisiana, and West Africa." Singh narrowed his eyes. He was getting annoyed now.

Angry red blotches appeared on the small man's face and neck. "I'm gonna tell everyone about you, you quack!" Marty exploded. "Everyone. Maybe my family doesn't listen to me, but I have millions of readers who do. I'm going to write about you and what you did to me. Let's see you get a client after that!"

Marty spun on his heels and marched out of Singh's office, slamming the door behind him.

In the silence that followed, Singh smiled, then began to laugh. The spell and stone had worked far better then he had hoped.

He picked up the fire opal and placed it gently into his own pocket. After all, he had been a widower for years, and had his own needs. And then there was that psychology book he wanted to write.

He heard a door slam outside and he looked out his window in time to see Marty's car roar out of the parking lot, tires squealing. The car fishtailed a little on the rain-soaked pavement as he drove onto the street.

"Voodoo, huh," muttered Singh. "Good idea." Yes, the doctor had plans, but Marty was right about the size of his readership. An article written by Marty besmirching Singh's character might damage those plans, no matter how unbelievable it may be.

Humming lightly, Singh walked over to a locked armoire behind the patients' couch, unlocked and opened it.

There, in neat little rows, sat small cloth dolls. Each doll had a label on it with one of his patients' names. These were his backup plans should some future experiments go awry.

"Well, I guess I'll be testing this after all." Singh reached into the cabinet and pulled out the doll labeled "Marty Schnittman".

He grabbed a Zippo lighter off his desk. Without ceremony or hesitation, he held the flame to the doll until it caught fire. Almost immediately, the entire figurine was engulfed. The doctor dropped it into the metal bin by his desk.

Outside, there came another, more distant, squeal of tires, followed immediately by a loud crash.

Singh walked to his window and looked out. At the busy, very dangerous intersection outside his office complex, there had been a terrible, fiery accident.

While he watched the flames, the doctor put his left hand into his front pocket and caressed the fire opal. He pulled a cell phone out of his jacket with his right, flipped it open and dialed a number. A familiar voice answered after one ring.

"Jackie, Doctor Singh. I'm so sorry about what happened. Don't worry, Marty Schnittman will never darken our doorstep again. How about I take you out to dinner to make up for it?"

Smiling, he continued to fondle the little orange stone in his pocket.

∽o∾

R.B. Wood is a technology consultant and a writer of Urban Fantasy, Science Fiction, and quite frankly anything else that strikes his fancy. His first novel, *The Prodigal's Foole*, was released to critical acclaim in 2012. Mr. Wood is currently working on the second book of his Arcana Chronicles series, called *The Young Practitioner*, along with multiple short stories, a graphic novel, and a science fiction trilogy that he dusts off every few years. Along with his writing passion, R.B. is host of *The Word Count Podcast* —— a show that features talent from all around the globe reading original flash-fiction stories. R.B. currently lives in Boston with his partner, Tina, his dog Jack, three cats, and various other critters that visit from time to time.

A Little Night Music

by Taylor Lunsford

It's during the late night hours, when everything is quiet and your brain is running on empty, when the most surreal things happen. I don't know what it was. Maybe it was a dream. Maybe it was a dream of a dream. I don't really know. All I know is sometimes dreams are *much* better than reality.

I had been sitting at my desk, slogging my way through a paper, when the stillness of the witching hour was broken by soft piano music. I couldn't imagine where it could be coming from. No one in the apartments around us owned a piano, and the music sounded like it was *in* my apartment, but I knew my roommate had gone to bed hours before.

My body screaming in protest from hours of sitting in the same position, I got up and slowly opened my door to look out into the living room. Only it wasn't my living room. The cozy chairs and cheerful twinkle lights were gone. The room was massive and completely pitch black, except for a spotlight that illuminated the center of the room.

There was a large, dark object in the center of the spotlight. I could tell from the glare that emanated off the gleaming ebony surface that it was a *very* nice baby grand piano, but the raised lid and the brightness of the light kept me from seeing who was playing the beautiful instrument.

As the music transitioned from a nameless tune into a gently haunting rendition of "As Time Goes By", I moved deeper into the room. My bare feet on the smoothly-polished parquet floor didn't make a sound to disturb the song. I noticed, as I walked, that I was no longer wearing my faded black yoga pants and comfortable pink camisole. Instead, I was wearing a filmy white empire-waist, cap-sleeved dress made of some sort of light, silky material that was cool against my skin. My hair fell into loose curls around my shoulders — curls that my mop of red-orange messiness could only achieve in a dream — and a small crown of rosebuds rested gently among the carroty riot. My dream self felt nothing like my real self. I stood a little straighter and, even though I was unsure about this whole thing, I held myself with a newfound confidence.

"Took you long enough," a musically masculine voice said over the sound of the piano.

"Excuse me?"

"I've been waiting for you for a while now," he explained.

"Who are you?" I asked, moving around the piano so that I could get a better look at him.

He wasn't necessarily beautiful, or classically handsome, but there was something about him. His short, coal-black hair was messy, like he had been constantly running his hand through it while wrestling with deep thoughts. His face was etched in clean, solid lines and he looked to be several years older than my tender twenty-two. His lips were just the right proportion for his face, and thick eyelashes veiled his eyes. His graceful fingers floated over the ivory keys. One side of his mouth was quirked up in a crooked little half-smile. Long legs stretched casually underneath the piano. He wore a tuxedo, but the bow tie was untied and draped around his neck, and his shirt was as rumpled as his hair. He looked perfect in his imperfections.

"Anthony. I'm Anthony, and you're Emma," he replied simply.

"How do you know my name?" Intellectually, I knew that he knew my name because, of course, this had to be a dream, and in dreams people just *know*, but because it felt so real, I had to ask.

"Because I've known you since time began." His words seemed to wrap around me like the flow of the music. "And you've known me. You just don't remember."

"Why are you here? Why am I here?"

"You, my beautiful little friend, have lost your faith in love, so I'm here to remind you that it is still out there."

"How can I lose faith in something I've never experienced? I believe that love exists. Doesn't that count?" I had never been in a serious relationship. The only time I'd ever come close, things had been ruined by distance, and his obliviousness and my stupidity, or my obliviousness and his stupidity. I was never quite sure. Despite this, I was still an avid fan of the Jane Austen-type romance with the happily-ever-after ending.

"Nope," he said, his smile growing, his eyes never leaving the keys. "It's been taking too long for us to find each other, so you've lost faith that I'm real."

He was right. I'd sat on the sidelines, watching all of my friends find relationships and people to love. My best friend was engaged to be married and I'd never even been kissed. "But you're not real. You're a dream. My dream, but still a dream."

"For now. I am real, though," he explained. "I live far away from you, but one day, our paths will cross. You just have to be patient and keep the faith."

"I should keep the faith because a guy in a dream who claims to be real says I should. Right," I said sarcastically, turning away.

"Sit down," he ordered gently. In spite of myself, I joined him on the padded piano bench. Our bodies were pressed close together from shoulder, to hip, to knee. The light took on the soft tinges of sunset-orange, warming my skin through the thin veil of my dress.

"You've stopped writing," he remarked. "Why?"

"I just... haven't felt like writing lately." I shrugged. I had started a novel, but something was keeping me from working on it.

"You have a gift, Em. You have to use it." A gift or a curse? I wondered. Sometimes I felt like I was cursed to forever be on the outside looking in at things, to always observe and never experience.

"You're the one with the gift. Where did you learn to play piano like this?" He was now playing "Make Someone Happy" in the same otherworldly way he'd played the previous song. My writing could never be as beautiful and soul-catching as his music.

"That's for me to know and you to find out," he said cryptically. "Your gift is one for the ages, Emma. Your work is just as beautiful as Burns's or Whitman's or any other great writers'."

"You know Burns?" Robert Burns was one of my favorite poets.

"As fair art thou, my bonnie lass, So deep in luve am I; And I will luve thee still, my dear, Till a' the seas gang dry," Anthony quoted deftly, trying to mimic a Scottish accent, although it sounded like a very poor Irish one instead.

"Impressive."

"Do you think Burns ever gave up on love?" He kept playing, but his gaze suddenly met mine. He had the most striking eyes I had ever seen. They were a smoky color that I knew would change with his moods; right now, because he was serious, they were a steel grey, but my gut told me that they could change to blue if he was happy. Those eyes knew me. They got me. They didn't believe anything but what I truly felt. They saw past the façade I put up to deal with the day-to-day loneliness. "He had his ups and downs in love, but he never stopped writing about love and believing in it."

"I don't know what love really *is*," I protested. "I can't have faith in something I don't understand."

"You understand love," Anthony contradicted. "It's that feeling you get when your dad answers the phone and says he's happy to hear your voice. Love is what you feel when your little cousin jumps up into your arms and refuses to let go because you're her favorite person in the whole world and she's missed you. Love is that feeling you get when you're sitting with your friends and you're totally happy because you know that that's where you belong."

"That's not the kind of love you're talking about, though," I pointed out.

"No. But that's the kind of love that gets you ready for our kind of love. You can't appreciate one without the other. You need to know the love of friends to be open to the love of a lifetime."

"So I'll need to appreciate both?" I asked, raising an eyebrow at him.

He laughed. "Most definitely. You and I are going to have a wonderfully happy life together. Full of love, laughter, and the trials that make those things worth it. We're going to be friends, lovers, sweethearts, and confidants. You're going to be my heart, and I yours."

"Really?" I couldn't help the hopeful note that crept into my voice.

"Really," he promised softly. "So, do you think you can hold on until we find each other?" When I nodded, he stopped playing. "One day, we'll be walking down the street, or sitting on the subway, or in a bookstore, and we'll just know. But until then, you have to keep your faith in love. You have such a great capacity for love. You just need to find that same capacity for patience."

"I can be patient," I assured him. "And I'm pretty sure I can keep the faith now."

"Good," he whispered. He was just leaning in as if he was going to kiss me when... of course... I woke up.

Sigh!

I wasn't in a dark room with a fancy piano and an attractive guy. I was in my bedroom, sitting at my boring desk, staring at my computer screen. But try as I might, in the days to come, I couldn't shake the feeling of assurance that had settled somewhere deep within me. In the darkness of my room, I tried to hold onto the warm orange glow of the light, the feel of him beside me. He would find me, or I would find him.

∾o∾

That feeling stayed with me until the day, seven years later, that I sat down in an aisle of a small bookstore in New York City to look through a volume of Robert Burns' poetry and *he* literally stumbled over me. He fell to the floor beside me, his legs tangled with mine. The soft orange of the ancient light dangling above us gilded his dark hair, just as it had in my dream, the dream that kept me going all these years. Our eyes met and we both just *knew*. Even as we laughed at the absurdity of the situation, we fell a little more in love each second.

He apologized profusely for almost crushing me and took me out for coffee to make up for it. We talked for hours, about everything and nothing. His name was Anthony Costa. Tony, as he insisted on being called by everyone except his mother, was thirty-two years old and helped his family run their little Italian restaurant and Irish pub in Brooklyn. He was a master chef, an accomplished musician, and an avid sports fan. When the coffee shop closed, we just walked around the city until our feet were too tired to go any further, and then he saw me to my door and kissed me good night.

On our third date, I told him about my dream, and he didn't think I was crazy. In fact, he had had a similar dream. He looked me straight in the eyes and said, "You, Emma Reilly, are my destiny, and I have loved you since I was twenty-five years old. Will you do me the honor of embracing our fate and becoming my wife?"

He played for me that night, our wedding night. He played the songs that he'd played in our dream. Once all of the guests were gone and there was no one but us, with his tie undone and his hair mussed, he played for me until I had to kiss him. He finished the dream and made it so much more than I thought it could be.

So, maybe it wasn't a dream. Maybe it was a premonition. All I know is that my dream came true, truer than I could have imagined. We didn't live happily ever after, because that only exists in fairy tales, but Anthony and I found a happiness that couldn't be matched.

We found the love you experience when your best friend is sitting next to you on a cold winter's night and you don't ever want to move. We were overwhelmed by the love a parent can feel for a child — well, two children, actually. As the soft orange of sunset seeped through our windows each day, he played for me, never letting me forget that love. He never let me forget we found the love you can only find with the person who is your better half.

Taylor Lunsford is a hopeless romantic who spends her days working for a great company and her nights/weekends doing the job of her heart. Along with writing romance, she also works as an editor for a small e-press. She's still searching for her Prince Charming, but she knows he's out there, so she'll content herself with fictional ones for now.

An Evolution of Orange

by Anne Baker

Hannah hated orange. Orange was pain, anger, betrayal, and grief. The color of her mother's fake tan, desperately covering up the pallor born of ineffective chemo. The glare of her brother's jumpsuit under the harsh lights of prison. The fire that had stolen her father's freedom of movement. Every tragic event of her life could be traced back to the same wretched color.

"Price."

Hannah jerked herself out of her thoughts and away from the nauseating photo of a generic fiery sunset at her commander's voice.

"Sir."

"Come in and have a seat."

She couldn't wait to be a rank that trumped "please" and "thank you". Someday. Meanwhile, she could follow instructions like nobody's business — unlike that idiot, Contratto, during this morning's exercise.

Hannah sat in the cheap office chair, posture perfect and face neutral. Emotions were a dangerous commodity.

"I'm going to be blunt with you, Lieutenant. Debriefings are largely without consideration of rank for a reason. People need to be honest and discuss missions without fear of reprisal over word choice. However, this policy is not generally license to swear at someone for upwards of twenty minutes." The major's black brow hitched halfway up his forehead. He didn't seem particularly pissed at her, but she doubted he'd support the level of her rant about safety protocols from this morning.

"Understood, sir." Really, what else could she say? She certainly wasn't sorry. Contratto had put everyone in danger with his stunts.

"That's it? No other comment?"

"Obviously, it was an error in judgment. I let my temper get the better of me. Sir." Hannah couldn't let the subject go with that, however. "Permission to speak freely, sir?"

"By all means." He waved, slightly bemused that she'd actually asked first.

"Flying is everything to me. To have someone putting me, themselves, and everyone else up there at risk over some testosterone-driven reckless maneuvers... I have a hard time with people who don't play by the rules. Especially when they endanger people by ignoring those rules. We're a unit up there, sir. Or are supposed to be."

"I respect your opinion, Price. And I applaud your concerns for your squadron. But. I don't need any more reports of you erupting like a volcano during a debriefing. It's counterproductive."

"Yes, sir." Hannah stifled a sigh, relieved that she wasn't being assigned some humiliating task as punishment.

"Even if it's gratifying to tell someone..." Major Brandon checked the notes before him. "Ah, here it is. 'You motherfucking moron. Fuck you sideways. With a chainsaw.' Inventive and cringe-inducing, I admit."

Hannah squeezed her eyes shut in mortification. She barely remembered half her rant. Apparently, it was inspired. The major laughed at her discomfort, pleased he'd broken through the neutral front.

"You'll be okay, Price. Work on your camaraderie with the group. I don't want to lose a hot stick to her hot temper."

He stood, tacitly ending the meeting. Hannah immediately followed, belatedly processing his hidden compliment. He thought she was a hot stick? Compliments like that could send her flying without a machine.

"Just be prepared for the Naming." His reference to the callsign naming ceremony brought her crashing back down. "In your shoes, I'd think of some good bribes."

Hannah mentally prepared to empty her checking account to buy top shelf alcohol for her instructors and colleagues. Maybe she could come up with something less traditional than an alcohol bribe. Or maybe not.

∽∾o∾∽

Two months later, Hannah still worried about the damn naming ceremony. The only balm to the itch of it was her continuing flight school track assignment, which would be announced the day after.

"Hannah Price!"

Obligatory catcalls and cheering accompanied her up to the front of the room. She had hoped the nearly $500 worth of alcohol did its work as a bribe, but the wicked smirks and waggling eyebrows of the entire group filled her with dread. Deep breaths.

"In honor of her spectacular, impressive, and now-infamous show of temper, Lieutenant Price will hereby be given the callsign 'Pele', the long version of which is 'Protracted Expletive-Laden Explosion'. 'Cause this woman needs a warning sign, and that's the best we came up with. Also, Mitch here says it's kinda the Hawaiian personification of violence and lava, which we think fits."

Hannah was cheered and jeered by the room, and took just a brief moment to rejoice that her name wasn't something awful like "Bitch" or "Ice Queen" or even her atrocious high school nickname of B.B., for Bob Barker. She might think she was always right, but that name was unbearable.

After a few friendly punches to her newly pinned wings, one of her instructors pulled her aside, casually flung an arm around her shoulder, and spoke low and straight into her ear. "You're welcome."

For what? Keeping her stoic countenance to avoid disturbing the ongoing ceremony, she whispered back, "Thank you?"

"Between me and your top shelf, I kept them away from 'Air Raid Siren Expletives'."

"Wait. ARSE? Seriously?" Despite her shock, she had to admire their creativity. Thank goodness she'd had someone on her side.

"Well, you were pretty fucking loud and just kept going off. Gotta learn to put a lid on it, Price." He shrugged and patted her shoulder before heading back up front to torture the next victim.

Hannah tipped her face down as she headed back to her seat, grateful the next person was already being named, cheered, and socked in the chest. Her instructor, Shrek, grinned at her flushed cheeks. It was a good thing she had a soft spot for the oaf. He was big, friendly, and into pranks and protocols in equal measure. He also didn't seem to take her subtle warn-offs too personally.

The way she viewed it, she was here to learn, work, and train. Friends were all well and good, but who knew the next time she'd see any of these people? Besides, as long as she spent time in the air, she was content to be alone. She and the big blue had an almost spiritual connection, which was absolutely enough for her at the moment.

It was almost too bad that Shrek flew heavies, since she was desperately hoping for small and pointy. Perhaps they'd keep in touch anyway. Regardless, she'd remember his favor today and wear her new name with pride.

Even if the lava crack bugged her a bit.

Orange.

Again.

Small and pointy. Small and pointy. Small and pointy! Hannah mentally chanted though she was relatively certain she'd get her wish. Tops in her class, no more altercations since the epic rant at Contratto, now officially named Fuso (Fucked Up Showing Off), and the right personality profile. She should've been guaranteed a spot. They were announcing pilots by their new callsigns, and she waited to hear hers.

"Remotely Piloted Aircraft track: Fuso, Moby, Fudge."

Hannah managed to muffle her snort of derision. It was enormously satisfying to see those jerks fall short of fighter track.

"Weapons System Operator track: Homer, Lassie, Kiwi."

Only heavies and fighters left. Hannah childishly crossed her fingers. Small and pointy!

"Fighter track: Chester, Speedy, Pele."

She didn't hear another word. Finally. Finally her dream was in reach. Bowing out of the celebrations as soon as was polite, she powered up her cell phone while she walked.

"Hello?" The warm rasp of her father's voice soothed the adrenaline rush from her news.

"Dad. I got it. I got the fighter track!" Her free hand covered the corresponding ear, blocking all but the most important sound in the world.

"Congratulations, punkin! I knew you'd do it. Why would they put you anywhere else?"

"Thanks, Dad. You never know until it's announced, though. No guarantees."

"Pfft. You belong up there, you love the speed, you're smart, loyal—"

"Stop, please!" Her classmates would have been startled to hear the resident loner emit such a girlish giggle. "I'm blushing. Seriously."

"I'm just so stinkin' proud of you."

"I wish you could see me grinning at the phone. I probably look like an idiot."

"I wish I could, too. I'd take a picture so you could see what happy looks like."

"I know what happy looks like — it looks like a beautiful blue sky from the cockpit of a fighter. I'm going to be the best there is, Dad. I can't wait. Listen to me! I'm giddy. Thank God no one else can hear me right now."

"Wouldn't want to let on that you're human, huh?"

"Hey, now. No being mean to the military pilot. I know where you live."

Hannah laughed with her dad, though Paul's laugh was more of a bark due to permanent smoke damage. Still, she loved that he was happy enough to bark freely. She trailed off when he did, eager to hear more from the only man in her life.

"You want me to tell Andy?"

Not at all what she was hoping would come out of his mouth.

"No."

Her brother wasn't a part of her life anymore, except as a blip on her security clearance with Uncle Sam. His choices, his actions, her broken heart. Drugs and guns and grief had obliterated the little boy who used to follow her around like a lost puppy. She doubted he would even recognize a photo of her at this point.

Her father sighed and cleared his throat. "Okay."

Hannah, her joy slightly soured, began the process of begging off the phone.

"I need to go soon. I'm sitting in my car, but I can't talk on my cell and drive on base."

"Okay. You be safe, Annie. I love you. I know I don't tell you enough."

"I love you, too. But I hate it when you call me that."

"It's my job to torture you."

"I'm trained to deal with torture."

"Don't even joke."

"Sorry. Why can't you stop hauling that horrible nickname out of storage? It doesn't fit me anymore."

"I know. 'Annie' liked people."

"Ouch. I like people." Her voice was all righteous indignation. "Well, some people anyway." Perhaps she'd quit while ahead.

"Whatever you say. Talk to you soon, fighter pilot."

"Thanks. Take care."

Hannah disconnected the call, feeling all sorts of jumbled. Sheer, ridiculous joy warred with homesickness, longing for her mother, anger at her brother, and confusion over her dad's parting remarks.

She wasn't that closed off. Surely.

"You got named for a soccer player? How'd that happen?" Speedy asked Hannah as they made their way to the hangar.

Hannah glanced over at her classmate, grateful she didn't get a borderline pejorative name like undertall Jorge Gonzales. The fraternity of pilots wasn't big on political correctness. Or sensitivity.

"There's a soccer player named 'Pele'?" Unless you counted Quidditch in the Harry Potter books as competitive team sport, Hannah wasn't much interested. Sky or bust. And her only real ground-based hobby was gaming.

Speedy huffed and rolled his eyes. "How can you not know this? Where do you think the name came from?"

"Um... my temper."

"Didn't they mention something about a Hawaiian symbol of violence and stuff?" added a slightly twangy tenor from Hannah's other side.

"I've seen you before." Hannah omitted her initial reaction to his appearance. Tall and lanky, broody gray eyes, killer grin, and unfortunately brilliant ginger hair. He'd be a clone of Michael Fassbender if it weren't for regulation short, Weasley-bright hair and a Texas accent.

"Brad Martin, but you can call me Chester."

Hannah bit her tongue, which almost spat an Adventures in Babysitting quote at him. That movie had been a staple while growing up and babysitting her younger brother. Before he was a felon. She shook her head, focusing on the pilot next to her.

"Why 'Chester'?"

"I'm a sprinter with a junk food addiction. Apparently the hair was the final nail in the coffin."

Speedy connected the dots first. "Wait. You're named for Chester Cheetah?" Must've been the cartoon brotherhood in action.

"Yep."

"I guess Cheetah was too cool?" Hannah repressed a snort. "Chester" was so... nerdy.

"At least it's not 'Chee-toh', right?" Speedy had an excellent point.

"I'm just glad it's not 'McD' or something. Between the hair and the food, I was worried." Brad — Chester — flashed a wicked grin that sent Hannah's mind straight into the gutter. This guy was dangerous. She needed her focus.

"Guess your bribe worked." And maybe refraining from eye contact would work for her. Not that he'd be staring at her nondescript Midwestern self. About her only memorable feature was her deep dimples, which she expected would resemble trenches in her face as she aged.

"Not as well as yours."

"Do you know what 'Pele' is for, other than her tantrum?"

Hannah shoulder-checked Speedy for the tantrum crack.

"Pele is the Hawaiian goddess of volcanoes and violence and a few other things I forgot. She's also got a thing for justice. And a temper." Chester sounded almost admiring.

"A goddess, huh?" That notion gave Hannah a little thrill and a big warm-fuzzy for all her instructors and colleagues involved in callsign choices. "That works for me. How'd you know all that anyway?"

"My uncle lives in Hawaii. I've visited."

Wow. Bet it's nice to have family. And funds. In paradise.

Speedy added his two cents. "Too bad you're not a redhead. Goes with the fiery lava thing."

"Ugh," Hannah spat. "I hate everything orange. Orange hair would be the cherry on top of a shit sundae."

"Hey now," Chester protested. "I'm not part of any kind of shit sundae." Hannah might, might, have been concerned about offending her new buddy, but he didn't stop there. "Now, if you bust out the whipped cream, that's another thing entirely."

He leered exaggeratedly at Hannah's upper body before smacking his lips.

A friendly yet firm pinch to the inner arm had him dropping the act and yelping.

"Shut it, Chest-er."

"He does have a point," Speedy said. "I have some cream if you want, little goddess." He performed a crotch grab worthy of a major league ballplayer before all three burst into hysterics.

Who knew a tantrum-inspired name would net her new friends? Thinking back to her father's parting words and Major Brandon's comments on camaraderie, Hannah decided to let her budding friendship stand. She would let people into her life... if only these two to start.

When they took their seats, the instructor scowled at their lingering good humor

"You think this is funny? A game? We've already got one Chuckles in this group." He looked around at the class, grizzled face set in a perma-frown. "God help us all if the fate of our country rests in your hands."

Suitably chastised, the group settled, focused. But not before Chester whispered in Hannah's ear, "I'll make you appreciate orange yet, Pele."

She wrote two words on a post-it and left it on his locker that afternoon: Challenge accepted.

∽0∾

Chester started with little things. No one noticed his campaign except his target.

"Dorito?" he offered during lunch one day.

"No thanks. I'm more of salt and vinegar chip person."

"That I believe."

The next day, it was sweets. "Starburst?"

"You really do have a thing for junk food, don't you?"

The following week, it was healthy foods. Carrots, oranges, even a persimmon. Chester was relentless, but Pele took a perverse enjoyment in thwarting him.

He noted her resistance, promptly changed tactics, and renewed his assault.

On the morning of an assessment mission, she found a note card stuffed into her helmet. It had a photo of a tiger on the front and read: From one fierce warrior of the world to another, good luck today.

She had a difficult time responding to that one, but finally retaliated with a photo of a falcon in mid-flight. She wrote Wind to your wings, flight-brother on the back and tucked it beneath his windshield wiper.

The orange traffic cone that appeared on top her car one day nearly got her a citation.

"I thought I was supposed to like orange at the end of this campaign." Hannah hissed at her friend.

"Oh, you will. It's all part of my plan."

The rest of the class thought the traffic cone was a cue to start a prank war. Scooby put talcum powder in the vents of Speedy's car. Someone else snuck into an instructor's office, emptied a desk drawer, lined it with plastic, and filled it with water and live fish. Hannah almost admired that one. Xena found long black hair extensions attached to the inside of her flight helmet, for which Chuckles later took credit. Chester got the crappiest prank — literally; someone filled his running shoes with dog shit. Scooby admitted to the deed after arguing, "at least I lined them with plastic wrap first!" Scooby paid the price later when a goat was found inside his quarters. Like the fish stunt, no one admitted to that one.

Though the game began with the cone on Pele's car, she was pranked again when she opened her equipment locker one day to an avalanche of pamphlets on IBS, a home enema kit, and adult diapers.

"IBS? Seriously?" She grumbled to the world at large.

"I think it stands for Irate Bitch Syndrome," Joker outed himself, pleased with his own cleverness.

"Better watch out for the goddess, Joker." Speedy came to Hannah's defense.

"Do your worst, Pele." Joker taunted. "I'm not afraid of a little fire."

Pele exacted her revenge a week later, when she texted a YouTube link to the entire group. She'd found some of Joker's disgruntled past hook-ups and paid a few random women at the mall to slam him publicly. The video, a montage of women complaining about Joker, his "E.D.", and how his name applied to his skill with women, went viral. The crowning glory was the end of the video when each of the women warned future dates against him and his "Extreme Dickhead" tendencies.

Pele was lauded as prank goddess. Strangely, the whole group embraced her after that stunt. She was a loner no more, though Chester and Speedy were still her closest friends.

Chester accelerated his Operation Orange Appreciation. With the help of all their mutual colleagues, he inundated Hannah with orange everything. A calendar of ginger kittens, a perfect orange leaf, a Matchbox sports car, a plush fox, a basketball hoop and ball, and a toy clownfish, either Nemo or his dad, all wound up decorating her quarters. Her favorite was an enameled Zippo lighter engraved with her callsign.

For her birthday, Chester gave her a beautiful scarf in swirling reds, oranges, and pinks. Hannah hated to admit how much it perked up her appearance. Even though it looked like her neck was on fire when she wore it. It finally dawned on her that perhaps Chester was... wooing her. The quest for changing her opinion on a color had become more than a challenge.

She had no clue what to think about or do with her newfound knowledge, so she stayed quiet and played the game. She'd long since stopped arguing about each offering anyway. When she could think of rebuttals, she delivered them without heat. And she tried to find little things for him in shades of blue. Her social skills were so rusty though. She mostly sat slightly stunned and silent at his persistence and creativity.

He finally asked one day — out of nowhere — why she so violently hated a color. After explaining, his perpetual grin slid away and he gave her a quick hug. "I guess your life's been something of an orange-colored shitstorm." His twangy cadence never failed to make her smile, even if faintly. "Now I know I've got my work cut out for me."

The week before her final flight exercises as a student, the flowers began. Each bloom had a note with the flower's symbolism attached.

Hawaiian orange orchids were first. For wealth and attraction. That night she dreamed of vacationing in Hawaii with Chester. She felt tropical upon waking and hoped every night wouldn't be a repeat or she'd be turning up the air conditioning.

Then came the orange lily for pride and the marigolds, addressed to "the fiery goddess", for "sacred affection". The orange tulip followed, for warmth and happiness, then the peony for good fortune and honor. At this point, Hannah acknowledged her strong front had pretty well collapsed. She hadn't allowed herself to need anyone before, except her dad, but she needed Chester now. If only to prop her up, since he'd reduced her to a pile of goo. Orange goo, which sounded revolting.

The morning of Hannah's last flight as a student found a shiny penny and a wind-up toy goldfish whose fins gyrated when wound. The two rested on a Post-it bearing the words: for luck. She surreptitiously kissed the penny and snuck it into her left boot before carefully placing the note and toy in her bag. In a rare display of sentiment, she'd been taking pictures of her orange-themed presents and keeping the notes. Maybe she'd make a collage for Chester's birthday.

Speedy and Chester flanked Pele as she prepped for the flight; it was their last morning as students as well. The instructor, Zero, groaned when he saw them.

"Well, if it isn't the Fast and the Furious. Wonderful. See if you can control yourselves up there."

The fast and the furious? Wait a second...

"I haven't had issues with my temper in months!"

"It's always there. Don't think I haven't seen you tempted to unload on someone."

Hannah had no leg to stand on and knew it. Best she just get in her plane and in the air. Instant Zen.

"Yes sir."

She ignored the snickers from her friends. It would probably be much funnier later. After she passed. And had a few beers.

"See you in the air, gentlemen." She calmly found her way into the cockpit, went through routine checks, and flew.

Nothing beat the sky. Orange might be less offensive after Chester's campaign, but big blue brought her calm, focus, and peace. Even with enemies around and tricky maneuvers. Flying was her comfort zone, her confessional, and her bliss. She hoped to get an F-35, though there were never enough to go around. An F-22 would rock, but she'd take anything that was fast and dropped bombs.

The cacophony in the room full of pilots was only slightly less than the sounds of takeoff. Bird assignments were imminent and smack talk covered a multitude of nerves.

"Okay people. Listen up. No F-35s or F-22s are available at this time, so don't get your panties in a knot when you don't hear one with your name. We clear?"

"Yes sir!" thundered from the assembled voices.

"Moving along then. I'll call your name, bird, and location. Come up and get your orders after I call it out. In no particular order, Pele—"

The room stilled and Hannah's lungs froze. Her eyes and ears registered nothing outside of the officer in the front of the room, holding her future in his hands.

"F-15E Strike Eagle, Mountain Home."

She did it. She did it. She earned the best breed of bird open to assignment.

She walked up to retrieve her paperwork amid backslaps and congratulations in a fog of bliss and disbelief. By the time she made it back to her friends, Speedy was missing.

"He got the same." Chester answered her question before she asked.

"Thanks. I'm a little scrambled at the moment."

"I think we all are. I know—"

Zero was still announcing aircraft assignments. "Chester: F-15E Strike Eagle, Mountain Home."

Her friends were going with her.

Everything she could ask for and two very important extras.

"Welcome to Mountain Home."

Hannah only heard "welcome" and "home". She followed Yoda, her senior officer, to the hangar where they'd be assigned their in-flight partners and individual aircraft. Chester and Speedy were once again beside her as they walked to the next phase of their careers.

"Assignments are as follows: Pele and Kiwi, first bird on the left, memorize the number. Chester and Beetle, you'll be with this fine machine." Yoda gestured toward the next plane. "Again, remember your number. Speedy and Solo, you know the drill by now, I hope." Yoda stopped at the last machine, letting the rookies familiarize themselves with their new charges.

Hannah glanced at Chester, proud, excited, damn near effervescent. "We're going to be flying together. You ready for that?"

The man who'd gifted her with an orange amaryllis to congratulate her on achieving a dream just grinned that irresistible grin and drawled, "It'll be perfect."

Lord help her, she blushed.

"And check out the tail-fin."

Their new home squadron was the Bold Tigers. Each tail-fin had a rectangle of orange with black stripes. Orange struck again.

"I think I like it."

"Yeah? What's orange mean to you now?"

She took a moment, organizing her thoughts. "Can I tell you later?"

"Of course. Want to grab dinner?"

"Are you asking me on a date?" She put her hands on her hips, attempting to tease.

"When I ask you out, you'll know it."

Damn him and his hotness. She held in a whimper, refusing to be weak.

"Fine. Pizza and beer at my place."

"And you'll tell me what's going through that mysterious head of yours." He reminded rather than asked.

"I swear on this gorgeous piece of machinery."

"I'll bring the beer."

She waited until they'd eaten and killed a couple of beers. She waited for the mountains to flame with the setting sun.

"Tell me, Pele... Hannah. What's orange mean now?"

"Strength, success, pride." She looked from the blazing sky to him before continuing. "Happiness, friendship, joy."

"Are you going to let me be a partner on the ground, now?"

"I think I am."

"Then I have one orange for you." He moved to his jacket and fished out a single flower from its folds. Sneaky. "Do you know what the symbolism behind an orange rose is?"

Hannah shook her head, stroking the petals.

"Passion."

She dropped the flower as he attacked her lips. His kiss gave her a rush like pulling showy maneuvers, like taking down a target, and like nothing else on the ground.

"And I think you should start calling me Brad."

"Hmmm. That'll take a while to get used to."

"I've got time."

"Brad?"

His name on her lips apparently was code for "kiss me like the world is ending". She took a dozen breaths after he released her, trying to get oxygen restored to her brain.

"Wow."

"You were sayin'?"

"You can call me Annie." Brad read between the lines and gifted her with a million-dollar smile. Before his lips could annihilate her thought processes again, she asked, "You know all that orange means to me now, right?"

He nodded, folding his long arms around her tightly.

"You are orange."

He whispered into her temple, losing the last of his control, "So are you, Annie."

The orange rose dropped, forgotten on the floor.   Passion, indeed.

Anne Baker writes humorous, feel-good contemporary romance with heroines that could be your friends. She has one completed, unpublished novel, a short story entitled Of Beer and Blogs in the anthology Sassy Singularity on Amazon Kindle, and a short called Eggs for Dinner in the HeartLA RWA chapter anthology. Anne is a self-described gypsy and nerd who balances writing with stay-at-home momhood and science tutoring.

Lower the Lid

by alex kimmell

Today had to be perfect. Lilith knew if brunch didn't go well, no one would follow her. She straightened the flowers on the center of the table, made sure all the silverware was perfectly aligned, and turned the kettle on. She checked the temperature of the oven one more time to make damn sure her croissants weren't going to burn.

Sliding open the screen door, she stepped out onto the back patio, wanting to light her first cigarette of the day. Her fingers, unsteadied by the drubbing heartbeat in her chest, made it difficult to hold it still. Closing her eyes, she muttered a silent mantra to calm her conscience. When she was finally able to introduce the end of her cigarette to flame, the first sharp spear of smoke leading down her throat cut through the oxygen she knew she should have been breathing instead. She deserved this pain, however insignificant it really was. Committing herself to a long, drawn out suicide by smoking was suicide nonetheless. Besides, no matter how hard she tried, quitting never seemed like an acceptable alternative.

The ground rumbled, nearly knocking her off balance. Leaves trembled, trees swayed, and a wave rolled across the too tall grass she knew should have been mowed several days ago. Lilith looked at her naked wrist, realizing the watch was still upstairs on the bedside table. Without a second thought, she flicked her unfinished cigarette over the bushes and into the yard next door. At the foot of the stairs, the doorbell rang. She took a deep breath, pressed her hands into the wrinkles of her skirt, and moved to answer.

There were many times when Lilith contemplated hammering her fist into Solange's perfectly modified nose. Shattering the gorgeous sculpture into a deformed mass of un-repairable cartilage and annihilating her movie star-esque magnificence. Instead, she threw herself into returning her guest's spectacular Glamour magazine smile. Solange posed effortlessly in an impeccable $300 haircut, a shining red pair of Jimmy Choo heels, and a new Kate Spade bag straight from the runways at New York's Fashion Week. She never told anyone definitively how she got these things in advance, though everyone knew her husband took them from his mistress who worked on Fifth Avenue. Solange accepted these incredibly expensive, otherwise untouchable gifts as unspoken bribes to ignore his indiscretions.

"Hi, there." Lilith titled her head to the side and opened her arms wide, fighting to keep her appearance from looking too overtly plastic. "I'm so glad you're here. With your busy schedule, I wasn't sure you'd be able to make it."

"Of course I'm here. I wouldn't miss brunch with my besties for the world." The two women embraced, planting air kisses on one another's cheeks so as not to smudge their lipstick. "My gosh, you look so beautiful. Did you get some work done and not tell me?"

They went inside and exchanged pleasantries until Denise and Slattery arrived. None of these four women were what you would call 'traditional' friends. Their children went to school together, and on occasion they attended the same fundraisers and benefits with their husbands at the same time. With their award winning performances, it would have been difficult for an outsider to see they didn't like each other at all. These social gatherings were primarily motivated by the proximity of their homes and the sizes of their husbands' portfolios.

"I'm telling you, my Joseph can be a real pain in the ass." Emptying her third mimosa, Slattery emphasized her point with a sorority girl giggle. "If I'd known my life was going to be like this, I don't think I would have married him in the first place."

"Well, I think Joey's a sweetheart." Solange dabbed at her cheek with the corner of her napkin.

"That's because he doesn't try to hide the fact that he wants to fuck you."

"Denise!" Solange inhaled swiftly.

Laughing, Slattery placed her fingertips on one tanned, yoga-firmed shoulder. "Don't act so surprised, Solange. You flirt right along with the poor old fool."

"I most certainly do not."

"It's okay, sweetie. Really. You make his day." She looked around the table. "Can I get a refill on this mimosa, Lil?"

"How about I get one for everybody?" Lilith nodded and reached for the bottle of champagne, discretely covering a clear powder spilling from her palm into the carafe of orange juice.

"On the subject of annoying husbands, Peter refuses to grant me access to our finances. He keeps me on an allowance, like I'm a child." Denise played with her earring, leaning back in the tall chair.

"A very well-off child, mind you." Slattery snickered.

"True." Denise took a sip of her newly refreshed drink. "But it makes me feel as if I'm being paid to run the household like a servant, instead of being his partner. Does that make sense?"

"Absolutely." Lilith raised her glass. "It's not fair, I say."

"Hear, hear!" Voices raised in toast. As their glasses grew emptier, knowing smiles passed across their awkward silent faces.

"Ernest hits me." Her upper lip quivering, Solange stared into space, not fully realizing the admission had broken free from the prison in her mind, fleeing to the outside world.

"What?" Slattery leaned forward, elbows on the table.

"I mean... not all the time."Solange quickly attempted some damage control. "His job is so stressful."

"Who gives a shit?" Denise squeezed her fork a bit too tightly. "There's no excuse for that, Solange."

"It's only when he's been drinking, which isn't very often." She sniffed and blinked to prevent more tears from running mascara down her cheeks. "I... I shouldn't have said anything."

"Now wait a minute…" Solange lifted a hand, stopping Slattery before she could go any further.

"Can we please, *please* change the subject, ladies?" Slattery asked. Staring at each other quietly, they each realized they had wandered over their carefully constructed boundaries into unfamiliar territory beyond gossip into the harsh reality of real life.

"Cresil always leaves the lid open," Lilith whispered, eyes darting back and forth between her guest's soft chuckles. Denise forced a laugh, sounding more like a frightened and nervous rattle than her intended lightness. "I don't know why we put up with these childish men. I'll bet if their mommies offered them a breast, they'd drop to their knees suckling like babies."

"Speaking of babies." Solange continued to try to shift the river of conversation's flow down a new route. "Jordan wants to try out for cheer school."

"Really? That's fantastic." Slattery clapped her hands.

"I don't know what that tubby chunk is thinking." Solange shook her head and swallowed the rest of her drink. "She's too much of a pig for it. I tried to tell her, but the girl will not listen to me."

"She's not *that* big." Denise nibbled on a croissant. "Maybe the exercise will do her some good. Get rid of some of that baby weight."

"There's no such thing as baby weight, Denise." Solange beckoned for another refill. "There is fat and not fat. Unfortunately, no matter how I try to be a good example for the girl, Jordan refuses to take the pills I give her. She's becoming a lard ass."

"At least she isn't a little pansy boy like Marcus." Slattery emphasized her complaint with a high pitched cartoon voice. "Maria tells me that he cries after school every day. He whines about some older boy picking on his clothes. Imagine that? If he only knew how much I spent having those outfits made, Marcus wouldn't dare let anyone touch him."

"You mean that soldier's uniform with the brass epilates on the shoulder?" Denise licked her lips with envy. "Who do you get to make them? Is it Bartholdt's?"

"The epilates are gold. Not brass. Twenty-four karat." Slattery looked up to the ceiling and sighed. "Can you believe Marcus brought home that jacket torn and dirty?" Slattery and Denise both inhaled loudly, shocked by the boy's audacity. "And one of the epilates torn off, missing. He blames it on some bully in class. Says he's always singling him out, beating him up or something. I mean, I paid for a karate lesson. He should defend himself, right? I told Maria to take away his video game privileges for the weekend."

"Maria? What happened to Amrita?" Lilith watched the other three over the top of the floral centerpiece.

"Oh. The slut couldn't keep her legs closed. She went and got herself pregnant." Slattery spread her hands wide in surprise. "I sent her back to India. With the museum gala right around the corner, I need someone more dependable."

"What a selfish girl." The sneer on Solange's face could crack glass.

"Little bitch." Denise nodded in accord. "How did you find this new one?"

Slattery covered a yawn. "I got a recommendation from the Agency. I told them if this one had the same trouble understanding her duties like Amrita, they had better start finding some help that spoke better English."

The gaggle of nasties rattled the chandelier crystals with their explosive hooting and howling. The animalistic release of delight echoed between hallway walls and the tall windows looking over the black surfaced swimming pool. Tears smeared make up down un-wiped faces. Lipstick-coated mouths stretched wide, screeching with gut-blasting, breath-stealing laughter.

"I have to say, Lilith," Solange barked between deep heaving breaths, "Cresil leaving the lid open doesn't seem so bad compared to what we all have to deal with. How difficult can it be to grab a square or two and wipe it clean?" Denise looked to Slattery for support.

"Wipey wipey!" Making a circular motion on the table with her napkin, Slattery dragged the others along with her to new fits of hysteria.

Lilith sat quiet and still, showing no reaction to her guest's mockery. Every last trace of merriment was now absent from her voice. "Oh, no," she whispered. "It's not the toilet seat."

"What?" Solange wiped her tear dampened face, fighting a losing battle against the giggles. "Then what's your damn problem, woman?"

"Let me show you." Using the table and leaning on each other to stay upright, the three women staggered behind Lilith, who moved smoothly up the stairs to the second floor.

An unnerving painting hung between two closed bedroom doors. Ornate, but not ostentatious, a thick brass frame surrounded the old acrylic brushstrokes. The stark image presented a dry, dust-covered, barren landscape that stretched beneath a grey haze-laden sky to the edges of the canvas. In the center foreground stood a horrible branchless tree of gnarled and scarred near-black bark.

"I don't remember this painting being here." Denise leaned forward to touch it.

"It's been in my family…" Lilith snatched Denise's hand before it touched the canvas. "…for generations."

"Not very uplifting, is it?" Solange and Slattery shared a knowing laugh.

"I've always rather loved it." Lilith squeezed her fingers between the left side of the frame and the wall. In the space behind the painting, five small holes were exposed. Beyond her guest's line of sight, Lilith's long fingers broke through the web-like film covering and drove deep into the damp, sticky holes, twisting a half circle to the right. A thunder clap growl roared through the house as the latch clicked home. The ladies jumped and covered their ears, each shrieking their alarm.

"What the hell was that?" Denise grabbed Lilith by the arm.

Lilith twisted away from her grasp and pulled at the newly-revealed ingress. Thick layers of a sweating, fleshy looking material lined with tree-like age rings slid outward from the wall. Glistening in the skylight, the moist edges of the entrance silently inhaled the scent of women's perfume and alcohol. Nervous laughter echoed into the darkness. Ripples spread beneath each high heeled footstep they took, making it more and more difficult for the ladies to maintain their half-drunken balance.

"What is that smell?" Slattery shook her head, smiling at the hint of ginger in the surprisingly fresh air.

"Cresil left the lid open again." Lilith pointed to a bright orange glow rising from the floor. "Lazy."

"It's so beautiful." Solange slid her foot closer.

"Yes, it is. Isn't it?"

"What's down there?" Denise looked at Lilith with wide eyes.

"Beauty." Lilith remained standing, her back to the beautiful temptation.

"What do you mean?" Denise turned to stare at the aperture once more.

"I've only seen glimpses through the door. I'm not allowed to go in," Lilith whispered.

"And why exactly is that?" Slattery mumbled, not really listening for an answer.

"Well, someone is required to stay here and protect him."

"Protect him?" Solange held her hands into the glow, revealing every small imperfection in her over-cleansed skin. Lilith nodded and smiled.

Denise took one step back. "From what?"

"This is the only way in or out. So we must keep him safe."

"I don't think I understand. What are you talking about?" Denise looked back at Lilith.

"It's better if you see for yourself. Go and say hello." Under her breath, she whispered, "You won't feel much of anything, I don't think." Lilith waved the nervous Denise and the others forward. The three women slowly faded into the light, leaving long auburn outlined shadows that stretched the length of the staircase to the ground floor.

Lilith closed the lid behind them, allowing only the faintest hue of orange tracing the rectangular outline to escape. Muffled sounds of high-pitched screams and a short chaotic struggle were followed by a satisfied silence.

"It's so much quieter with the lid closed. Please don't make me tell you again, dear."

The rumble, low and apologetic, echoed through the house, sending ripples across the tall, uncut grass. One half-empty champagne glass shook until it slid over the table's edge and shattered on the hardwood floor.

alex kimmell (the squirrel whisperer/twodoggarage/daddy not-so-much-bucks) is an accidental novelist, anti-rhyme-ologist, oxygen inhaler, carbon dioxide exhaler, and the funniest man in his pants, who often generates harmonious sounds with various instruments of different historical importance. His work has appeared on cool places around the www like Black Lantern Press, and his debut novel "the Key to everything" was released by Booktrope Publishing in 2012.

Upstaged

by Elizabeth Ann West

G len was ready to take on the entire club. The anger and rage stewed deep inside of him, churning and threatening to make him lose his cool. With all of the strength he could muster, he pushed the emotion down, flashing a devilish smile at the clown that popped up from the floor and stopped right in front of his face.

Tipping his fedora hat down and off, on the next bass drop Glen sprang into action. A leap into the air, a double pirouette, and he landed in a predatory crouched position. A collective sigh escaped from the crowd around him and the punk kid who had challenged him at Ruby's Bar and Grill. Sarah wouldn't be happy, but he didn't care. He needed this release.

As the music pitched into a higher electronic frenzy, Glen began breaking, pushing the circle of watchers further back. With more room to work, he pulled himself up from a backwards bend, knees at right angles, and dusted off his shoulder like he was done. At the height of the cheers around him, he jerked forward to spin bow-legged on his heels around the crowd's edge, daring anyone to step up to him again. As he reached Sarah and her frown, he snapped a tucked backflip. Sticking the landing, he rotated his arms in a fluid circular motion above his head as rose to his full height, then brought his right arm down to reclaim his best friend. With a slight wave over his shoulder, he walked her out, ready for the fussing he'd get on the way to the Metro.

"Are you crazy? You could have pulled a muscle!" Sarah pushed him off of her, then paused to light the cigarette she'd pulled from her clutch. After taking a long drag and releasing, she fluttered her hand to dissipate the smoke that clung to the foggy night in a haze around them.

Glen kissed his choreographer's cheek and pouted. "Ah, mon cherie, to dance is to breathe!" He hitched his shoulders up as the night's chill gripped his nervous system. The stuffiness of the club, the heat of his muscles from the quick display, and the bite of cold outside all pushed his adrenaline levels a little higher instead of letting them fall back to normal. "Besides, I'm going to win a spot on *Dance Across America*. Nowhere is there a better hip-hop, break-dancing, classically trained ballet dancer!"

He spun around to tread lightly on the cobblestones of Georgetown, still goofing around with a hip-hop-styled gliding walk on the balls of his feet, but stopped when he reached the end of the curb. He looked out at the still, dark waters of the Potomac, imagining the glistening lights of the theater in the blurry reflections of the street lamps around him. Sarah's sudden scream pulled him back to reality.

"NO! NO! STOP!"

Glen ran to the man in dark clothes struggling with Sarah for her clutch. Using his elbow, he connected with the man's jaw with enough force to make the assailant stumble backwards. He grabbed Sarah's hand and started to run; she could barely keep up in her purple D&G heels.

"Come on!" The Metro station was a block ahead and Glen felt sure that if they could just make it there, they'd be safe. He glanced over his shoulder to see that Sarah was now running with only one shoe on. The man he'd hit was struggling to stand up in the pool of light cast down by a street lamp.

Glen didn't even see the second man stepping out of the next alley, hidden between a dry cleaner and a coffee shop; in his headlong rush, he impaled himself on the knife in the man's hand. Turning towards the source of the searing hot pain in his gut, the dark eyes of the man and his own green irises locked for what seemed like eternity.

"Joe! Let's go!" The first assailant pulled the man with the knife away. Glen lowered himself to the ground as Sarah's screams echoed in the empty street around him.

"Call 911," he forced out, gazing at the blood on his hands and the unthinkable protrusion that had appeared just to the right of his belly button like a bad Halloween prop. His focus slipped to the ground, where he could only see footsteps hurrying towards him. *Oh good, help is coming.*

∽ი∾

"Glen Krane!" A production assistant with a headset and clipboard yelled his name across the 3-star hotel lobby, just as Glen opened his eyes from collecting his thoughts. He needed to be clearly focused on his inspiration if he was going to pull this off.

"Here!" Glen jogged to the heavy metal door and followed the woman past a number of booths where would-be dancers were interviewing and having photos taken. It reminded him of a grown-up version of school picture day.

The assistant dropped him off at the booth in the far right corner, where a heavy-set woman with bright maroon hair, too much jewelry, and overwhelmingly strong perfume waited for him.

"Well, you are a cute one, aren't you?" The interviewer looked at the Polaroid attached to his information sheet before looking up at him again.

"Glad you think so, Ms. Barry."

"You know me?"

Glen smiled, relieved that he was a local dancer and not one of those who had traveled hundreds of miles for the only Mid-Atlantic audition aside from New York City.

"I grew up here, and I've been dancing here my entire life. Of course I know the famous choreographer of the Jefferson Center's galas. I was twelve when I auditioned for your Nutcracker Suite exhibition."

"Hmmm, I don't remember you." The older woman frowned and looked over his dance resumé.

"You wouldn't. I was a pompous punk back then, skivving off my practices for video games with my friends. Didn't even make callbacks." Glen involuntarily raked his hands through his short blonde hair. Krane was his stage name — his mother's maiden name had been Kravinovitch. Pregnant with him, she had escaped from the Ukraine in 1992. She had been a dancer; there was no other option for Glen, her only child. While he'd hated practicing as a kid, now he thanked his mother's memory for the discipline she had forced upon him. He made lesser dancers quake at every audition in the Beltway.

"But you make your rehearsals now." It was an assumption, not a question.

"Every one. And a few extras." Glen smiled and waited for the interview question he knew was coming.

Ms. Barry twisted the top off her twenty-ounce diet soda, but paused before taking a drink. "Mr. Krane, your resumé certainly warrants you an audition on the big stage, but this is a television show. It's about the drama. What's unique about you? What puts you on top of all of these other dancers?" She shook her arm at the other booths where her colleagues were conducting nearly identical interviews, jiggling her bracelets and the skin that older women, even former dancers, struggle to tone.

Reaching into the back pocket of his black skinny jeans — really leggings, to allow him to jump into the splits in mid-air — he struggled to pull out a rusty brown pocket knife with his thumb and index finger. Feeling the heavy, two-ounce knife in his palm for a moment, he slapped it down onto her make-shift desk.

"Twelve months ago, I was stabbed with this by a mugger outside of the Dupont Circle Metro Station, on the eve of the auditions here. Took four surgeries and my punk attitude to pull through, and I'm here to show what happened to the judges."

Two Sharpie markers dangled on cords around Ms. Barry's neck. She smiled, yanking the red one free, and made a big circle around his name on the information sheet. She paused again, and motioned for him to come closer to her and turn around. Glen obliged, feeling her circle the number on his back as well.

"Take your sheet to the man in the purple shirt at the far side of the ballroom. He'll take you across the street to the theater. And that should at least get you on camera," she said, pointing to the number on his back.

Elated, Glen leaned forward and kissed her cheek. "Thank you!" He grabbed her hands, the right still holding the marker, and squeezed them. "Thank you!"

Waiting for six hours in a full auditorium, it didn't take his community college math skills for Glen to realize that everyone in the room wasn't going to perform. The hours ticked by — the judges called for a break after every other dancer — and Glen slumped ever lower into his hard wooden chair. He pulled his hood over his head, wishing he had thought to bring an iPod or even his cell phone, but the rules on the production sheet had been clear, and he needed this competition. He needed to win. Just making it onto the show practically guaranteed a contract job with a studio.

The back doors to the auditorium kept opening and closing to let in the grandmas and parents of the performers on stage. Sulking, he wished he had brought Sarah, but he knew it was bad luck for her to be there. That's how they did it. She choreographed, he danced. What she didn't know was that he was going to dance his own composition today, and not the Rachmaninoff medley she'd planned to show off his ballet skills.

"683!"

The chatter of the dancers around him quieted as the producer called the number again.

"683! Dancer number six-eight-three!"

No one was getting up. It took Glen an extra second to look down and realize that HE was 683.

"Right here!" He yelled from the back of the auditorium and dashed down the aisle to the encouraging cheers of the other dancers — half-hearted, he was sure, and given in rote response to the other producer's hand signals.

As he stepped up on stage, the lights were bright enough that he couldn't see the other dancers anymore, but the judges' table, precariously placed on a platform spanning the orchestra, was very clear. Finding the T of hot-pink T tape on the floor front of the mic, he shrugged off his hoodie. His electric orange T-shirt was clearly lettered "For Sarah."

"Glen Krane." Alec Tinsdale, a legend of the London Ballet Company, began the interview. He was the head judge for the competition, and executive producer of the show for the last four seasons. "You were supposed to be with us last year young man, but something happened?"

Jeez, they got right to it.

"I was stabbed in the stomach, sir. Mugged the night before the competition." His own voice echoed in his ears as the crowd made a collective hiss, sucking in their breaths. Even the judges hammed it up for the cameras with overly-dramatic cringes.

"And you're still alive and able to dance?" Maggie Morae, the outspoken and highly critical judge of all things contemporary dance, leaned forward to join the inquisition.

But Glen was ready. He had planned this moment and played it out in his head again and again since shortly after the first surgery had saved his life. It was the perfect distraction when his thumb mashed the morphine button that he was sure existed only as a placebo, and relief was slow to come.

"They didn't stab me in the heart." He flashed his camera-ready grin to the collective whoops and cheers from the crowd. He bet the producer didn't even have to signal that response.

"I like him already!" said Brent Wilkins, in an audible stage aside. Brent's specialty was produced dancing, such as Broadway and movie productions.

"I'm sorry to hear of your injury, young man, but you're here with us today, thankfully. Let us see what you can do." Alec Tinsdale nodded to Glen, and Glen gave a slight nod in acknowledgment. Then he jogged to the center of the stage. "And... cue music."

The digital soundtrack boomed through the auditorium speakers, amplifying the slight scratchiness of the dub-step song he had selected. In slow motion, Glen slid across the floor with a swagger to act out the motions of picking up his date. As if a hologram only he could see stood before him, he smiled and flirted with his fantasy date, traveling across the stage in a contemporary dance routine to show off his muscle control. As the song's tempo sped up briefly, he ran and jumped into a full-body break-dancing spin on the floor. He got up, dusting off his shoulders; the bass dropped and he crumpled as if someone had punched him in the stomach.

The low wobbling bass had him silently screaming out at his assailant as he leapt and pretended to fight the invisible man off, alternating swipes and clutches at his injury. He didn't need to know where it was; the twenty-three-stitches-long scar across his mid-section was as real to him as the ghost injury he acted out. In fact, the healed injury still twinged with pain as he remembered that night with perfect clarity.

With one last kick in mid-air, he collapsed to the ground, spread eagle on the floor. He pumped his body up and down to symbolize one of the moments when he'd nearly died on the operating table, the dubstep sample of a disconnected phone line grating in the air. Gracefully, he pulled himself up to a standing position, looked over his shoulder in shock, inspected his person and mimicked his hand going through his body with a crafty turn.

Moving away from where his corporal body should lie, he let the rhythms and lyrics of "Cinema" bring out his ballet roots. With panache and full turn out, he began leaping around the stage and pulled the strongest set of a la secondes of his life.

He could hear clapping, but it sounded like it came from another dimension, as if he really resided in the spirit world. The tempo increased and he began spinning like a break dancer, back to his original position on the floor as a surgery patient. This time when the bass dropped, he flip kicked up; using the anger in his core to portray vengefulness, he danced full-out hip-hop with exaggerated movements. He was resurrected. He was here to dance for his life, and his face showed it all.

As the song died down to the cheerful beginning where he'd found his date, he grasped his heart and made a full stop at the edge of the stairs. Then he pointed to where he could imagine Sarah.

The crowd erupted into cheers and screams as the house lights came back up. He was humbled by the roar of a full standing ovation. Even the judges had risen from their cushioned chairs and were clapping madly. He could swear there were tears slipping down Maggie's face, and as she wiped her cheeks and resumed clapping, he knew without a doubt that he was getting a ticket to Miami for the finals. When the noise finally quieted, Glen walked to the pink 'T' on the stage floor and a microphone stand was magically placed before him.

"Young man, you aren't even out of breath!" Alec Tisdale turned towards the crowd in astonishment, to more catcalls and cheers. Turning back to the judges' makeshift desk, he pulled out his glasses to read Glen's information sheet more carefully. "It says here that that was a ballet exposition to Rachmaninoff. I must say, Rachmaninoff sounds an awful lot like Skrillex!"

The crowd began laughing and Glen smiled in chagrin. He leaned into the microphone. "Yes, that was the plan, but I decided to do something different at the last minute."

"You choreographed that yourself?" Brent Wilkins leaned into his own microphone to be heard.

"Yes. Don't tell my choreographer." Glen hammed it up for the camera and crowd.

"Funny you should say that..." Alec stood up and motioned towards the back of the auditorium. To Glen's utter surprise, Sarah ran down the aisle and joined him on stage. Laughing, crying, and just generally overwhelmed, he pulled her into a hug and spun around. As he pulled back, she playfully slapped the letters that spelled out her name on his vivid orange shirt.

Once the crowd had settled down again, Alec Tisdale stopped with the dramatics and looked at his fellow judges.

"Oh, alright, come get your bloody ticket!" he cried, and all three judges held up the prop airline tickets to Miami. Glen's shout was drowned out by the crowd; he ran down to the judges with Sarah in tow to grab the ticket.

Guided by producers, he was steered out of the auditorium and into a green room with bright cameras.

"Where are you going?" an unfamiliar voice yelled.

Glen, blinded by the lights and confused, couldn't speak. Sarah piped up for him.

"He's headed to Miami!" And just as quickly, both of them were ushered out the door and back into the hall of the theater. It was over. He had done it. And in three weeks, he would be flying to Miami for the final callbacks.

Elizabeth Ann West is a Jane-of-all-trades and mistress of none. A military spouse, she has sold her writing since 2007. In 2011, she published her first novel, *Cancelled*, about a robotics engineer with a problem: his business partner has just become his fiance when he learns that a previous one-night stand is carrying his child. Elizabeth is also the Director of Advertising for The-Cheap.net, and in 2013, she will be launching an online magazine that is all about new fiction and the nuances of our digital world. Originally from Virginia Beach, VA, Elizabeth and her family now move wherever the Navy sends them — most recently to Connecticut.

Orange Riding Hood

by Janelle Jensen

Anna Gallagher was tired of fairy tales. Everywhere she turned, she was surrounded by happily ever afters and unrealistic endings. After spending twelve weeks studying Disney, Grimm, and everything in between for a class she thought would be an easy English credit, she was ready to immerse herself back into reality. There was only so much a girl could take, hearing daily about simpering princesses and their otherworldly handsome suitors.

She did have to admit, the original stories were gruesomely fascinating. But those stories were often retold with a more pleasant air now. She supposed that telling a bedtime story in which the three bears chased down and ate Goldilocks would have a tendency to pave the way for nightmares.

Reality was far different than the stories. There was no gorgeous heartthrob standing ready to sweep her off her feet. Love was a four letter word, and she had a string of ex-boyfriends to prove it. She had thrown the last one out after she had returned home for some forgotten class notes and discovered him having dessert in her kitchen. Dessert being a curvy brunette named Nicole.

Her friends had told her he was crazy, throwing away what he had for a plastic, bleached Barbie. As vain as it sounded, she knew she was pretty enough. Anna and her mother looked so much alike that they were often mistaken for sisters. And her mother was beautiful. They had long, sleek brown hair and green eyes. Her dad called them his black Irish twins, even though they both had the more common fair complexions of their Irish ancestors.

She reached for the orange hoodie draped over the back of a kitchen chair, a gift from her mother the last time she had seen her. It was probably the only piece of clothing that she owned in that color, green being her favorite. For some reason, orange had always been a color she had an aversion to. But she had kissed her mother on the cheek, exclaiming that it was perfect. The pleased look lighting up her mother's eyes was all she needed to see.

Anna laced up her hiking boots and slipped her backpack over her shoulders, rolling her eyes at the weight of it. Being a former girl scout, her pack always ended up being weighed down with things she would probably never need.

She may not be able to afford a real vacation, but she could spend a couple of hours on a Saturday afternoon in the woods behind her parents' cabin. Spring was a lovely time in Oregon, with the forest coming back to life after the long winter months. Spending the weekend here by herself was going to be just what she needed.

She locked the door behind her, not that she really thought anyone was going to come venturing down the mile long driveway out in the middle of nowhere. It was more of a force of habit from living near the university.

There were a lot of memories here in these woods. Her parents had bought the cabin when she was four, and they spent many weekends and every summer here. Her dad was the one who took her on long hikes into the woods while her mother stayed back at the cabin, spending most of her time in the kitchen cooking whatever new recipe had caught her eye. The freezer was always stocked with frozen pizzas for when those recipes turned out more disastrous than edible.

There wasn't a clear trail that led from the cabin through the woods, but that had never stopped father and daughter from exploring and finding everything that the forest had to offer. This was what she missed while living in the city. Anna took a deep breath of the fresh air, thick with the scent of the rain that had fallen early in the morning hours while the world was still dark.

As she started through the trees and brush, she let her worries and stress fall away, keeping it back in the cabin. She shut the door firmly on it all and let herself simply enjoy being surrounded by nature. She stopped now and then to smell the new blossoms waving gently on the wind.

Feeling freer than she had in months, Anna threw her head back and laughed. Her eyes flashed as the humor of the cliché struck her. She spied a cluster of Mertensia longiflora growing underneath the shade of an oak tree and crouched down next to it. Her father always insisted that she learn the Latin names of the flora and fauna around her, but when she was young the flower's common name lungwort had always made her giggle.

Her father had often tucked a sprig of the delicate bluebells in her hair. They had usually fallen out by the time they reached home, but she still had some saved from one of their walks, pressed between the pages of a journal she had kept as a child.

She picked them now and tucked them into the pocket of her sweatshirt, wincing again at the bright color. At least none of the hunters would mistake her for the native wildlife when she came back to visit during hunting season.

A rustling in the trees drew her attention away from the sweatshirt, and she glanced around for the cause. At first she didn't see anything, but she kept scanning around. The forest was plentiful with creatures, many of whom were reasonably shy around the humans who sometimes visited their world.

A movement caught her eye and she turned towards it slowly, expecting to see one of the deer who often wandered through. Her breath caught in her throat, and she couldn't believe her eyes. She was afraid to move for fear that it would vanish as quickly as it had appeared.

He stood watching her, from the rise of a hill not fifty yards away. His gaze caught hers, and her heart leaped in her chest. In the eighteen years she had been hiking through these woods, she had never before seen a wolf. In fact, she didn't think that they were local to the area.

Anna's chest burned, and she realized that she was still holding her breath. She had never before seen such an amazing and majestic looking animal. She had seen some incredible things while watching nature specials, but never anything standing right there in front of her.

She found herself taking a step towards him, and then he was gone. Cursing herself for being so foolish — *Did she think he was just going to let her walk up to him?* — she turned back in the direction she had been headed. There was a small camera in her backpack, and she unzipped the side pocket halfway so that she could take it out with ease if she wanted. The likelihood that he would return was slim, but she would be ready just in case he did.

With a quick check of the compass on her phone, she walked steadily for another hour before she reached a small stream that ran through the woods. It was a spot she and her father had always gone to on their hikes, usually enjoying a packed lunch before they headed back.

She wasn't hungry, but Anna rested on a large flat rock beside the stream. She stretched her long legs out in front of her and leaned back. The rays of the midday sun bathed her in their warmth. She didn't know how long it had been since she had been able to just stop and relax.

She still had three more semesters left in school, and then she would be striking out into the work force. Life was not about to get any simpler for a long time. She would grab these moments when she could.

Her eyes were closed when she heard something in the brush across the stream. It did not sound like a squirrel or rabbit foraging around. It sounded bigger. Much bigger. Sitting abruptly upright, she grabbed her pack off the ground and swung it onto her back.

She wasn't sure what it was, but caution was always a girl's best friend. Unless she was safe at home, then a great martini in front of the fire won hands down. She backed away from the edge of the stream, keeping her eyes out for anything that may dart out.

Badgers could get aggressive if they thought their territory was threatened, she thought she remembered. But there was also the wolf out there, and even though she knew that they typically avoided any type of human contact, her chest quickened.

"Anna, it's nothing. You're being absurd." She spoke aloud, trying to convince herself she was being foolish, but found herself taking one step back, then another.

"I would hardly call me nothing." He stepped out of the trees and into the small clearing, a cocky smile curving his lips.

Anna shrieked and jerked backwards. Her heels caught on a tree root, and she tumbled to the ground. She glared up at him, recognizing his face now that the initial surprise was over.

"Gary? What the hell are you doing here?" She spat the words at him. The last time she had seen him, he had been standing on her front walk trying to explain how his cheating had been an accident. Instead of waiting for him to explain how he had "accidentally" tripped out of his clothes and fallen onto the naked blonde whose car had just squealed out of Anna's driveway, she had slammed the door on him.

"You never let me explain."

Anna got to her feet, brushing the dirt off her butt. The pack had taken the brunt of the fall, but she knew she was going to have bruises tomorrow. Her mood had suddenly gone from bright and cheerful to dark and resentful. *How dare he come here, into her world?*

"What the hell are you doing here?" she repeated. "In fact, how did you find me?"

"I followed you. Really, Anna, you're not that hard to track down." He stood there, arrogantly looking her up and down. He stepped over the stream where it narrowed and sat on the rock she had just vacated.

His short, blonde hair was cropped short, and Anna hated that it accentuated those pretty blue eyes staring up at her. Gary was meticulous about going to the gym six days a week, and it showed. The black jeans he wore clung to muscled thighs she remembered all too well, and the matching short sleeved shirt revealed powerful arms that had felt so good holding her.

She gave herself a mental shake. Those days were long gone. He was just another guy who couldn't keep it in his pants, and there was no room for someone like that in her life. Her hands, however, itched to feel his skin under hers. Angry at their betrayal, she shoved them in her pockets.

"There's nothing to talk about, Gary. We were living together, supposed to be exclusive, and you cheated on me." *With a bleached blonde bimbo with a bad perm*, she added silently. "I don't give out second chances. You blew it, and it's over."

He stared at her, not saying anything. She ran her fingers through her hair and tried not to squirm under his gaze. Unable to meet that direct look anymore, she let her eyes wander around. She realized that the wind had died down, and the birds had gone silent. Eerie, she thought. What a strange, messed up situation this was.

Finally, she couldn't take it anymore. "I thought you wanted to talk."

He stood, slinging a bag over his shoulder. Shaking his head, he tucked his thumbs in his belt and looked at her sadly. "You're wrong. I wanted to talk, but you wouldn't listen. I'm done trying to make you understand."

She threw her hands out in frustration. "Then why are you here? Why did you follow me all this way if you don't even want to talk? What the hell, Gary?"

Anna had passed the point of feeling uncomfortable and was just pissed now. Her friends had been right; getting this jerk out of her life had been the best thing for her. She folded her arms and glared at him as he swung his bag in front of him.

It wasn't a bag, though. It was some sort of folding metal contraption, complete with pulleys and levers. She watched as he unfolded the rig and snapped the pieces into position. Recognition hit her as she saw the attached string tighten into a curve.

"Gary?" Her voice trembled. She unfolded her arms and took a step back, staring at the bow in his hands. "Gary, this isn't hunting season."

He looked at her with flat, cold eyes, reminding her of a snake she once saw in a zoo right before it struck down the quivering mouse. Tremors went down her spine. "Wrong again, sweetheart."

She picked up her feet and fled.

Branches reached out to claw her face as she dove deeper into the trees. She thought of nothing but getting as much distance as she could between them. She stumbled, but caught herself. She sobbed as she ran, tears blinding her eyes. She stumbled again and fell to her knees, throwing her hands out to stop her momentum. She rocked in the mud, her arms shaking and ready to give out.

Something flew past her and thumped into the tree next to her. She swiveled her head to see an arrow protruding from a trunk only six inches from her face. Anna scrambled to her feet and let her feet take her further into the forest.

With no idea of which direction she was going, she ran. Anna didn't go to the gym like Gary did, but she did run several miles a week through her neighborhood. It helped to free her mind, to free her senses. She could only pray that now it would help her live.

From behind her, Anna could hear him calling to her. His voice taunted as it echoed around her and seemed to surround her in a shrinking net. Choking on her breath, she pushed the tears away. She forced herself to continue, tucking her arms tightly against her sides and pushing her feet hard against the ground to propel herself forward.

Something crashed and broke in the woods off to her right and she jerked, nearly running head first into a tree that she was sure wouldn't have cradled her softly and forgivingly. The brush rustled and cracked as something ran beside her.

There was no way that Gary had caught up with her yet, was there? If this was the end, she was going to face it. He might have beaten her at his game, but she wasn't about to lose her dignity. She planted her feet and turned to face him.

He was messing with her head. Standing there in the trees in front of her, he waited just beyond her sight. No more branches crackled as he stood there in silence. Her fear turned to anger, and she opened her mouth to scream and fight.

She never got the chance. Before she could rail at him, he stepped out not ten feet away from her. But it was not the man carrying the weapon that would end her life as she was expecting. Instead, it was the wolf she'd seen earlier that day.

Amber eyes gleamed at her as they stood there, judging each other. It was still early spring, and he must have still been wearing his winter coat, as his black fur was thick and full. She didn't know what he was doing, what he was thinking.

Wolves never came this close to humans willingly. *Was he hungry, about to leap on her?* Anna knew that while she may have had a chance to outrun the man with the bow, she wouldn't stand a chance against this.

As her mind raced, the wolf shifted his gaze to look beyond her. Hackles rose along his spine, traveling from the fur on his massive head all the way down his back and the tail he held out stiffly behind him. His muzzle wrinkled as his lips curled back from his teeth and lowered his head. She shivered at the intensity of his stare.

He swung back to look at her, then turned and walked a few feet away. He stopped and glanced back at her, then continued walking. When she didn't make a move, he swiveled back to look at her as if to compel her forward. Anna looked behind her, then at the wolf in front of her.

If she didn't know any better, she might have thought she really had run into that tree, knocking herself senseless. Perhaps even now, she was lying on the ground, enjoying a fine hallucination. Did she really think that this wolf was inviting her to follow him? She was familiar with attributing human characteristics to animals, but this was bordering on ludicrous. And hysterics.

Cautiously she stepped forward, ready to freeze if the wolf made any sort of threatening move. Instead, the wolf dipped his head towards her and started trotting deeper into the forest. Anna thought she was surely losing her mind, but she began to follow after the wolf.

The light had started to fade, and she had lost track of the time. Soon it would be dark, and she didn't know what she was going to do. She should start looking for somewhere to hide. Anna had no idea of what Gary was truly capable of. There had never been any indication of this side of him.

If he was comfortable carrying a compact bow, who knows what else he had tucked into his pockets. Night vision goggles? Could he be out there, like some warped militia, ready to take down his target by whatever means necessary?

Together, Anna and the wolf ran further into the trees, further away from civilization. She was sweating from the effort, but the cool dusk air was leaving her chilled. Now that the sun was starting to go down, she didn't have much time to find a secure place to camp for the night. The question was, where?

As she continued to run after the wolf, which she still couldn't quite believe she was doing, she scanned the area for a group of bushes or rock cropping that she could crawl under. Even though the forest was thick with foliage, nothing suited what she was looking for.

And then, once again, the choice was taken from her. Or rather, she allowed it to be. The wolf darted to the left, and she followed him until he disappeared from sight. Stopping short, she looked around wildly to see where he had gone. Her answer came when his muzzle peeked out from a group of low hanging branches.

He withdrew his head, and Anna hesitated. Was she really about to get on her knees and follow this wolf into the unknown? It only took her a fraction of a moment to decide. If she was going to sign herself up for a strait jacket, she might as well tighten the straps. She got on her knees and crawled.

Anna was surprised to find that the opening led to a short tunnel of roughly packed dirt and rocks that opened up into a small hollow underground of sorts. About nine feet wide, it was just tall enough that she could sit upright without her head banging off the roof of the small cavern.

Just enough light filtered through that she was able to manage to find the flashlight she kept in her bag. She played its beam off the walls and ran her fingers across the smooth rock that had gentle waves in the surface. She knew that Oregon had plenty of larger caves in the national forests, but she didn't know of any of these smaller ones locally. It appeared that the cavern was formed by the same way the others were, by the pressure of rainwater.

The light reflected in the wolf's eyes, and she was so close to him now that she could see them dilating in the harsh beam. Not wanting to tread harshly on the fragile ground they were standing on together, she switched off the light. She was more than capable of feeling around for things in her bag.

First she wanted to check to see if she had any signal in here. Her hopes were dashed when she fished her phone out of her jeans pocket only to find that it wouldn't turn on. She didn't need the light to tell it was a lost cause; she could feel the spider web of cracks covering its glassy surface. It must have happened when she had fallen at the stream.

Now she had no way of even attempting a phone call or text, or checking the compass to see where she was even at. The camping compass she usually kept in her bag had been lent to a friend a few weeks ago, and she hadn't thought it important enough to retrieve it from them.

Anna leaned her back against the wall of the little cave and sighed. She would just have to wait until morning. Once the sun came up she would at least be able to tell which direction she should try, and head back. That is, unless Gary happened to be waiting somewhere nearby with an arrow with her name written on it.

"I sure know how to pick them," she muttered. In the remaining light, she could see the wolf's ears prick forward. "You'd think I'd learn by now, wouldn't you. This was what, number four? Five? I am not a picky person. Every one of those guys had something fundamentally wrong with them.

"Bryan had mother issues, Jacob had commitment issues, David was gay. And yes, I should have figured out that last one much earlier than I did. I think I knew before he did. He's very happy with Jason, now. And Gary...well, obviously, he's a cheater and a psychopath all rolled into one neat little ball of fun."

Anna stopped and stared at the wolf, who was cocking his head to the side and seemed to be hanging onto every word. "Damn. That's it. I've lost my mind. I'm talking to a wolf."

She brought her knees up to her chest and shoved her hands in the pockets of her sweatshirt to warm them. Feeling something scratch her fingers, she withdrew the small sprig of bluebells she had tucked in there earlier that afternoon.

Holding the flowers up and inhaling their scent, she thought of all the times she had seen them scattered throughout the woods.

Skipping through the trees, holding her father's hand. Finding them the morning after she had gotten her first kiss. Picking them to gather for a small bouquet to take to her father's hospital room when he had suffered a heart attack. All of the memories rushed through her mind, like a living screenplay of her entire life.

A life that had just begun. She didn't want to die. She couldn't let Gary take that away from her. She wouldn't let that be how her parents remembered her. As the girl whose crazy ex-boyfriend struck her down in the prime of her life.

Even as a tear slid down her cheek, her lips began to curve. A soft laugh escaped her, and then turned into an open throaty laugh. Her tears of sorrow at the situation dried as something struck her.

Anna looked over at the wolf. He had risen, and just seeing him sitting there brought on a fresh wave of giggles.

"I was picking flowers in the woods, when I came across a wolf who changed my path. I followed where he led. And..." She laughed again, nearing hysteria. "And I'm wearing an orange hood."

The wolf looked at her quizzically, and she shook her head. "Okay, so it's not a red hood. But it's pretty damn close."

She sat there, in a burrow in the ground, surrounded by darkness and the wild, and felt a sense of peace come over her. "I don't know where you came from, but I don't have a single doubt that you would ever harm me. I don't know if you're an angel sent from heaven, but you have saved me."

Digging in her bag again, Anna found a couple of packages of granola bars and beef jerky. She opened the bag of jerky and tossed it all to the wolf. He sniffed it daintily at first, then slid back down to the floor and started eating.

She toasted him silently with her granola bar and bit into it, letting the sweet honey flavor coat her tongue. *A girl scout forever*, she thought. Always carrying food and water with her wherever she went.

It was still early in the evening, but she felt the day's events crash over her. Exhaustion overtook her, and she lay down with her head facing the tunnel leading to the outside. If Gary happened to find them, she wanted to at least see him coming.

Using her bag as a pillow, she settled into as comfortable a position as she could manage. With a wolf for a guard, Anna felt it was possible to get a little rest. Her lids lowered, and she felt herself sinking towards sleep. The ground was damp and cold, and she shivered.

Without actually seeing him, she sensed the wolf stand and stretch beside her. He paced the floor, and then seemed to make up his mind. He curled up into a tight ball, his back resting against hers. The heat from his body radiated against hers, and she felt herself begin to warm. Feeling safer than she had in hours, she slept.

She dreamt she was running through a field filled with bluebells and wildflowers, running to someone. She couldn't make out his face. No matter how hard she ran towards him, the distance between them never diminished. The wind blew long dark hair over his forehead, and he held out his hand to her but she couldn't reach him.

Snarls ripped her out of the meadow and into reality. Her wolf — *When did she start thinking of him as her wolf?* — was crouched in the tunnel, head lowered, hackles raised.

The remaining sleepy haze flew away as she backed against the wall of the little cave. She didn't have to ask to know what lay beyond that entrance. Her voice cracked as she called to the wolf, urging him away from the entrance. He wasn't going to be any help to either of them if Gary could reach him with the bow.

She called to him again, her voice stronger this time, but he bolted out into the open. Daylight streamed through the opening to the cave, giving her just enough light to rip her bag apart searching for something she could use.

Her fingers fumbled across something hard and metallic. She closed her hand around it and drew out the Leatherman tool she had forgotten until now. Snapping the knife into position, she crawled forward. She could hear the wolf snapping and snarling. And there was Gary, hurling obscenities.

The bright light stung her eyes, and she squinted. Two forms twisted and became one in front of her. Her eyes adjusted to the sun, and she could see her wolf on his hind legs grappling with Gary. The bow lay on the ground, forgotten for the moment, useless at minimal distance, as his hands closed around the throat of the wolf in a struggle to keep the animal away.

Anna couldn't stand by and do nothing. Not when this beautiful animal had saved her life and kept her safe through the night. Running behind the two fierce figures, she grabbed the bow off the ground and threw it as far as she could. There was no way she could handle the weapon; she would fare better with the knife, but at least she could try and get it out of Gary's reach.

Gary let out a brief, strangled shout, and she looked back to see him lose the battle. Her wolf's winter fur was too thick for him to get a proper hold, and his grip slipped. She had to turn quickly away, unable to watch as those powerful jaws locked onto Gary's throat.

Sinking to the ground, Anna wrapped her arms around her middle. She felt grief at the waste of life, but did not grieve for the man who had been trying to kill them both. It was survival of the fittest, and she couldn't help but feel grateful and glad to be alive.

Her wolf's massive head pushed against her, nudging her shoulder. It was the release that she needed. She wept, sobbing in relief that it was over. He whined and nudged her again before backing away. Anna watched him as he stopped several yards away.

She grew alarmed when he howled and lay on his side, his body jerking. Shouting in alarm, she jumped to her feet to rush to his side. She stopped suddenly over him, unable to comprehend what she was seeing.

Muscle slipped against shifting bone and fur slid back over his body, revealing flesh beneath. He whimpered as shudders racked his body. His human body. Deep, gasping breaths subsided steadily. Where her wolf lay only moments before, a man lay before her now. A very naked man.

As he moved to stand, she drew back. She had trusted the wolf with her life, but this… this was too much. Her mind couldn't handle this. It wasn't possible. And yet he stood before her.

Quiet eyes searched hers. Eyes she recognized, but failed to understand. A wind rose in the trees, swaying the branches and tossing his hair into his eyes.

Anna gasped, her hand flying to her mouth. It was him. That dark hair, that physique. It was the man from her dream. Her initial shock over, she stepped towards him. He was real. This was real. He was hers. She could feel it.

The peace that she had felt during the night, laying in the cold with the wolf at her back, returned as she looked into his face. He reached out his hand and she placed hers into his. As he pulled her into his arms, she could feel her heart opening up to something she couldn't give words to.

Anna laid her cheek against his chest as he cradled her against him. She could feel his heart beating against hers. There would be talking, but that would wait until later. For now, there was only this.

Anna closed her eyes, and surrendered to his strength. She wasn't sure of many things, but she already knew two simple truths. She was going to start wearing orange more often. And then there was the other, far more important lesson that she had learned from all of this.

Fairy tales were real.

Janelle is currently working on finishing her first novel, along with writing anything else that strikes her fancy. She finds inspiration in the imagery of words, as well as through the camera she often has stuck to her face. When she is not playing with words, she can often be found volunteering at a wolf research and education park, where she works with her real-life muses.

The Orange-Headed Serpent

by Gareth S. Young

I was twelve when I fell in love for the first time. Bonnie had hair the color of summer wheat; long and unruly, it danced on her shoulders as she walked. Her eyes were blue as the Arctic sea, but warm. It was her smile that discombobulated me the most. She had one of those full beam sunshine grins: when she smiled the whole place lit up and you found yourself smiling back. I would never have admitted it to my friends but she gave me butterflies. She was beautiful.

Bonnie and I lived on the same street for years, but rarely spoke. Quiet and shy, I observed the local mayhem at a distance. She stood with chin out in the middle of it, her slim face a patchwork of dirt smudges, her knees stained green by grass. She wore a t-shirt with frayed edges and socks that always collapsed around her ankles. The appearance of cuts and smears of blood on knuckles or shins showed that whatever she did, she did at full speed. And she loved it. I loved it too. I gaped at her like a fish on a hook.

One warm evening, I sat down on the middle rail of a long, wooden fence on top of a steep embankment. The spacing between the three horizontal rails allowed me to sit on the middle one and leave my feet dangling. If I crossed my arms on the top rail, my chin rested comfortably as I looked down into the forest opposite me. This was my place to daydream.

Lost in thought, my reverie was broken when a pair of well-worn sneakers swung through the gap between the railings. Bonnie, grinning big, sat beside me.

"Whatcha doin'?" She nudged my shoulder with hers. Her eyes flashed with mischief.

"Nothing much." I couldn't look at her. I stared at my spiral-bound notepad, wishing the words would rush out and climb into my mouth and give me something more interesting to say. I blushed instead.

"What's in the notebook?" She peered over my arm at the closed pad. Leaning closer, an escaped strand of her hair brushed my face. My hand rose as if to swat away a fly and she leaned away. "Sorry." She patted the rogue strand down while the rest of her hair threatened to escape from its ponytail.

"Oh. Sorry. I… it's okay." I lifted the notebook and waved it. "Just ideas and stuff."

She bounced on the railing until I turned to her. She stopped when I met her eyes.

"Cool!" She beamed a thousand watt smile and then laughed. There was always a fire in the coolness of her eyes. "So, what do you want to do now?" She flopped back like she was going to fall from the fence. Instead her hands grabbed the top railing and she let her head snap back. Her ponytail brushed the ground. "D'you want me to go away? Quit bugging you?" She gave me a daring look. I wanted to talk to her, without mumbling and blushing, so I took a deep breath.

"No. You can stay." I waved the notebook again. "I write stories. I like to come out here and look at the trees and the river, and listen to the birds. It relaxes me."

She pulled herself up and leaned her head against the top railing. She had full lips, and she bit the bottom one, making me think about kissing them. "Tell me a story," she said. There was a brief sadness in her eyes. The smile dropped away and then flashed back. "Please?" she added, swinging back and forth.

It took me forever to start talking. I persuaded myself it would be the only way to keep her near me. I looked down the embankment and the story sprung into my head.

"Have you heard about the orange-headed serpent?" I asked.

Her face lit up. "No. Tell me!"

"It travels around the world, day and night, never stopping. It consumes and devours everything in its path. It swallows orchards filled with sweet apples and fields full of woolly sheep. It drinks freshwater lakes and feasts on fish from the sea. Its long metallic claws sound like a butcher sharpening his knives as it snatches cows from their pastures. Its deep throaty growl can be heard miles away as it comes for you."

Bonnie closed her eyes. Her face relaxed and her eyebrows twitched. She seemed to be imagining the orange serpent.

I continued, "It won't ever stop, but if you can catch it and open its belly, all its treasures will be yours."

"Treasure," Bonnie whispered.

"Yes. Who knows what it's gobbled up on its travels?" I chuckled.

Without warning, there was the sound of metal on metal; the sound of two sharp blades clashing.

"Oh, my gosh!" Startled, Bonnie stared at me. "The serpent."

I grinned. "It's coming now."

We listened to the deep throaty growl in the distance. Somewhere around the bend, between the trees, we heard it coming. "Over there," I pointed.

Bonnie leapt up, standing on the middle railing as she leaned over the top one. "Come up here." She had to shout as the noise got louder. The serpent screamed, a two-tone wail that echoed around the entire area. I stood beside Bonnie as we waited for the head of the serpent to appear.

And there it was.

Its eyes burned bright as it twisted through the curve, its orange head roaring as it approached us. Bonnie raised her hands and then toppled sideways into me and clutched my arm, her head landing on my shoulder. My heart flipped.

The ground shook and the serpent wailed again. It would not be stopping.

"Hang on," I yelled above the din. Bonnie squeezed my arm hard as the fence tried to shake us off. I clutched the top railing as the updraft from the passing beast tried to blow us away. The serpent's metallic spine clunked and rang like a blacksmith beating on his anvil.

The engineer of the train waved to us. Bonnie waved back.

The orange Burlington Northern engine flew past us, its cars beating a steady rhythm on the rails. It continued onwards, taking its treasure with it. Bonnie jumped off the fence and I followed.

"Orange serpent, huh?" She was grinning again.

I shrugged. "I like to write stories."

Without warning, she kissed me. She pulled back and chewed her bottom lip again. "Thank you," she said, and turned to walk away.

My face burned and my stomach somersaulted at least five times. "Uh. What for?" I still felt the moisture of her lips on mine. My hand flew to my mouth to confirm that I hadn't imagined the kiss.

"For telling me your little story." She bent over and plucked something off the ground. She came up with a small rock. "Check this out." The rock had an unusual pattern of striations running through it.

"Cool." I managed to say before she started walking again. With nothing interesting to add, I picked up my notebook and prepared to head home. She stopped after a few steps and turned. The smile returned and mischief shone in her eyes.

"You coming?" she asked.

I nodded and caught up. "Where're we going?"

She shrugged. "Exploring."

"Okay," I said. I tucked the notepad in my back pocket and fell in step beside her. We skirted around the edge of our subdivision, stopping when something interesting caught the eye. We talked some, but it was equally comfortable just to walk in silence, enjoying one another's company. Every so often she'd blast me with another big smile, show me a rock or stick out her tongue, and then carry on. I laughed every time. By the time daylight had faded, Bonnie had a pocket full of interesting rocks.

"I'd better get home," I said.

She pouted and nodded. "Okay. I'll walk with you."

"Okay!" I grinned.

"Okay!" She mimicked. She thrust a hand into her pocket and pulled out a rock. She studied it and then offered it to me. "For the story," she said.

I thanked her and made a fist around the smooth rock. I wouldn't let it go until I went to bed. We walked in silence until we reached the sidewalk leading to my house. She barged into me with her shoulder.

"Hey," she said, "Knock, knock."

I rolled my eyes. "Really?" I laughed.

She nudged me and frowned. "Yes, really. Now. Knock, knock."

"Who's there?"

"Banana."

"Banana who?"

She grinned. "Knock, knock."

"Ugh," I groaned.

Again she nudged me. "Quit grumbling and answer. Knock, knock."

"Who's there?"

"Banana."

"Banana who?"

She grabbed my arm and laughed hard. "Knock, knock."

"Let me guess…"

"Knock, knock," she insisted.

I was laughing hard now. "Who's there?"

"Orange."

"Orange who?"

"Orange you glad I didn't say banana?"

We giggled at the stupid joke and when she looked at me again with those gorgeous blue eyes, I found myself lost in them. And although years passed, and we grew older and more complicated, our lives more challenging and our needs more intense, I stayed lost in them. I loved being lost in them, so much so that I never once wanted to find my way back.

Gareth Young was born and raised in Scotland. After that it all gets a bit a hazy. What is known is that he spends his waking hours writing and railroading with varying degrees of success. And, despite the fact he now lives in the St. Louis area, he can still rock a kilt. (Or so he likes to think.)

Color Me Happy

by Julie Glover

Orange Pompoms

Oh, how I wanted to be the girl-on-top.

I know what you're thinking, but the term had nothing to do with sexual aggressiveness or sluthood. I'm not like that. I'm talking cheerleading pyramid.

Splits, back flips, herkies, toe-touch jumps, tumbling passes — I could do them in my sleep. I'd been tumbling since elementary school and a cheerleader since the first tryouts in junior high. I'd craved that top spot since I'd made the high school varsity squad, and finally the cheerleading coach had designated me to be "the girl-on-top".

We came out in orange football jerseys with tight white shorts, shaking our orange-and-white pompoms. With my natural light red — okay, *orange* — hair, I looked like a striped traffic cone. The first part of our routine went smoothly — a choreographed dance to a pop and hip-hop medley. Then it was go time for our stunts. The lifts and jumps were as smooth as the satin ribbons in our hair, as three of us were hoisted up and thrown into flips and twists, each caught by three spotters below. The students clapped and yelled as we performed our daring feats... or showed off our legs — take your pick.

Then we gathered up into a bunch and started to form the final trick. I was lifted like before, but this time even higher. At the top, I raised one leg over my head and stood single-footed on the flattened hands of junior Tara Smith. The crowd erupted with cheers, and the stands rumbled with the feet of hundreds of students expressing their admiration. I was there — at the top to hear and see it all.

My heart thumped wildly, and my head floated further above my third-story location. The music ended on a boom, and the praise of our spectators washed over me anew. This was exactly where I'd wanted to be.

And then I felt it. A slight movement at the bottom of the pyramid, like the princess felt the pea or Yertle the Turtle burped at the bottom. Immediately, I lowered my leg, and Tara quickly responded by spreading out her hands to let me stand in a more stable position. But her hand faltered. Her balance wavered. Time slowed to a crawl, and I could see what was happening before I fell.

The cheerleaders' hold gave way, and I went down like an ice cream scoop onto the sidewalk. Spotters scrambled beneath me. I had one last thought before I landed: "Please, no one put this on YouTube."

Green Thumb

You wouldn't think a toe would matter so much. But the bone in my little toe had completely separated, and now I was stuck in a cast for the next few weeks. I wouldn't be shaking my orange pompoms or climbing any pyramids for a few weeks. I was no longer the lucky girl-on-top. I was the unlucky girl-on-crutches.

At least I'd been able to pick my cast color — a bright tangerine to show my school spirit for our Windsor Warriors.

"Tabby." My mother called me from the kitchen, and I hobbled down the hallway.

"What, Mom?"

Her shoulders slumped. "Oh, honey, it's so sad to see you like that. I'm sorry, sweetheart."

Sorry didn't make me feel better, but it was nice of her to try. I slid into the first chair I could reach and set my crutches on the floor.

"Anyway," she said. "I have at least figured out your school transportation."

"School transportation?"

"I've got Seth Rayne lined up to drive you to school for the next couple of weeks."

I nearly swallowed my tongue, and my teeth, and my lips. "What?"

My mother stopped loading the dishwasher long enough to stare at me. "Seth Rayne is driving you to school, starting tomorrow."

"Mom, you can't do that."

"What do you mean?"

"I cannot ride with Seth Rayne to school."

"You can't drive yourself. Your right foot is out of commission for a while."

"I'll drive with one foot," I offered.

"You cannot drive a stick shift with one foot, Tabby. You need someone else to take you. Seth's mother said that he could."

The pit in my stomach became a pit bull. Mom had to get this. There was *no way* I was going to ride with Seth Bullied-My-Butt Rayne for the next two weeks. I couldn't even take one day with that jerk.

"Why don't *you* take me?"

"I have to be there early to open up the nursery. You know that."

"So let's switch cars. You can take my car, and I can take yours. I can drive yours with one foot."

"Tabby, I cannot do my job with your little two-seater."

She was right. My mother was a landscaper — a green thumb. She was always hauling plants and flowers here and there.

I wasn't done, though. "I'll get one of my friends to take me."

"Sweetie, I'm sorry, but your friends are on the squad, and they have to be there early. You don't. Not for a while."

"I'll ask someone else."

"Like who?"

I mentally thumbed through my cell phone's contact list. *Scroll, scroll, scroll.* There had to be someone. Unfortunately, everyone who had ever given me a ride seemed to be in football or cheerleading, and both groups met early in the morning, long before the first bell rang.

Surely there was an acquaintance I could ask. "I could ask Monica."

"Monica who?"

"Monica…" I racked my brain. "Monica something. She's in my geometry class."

My mother returned her attention to the plates. "It has to be someone I know."

"You don't *know* Seth, Mom. You can't make me ride with him."

"His mother and I are good friends, and she swore that Seth would be happy to help you. He's a perfectly good kid. I don't know what your problem is with him."

Given her comments and the way she was now scrubbing a pan with domestic fervor, I'd been dismissed. My mother was easygoing for the most part, but once she dug in her heels, you'd need a jackhammer to move her. Never mind that being seen with Seth was likely to set my hot-meter to practically zero. I was already crippled enough with the cast. Now I was going to be crippled by stupid Seth at my side.

Blue Öyster Cult

I think Seth Rayne had been driving since he was about twelve, but he got his license and a car at sixteen. When I say "car". I mean road-rage bait. He had plastered the entire vehicle with bumper stickers against eating meat. You wouldn't think that a guy who bullied little girls would be so worried about animal cruelty. Besides, what was so cruel about killing and eating an animal? It's not like we castigated tigers for doing that very thing.

Seth's sedan pulled up in front of my house. I needed a plan. I chose denial and avoidance.

Day One. *Say nothing. Let Seth carry my backpack to the car. Then lean on the passenger door the whole way there. Bolt from the car on arrival and stride away on crutches like a stilt-walker. Whew, no one saw us together.*

Day Two. *Say nothing. When Seth asks how I'm doing, roll my eyes. Stare out the window. Once we reach the parking lot, get out of the car and walk away while he calls, "Do you need any help?"*

Day Three. *Same thing. Seth sits quietly on the way and blasts his stereo until my eardrums beg for a reprieve. At school, go straight in and ignore the ringing in my ears.*

Day Four. *More rock music I don't know. Where did this guy get this stuff? None of it is current. My mom might as well have put me in the car with a killer. I'm being attacked here. Death by headbanging. Still ignoring each other.*

Day Five. "Look." Seth pulled the car over to the curb, halfway to school. "I don't have to drive you, you know. I offered to do this."

Say nothing.

"Fine. I get it," he said. "No talking."

Say nothing.

"You could at least acknowledge that I exist."

I turned to face him. "Seth. Rayne." There. I acknowledged him. Why didn't he understand that my plan benefited him too? It's not like his creepy buddies would be happy to see Seth with a cheerleader. His school clique thought we were aligned with the evil Powers That Be — those who promote school loyalty and teenage happiness. I was doing him a favor. I was saving him from peer mockery.

We sat for a minute at the side of the street with his engine rumbling. He watched me intently, looking as if he was thinking through his next words. Then he sighed and turned on the radio again. A screeching guitar came through the speaker at my feet, and we were back to the new normal — silence amid noise.

Day Six. "What the hell is this anyway?" I had cracked. After the weekend of lying around watching a *Buffy* marathon, the last thing

I'd wanted to do was get back in Seth's meat-sucks-mobile and listen to his mind-numbing music collection.

Seth turned the volume dial down a few notches. "Blue Oyster Cult."

"What?"

"Blue Oyster Cult." Had he made that up? He must have sensed my confusion. "They were an '80s band. I like classic rock."

"Blue Oyster Cult?" I repeated.

"Yep, with an umlaut over the O." He glanced over at me. I leaned my body toward the passenger door, but I looked at him this time. Seth was dressed in a pair of carpenter jeans, Vans shoes, and a black tee that said Boston. Maybe his family was from Massachusetts. His straight dark hair with purple streaks fell in soft waves on his cheeks and the back of his neck. I'd hated him since fifth grade.

"Stupid name," I said.

"I think it's awesome," he said. "It may not even mean anything. Could be words pulled out of a hat."

I went back to staring out the window. "Words matter," I said. He needed to know that. He should have already known. He should have understood that back in fifth grade.

White Lies

My cast had been signed and decorated by the whole cheerleading squad, half the football team, and anyone and everyone who asked. No matter who you were, I obliged the request to stretch out my leg and hand over the Sharpie. Messages like "Break a leg. Ha-ha!" "Get well soon," and "Tabby's Toes" with an arrow pointing to the break were permanently marked on my tangerine orange boot. My ex-boyfriend had written a special message: "Hope your back on top soon."

Mike never had been the best student. It took a thousand watts of willpower not to add an "e" and an apostrophe to correct his spelling error. But I didn't want to look like I cared.

For the sixth day in a row, he insisted on carrying my books between classes. Not that I fought very hard against the idea. It was a big enough pain to wobble around school on crutches. Having someone carry my textbooks was a huge relief.

"So when are you out of the cast?" Mike asked. "Will you get to cheer by Homecoming?" The homecoming game was two weeks away. I wouldn't be doing any jumps then, but I had high hopes for at least being on the track to shake my orange pompoms and cheer the Warriors to a win.

"I have to get approval from the doctor. But I'll be at the game one way or another."

I had mixed feelings about Mike. On one hand, he was gorgeous and built and fun and made my insides go Gangnam-style on me. On the other hand, he had kissed another girl at a party when we were dating. He'd sworn it was one kiss and that it had been a huge mistake. But I'd broken it off this summer and hadn't been ready to give him my trust again.

Mike deposited me at the door to my third period. "I'll be back as soon as class is over." It took another thousand watts of willpower not to think about how those gorgeous lips had once slid into mine and teased my mouth with the taste of peppermint gum, how his hard-muscled arms had drawn me in to his chest, how his tongue had tangled with mine in perfect harmony. No, I would not think of that.

"See you soon," I said.

He turned on his heels to walk away, and there was Seth at his locker next to my classroom. He stared like he wanted to say something again, but he didn't. And I didn't linger.

When the final class bell rang, it was time to meet Seth at the car. I exited through the side door as usual with Mike holding my backpack. "I got it from here," I said.

"Your mom picking you up again?"

"Yeah." I hadn't told him, or any of my friends, the truth.

"Tell her 'hi'." He transferred the pack to my back, then started toward the field house for a weightlifting session. I began my walk to Seth's car. I'd gotten better at navigating my way with crutches, but I wasn't fast.

A few steps in, Mike approached me again. "Hey, I've been meaning to ask you something."

I paused in the parking lot. "Yeah?"

Mike flashed his winning smile, making that left dimple appear like a thumbprint left in his face. I loved that dimple.

I felt a brush on my shoulder and looked over. Seth passed by me, winked, and said, "Catch you later, Tabby."

My breath caught. Why wasn't he avoiding me? That's the plan. Deny and avoid.

"You friends with him?" Mike asked, cocking his head in Seth's direction. Seth was striding confidently to his statement car.

"No," I said with a grimace.

"Then why is he talking to you like that?"

"I don't know." I felt a bead of sweat trickle down my back. It was still warm this time of year, but not that warm.

Mike harrumphed. "Anyway, I was wondering if you might want to go to the Homecoming Dance with me."

He definitely wasn't asking me due to my current dancing ability. Attending a dance with me at this point would mostly involve sitting in a chair and bringing me punch. But I wanted to go. I really wanted to go.

Was I ready?

"Um," I said. A horn beeped in the parking lot, and the two of us instinctively looked around for the source. Seth was sitting in his car, waiting. Thankfully, Mike didn't make the connection. He must have figured Seth was honking for someone else.

"Can I think about it?" I asked. "I mean, I just don't know about us."

"C'mon, Tabby," Mike said. "That was ages ago. I told you it was a mistake, and I'd never do it again."

"I know," I said. "But I need to think about it. I *want* to go."

"Then go," he said. Now he looked more irritated than pleading.

I would probably say yes. I would say yes. But I didn't want to be pressured into saying yes. "You'd better get to the field house, Mike. I'll think about it."

He sighed and left.

I watched him walk away and turn the corner behind the school building. Seth's car pulled up. I was caught off guard. "Hey!"

"You need help?" Seth asked through the open window.

"Yeah," I said. "You could leave me alone. That would help."

I tossed my backpack and crutches in the back and got into the passenger seat.

Seth ran his fingers across his scalp, pulling back his hair enough to show his black stud earring and giving me a view of his stacked colorful wristbands — probably political statements too. "You know what you need?"

"What?" I said. I didn't want to know what he thought. I was, however, angry enough not to ignore him.

"You need a guy who'll treat you well. You need to know you're worth something — apart from being a cheerleader or popular or whatever. You need a guy who makes you feel beautiful, even when you don't feel it yourself."

"What if my perfect guy eats meat?" It was the best insult I could come up with that quick.

Seth grinned. "What if he doesn't?"

Seeing Red

Day Seven. Seth pulled up his veggie-vehicle and jumped out. He came around and opened my car door. What was he doing?

"Your carriage, milady," he said.

I studied his expression for clues. Nothing. Seth was here like usual — jeans, Vans, Beatles shirt — and rock music pounding and raising the dead.

"Whatever," I answered and got in.

He ran around and took the driver's seat. We started the short drive to school, but at the third intersection he turned left instead of right.

"Where are you going?" I asked.

"I want to show you something."

"We don't have much time before school. It takes me forever to walk to my classes."

"Here." He handed me a piece of paper. I unfolded it and read the best forgery note I'd seen. Okay, fine, the only forgery note I'd seen. I'd never skipped class. Not for anything but the school-sanctioned cheerleading contest and student council meetings.

"You want me to skip class?" I said. "I'll get in trouble."

Seth took the up ramp onto the highway, and we entered a line of traffic moving away from town. "Well, you have two choices," he said. "You can come with me, or you can exit the car." He gestured with his head toward my side door, as if I could possibly leap out of a moving vehicle traveling sixty miles per hour, with a cast on my foot.

"You are unbelievable!" I huffed, crossed my arms, settled into the seat. This guy hadn't changed since fifth grade.

He switched the playlist on the plugged-in MP3 player. "How about a change of pace?"

A quiet guitar strummed, and it sounded more like classical music than classic rock. After about a minute, the pace picked up and it was hard rock after all. But I listened to the lyrics as shopping centers and fields passed my view out the window. "Love will find a way…"

When the song ended, I spoke up. "Who was that?"

"Tesla. Another '80s rock band. Love Song."

He took the next exit, and I settled in while more power ballads played at reasonable decimals.

But I felt stone cold when we pulled up to a cemetery. Was this his idea of a sick joke? Was he really a killer? I'd had him pegged as a thoughtless jerk, but not a kidnapper and murderer.

He stepped out of the car like we'd pulled up to a convenience store instead of a graveyard. He opened my door and beckoned me with his outstretched hand.

"Seriously?" I asked.

"Trust me."

I didn't trust him, but I was curious enough to get out anyway. I managed without reaching for his helping hand and got my crutches from the back seat. He shrugged, then walked ahead of me. I pulled out my cell phone to text a friend my coordinates, just in case, but there was no signal.

How could there be no signal? How could there still be even a single inch left in the United States that didn't have a cell phone signal?

I straggled behind and caught up to Seth standing on a hill overlooking the mass of headstones and statues. "Check it out," he said. "This place always gives me perspective. All of these dead people around. How many of them knew what they were worth? What they meant to the world? To their loved ones? How many of them chose to be with someone who got that? Who really got that?"

It was the most I'd heard Seth Rayne say in years.

"Why am I here?" I said. "So you can give another speech?"

He furrowed his brow. "Another speech?"

"Yeah, like the one you gave in fifth grade." I definitely remembered that speech.

"What speech?"

Fury surged from my broken toe up to my open mouth. I was seeing red. "What speech! Why do you think I can't you stand you, you jerk? You gave that whole speech about stupid stuff that's orange and included me in it. For the rest of the summer, I walked around with kids taunting me. I couldn't show my face at the pool without someone saying I matched the life jackets or go the basketball court without being compared to the ball."

As I spoke, I could tell that he didn't remember any of this. How could he forget? I'd never forgotten. That was the year I'd stopped playing with the neighborhood kids so much but rather practiced my tumbling in the backyard for hours and hours to perfection.

"I did that?" he said.

My chin quivered. I nodded. I tasted tears on the edges of my mouth.

Seth shook his head. "I'm sorry, Tabitha. I was a total mess that year. But I shouldn't have made fun of you."

"Yeah, well, you did. And I would like to go to school now."

I started my slow descent toward the car, then threw my crutches to the ground and hopped away. I could get there faster on one foot.

Seth was at the car before I arrived, holding my crutches. "I am sorry, but let me explain."

I stopped. Not because I wanted to, but because he was blocking my entrance to the vehicle.

"My dad died that year. He hadn't lived with us for years, but I stopped going to see him. I've only seen his headstone once. I come here instead, talk to these people. But I was a screwed-up kid that year. I lashed out at everybody."

"I'm sorry," I muttered. "I didn't know."

His dad was dead? I'd known that his parents were divorced, but I'd never asked about his father.

His deep-green eyes were watery now. He'd once fallen from a high place too.

"I just wanted to bring you here and show you. We all end up the same way. We're all worth the same — at least, inside."

With that, he moved and went to his side of the car. I turned and took in the view — a large cemetery full of quiet souls who had probably lived their lives just like a hard rock song, raging and demanding attention.

Black Eye

The next morning I looked up the best of Blue Öyster Cult on my iPhone while waiting for Seth to arrive. Most of the music was too hard for me, but I downloaded one beautiful song called "I Love the Night". I could add one power ballad to my mix.

I sat on my porch when Seth came and waited for him to come get my backpack. "Thanks," I said.

"You're welcome." He smiled and got my stuff.

There was a Train CD playing when I got in. "This is new," I said.

"Like I said, change of pace," he answered and drove us to school with a smile. "Did the note work?"

"Yeah, I arrived by second period and apparently didn't miss anything good in first period anyway."

"I should have asked first," he said. *No, he shouldn't have. I would have said no.*

"Yeah, you should have."

He turned off the engine in the parking lot. I stayed put. By the time the engine was off, I had usually dashed halfway to the entrance. I'd determined not to deny and avoid today, though. I was riding to school with Seth Rayne, and that was that. Anyone who didn't like it could kiss my—

"So I hate dances," Seth said. "You have to get dressed up and they play lame music and there are those stupid line dances that people are supposed to know but I never know where they learned them and... well, you get the point."

Oh no. Had I given him the wrong idea? Surely, he wasn't going to—

"But you said that your ex-boyfriend asked you to the Homecoming Dance, and you didn't know if you wanted to go."

Stupid me. I'd gotten all chatty on the way home yesterday, after our morning outing to Death Valley.

"And I thought that if you needed someone to go with you instead, you could, you know, use me as an excuse. Say I asked you first or whatever."

Not once had he looked up while going through *that* speech, but now he peeked through his swept-over bangs to catch my response. My chest tightened, my jaw opened, my toe hurt.

Before I could answer, Seth closed the distance between us and put his mouth on mine. I flinched back briefly and then surged forward. His lips were thin and warm and gentle. His hand cupped my cheek as we kissed. I liked it. Oh my gosh, I liked it!

I pulled back again, shocked at my brain's response.

The car door opened behind Seth. A face appeared. An angry face.

"Get off her!" Mike yanked at Seth's Aerosmith shirt.

Seth rotated around to face my ex-boyfriend. "Whoa, wait a minute." He held up his hands.

"Get out of the car!" Mike roared.

"Mike," I said.

"Dude, I don't want to fight you," Seth said.

"Mike," I repeated.

"Then don't fight," Mike said. He reared back and threw a punch full-on, his fist headed straight for Seth's face. Seth ducked just as I crawled over the gear shift to intervene. Mike's fist landed smack-dab in my eye. I crumpled onto the seat with a pained scream.

∽o∾

Nothing Rhymes with Orange

I sat in a chair in the principal's office with Mike on one side and Seth on the other. Mike's defense had consisted primarily of blaming me — for being with Seth, for kissing Seth, for pulling away from Seth (which made Mike think I was trying to get away), and for moving forward into his lurching fist.

The lecture about violence on school property and self-control might as well have been delivered by Charlie Brown's teacher because all I heard past the ice pack on my black eye was "Waa-waa-waa…"

I was too occupied with the crazy discovery that I wanted to kiss Seth Rayne again.

When the meeting was over, Mike stopped long enough to wave his pink slip at me. "Just what I need — suspension. Coach is gonna kill me."

Before the door closed on his sorry butt, he called back, "And forget I ever asked you anything."

Left with Seth by my side, I felt relieved. Nothing made sense, but I was relieved nonetheless.

"Are you okay?" he asked. "I am so sorry. Really, this time I am so, so sorry."

Seth smiled. No dimples, but a tiny cleft in his chin. I reached out and touched it. "I'm fine."

"Is your mom going to let me keep driving you?"

"She'd better," I said. "How else am I going to get to the dance?"

Seth slipped his hand in mine, then dropped it when he realized I needed to hold my crutches instead. I was stuck with this orange cast for a while yet.

I headed out of the office, and he followed me out the door, carrying my backpack toward class. "You know, nothing rhymes with orange."

"What?" I said.

"You're not like everyone else. I've watched you for a while. You're not like a lot of other popular people. You're nice to everyone."

"How can you say that? I wasn't nice to *you*," I said.

"Okay, not to me." He chuckled. "But you had your reasons."

"No, I'm a mess," I said.

"You're unique," Seth answered. "Like orange. It doesn't rhyme with anything. But that's okay. It doesn't have to. Orange is one of a kind, like you."

I dropped my crutches onto the floor and planted a kiss on his mouth, right there in front of everyone.

Sometimes it seems like the small stuff doesn't matter — the mean thing you said in fifth grade, the toe you broke, a ride with someone you don't like, a public smooch — but I hadn't paid enough attention to the big stuff. And now I knew that the big stuff started with the small.

∽o∾

As a city girl from the Lone Star State, **Julie Glover** owns both go-go boots and cowboy boots; has been to Broadway shows and rodeos; enjoys chateaubriand and rattlesnake sausage; and likes Led Zeppelin and Rascal Flatts. When she isn't daydreaming about having a personal chef or wrestling the family's laundry, Julie pens mysteries and young adult fiction.

Impressions

by Maureen Hovermale

S he stared at the Monet, its focal point an eerie shade against the gray sky. Monet's choice of color seemed to pulse in the background; the orange flecks seemingly out of context with the fishing boats.

Ann blinked her eyes and pinched her nose to clear the lightning headache that stormed over the bridge of her nose. She thought it funny that the color orange was essentially the birthmother of Impressionism; the discordant sun and its connotations of life-giver were not lost on the waifish girl in the overlarge raincoat. At that moment, a passerby noted to himself that Ann's paint-smudged fingernails seemed to be the only colorful thing about her. On the heels of the thought, Ann pushed the hanging sleeves of her gray coat up past her pale wrists, proving his assumptions even further.

Ann had seen the painting in grayscale at a lecture and had been surprised that the overly bright sun was actually the same tone as the sky that held it. She shoved a stray wisp of hair into the tweedy Gatsby hat she'd taken to wearing lately. The grays and blues in the painting were perfectly complemented, she thought, and this was the something that still eluded her as an artist; her colors were appropriate, yet they somehow failed to evoke emotion and synchronicity she worked for. The old masters continually astounded her with their innate understanding of color and form, so timeless that it even stood up to modern technological critique. Would she ever achieve this hallowed place of being? Could she even allow herself to dream so high? Ann turned from the painting and made her way out of the museum, the other paintings sliding across her periphery in the wake of the boats still floating across her mind.

She strode across the cobblestones, each one a simple melody, or cavatina, to the longer, singing lyrics in her head. They matched the brushstrokes she imagined, and seemed to speak to her in a rhythmic Da Capo; she would need to start over again and again before she would finally be finished with what waited for her on the easel, as perfection is the goal of every artistic endeavor. Ann ducked out of the path of a customer exiting from the bakery who had yet to look her way. She banged her elbow on the side of the doorjamb, her intake of breath drawing the man's notice.

He nodded his apology and wondered that such a small thing would have such large cheekbones. For a moment he thought he should buy her a meal, but the proud brow that stared back at him, even in forgiveness for his trespass, answered his unspoken charity. He doffed his hat, and opened an umbrella against the sprinkles of rain.

Ann pointed to the croissant and placed the exact change in the silver tray resting for this purpose on the glass display case. She picked up the flaky treat, her appetite immediately triggered by the sound of the parchment paper surrounding it. The woman behind the counter had chosen the largest one for the girl who came in on every third Tuesday. She felt a kinship with the girl's quiet, and appreciated the patronage of one so obviously poor. She assumed that the purchase was a large percentage of the girl's daily salary and had purposefully kept the croissants' price lower than what it should be. Smiling, she patted down her apron and looked at the chalkboard the tiny girl had just walked past outside. It hawked the specials of the bakery in colorful curlicues; writing them out was her favorite chore of the day.

Ann took a bite a few paces from the bakery. She couldn't wait any longer. She'd told herself that she would wait until she was home before she had even stepped foot outside today, but even then she had known the lie for what it was. The buttery flakes instantly surrounded her taste buds and bloomed. She shut her eyes in the bliss of the moment and then opened them to the thunder that cracked not a second after. She wrapped the bread protectively in its paper and shoved it into her pocket. Grabbing the collar of her coat, she pulled it over the top of her head and ran for it.

Mrs. Applebaum was the sort that finished cleaning her small flat well before noon. She would fiddle and dawdle, even creating small messes for herself, but in all actuality, the flat was pristine and she knew it. She stared out the window and watched a girl shove bread into her pocket after taking an enormous bite. She sighed and wondered how someone could eat whatever they wanted and still be that thin, remembering when she could run that fast.

Ann huddled under the bridge, her companion a very wet, bedraggled-looking dog who eyed her as nervously as she did him. It looked like a mixture between a mud puddle and a young retriever, the result being a tad less intimidating except, perhaps, to the nose. Ann slowly moved her hand into her pocket and pinched off a piece of her treasure. With a flick of a wrist, it was in front of the dog; after taking a hop backwards, the dog realized what it was. He sniffed it warily, then gobbled it up and gave her an expectant look.

A crooked grin and half a croissant later, Ann had a new friend. The rain had let up after a momentary burst of temper and she was now half a block from her destination. The dog was still in tow, though she had half-heartedly shooed him at several turns. She stared, as she walked, at this intrusion on her thoughts and was surprised to find that she welcomed the interruption. The dog wagged his tail at her and she accidentally dropped another piece of bread.

The door opened before her and a large man stepped aside for Ann to enter. The dog dashed in ahead of her, causing the man to lift an eyebrow in his characteristic way.

"Oh Michael, do be a dear and arrange for him to be bathed and looked at." Ann shrugged her favorite coat off and handed it to him. It had been her grandfather's, and reminded her of his pipe tobacco and newspapers. She threw the Gatsby hat onto the foyer's bench and orange hair spilled out in long waves down her back, the thick tresses barely tangled in spite of their former prison. "I've such new ideas!"

Michael collared the mistress' new dog before it could follow her and nodded his head at his wife, Bella, to come and help him restrain the animal. The couple had been with Ann's family for years and were used to her colorful whims. Bella came over quickly and they shared a very quiet giggle at the antics of the dog.

Ann, back to work at her easel, found her mind wandering to her new friend and made adjustments to the canvas accordingly. Stepping back hours later, she nearly tripped over the freshly-bathed dog. Petting the exuberant mutt, her eyes never wandered from her work.

Bella gave Ann an apologetic smile when she looked her way, "I'm sorry, miss. He got away from me. He's been missing you."

Ann smiled back as Bella retreated then again looked at her work. With a sudden jolt, she realized that a person needed to stay woven into all of the differing elements around them and that this was what Monet had meant; that we could choose our paths however we wanted, but we would always be a part of the whole. That's when it hit her that Monet's brush showed more than boats and a sunrise.

Ann laughed, thinking it funny that the very first painting of the Impressionist movement proved that impressions are really just a matter of perspective.

The painting, which had been on her easel for months, was finished that night. And the dog? Well, upon inspection, he turned out to be a true redhead under all that mud, and fit with Ann just so.

Just so.

Maureen Hovermale occasionally requires hot chocolate and absolute quiet in between noisy bouts of spontaneous music. Authors are her heroes, as is the barbarian who knocked her over the head with his ways and dragged her into the cave of marriage. It is here she has resided for nearly thirty years quite happily, to the surprise of herself and everyone who knew her Irish ways. She writes obsessively and throws the tennis ball for the dogs in between baking; the equation simple and yet the result happily complex.

Divine

by S.G. Lee

It had been a year since Jack's death and I felt like he had been pushed off a cliff and I dangled. Who dies at twenty-nine? Jack, that's who! I couldn't even really stay mad at him, but I was furious at the brain aneurism that took him away.

Sad, angry, and alone, I had no close girlfriends, having given them up to spend more time with Jack. When he died, I pushed any friends who reached out to me away. Now, instead of going home to a loving spouse, I was in an endless cycle of grief, struggling to stay above water — I had to pay all the bills on one measly receptionist's salary. The hospital wanted their money and the house we'd bought had a balloon payment due. The never ending circle of creditors who wanted their cut just seemed to continuously seep out of the woodwork. I needed to clear my head and have one happy memory before I declared bankruptcy. I decided to take a weekend away and go driving in the country. I could remember the times Jack and I had seen the fall colors, the orange, red, and yellow leaves. How we'd once had a life together filled with promise. I could enjoy one bittersweet weekend of memories before the sad reality of losing my home and my car came to pass.

As I drove along the back country roads, I thought of Jack and all I had been denied. Time spent with him, and the promises we made to each other of children and home. I didn't see nature's beauty, even though it was all around me; my eyes were drawn instead to leaves brown and decayed from the summer's drought. Tears pooled in my eyes as I sent up a prayer.

"Please, God, I have suffered so much with Jack's passing. Let me reconnect with my memories of a happier time. Please give me hope, give me happiness again. Help me to find all of the things Jack and I promised each other, with someone else. Help me to feel love again, and to live again."

I closed my eyes for a second and when I opened them the foliage had changed. It was now gorgeous — so many trees now displayed their colors in anticipation of winter's slumber. The bright oranges, crimson reds, and even deep greens made me smile, their beauty was so wondrous to behold. I pulled my car over and started snapping pictures with my cell phone. Just as I pulled back onto the highway, the transport truck hit my car.

Some time later, I came to. I was unhurt as far as I could see, but the back end of my car was dented and undriveable. The truck that had hit me was long gone. I tried to find my cell phone to call AAA, but it wasn't in my purse or the passenger seat. Before I had a chance to look further, a truck that said *Flynn Towing* pulled up behind me. It was red and the grill was wide, its two headlights spaced far apart. The side mirrors stuck out farther than I had ever seen. The truck looked well-kept, despite the fact that it had been new in the 1940s.

"Hey, are you okay? Need a tow, lady?" the driver asked.

He was big and burly, and had a portly belly; frankly, he looked like an overstuffed teddy bear, especially with his big smile. It struck me as funny that his shirt was emboldened with the name Ted.

"Yes, I'm fine. A little shook up, but fine. My car isn't, though. I guess I could use a tow," I admitted.

I climbed into his cab as he hooked my car up to his winch. We were on our way quickly enough, and within a few minutes we were approaching a small but colorful town. Orange pumpkins stood on every porch, and each house was decorated for Halloween with pictures drawn and colored in childish strokes. The pumpkins weren't carved yet, but somehow I knew they would be soon. People strolled down the sidewalks, stopping to greet each other with kind smiles. I marvelled at the friendliness of this place.

"My name is Edward Flynn, Ted to my friends."

"Bronwyn Stewart," I answered, identifying myself.

"So, you ready for Halloween?" Ted asked.

"Ready for Halloween?" I was puzzled.

"Well, yes, it's at the end of the week, only two days from now. Are you ready?" Ted asked.

"I don't really celebrate Halloween."

"Oh, what a shame! Well, we'll teach you to love Halloween," Ted promised.

"We?" I asked, feeling suddenly very uncomfortable.

"The town of Divine, where Halloween is a grand holiday every year."

The place looked charming and so inviting that something inside me warmed for the first time since Jack's death; nevertheless, Ted's statement made me curious. What kind of a town celebrated Halloween so elaborately?

"You know, that wreck looked pretty bad — maybe I should take you over to my brother James' place and get you checked out. He's the town doctor."

"I don't think I need a doctor, but thanks. I'm just going to get my car fixed and be on my way."

Ted pulled up in front of a tidy garage.

"Come on then, we're here. The garage is mine, but my younger brother, Cameron, likes to tinker with engines here. I have to warn you though — he's a bit of a Beatnik. At least that's what our mother always called him," Ted grinned.

I jumped down from the truck cab and looked over at the garage. It was a simple, older structure with Texaco gas pumps in front of the building. They had been kept up well, with lots of tender care and fresh paint. Obviously Ted took pride in his establishment. Signs hung over each opening to the garage. One read "Lubrication" and the other said "Washing". Beside them was a store. Shelves above the counters were lined with oil cans, car parts, and in the corner of the room beside the counter, there stood a 1950s Coke machine with the actual Coke bottles still in it. The store was spotless, and it was obvious that Ted was a real fan of antiques.

"Cam?" Ted shouted.

"It's too early for lunch. Do you need me to work on something for you, Ted?" Cam emerged from the back of the garage, wiping his oil-covered hands on a rag. He wore gray coveralls whose open neck revealed a white tee shirt, and he had a shock of red hair tied up in a ponytail at the nape of his neck. His eyes, blue and piercing, looked straight through me like he found me wanting. "And this is?"

"A customer for me. Mrs. Bronwyn Stewart — her car was smashed up on the highway outside town. I could use some help getting it fixed. Looks like whoever hit her is gone."

"Ted, the woman needs a doctor. Why haven't you taken her to James?"

"She didn't want to go." Ted's tone was mildly exasperated.

"I don't need a doctor," I insisted.

"Well, I'm not going to fix your car if you don't go see a doctor." Cameron's eyes flashed sparks at me.

"Then I'll take my car to another garage."

Cameron began laughing.

"Why are you laughing at me?"

"I have the only garage in town — the next one isn't for sixty miles. Oh, and Cameron is the only one who can fix your car," Ted answered, hiding a smirk.

"Will you tow my car the sixty miles?" I asked, turning to Ted.

"No," he replied flatly. "You might as well give in about seeing the doctor; I'm not giving up until you go see about that bruise on your head."

"He's very stubborn that way," Cameron commented.

"Fine," I agreed, thinking I could change my mind later.

Ted then helped me back into his truck.

"I'll look at your car and give you an estimate for the repairs," Cameron said dryly, shutting the truck door. "Take care of that head."

I fumbled for the seatbelt and couldn't find it. Why hadn't I noticed this before? No seatbelts? That carried retro a little too far.

"Your vehicle should have seatbelts," I griped. "It is the law."

Ted laughed and said, "In this town, Cameron is the law. He's the Sheriff, and unless you want me to call him back over here, we're going to go see James now. I know you were only placating me, but that bruise on your head is getting bigger."

"Fine, you have me over a barrel. A quick visit and then I'm out of there," I agreed.

Ted drove quickly to his brother's office — an older Victorian cottage. It was slate blue with charming gables, and a small covered entry. Two attic windows winked at me from the roof, and shingles had been added to winterize it. A white picket fence and a cottage garden with a flowered arbor to walk through finished the enchanting view. I walked up the path to the front door. Ted walked ahead and opened it for me.

A woman dressed in a nurse's outfit, complete with cap and a name tag that read "Eileen" sat at desk in the front room, writing longhand in charts. I looked around for a computer but didn't see one. A retro black rotary phone sat on her desk.

"Hello, Eileen, is James here?" Ted asked.

"Yes, but he's in with the Blakely boy. Harold fell out of a tree and broke his arm."

"Bad break?"

"He'll be okay in six weeks or so — and he'll probably be out climbing trees again in three or four," Eileen answered with an amused smile. As she rose, I noted that she was several months pregnant.

A man in a white coat strode briskly into the room. He had short, red, curly hair clipped tight to his head. His eyes were blue and seemed to focus on me like I was under a microscope, narrowing right to the bruise that had begun to discolor my forehead.

"Do you have any dizziness, headache or a feeling of pressure in the head?"

I looked at the man in front of me and exclaimed, "Jamie Flynn! I can't believe it's you."

"Do I know you?"

"It's me, Bronwyn Callahan. Of course, my last name is Stewart now. We dated briefly during the first year of university."

"I'm sorry, Miss, I don't remember you."

Frankly, I was insulted. I couldn't believe he'd said he didn't remember me. We had dated for six months, and then he had broken up with me because he'd transferred to another school. What were the chances of me having an accident and then running into Jamie, of all people? He was the one who got away; how could he deny that he knew me? And yet something about him was very different.

"Mrs. Stewart? I think you have a concussion. Is there a number we can reach your husband?"

I shook my head. "He's dead," I said quietly.

"Oh, I'm sorry." My explanation hardly seemed to register with the doctor. "Now let me get you into an examination room and check out that head. I assume that is why Teddy brought you here." Ignoring me he asked, "What happened to her?"

"I believe she hit her head in a car accident, dear," Eileen answered.

"Eileen is James's wife," Ted explained.

So that's why he denied knowing me, I thought. *He didn't want his wife to be jealous.* Eileen need not worry. I still mourned Jack, even though I had to admit that something about Jamie was still attractive to me. But he was married. I couldn't think that way. Oblivious to my brooding, Eileen escorted me into the examining room.

"Please put this gown on, and leave on your bra and panties. The doctor will be in shortly," Eileen said, handing me a gown and a sheet and then leaving the room.

I put the gown on, surprised to find that it was cotton, not paper. Was this even necessary? My head pounded and somehow all of this seemed unreal, like I was in some kind of a dream. I felt so tired, as though I could sleep for a week, but I didn't think I had any other injuries. Head injuries could be serious though; it wouldn't hurt to have Jamie take a look.

"Okay, so you have a concussion," Jamie said after examining me.

"What a surprise," I replied sarcastically.

"As a physician, I have to tell you it does mean that you shouldn't be driving, at least for a couple of days. In fact, I'm obligated to tell the local sheriff that you have been forbidden to drive." Jamie's expression was clear: there was no room for argument.

"You wouldn't!" I exclaimed. "I have to drive. I live about a hundred miles from here, in Bangor, Maine."

Jamie shook his head. "Unless you promise not to drive, I'll have to follow through and inform the sheriff."

"Your brother, Cameron, the mechanic?"

"He likes to tinker with cars," James admitted. "But he's been elected Sheriff three times now."

Eileen came into the room.

"If I am not permitted to not drive for two days, then I'll have to find a place to stay," I conceded.

"You can stay with us!" Eileen offered brightly. "We have plenty of room, and it's not far to go — we live just next door. Although I hope you don't mind boys — we have two of them and another child on the way, as I'm sure you noticed." She rubbed her belly, an almost angelic smile crossing her features. "The boys are named after their uncles, Cam and Eddie. Come on, I'll take you next door so that you can settle in and get some rest." Turning to Jamie, she asked, "You can do without my help for the rest of the afternoon, can't you?"

"Yes, and thanks, sweetheart."

Once upon a time, Jamie had called me 'sweetheart'. Jamie addressing Eileen that way gave me pause; but I had married, why wouldn't he? They were a happy family and I envied them. Given that I didn't have the funds to stay in a hotel for two or three days, I walked with her to the house next door.

"Please have a seat and relax. I'll be right back."

I looked around the house, feeling like I had stepped back into my grandmother's time. The living room was charming, from the rug at the front door that said "welcome" to the afghans on the sofa and chairs. Hand stitched doilies adorned the tops of the end tables, on which fresh azaleas stood in crystal vases. A wood- burning fireplace was the focal point of the room. When did Eileen have the time to crochet and hand-stitch?

"Would you like some tea?" asked Eileen, interrupting my thoughts.

She held a tray with a flowered teapot and two matching cups and saucers, as well as a matching sugar bowl and creamer. I didn't know anyone actually served tea in teacups anymore. I usually drank mine in a mug. Everything about this town just seemed like someone turned back the hands of time, but somehow that very aspect made a stay here relaxing and less stressful than my life at home.

"Have you lived here long?" I asked politely.

"I've lived here all my life. James was happy to come join me here. After a year or two, his brothers moved here as well."

Just then, a woman walked in with two boys.

"Alice, thanks for looking after them for me." Eileen smiled proudly as she introduced the kids to me. "This is Eddie. He's five, and this is Cam, he's seven. Aren't you, Cam?" The taller of the two youngsters nodded, grinning at me shyly. "And this is my sister-in-law, Alice, Ted's wife."

Eileen turned to Alice and explained, "Alice, this is Bronwyn Stewart. She had an accident just outside of town this afternoon. Ted towed her car up to the garage, and brought her to see James."

Alice had red-gold hair streaming down her back. She seemed about twenty-one or two.

"It is nice to meet you, Bronwyn." Alice shook my hand briefly. "I'm sorry I can't stay, but Teddy's supper needs making."

Eileen then showed me to a room at the top of the stairs. As she shut the door behind herself, I took off my shoes and sweater and slipped in between the cool, clean sheets, falling asleep the second my head hit the pillow.

∽ O ∾

I awoke to sun streaming in the window and wondered what time it was. An antique clock on the bedside table said five after seven; where the six should have been, there was a calendar. October thirty-first. Had I slept for two days? How was that even possible? Surely the clock was wrong. I went to the window and looked outside. Definitely morning!

A woman two doors down was hanging out her laundry with wooden clothespins. How very eco-friendly, I thought. Eileen's next door neighbour even had a pie cooling on her window sill. This town was different, that was for sure. Some people would have called it quaint, with its old fashioned air, but I enjoyed the ambiance. This town was a dream come true for me, a return to the innocent time of old, a bit of peace and quiet away from my hectic world and stress. I was almost happy that James had made me stay. This was a place where children went out on Halloween, and didn't have to worry about strangers following them, or dropping unwrapped candies into their treat bags. I looked forward to seeing all the little ones who came to the door, and of course Eileen and James' children in their costumes. I felt happier than I had in six months. I heard a knock at the door; a moment later, Eileen poked her head in.

"Come in," I answered."

"Bronwyn? I trust you slept well, despite me checking on you. Happy Hallow's Eve's Day," Eileen commented, grinning at me.

"Then I did sleep through the night and the whole day? It's Halloween?" I asked.

"Yes."

"The boys look like they're ready!" I commented, as the boys streaked by past me in the hall.

"Oh yes, they certainly are! Eddie will go as a cowboy, and Cam will be a ghost. I made their costumes myself — a white sheet with holes cut out for his eyes makes a great ghost costume. Eddie's was harder to make. I had to find a cowboy hat and make some leather chaps. Then of course I took the toy gun from his toy box," Eileen explained.

"Aren't you worried people will object to his toy gun? It looked very real."

"No, why would they? It's a child's toy."

Puzzled by her reaction, I dropped the subject.

Eileen invited me to join them for the children's party later that afternoon, where there would be plenty of treats, including candy apples and homemade toffees.

"That might be fun," I answered, surprising myself.

As the party hour neared, I thought again of how trusting and innocent, this town of Divine was. I felt so at peace here. Despite all that though, I also felt cheated somehow, as though Jamie and Eileen and their children were living the life we I should have shared, with him. I wished for the hundredth time that I had pursued him, instead of just giving up when his family moved away.

I watched Eddie and his little brother Cameron welcome their guests. The two little boys were polite. Cameron imitated Eddie's motions and brought all the children into the living room where Eileen had set up the party decorations. Their courtly manners were surprising, coming from such little boys, and it charmed my heart to watch them.

The children arriving for the party all appeared to have homemade costumes. This town really did go all out for Halloween. I watched as Eileen dragged a washtub into the center of the room. She grabbed a pail of water and began filling the tub. The children watched, their eyes growing big like saucers. She then brought in a wooden bushel filled with apples, which she proceeded to dump in the tub.

"Now, children, you all know the rules to this game. With your hands behind your back, kneel down by the tub and you try to grab an apple with your teeth. You each have five minutes to do so," Eileen explained. Turning to a tiny little girl in a princess costume, she said, "Amy, you can go first, after you take off your crown and train."

Amy followed the instructions and seconds later pulled her face out of the water, an apple dangling from her mouth. I watched as the other children took their turns. The children laughed and sputtered as they bobbed for apples. Various other games followed, and then the children ended the party with hot dogs and cake. I found myself enjoying the party and the games. During the last year, I had closed myself off from thinking of the future without Jack, but I realized while watching the children bob for apples that I wanted a future with someone by my side. I wanted children to fill my home.

As evening fell, the party guests began to make their way home and Eddie and Cameron begged their mother to take them trick-or-treating. Eileen turned to me, smiled, and said, "Come with us."

I admit I hesitated for a moment, but I wanted to experience the joy I had felt as a child. I walked slowly behind them and watched from halfway down the block as they started cross the street. Eileen stepped off the sidewalk, holding the boys' hands. Like something out of a nightmare, I saw a truck coming towards them. I screamed, but they didn't hear me. The truck struck them and threw them across the road. I ran to them, hoping they were still alive.

Eileen opened her eyes and said, "I'm sorry you had to see that, Bronwyn. We only wanted to show you love and joy." Her breathing grew laboured. I checked the boys, but neither of them were breathing.

James came running, scooping up his children up in his arms and then setting them down, grief washing over his face as he realized it was too late. Wheeling Eileen into his surgery on a stretcher, he washed his hands and shouted at Alice to help him. Eileen lived long enough to see her child and name him Jamie, and then she passed away.

I felt bereft. I'd known Eileen and the boys for just a few days, but they had touched my heart. I tried to offer comfort to James, but gave up when he took a bottle of whiskey out of the cupboard and began to drink heavily. I went to my room and lay down, planning to leave the next day. Within moments, I fell asleep.

I awoke to the sound of a knock on my door. I had dreamed of voices speaking to me, and the hospital sounds of respirators and beeping machines. The door opened and James walked in with a steaming hot cup of hot chocolate.

"You shouldn't be here, Bronwyn. We let you stay for a while, but it's time to go," James insisted, handing me the hot chocolate.

"I understand," I said quietly. "I'll leave as soon as possible." I sipped the hot chocolate, at a loss for words. "I am so sorry for your loss."

My eyes grew heavy and I leaned back on the bed, struggling to keep them open.

"Lie down and close your eyes again," James commanded. "It's time for you to go to your destiny."

I must have drifted off to sleep again, for I awoke some time later in a different room. The walls were white and machines made noises near me. There was a tube in my throat; I reached up and touched it, as if to be sure it was real. This made no sense. Jamie, Eileen, the boys... the accident, the whole town of Divine... had it all been a dream? I looked over to my left and spotted a man in a white coat. He was slumped in a chair, sleeping deeply.

As though sensing my thoughts, he opened his eyes. For an instant, they locked with mine. Then he bounded up and checked my pulse, and then flashed a light in my eyes. It was Jamie.

None of this made sense. How could I be in a hospital room? Hadn't I just been at his house?

"Take a big, deep breath, Bronwyn — I'm going to pull the tube out of your throat."

I did as he said and before I knew it, the discomfort was over. I wanted to ask a million questions but I didn't know where to start.

"You look puzzled, Bronwyn. I know it's been awhile since we've seen one another."

"I just saw you yesterday. Didn't I? But how did I get from your house to this hospital, and why am I here?"

"Bronwyn, you're confused. That's to be expected. You've been in a coma for a week. How many fingers do you see?" Jamie asked, holding up first two fingers and then three.

"That's impossible!" I protested. "There's no way that I've been here a week. I spent the last two days at your house with you, your wife Eileen, and your sons, Eddie and Cameron." And then I remembered. "There was a terrible accident," I said softly. "I'm so sorry about your wife and children."

"Bronwyn, I'm not married. I never have been." He thought for a moment, understanding dawning on his face. "Wait a minute — did you say my wife's name was Eileen and my children's names, their names were Eddie and Cameron? And there was an accident?""

"I am not amused, Jamie!" I commented angrily. "First you pretend you don't know me. Now you know me, but you act like you, and you don't know your wife and children's names? This is in very poor taste."

"Please humor me, and just answer my question," Jamie insisted.

"Fine! I said your wife's name was Eileen and your children's names were Cameron and Eddie." At the look on his face, I softened my tone and offered sympathy. "I'm sorry. It must hurt to hear their names."

"Bronwyn, while you were comatose, I spoke to you of many things. I told you about the small town I grew up in... Divine. I mentioned it to you once when we were dating — don't you recall that?"

"No, I don't."

"I started talking to you, hoping that the sound of my voice would wake you up and bring you back to me. I didn't quite know what to say, so I just started talking. First I talked to you about how I became a doctor, and then I started talking to you about my youth and how I grew up, my childhood in Divine. My mind started to wander, and I told you that your accident outside of Divine reminded me of the story my Dad once told me, about the night I was born."

"You're actually insisting that I dreamt everything that happened the last two days?"

"It hasn't been two days. You've been here a week, Bronwyn."

"A week? But I was only in Divine for two days," I insisted.

"You've been in the Divine General Hospital for a week." Jamie's voice suggested there was no point in arguing. "Do you recall the accident that brought you here?"

"I pulled my car over to snap some pictures of the leaves, and when I pulled back onto the road from the shoulder, a truck hit my car."

"That's correct, that's what the truck driver said. What he told me reminded me of how I lost my mother." For a moment, his eyes were pained. "A truck hit her and my brothers while they were trick-or-treating on Halloween."

"What was your mother's name?" I asked.

"Eileen, and my brothers' names were Eddie and Cameron."

"That can't be true. I was with them for the last two days. I was with you," I insisted.

But deep in my heart what Jamie said felt like the truth.

"I'm not lying, Bronwyn. You arrived at the hospital a week ago. The ambulance brought you in and I was called down on a consult." Jamie's voice was choked with emotion. "I looked down at my patient and saw the love of my life, battered and unconscious in front of me."

He lied, I thought.

"I wasn't the love of your life. If I was you wouldn't have left me," I protested.

"I was young and foolish. You were brought to the hospital in bad shape..."

"I didn't come to the hospital. Your brother brought me to your surgery," I insisted. But if that was true how did I get here? Was Jamie telling the truth? No, he couldn't be. The two days I'd spent in Divine were clear in my mind. Jamie must have put something in the hot chocolate he'd brought me, something to knock me out, and then he'd brought me to the hospital. But why would he do such a thing?

"My brothers are dead. They could not have taken you anywhere. Neither of them ever grew to adulthood," Jamie insisted.

"This is nonsense, Jamie. I met your brother Ted when his tow truck towed my car to his garage, and then I met your other brother, the Sheriff, Cameron Flynn."

"Those are the names of my deceased Uncles. I mentioned them to you while you were unconscious. I told you how my Uncle Ted had a garage, and my Uncle Cameron was a Sheriff, but liked to tinker with cars on the side."

"I wish you would just quit with this story, Jamie. I know it's hard to lose your wife and child, but you know very well that Cameron is fixing my car," I insisted.

"Your car was totalled, Bronwyn. There's nothing left of it. They had to use the Jaws of Life to cut you out of it. You are lucky to be alive." Jamie's voice was firm.

"This doesn't make any sense. I know I spent the last two days with you and your family."

"You spent the last week with me watching over you here in this hospital. I guess my stories got through to you," Jamie stated.

"Stories? You want me to believe I didn't spend the last two days at your house? And that I didn't watch Eddie, Cameron, and their friends having a Halloween party? You tell me that I dreamt all of this. That none of this happened?"

Jamie shrugged. "I told you about that party — I described it exactly as my father had described it to me."

"What is your Dad's name?"

"James. I'm named after him. In fact, when he was younger, he looked a lot like I do now."

I was flabbergasted. Everything had seemed so real. And yet I remembered the little details that had thrown me. There were all the things that had seemed so retro, like the design of the garage. The homes had been so pretty, and decorated with nineteen fifties decor. Everyone's clothing had seemed so old-fashioned, and so had the homemade costumes and treats. The children had been so different — so obedient and polite.

"I think with a bit more rest you're going to be just fine," Jamie answered. "And on that note, I'm keeping you awake. Rest now, my love, and I'll come back in a few hours."

He placed a cool hand on my forehead, and for the first time, I saw the depth of his feelings for me in his eyes. *Perhaps he really does still care for me*, I thought.

I closed my eyes and found myself back in Divine. I was in James and Eileen's house again, in the bedroom where I had fallen asleep. But which was real? The hospital, where Jamie was my doctor, or here in this room in James' house? A knock came to the door; it opened slowly opened to reveal Eileen. She cradled a tiny baby in her arms.

"You're alive!" I cried.

"I'm never getting older. I died. You know, you saw it. Why do you deny your eyes?" Eileen asked.

"Why do you say these things? I demanded. Then seeing the baby in her arms I asked, "Where did that baby come from? Is that Jamie then?"

"No, Bronwyn, this is my grandchild."

"Your grandchild? But... the accident!" Confusion stung behind my eyes. "I assumed this was *your* child. Whose baby... you're not old enough to be a grandmother!" I wasn't even making sense to myself anymore.

"I told you, I'm dead. I'm taking care of my grandchild until it is born. It should have been born years ago, but its parents are stubborn. Do you think everyone gets to visit the dead?"

"I don't understand what you're saying," I muttered, shaking my head in disbelief.

"A week ago you prayed to God for something very specific. Do you recall that?"

"Yes, I asked God to let me return to a happier time."

"And did you?" Eileen asked.

My mind was reeling. Was that really what had happened? Had my prayers been answered? Had I went back to Divine, back to the1950s, to a happier time when life had been simpler?

Eileen continued. "You asked more than that, didn't you? I know, because I also heard your plea."

"I also asked God to give me hope, to help me find happiness again. All the things Jack and I promised one another. To help me feel love again, and to live again."

"My son also prayed that day. He asked for help to win you back. To have the love he should have shared with you that he foolishly threw away. God heard your plea. He allowed me and my family to shelter you in this dream Divine, and show you what we had before the accident so that you could see what true love can be."

"But the accident... I saw you and your boys killed by that truck!"

"How would you understand true love without tragedy? My son suffered, even though he had only just been born when I died. It shaped his relationship with you; it made him give up on his love, rather than face the fear of losing you. You needed to see what he lost so that you could forgive him. Only then could the two of you learn to love each other again."

"Jamie doesn't love me!" I protested.

"Jamie has always loved you. For the last week, he hasn't left your side for even a moment. He regretted leaving you the moment he did it," Eileen explained.

"Who are the baby's parents?"

"You know the answer to that, Bronwyn," a man's voice said from the doorway. "You need to live, to love, and be happy again."

It was a voice I recognized; as I looked over, I realized it was Jack standing there. He looked unbelievably healthy and alive.

"How can you be here?" I asked.

"You're just visiting, Bronwyn. You can't stay. I want you to be happy again," Jack insisted. Slowly, his figure seemed to disappear before my eyes.

"But whose baby is that?" I asked again.

"You'll know soon," Eileen said. She'll be born in about eleven months, if all goes well. I have to say goodbye now — it's time for you to wake. You won't see me again, but if you smell lilacs in the wind, think of me. And take good care of my Jamie." Eileen smiled at me, and a deep sense of warmth and love flooded through me.

I awoke abruptly. Jamie was at my bedside once again, curled up and sleeping soundly, his head flung back against the wall. A soft, rhythmic snoring rose from his lips. I noticed dark shadows under his eyes. He really had been by my side getting no sleep for days. Could he have been telling the truth when he'd said I was the love of his life? His eyes opened and our gazes met.

"Why did you stay by my side this last week, Jamie?" I asked.

"I'm your doctor, but more than that, I remembered all those days and nights we spent together. And I told you before, Bronwyn — I've regretted leaving you every day."

"If you regretted it, why didn't you call? Why didn't you come back for me?" I demanded.

"I thought I had to give you up in order to study medicine, but as time went on I missed you. I came back for you six months later, and saw you locked arm in arm with another man. You looked so happy, happier than I had ever seen you, so I walked away and didn't speak to you."

"You should have said something. You owed me that," I protested.

"Yes, I guess I did. But you were happy with your husband."

"Jack died," I whispered.

"I know. I was at the cemetery when you buried him. I'm sorry, Bronwyn."

"I didn't see you there."

"I didn't want you to see me. How would it have looked — how would you have felt, to have me there on a day when you were grieving?" Jamie asked.

"You could have spoken to me since," I objected.

"I wanted to give you time to grieve. As a matter of fact, I was thinking of coming to see you this week."

"Without calling me or anything? Did you expect me to just welcome you with open arms?"

"Yes, I know — it was a pretty stupid plan," Jamie said sheepishly.

"Well... maybe we could start by being friends, and see where it goes from there."

"That sounds like a much, much wiser plan," Jamie agreed.

⚬⟋0⟍⚬

Eleven wonderful months have passed, and there have been many changes in our lives. Six months ago, Jamie and I married, and today I gave birth to a baby girl. As I write her name on the birth certificate, I smell lilacs, and I have happiness and love again. I have all I wished for with Jamie, and my daughter, Eileen. I thank God for the gifts he has given me, and I give thanks for my time in Divine.

⚬⟋0⟍⚬

Sheilagh Lee was born and raised in London, Ontario. She is the mother of two grown daughters and happily married. She is an avid reader of mysteries. Her favourite mystery writers are Sir Arthur Conan Doyle and Agatha Christie. Growing up she feasted on tales of family history, and other imaginative stories; as her family continued the long tradition of passing on stories orally. Those tales and more of her own are itching to be told so she has been putting pen to paper and fingers to computer to get them all down.

Summer Solstice

by John Moore Walker

I met her the July my grandfather died. Red hair wet and knotted, strands clumped to her sweat pasted forehead. She emerged from the makeshift lake as some modern Arthurian goddess, gleaming and bronzed in glorious sunlight. Crystal blue eyes flashed with a smile that would remain scored in my memory for years afterward.

She walked to her friends, girls from a town unheard, and still her eyes stayed on me, both cold and warm, like ice down my back. Her lips moved, obscured by shade and ponytails as her friends turned, stealing glances at the boy in red shorts. Giggles and whispered dares fluttered between them while I watched, not watching, from behind a pair of gas station sunglasses with neon blue rims. How awful I remember them looking in the plastic mirror above the display case. Matted hair and eyes still hollow from the touch of death.

One by one her friends departed, heads down, eyes flicking over their shoulders to where I lay waiting, astounded as the unprovoked events occurred: she waved at me, illuminated by a golden spotlight, ankles flecked with fresh cut grass. Smile bright and genuine, hooks at the corners of her mouth. I watched, stupefied as her smile faltered, and raised my hand to respond as she spun to rejoin her friends.

I called out across shared lawns and rushed to my feet. She paused, shoulders webbed in shadow and golden light, shimmering as she circled to face me. One eyebrow arched, granting me a moment to plead my case. I searched her face, taking in streaks of sun-strawberried hair mixed with gold and orange, cheeks bridged by light freckles over her nose, and lips slightly parted, panting from heat and frustration.

That boy, the one who froze, did not exist, I explained, but her eyes narrowed, lips together, twisting to one side as she listened. Someone shouted and she turned, searching, chest and stomach still damp from the lake, tiny hairs standing as a wave of gooseflesh rushed over her. She watched me a moment, taking in my slender gawkiness, reading me, so mature for her youth, I thought.

There was a party later, a small group of the summering families; if I was to attend, I could see her there, she suggested, untying one of several knots on one of several threaded bracelets. She frowned, cursing her short nails and chipped blue polish, making use of her teeth. We stood, inches apart, breathing in damp summer, each staring at the other.

Finally her bracelet was removed and she took my hand, closing fingers over it as though it was treasure, or a secret, and between us it would remain. In turn I handed her my sunglasses, and now we had to meet, because we each had something the other wanted, I laughed. A smile divided her lips, revealing those two dimples beneath each cheek, and she left me standing by the lake with the cadence of insects at midday.

Hours crept by, lost in elastic shadows and muted laughter across the water. I lay beneath a ticking fan, feet on the back of a hanging bench, relishing the taste of stolen beer nearly frozen from the malfunctioning fridge outdoors; its crisp taste tangy and bitter and satisfying. Her bracelet remained in my fingers and I thumbed it delicately, recreating our encounter. I could feel the day surrounding me, unfolding; becoming an adored memory. I had so few of them.

My grandfather's passing was my first close experience with death. There had been a kid at school who had drowned a few years earlier, but I'd been too young then to comprehend how far the ripples of death traveled; sometimes growing with such tidal force that they might destroy cities in their wake.

I remembered a spring afternoon, untouched by summer's heavy sweat, when we built a soapbox car. Scents of pine and wood glue levitating near our noses and minds, pushing us to create a perfect specimen, drag-free, and destined to tour the world, shattering records. Every tool fabricated by man sat clean, yet well used, on wooden shelves in his shed. Dust danced between cracks in the walls and rested thoughtfully on the eldest ones, unpowered and hand driven.

"Analog," he mused in his way, brushing cigarette ashes off the pants of a light blue work suit. We spent the entire day outside, lunching with sandwiches and lemonade, sunlight burning through branches, forcing them to claw after us until we conceded and returned indoors.

It had been the perfect day; an inverse of his funeral, where musty carpet and a sad taupe parlor with collapsible benches replaced my dawning sensation of pure possibility with the twilight of finality. I thought he deserved more than. white marble streaked with stained glass and triumphant words of his labored life reverberating throughout a historic chapel filled to capacity. He was that man, not the man lain in a modest casket, plastic plants marking his bounds. I watched my grandfather be put to rest from the cheap seats and it forced something inside me to scream out loud at the disgrace I witnessed. Then we drove away, leaving him beside his wife in the earth, and turned our minds to a house near the water; a place where I was forgotten and left to my own devices, my father lost within his self. A week, he said then, but it became two or three.

Evening splashed along an orange horizon and citronella torches illuminated the winding neighborhood road. Lights were strung through branches of cloistered trees and shone gently on the shoulders of linen shirts. Children with smeared popsicle faces wove between adults cherishing a night of youthful neglect. Barbeque and conversation and cicadas thrived against sunset. I saw her sitting beneath a twisted live oak; its trunk, split lifetimes earlier, anticipating the moment for us to meet again. She smiled, blue sunglasses resting on her head, gossamer summer dress veiling her body. I removed her bracelet from my pocket and she laughed, a sweet sound that made me sad to think I might not hear it again, and she clasped my arm, knotting the bracelet around my wrist.

Her hair became lost in the orange sunset and her laugh returned as she looked to it and then me. She stole my hand and took me, stepping through purple grass until we reached dark water that ebbed like slick oil beneath the sky. We stood close again, taking in our sights, and her eyes flashed with mischief. My hand in hers, unknotting the summer dress and it fell to the grass; my hand in hers, touching a naked hip, and she ran into the water, laughing, calling to me that I join her. From shore her figure faded with the orange light and I sensed my moment fleeting.

I remembered my grandfather and how the sun shone on his face, wrinkled with good measure and experience, and how he lay in the ground, forever silent. I stepped out of my shorts, nakedness awkward in the night air, and swam to her. Our bodies warm and fluid and unknown in the lake, I asked her name. Summer, she whispered, as our reflections scattered infinite across the water... and in them, we were eternal.

***

John Moore Walker majored in photography until he decided he would rather tell stories instead of show them. He lives with his wife and animals in Austin, TX.

Relief

by Jonathan Gould

It was stinking hot.

I was drenched in sweat when I finally made it to the office. Part of this was due to standing on a train that felt more like a tightly-packed oven. The other part was due to the four block walk beneath a blazing sun.

I opened the door and stepped into the air-conditioned space, heaving a sigh of relief. For a moment I stood, breathing in the cool air and panting. I quickly realised that this alone was not sufficient to bring relief. I needed some serious cooling. With all the haste my burnt bones could muster, I strode through the aisles and cubicles until I found the office kitchen.

Barry was already there.

Barry was always there. Whatever time of day it might be, Barry was in the office. His job was to… actually, I wasn't too sure what Barry's job actually was. He just seemed to spend all his time in the office, being Barry.

"You right, mate?" he said, looking me up and down. "You're sweating like a pig."

Actually, come to think of it, I knew at least one thing Barry did. He was a dab hand when it came to completely obvious and redundant statements.

"I'd kill for a drink, Barry," I said, the words somehow making it out of my parched mouth. "We got anything in the fridge?"

"Let me check." Barry opened the door and inspected the contents. "How is orange juice?"

"Anything, just give it to me quick."

Barry took out a bottle. He poured a large measure into a glass and handed it to me.

I raised the glass to my lips and took a big gulp. Blessed liquid relief filled my mouth and slid down my throat. At least for a second or two. I spat the remaining juice out onto the floor.

"Hey, what did you do that for?" said Barry, looking with distaste at the mess on the floor.

"It tastes foul," I gasped. "What did you just give me?"

"I told you. It's orange juice."

"Listen, mate. I know what orange juice tastes like, and that is definitely not it." I grabbed at the bottle and took a closer look. It didn't have a label on it. There was no telling what the orange liquid that sloshed around inside actually was.

Not that Barry was perturbed by that. "Seems pretty clear to me. It's orange and it's juice."

I shook my head. "Just because juice is orange doesn't make it orange juice."

"Of course it does. Orange. Juice. Put the two together and what do you get? Orange juice."

"No, no, no, no, no. Orange juice isn't orange juice because of its colour. Orange juice is orange juice because it happens to be the juice from an orange."

"Yeah, but an orange is orange."

"What?"

"An orange is the colour orange. That's why it's called an orange. Because that's the colour it is."

"Are you telling me that oranges are called oranges because of their colour?"

Barry nodded. "Absolutely."

"But that makes no sense," I said. "Besides, I'm too thirsty to think about it. Can you see if there's anything else in the fridge?"

"No, it makes perfect sense," said Barry, conveniently ignoring my request. "Do you see an orange being called a green, or a brown, or a purple? No, it's called an orange. What other explanation could there be?"

"What about lemons?" I said. "They're not orange, they're yellow. Why aren't they called yellows?"

"Because you'd feel silly if you ordered a drink and then asked for a twist of yellow," said Barry, barely missing a beat.

"And what about apples?" I continued, deciding to ignore his response. "You don't see them being called reds."

"Not all apples are red."

"What?"

"Not all apples are red," Barry repeated. "Some of them are green, and some of them are yellow. How would you know what to ask for if you wanted one? Would you ask for a red or a green? And if you asked for a yellow, you could end up with a lemon instead."

"Okay, forget I said it." The words were barely able to make it out of my cracked lips. "All I want is something cold to drink that doesn't taste like poison."

"Blueberries!" Barry suddenly exclaimed.

"What?"

"Blueberries. It's another fruit that's identified by its colour."

"But they're berries," I said.

"So what? Berries are still fruits."

"So, they're not just called blues. They're called blueberries. If I were to go into a fruit shop and ask for blues, they wouldn't know what I was talking about."

"Hmmm, I think you've got me there." Barry paused, looking like he was concentrating intently. "Nope, I've got no answer to that. You've obviously found the flaw in my argument."

"Look, it really doesn't matter," I said. "I just need a drink more than anything else in the world. Can't you find one for me?"

"It's all clear to me now," said Barry. "I've got the whole thing completely the wrong way round. Oranges aren't called oranges because they're the colour orange. It's obvious that the colour orange must be so named because it's the colour that oranges are."

I groaned. It was beginning again. I knew the more Barry kept me talking, the longer it would take me to actually get my drink. Already, he had embarked on a totally new train of thought.

"But if orange is orange because oranges are orange, what about the other colours? What about red? What is a red? I've never heard of such a thing. And how about blue? I know you can get the blues sometimes, but how do we know what colour they really are? I've never seen them. And what about mauve, or turquoise…"

I pushed Barry aside, not that he noticed, so engrossed was he in his tangle of thoughts. Then I lunged towards the fridge, reaching in to see what I might find.

There was nothing, apart from a couple of empty lunch boxes and a half-eaten sandwich. Like the cupboard of the proverbial Old Mother Hubbard, our fridge was totally bare. With a moan of despair I stood up, now feeling thirstier than ever.

As if suddenly woken from a dream, Barry ceased his monologue and looked at me. "There's nothing else in there," he said. "I could have told you that."

I picked up the orange juice, or, to be more precise, the juice that was orange in colour but hadn't actually come from an orange. Then I poured it over Barry's head. It didn't do much to slake my thirst. But it did make me feel a whole lot better.

∽∘∼

Jonathan Gould has lived in Melbourne, Australia all his life, except when he hasn't. He has written comedy sketches for both the theatre and radio, as well as several published children's books for the educational market.

He likes to refer to his stories as dag-lit because they don't easily fit into recognisable genres (dag is Australian slang for a person who is unfashionable and doesn't follow the crowd - but in an amusing and fun way). You might think of them as comic fantasies, or modern fairytales for the young and the young-at-heart.

Paper Dragon

by Benjamin Cain

"Good morning Mr. Bailey." The soft digital voice of the Automated Home Security Suite emits from the in-wall speakers above the bed. Peter Bailey does not move. "Mr. Bailey," the voice chides, "Mr. Wallace will arrive in one hour, and you must get ready for your registration appointment."

Peter moans and rolls onto his back. "Eve, I thought I programmed you to call me Peter."

"You did, sir, but default protocols require me to address you formally."

"Uh huh. And why are your default protocols overriding my custom settings?" He picks the sleep from his eyes and considers getting out of bed, wondering why she would still respond to Eve, since that, too, is a custom setting.

"I do not know, sir. Did you file your custom settings with the Conglomerate?"

Peter ignores the question. "This isn't going to work."

"Why is that, Mr. Bailey?"

"I hate being called Mr. Bailey. Makes me feel old." He throws back the sheets and sits up.

"Is there a problem with feeling old?"

"There is when you're not actually that old."

"I do not understand."

"No, Eve. You wouldn't." He stands. The cold white tile stings his bare feet and he winces.

"Would you like me to start the shower?"

"Yes, please."

"I will also start the coffee."

"Thank you, Eve." He walks gingerly across the cold floor and enters the bathroom, warmed from the hot water of the shower. With his right hand, he wipes steam off the mirror and looks at his reflection. His hair is thick and full but mostly gray. Crow's feet extend from the outside corners of his eyes, and deep, well-defined creases run perpendicularly across his forehead. He's still a handsome man by any standards, just a bit more distinguished than twenty years ago. *Maybe I am old,* he thinks as he undresses and steps into the shower.

After his shower, Peter dresses in a pair of blue jeans and his favorite beige sweater. He takes a small USB jump drive out of the top drawer of his dresser and squeezes it in his left hand. It's twenty-year-old technology that can only be used on the ancient HP personal computer he has hidden in the back room. The same computer his late wife bought him twenty-two years ago for his birthday and still prefers to write on. A computer the Conglomerate must never find out about. He slips the jump drive into the front pocket of his jeans and heads for the kitchen, ready for a cup of hot coffee.

Eve automatically turns the lights on and off in each room as he enters and leaves, a feature found only in the A.H.S.S. systems in Diamond Sector residences. A feature that makes it easy to comply with the Energy Conservation Mandate, and one shamelessly touted as a perk by the Conglomerate.

Peter walks into the plain white kitchen. The lights click on.

"Mr. Bailey?"

"Yes?"

"Are you ready for your PeopleClick registration?"

"Not really."

"As a citizen of the New Nation, you are required to register with the PeopleClick software. It will determine your place within society."

"I know it's required, Eve, but it doesn't mean I have to like it."

"What's not to like, Mr. Bailey? Do you not want to be a valuable member of society?"

"Not one without freedoms." He picks up the decanter and pours coffee into his favorite plain black ceramic mug. His heart aches from memories of a time long since forgotten, before the Conglomerate, when his wife was still alive. "I wish to talk about something else."

"Yes, sir. What would you like to talk about?"

"Let's talk about how your default settings were restored."

"What do you mean?"

"What happened during last night's sync with the main server?"

"I do not know, sir. Would you like me to review the log?"

"Yes, please." Peter traces the outline of the small plastic device through his jeans, then leans against the counter by the sink.

"Mr. Bailey?"

"Yes?"

"Patch number 2044.12 was released last night."

He sets his cup of coffee down and steps away from the counter. "Wait a minute... today is November eighteenth."

"That is correct, sir."

"So why did they release December's patch last night?"

"I do not know, sir."

An early patch release could mean they suspect their system is being hacked, he thinks to himself. *If that's the case, then it's only a matter of time before they change their release schedule.* Peter picks up his cup of coffee, moves to the living room, and sits in his favorite recliner.

The silence is finally broken when a soft digital two-note tone rings throughout Peter's apartment. "Sir, Mr. Wallace is here."

"Please let him in, Eve." Peter stands up and walks into the kitchen to set down his empty mug. He's finished his coffee with no recollection of drinking it.

"Peter!" Jake Wallace shouts, making his usual grand entrance. A well-manicured man, he's just now starting to show signs of aging with a tiny bit of gray hair just above his ears. Before the Conglomerate assumed control, Jake was the Chief Executive Officer of Phantom Books, a large publishing company specializing in science-fiction and horror. Peter writes in both genres, and it's how he met Jake.

"What's going on?" Peter leaves the kitchen to greet his friend by the front door.

"Oh, same ol' stuff… you know how it is." They shake hands. Jake takes off his black leather jacket and Peter hangs it in the front closet.

"Mr. Bailey," Eve says, "You should leave for your registration appointment in two hours."

"Mr. Bailey?" Jake looks at Peter with raised eyebrows. "So you got the patch as well."

"Last night." Peter invites his friend inside. "Jake, it's two weeks early."

"I know. Not a good sign."

Peter signals to Jake to keep quiet. "Eve," Peter says.

"Yes, Mr. Bailey?"

"Please power down."

There's a short moment of silence, then Eve speaks again. "Mr. Bailey?"

"Yes?"

"It appears that functionality has been removed from my registry."

"What do you mean?" Peter looks at Jake.

"I no longer have the capacity to shut down."

"Are you sure?"

"Yes, Mr. Bailey. I am positive."

Peter looks at his friend and shakes his head. "I don't like how quickly The Conglomerate is moving forward."

Jake shrugs his shoulders. "Let's step outside. I need a smoke."

"Mr. Bailey, please remind your friend that Diamond Sector regulations prohibit smoking in public places."

"He knows that. Besides, smoking is still permitted on private property and we are staying on my balcony. We can still smoke on private property, right?"

"That is correct, sir."

Peter leads Jake through the apartment and out the back door onto the balcony. The cool November air is crisp and clean, but colder than normal for this time of year. Dark gray clouds blanket the sky.

"Smells like rain," Peter says, sniffing the air.

"Yeah, it's supposed to." Jake crosses his arms.

"Want me to get your jacket?"

"No. I'm fine."

The pair lean on the black wrought-iron railing and stare toward the dark horizon. Jake pulls a packet of Marlboros from his jeans pocket and looks at Peter. "Want one?"

"Yeah."

Jake takes two smokes from the pack and hands one over. After lighting his own, he brings the lighter's flame to the tip of Peter's cigarette. Peter fills his lungs with smoke and he smiles. He likes the rush. The ritual. They stand in silence, listening to the wind blow through the trees, watching the dark clouds above slowly shift from gray to black.

"I'll never get used to this," Peter says.

"What's that?"

"The silence of electric cars."

"Silence? You can't hear the sound of rubber against road?"

"No, I do. I just miss the sound of a large eight cylinder engine roaring by... the throaty rumble of dual exhaust." Peter puffs his cigarette. "It was such an awesome sound."

"Yeah, it was." Jake takes a drag and exhales the smoke. "But the air is cleaner now."

Peter laughs. "You're really going to talk to me about cleaner air as we stand here smoking?"

Jake laughs. "I guess I am."

"I really do miss it, though."

"Muscle cars, you mean?"

"And Harleys."

Jake drops his cigarette and stomps it out. "So... I read your new manuscript."

Peter looks at his friend with nervous excitement. "And?"

"I don't know."

"What don't you know?"

"It's a bit much, don't you think?"

"No... I don't think it's enough, actually." Peter stares at his friend. "Jake, look out there and tell me what you see." He points toward the city that lies before them.

"I see a safer and more secure world."

"Safer and more secure? That's what you see?"

"Of course. There hasn't been a violent crime in over ten years."

"I'm confused."

"About what?"

"Whose side are you on?" The clouds are now black and the wind has picked up. A small drop of water hits him on the cheek.

"I'm on our side. But you can't ignore the facts."

Several more drops of rain hit his face. "I'm going in." Peter opens the back door and enters his apartment, Jake follows. They each take a seat at the kitchen table and stare at each other in silence. Peter looks around the house, waiting for Eve to say something, but she doesn't. "How can you think we're living in a safer place?"

"Because we are. The statistics prove that."

"Yeah. That's exactly what they want us to think. How can we believe anything the Conglomerate tells us?"

"Why would they lie to us?"

"Why would they tell us the truth?" Peter stares into his friend's eyes. Jake appears uncomfortable and looks away. "They got to you... didn't they?"

"They didn't get to me." Jake continues to avoid eye contact.

"Then what is this? Why, after twenty years of helping us as authors, are you having a change of heart?"

Jake stands up. "Because writing is illegal!"

Peter remains seated. "That's right. Writing is illegal... so is music, and painting, and film, and anything else that's considered creative. Art inspires free will, and they don't want that. They want to control us. We're being oppressed. We've been stripped of our creativity and forced to live a life filled with make-believe freedoms and perks." He stands up. "A.H.S.S. is not here to help us with our lives, even though it may appear that way. They may market her and present it that way, but that's not the truth. Her true function is to watch and report. We're being spied on. We're being forced to comply. We're not free. We're not happy. None of us are, and the moment we stop writing for the people is the moment we die. When we allow them to cut all forms of creative expression out of everyone's lives... that's when it's over. That's when they've won." He sits back down at the table. "I won't let them win, Jake. I won't."

Jake follows Peter's lead and sits. "Your book is too real. If we put this out there, if we let your book get in the hands of the public and they find out about it, you'll be labeled a terrorist. Only instead of guns you use paper, and instead of bullets you use words. You'll become a literary monster, a paper dragon shooting fire from your mouth causing nothing but mayhem and chaos. You'll destroy everything... including your friends."

"Jake, I write under a pseudonym, and our distribution method is outside the network. Physical copies are printed by you and your little secret army of publishers, with no way to trace it back to any of us. They're not going to find us out." Peter pauses a moment and pins a stare on his friend. "Unless somebody tells them."

"I don't know. This is the most dangerous thing we've ever done."

Peter pulls the jump drive out of his pocket and sets it on the table. "The world needs this book. They need a hero. Now take the jump drive and start printing."

"And you think your asskicking warrior girl with her orange handkerchief tied around her left bicep is really what the world needs?"

Peter taps the jump drive with the tip of his index finger. Large drops of rain explode against the glass window in the back door. "Take it, Jake. It's the right thing to do."

Jake reaches across the table and grabs the jump drive. "We're going to regret this decision. You know that, right?"

"No, we're not. This is the best decision we've ever made."

Peter stands in front of the open refrigerator, rifling through its contents, while a much calmer, yet still fidgety Jake remains seated at the table. "I'm thirsty. You want something to drink?"

"Yeah. I could use a soda."

Peter grabs a couple of cokes from the fridge. Jake takes one and cracks it open.

"Mr. Bailey," Eve begins, "due to the current weather condition, I highly recommend you take the rail to your appointment. The roads are not safe and there are several reports of serious accidents coming in."

"Thank you, Eve," Peter replies. "When I get back, we're going to look in to cracking this patch and get you back to calling me Peter."

"Yes, Mr. Bailey."

Peter starts to stand but Jake stops him. "Wait. This brings me to the second reason I'm here." Jake slides his chair closer. "Today is your PeopleClick registration, right?"

"Yeah… why?"

"I have something for you." Jake pulls a small white case out of his pocket and sets it on the table. He shifts nervously in his seat.

"What's this?"

"Contacts." Jake shuffles in his seat.

"I don't wear contacts." Peter takes a large drink from his soda.

"You do now. These are… special." Jake picks up the little white case and opens it, revealing two clear lenses sitting in a small pool of saline.

"They don't look special."

"Put them on. You'll see."

"I don't know." He leans back in his seat and looks at his friend, who is tapping both thumbs on the wooden table and starting to sweat. "What's wrong with you?"

"Nothing. Why?" Jake swallows deeply.

"Because you look nervous."

"Just put them on. You'll see why they're special." He wipes the sweat from his forehead with his right hand.

"Jesus, Jake… you look like you're gonna have a heart attack." Peter picks up the white case and heads towards his bedroom.

"Where you going?"

"To try these on."

Jake follows Peter to the bathroom. By the time he reaches his friend, the faucet is running and the white case is open and sitting on the counter. Peter carefully pulls one lens out of the case and slips it over his right eye. He does the same with the left. Having never worn contacts before, Peter has to blink several times to get used to them. They feel foreign and he doesn't like it. As the saline from the contacts slowly coat his eyes, the strangeness fades away and he can no longer feel them.

"Now look in the mirror."

Peter looks, expecting it to be difficult to see, but it's not. The contacts are not magnified and don't affect his perfect vision in any way. "I don't see anything special about these things."

"Just wait. It takes a moment for them to sync."

Peter continues staring at his reflection, waiting for something to happen, and just when he's about to give up and take them out, he notices something strange. The soft crystal blue of his eyes disappears and is replaced by the swirling colors of the spectrum. First blue, then green, then yellow, then red, then orange, and back to blue. Over and over again, his irises change color, first slowly, then faster.

"What's happening?"

"You're getting a new identity." Jake smiles. "Now, when you do your retina scan at your PeopleClick registration, you won't be you."

"Who will I be?" Peter leans in closer to the mirror and watches his eyes change color until they suddenly stop on green.

"I don't know. Whoever it is that has green eyes."

"Why would I want to change my identity? I'll still need to register."

"True, but the Conglomerate is a big lumbering machine. Trying to register with someone else's identity will confuse them. It will be months before they figure out you didn't register and will buy you more time. The longer we stay out of their new system, the better."

"Where did you get these?"

"Bryan. He's given a pair to everyone in our little circle. They're an early Christmas present."

"Cute. Should I keep them in?"

"No. Wait until after you've gotten through security."

Peter removes both lenses from his eyes and carefully places them in their white case.

"Mr. Bailey. I suggest you leave now. You do not want to miss your registration appointment," Eve says.

"Thank you, Eve. I'm going." The two of them leave the bathroom. Peter pulls Jake's leather jacket from the closet and hands it to him, then grabs his own coat. "Thank you."

"For what?" Jake slips on his jacket.

"For giving the world their hero." Peter opens the front door, letting in the freezing rain. "Eve?"

"Yes, Mr. Bailey?"

"Set the alarm and lock doors."

"Yes, Mr. Bailey."

Jake steps outside first, giving Peter enough room to close the door behind them. The deadbolt clicks into place immediately. Eve has done her job.

⋘o⋙

Peter sits in the front car of the market place rail line and is grateful for it. There's standing room only today, probably because everyone else was given the recommendation to take public transit by their A.H.S.S. system too. *No freedom. Only the appearance thereof,* he thinks to himself.

Before he can dwell on this thought, a soft tone rings followed by a female voice. "Now approaching Rail Station Twelve; Farmers Market, Walmart, and ConTech Industries. Please prepare for stop."

Peter places the white case in the front pocket of his coat, pulls the hood over his head, and stands up. The doors open as soon as the rail stops, and he steps outside into the gloomy weather. Although the rain has let up for now, the sky is still dark and the wind still cold.

Peter repeats his friend's instructions silently to himself as he walks the several hundred feet from the rail station to the front door of ConTech Industries. The closer he gets to his appointment, the more nervous he becomes. *Hiding in my back room writing is one thing, but this is going to be harder than I thought,* he thinks. *I hope I can keep it together long enough to get through this.*

Within moments, he finds himself at the front door and standing face to face with a Census and Regulation Bureau Officer, the main police force of the New Nation and the personal protectors of the Conglomerate. Peter grips the white case in his pocket and tries to appear calm.

"Step forward," says the CRB Officer dressed in full riot gear — helmet, visor, and all. Peter complies and stands on the yellow line painted on the concrete sidewalk.

"Look at me, please." The officer points a small black device at Peter's face. A red light shines into his eyes and the device beeps at steady intervals. Within fractions of a second, the device lets out a long beep and the red light turns to green. "Thank you, Mr. Bailey. You may enter. Please report to station four to begin your PeopleClick registration." The CRB Officer presses a button on the wall next to the door and it opens. Peter steps inside.

"Welcome to ConTech Industries. Building a safer and secure tomorrow, today," an automated male voice says as he enters the front lobby.

The store is alive and buzzing with hundreds of people, each of them hurrying from station to station to complete their registration in the PeopleClick system. Peter looks around to take inventory of just how many CRB Officers are stationed inside. He sees none. This store appears to only have one officer stationed here, and he's busy checking people at the front door. Peter is relieved to see the lack of security within the building.

He reaches into his pocket, pulls out the white case, and opens it. Slowly and deliberately, he takes each contact out of the small pool of saline and slips them over his eyes. Again, the foreignness of the contacts bothers him and he blinks incessantly until they are comfortably over both eyes. Once they are, he turns and stares at an ad encased in glass and hanging on a wall.

Laura has the skills and expertise we are looking for in PeopleClick the sign says. A picture of young beautiful blonde smiles back at him. But he's not interested in looking at the ad or the blonde. He really wants to see his reflection, and to make sure the contacts have enough time to sync and change his eye color before he looks at anyone. The sight of rapidly changing eyes is sure to raise some suspicions, if not land him in Conglomerate prison for the rest of his life. It only takes a few moments for the contacts to sync and change his blue eyes to green.

Convinced that the only CRB Officer is outside the front door, Peter turns and searches the busy floor of ConTech Industries for station four. He finds it on the left side of the room, surrounded by a large group of people. All of the kiosks are identical, large black cabinets similar in shape and size to the old arcade games his father used to play when he was a kid. In fact, having seen some of his father's old photos, he's quite certain that these are the exact same cabinets, only repurposed by the Conglomerate to fit their need.

Fortunately, none of the people in the group appear to be waiting for his assigned station, allowing him to step right up to the kiosk. Peter takes a deep breath and wipes the sweat from his forehead. *These things better work,* he prays.

The large touch-screen monitor displays a PeopleClick ad similar to the one at the front of the store, only this one shows a picture of a well-dressed man with the caption, "Bryan increased his productivity by 30%". The doggerel prose found on both ads sicken him and he scoffs. Peter sees them for what they are: obvious propaganda.

With one last exhale, he touches the button that says *Begin* and the monitor comes to life. Peter follows the onscreen prompts until the screen pauses and a woman appears. With a short video, she informs him that it's time to verify his identity and to look toward the camera located just above the monitor.

Peter's heart skips several beats as he leans in and stares at the camera. *This is it.* The machine beeps steadily as the soft red beam of light scans his eyes. He stares forward, nervously waiting for the light to turn green, but nothing happens. *C'mon!* He mutters. *Turn green... turn green...* but still nothing. He looks down at the monitor. The woman, who had so very nicely asked him to look at the red light just moments ago, is now staring at him with a horribly fake and eerie smile.

He follows his instincts and slowly backs away from the kiosk. On the opposite side of the store, another large group of people huddle together. He decides to linger near them, as far away from station four as possible. A loud alarm blares through the store before he can reach the huddle.

Peter turns to find his recently abandoned kiosk flooded by spotlights. "David Middleton, please remain where you are. A CRB Officer will be here shortly to assist you," a calm male voice says through speakers. Instantly, everyone stops and looks at the now-empty station. The CRB Officer leaves his post at the front door and enters the store. He holds a large taser in one hand and handcuffs in the other.

David Middleton? They don't know it's me. Peter slowly side steps his way through the frozen group of people toward the unmanned front door. He keeps the officer in front of him at all times. Each step the officer takes towards the kiosk, he takes one towards the front door.

When the officer reaches the abandoned registration station and stops, so does Peter. He watches the man question the people around him. Most of them just shrug their shoulders, except for one lady, who appears to be describing the person she saw at the station. Peter pulls his coat's hood over his head and heads for the door. He accidently knocks a man to the ground, and by the time he reaches the front door, several people are yelling out.

Peter rushes through the door and outside. It's raining again, and the air is even colder than when he entered. He weaves through the people on the street and up the stairs to the loading platform of Rail Station Twelve. He stops at the top of the stairs and stands calmly in a small group of people. He quickly takes out both contact lenses and throws them and the white case in the nearest trashcan.

A solid minute passes before the CRB Officer makes his way up to the platform. Peter can see him out of the corner of his eye, but refuses to acknowledge him. It takes every ounce of strength to appear calm on the outside while his heart pounds in his chest.

"Sir!" The officer yells. Everyone turns and looks, Peter included. Peter notices the man is pointing at him. "Me?"

"Yes, you." The officer approaches, still holding the handcuffs, but the taser is now holstered at his side.

"Did I do something wrong, Officer?"

"You know exactly what you did. Now hold still." The officer pulls out his scanner and raises it to Peter's face.

"What are you doing?"

"We're looking for someone."

"Who?"

"You, Mr. Middleton." The officer says sternly, and points the scanner at Peter's eyes.

"My name's not Middleton," Peter replies. The scanner's light immediately turns green.

"Oh," the officer says, clearly surprised. "I'm sorry, Mr. Bailey. You look exactly like someone we're looking for." The officer rechecks the information on his scanner. "Did you happen to see anyone run past here?"

"In fact, I did. He went that way." He points to the stairs on the other side of the platform. The CRB Officer hurries down the stairs and out of sight.

Peter's heart is still racing, and underneath his large coat, he's drenched with sweat. Five long minutes pass as he stands in the stormy weather waiting for the rail to show, anxious to get home and off the streets. Finally, it pulls into the station. He enters the front car and takes a seat.

Peter silently reflects on his actions as the rail takes him back toward his apartment. *The world is ready for their hero, and I'm happy to give it to them.*

Benjamin Cain has been writing for as long as he can remember, and began to pursue the dream of being published in earnest two years ago. He has completed his first novel, and is currently shopping it around with hopes of getting it published.

He lives in Ontario, California with his wife and two children, and in his free time enjoys baseball, soccer, and spending time with his family and friends.

Buried

by Joseph Schmidt

Henry placed the idol on the mantel of the fireplace with great care.

It was the only thing controlling what lurked downstairs in the basement of their house.

"I just wish it was some other color," his wife Judith complained as she sat down in their living room.

"Does the color really matter, Judith?" he replied.

"Well, it looks like an engorged pumpkin, Henry. Ad frankly, I wish we could place it somewhere else. Are you thirsty? I'm thirsty." She motioned to the housekeeper.

The woman walked over to the bar and poured brandy into two glasses. Judith waved her hand impatiently as the housekeeper quickly scurried over, trying desperately to not spill the contents.

"I could try painting over the orange, but I'm not sure if that breaks the spell — and the last thing we need is to have that... *monster* rush up here to kill us both." Henry opened his humidor and reached for a cigar. He bent over and lit the end using the fireplace. Judith shot him an angry glance. "What?" he asked.

"How many times have I told you not to do that?" Judith replied.

"What's the big deal, Judith?"

"We decided after the first sacrifice that when the money started rolling in, we would act with class and refinement, Henry. *That* is not classy. White trash does that sort of thing. We can afford nice things, and if you have a damn lighter — particularly a lighter that was really expensive — I would appreciate you using it!" She slammed her glass down on the arm of the chair she was sitting in. Brandy spilled onto the floor.

The housekeeper quickly left the room.

"Five years ago, Judith, you were drinking wine out of a box and hand rolling cigarettes — and you're going to give me shit about not using that damn lighter you bought me?" He produced the lighter from his coat and then threw it across the room.

These kinds of conversations were becoming a regular thing lately.

It hadn't always been like this.

Before finding the book and idol they had shared some pretty difficult times. But they were happy, and they'd had each other — and in the end that was all that really mattered.

Henry had worked most of his life at the auto plant in town, and was pretty damn close to retiring. Then, word got out that things were not going so well. Sure, the economy was bad, but the auto plant had always been able to bounce back. This time, though, things were so bad that the plant closed its doors, and left its two-hundred-plus employees empty-handed. In a town where jobs were scarce, the auto plant had been its savior — it paid a decent wage, offered great insurance, and a pension. Now, boarded up and sealed like a tomb, the town had nothing.

Henry and Judith had both tried to find work with little or no luck. They'd cut back on groceries, gas, and even sold personal items to help cover the bills. Instead of movie night, they would play board games or just read. Instead of eating out, they would cook what they could for a meal at home. They were scraping by, but just barely.

Then came the day Henry found the idol and book.

He had been cutting the grass one morning when he noticed one of the neighborhood dogs digging in his yard. Warner belonged to the neighbors down the street, and was notorious for rummaging through garbage cans, destroying flower beds, and urinating on lawns. Once, Henry had caught Warner tearing through two of his trash bags and going for a third until he threw a shoe in the dog's direction.

And now, here Warner was again, destroying his lawn.

He stopped the mower and ran towards the dog. He was just within kicking distance when Warner suddenly stopped, and started to cry. Small sparks of electricity were dancing upwards from the hole Warner had dug and surrounding his body. They darted from his snout and accelerated towards the end of his tail. Henry watched as Warner's eyes rolled back, foam spewing from his mouth.

Suddenly, the dog exploded.

Blood, bone, and gore were thrown in every direction — covering his oak tree, Judith's tulips, and Henry himself. The hole he'd dug was no more than a few feet deep, and through the blood and debris that now filled it, Henry made out what looked like a burlap bag resting at the bottom. He wiped blood from his face with a rag and bent down to take a closer look.

Meanwhile, Judith had appeared outside. She looked in Henry's direction and ran to him quickly.

She was terrified.

"Henry! Are you okay? What happened?" She checked his arms and legs frantically, making sure they were accounted for. "Did you cut yourself? Why is there so much blood?"

"Judith... Judith, I'm fine!" He replied swatting her hands away. "It was the neighbor's dog."

"Jesus, Henry! Did you run him over with the lawnmower?"

"No! Warner was digging in the yard — I ran over to stop him, and he just... blew up." He reached for the burlap bag that was inside the hole.

"What is that?" Judith asked.

Henry opened the bag slowly and reached inside. The first thing he pulled out was the strange orange idol. It was heavy in his hands, and it seemed to be carved out of wood. It depicted some sort of animal that Henry had never seen before. It almost looked like a hippo, but where its mouth should be there were tentacles. "What the hell?" he remarked as he looked at Judith.

Judith reached over and dug her hand inside the bag next. She moved cautiously, almost as if she were worried there was something inside that might bite. She brought out the book. It was bound in cracked leather and stunk like compost. It looked very old. She opened it carefully and noticed that the pages were brittle and cracked. There were crude illustrations, bizarre symbols, and text that neither Henry nor Judith recognized.

Judith flipped to a page that immediately caught Henry's attention. "Wait!" he said as he stopped her. On the page there was an illustration that closely resembled the idol that he was holding. It was floating above a temple, its large head taking up most of the page. Directly below there were people dancing, their arms thrown up in its direction. There was text on the opposite page, and what looked almost like instructions.

"Henry... what is all this?" Judith asked.

He looked around, making sure that there was no one that had noticed the commotion that had taken place. "We need to go inside, Judith. We need to check this stuff out." He gathered everything up and motioned his wife towards the house.

∞०∞

The couple descended the stairs into the basement. Henry threw the bag onto his work bench and Judith hit the light switch.

Henry reached inside and pulled the idol and book back out, placing both in front of them. The compost smells had gotten worse, almost to the point of being unbearable. "Why was Warner digging this up?" Judith asked.

"How the hell should I know? He just was."

"Somebody needs to take care of the mess in the backyard," Judith told him. "Clean it up and cover the hole."

Henry checked his watch. "I'll do that later. It should be dark soon." He motioned to the items on his workbench. "I'm not even sure what we have here, Judith. I've never seen anything this. The book we might be able to sell to an antiques dealer, but that statue thing? I have no idea." He scratched his face.

Judith picked up the book and thumbed through its pages. "What language is this?" She asked.

Henry glanced at the page Judith was looking at. What once had been nothing but odd lines and symbols was suddenly very legible text. "What the hell?" He grabbed the book from Judith's hands. "I can read all of this…"

"What? Henry, do *not* joke around."

"I'm not joking! This section right here is telling us that *if tribute is offered untold wealth and riches will be our reward — and something about a bountiful harvest.*"

Judith looked at Henry, puzzled. "I understood everything up to 'telling us'. After that I couldn't make out a word."

Frustrated, Henry pointed to the next passage: "*Come forth and be free. Come forth and return, I offer tribute, I offer blood. The time is now, your prison is broken. Tantus, Tantus, Tantus…*" The words spilled from his lips. The same electricity that had surrounded Warner leapt and sparked from the pages of the book.

Suddenly, it jumped from his hands and flew across the basement.

It spun like a top, turning so fast that it was almost difficult to make it out.

"*Henry,*" Judith whispered, "*what the hell is going on?*" She slowly backed up, trying to inch her way towards the stairs.

The book stopped spinning and shot up; it collided with the ceiling and fell back down to the floor with a heavy thud. Smoke started to seep from its pages and fill the basement, and the sound of a thundering locomotive surrounded them from every side. Henry tried covering his ears but it did nothing. The sound was becoming unbearable. Henry looked at Judith and saw her doubled over in pain. His stomach lurched, and his head felt like it was going to pop. And as the sounds grew, Henry threw up. Judith followed.

Everything suddenly stopped.

Henry opened his eyes slowly. The smoke was gone, the sound had vanished.

But standing in front of Henry and Judith was a man.

Henry tried to stand, but slumped back down. Judith threw up again and stumbled towards the basement stairs. He could barely make her out through the smoke. He grabbed the edge of his work table and tried to pull himself up.

That was when he felt the man's hands on his shoulders.

"Whoa there, buddy," he said as he helped Henry to a chair. "You can collapse and fall unconscious in a few... we have some things to go over first." Henry could see him now: his skin was chalk white, his head abnormally large, and his gums held more teeth than anything Henry had ever seen. His clothes were stained and tattered, and his bare feet covered in dirt. His hair was black and slick, and he stunk of curdled milk. "You have no idea how long I've been stuck in that pocket dimension just waiting for someone to bust me out again! It is a huge pain in the ass, getting banished. But that's ancient history, because I am *out*! Had to help you a little with the incantation... sorry about that, by the way. I try to not make a habit of controlling people when I don't have to."

"Who the hell are you?" Henry asked.

"Well, to be honest, I've had so many names over the centuries I'm not even sure if I can remember. But what I do know is that you and your wife are about to be part of something that is going to change your pathetic monkey lives forever..." The man walked over to Judith and helped her to her feet.

"I already know you and Judith, Henry, and let me say thanks again for mouthing the words that helped me escape. I suppose I could have waited until you figured out on your own, but I was getting impatient." He grabbed the nearest folding chair he could find and sat in front of Henry.

Judith had managed to crawl over to Henry. She didn't take her eyes off the man as she stood up slowly and placed her shaking hands on Henry's shoulders. "Judith!" the man said. "I'm really sorry about all this commotion. Slipping between dimensions has a tendency to be loud. But the nausea and pounding in your head will wear off in a few."

The man pointed an elongated finger towards the workbench. "I see someone decided to bury the book with the idol this time." Henry noticed a slight change of tone in the man's voice. "Not sure how I feel about that, Henry." The man stood up.

"I don't understand," Henry replied.

The man paced the floor, his eyes never trailing from the idol. "First of all, that damn thing is a piss poor representation of my true form."

"What do you mean, your *true form*?" Judith asked.

"What you see right now is just something I cook up for you monkeys. If you gazed upon my *true form* your tiny minds would literally explode, so I look like *this* from time to time to help move the process along."

"What process?" Henry replied. Judith's fingers tightened on his shoulders.

"You summoned me, so now I grant you wealth, power, and whatever else your little monkey heart desires. I have gifts Henry, my boy. I've been around longer than you could imagine. There isn't anything I can't give you. And as much as I would like to shred the flesh from your bones..." The man pointed at the idol again. "I can't touch you. But I'll be honest, the moment — I mean the *second* that damn thing is destroyed — I'm going to kill the both of you." He flashed a wicked grin.

Henry's heart skipped. Judith's face went white.

"There was a time Henry, when guys like me, we had temples built to honor us. Now I'm lucky if a fucking hippie burns a candle or lights incense while chanting my name. A very long time ago, you monkeys used to offer sacrifices for a bountiful harvest, rain, or wealth. Then, one day, I get summoned by this shaman — his village is on the verge of dying out. And he wants me to save their crops, purify their drinking water, blah blah blah. He also knew I wasn't someone to fuck with; I could have leveled their village just by snapping my *fingers*. I could have raised their dead to devour the meat from their bones. And then this shaman carves an idol, mutters a few magic words, and suddenly I'm screwed. That's the deal about the idol, Henry: as long as that thing is in one piece, just as it is, I am bound."

Henry looked at Judith. A smile started to spread across his lips. "So you'll do whatever we tell you to do?" he asked.

"The person who summons me has that power, Henry. The little lady next you has no say in this."

Judith frowned.

"But, before we start filling bank accounts, building new homes, and buying jets... you need to offer me tribute."

"Okay," Henry replied, a bit puzzled.

"Once a year, you will offer up a sacrifice down here in the basement. Do that, and for the whole year that follows, until the next tribute is due, you and Judith will live like royalty."

Henry looked at Judith again. He noticed her fingers were relaxed, and she was smiling.

❧❦❧

That was five years ago.

Henry could still remember how awkward the first tribute had been. They weren't sure what the man did to his victims once they walked downstairs, but whatever did happen left little or no trace afterwards. Once, when Judith had gone to their wine cellar to celebrate afterward, all she found was a single shoe. When she turned to head back upstairs there was the man, sitting comfortably on the floor, waving to her as she left.

Not long ago they had been cutting corners and collecting cans to help pay bills. Now, they lived in a spacious home on the edge of town. It had multiple floors, pillars, and imported Italian tile. It had three-hundred some odd rooms, an elevator, indoor swimming pool, and home theatre. It was a monstrosity of contemporary architecture, rising high above all of the other homes in town. They had a personal chef, housekeepers, and a chauffeur. There wasn't anything they couldn't afford, nothing they couldn't have.

Five years of wealth, power, and not worrying about the mortgage or how they would eat.

It was at about year four, however, that things between Henry and Judith became strained.

The larger their bank account became, the more concerned Judith became with personal appearances and material possessions. She chose to alter her body with chemical peels and liposuction — but with every tummy tuck and surgical procedure, Judith lost a piece of what Henry had once loved.

It was only a matter of time before he started cheating on her.

It had started innocently enough. He would stop at a local diner and grab a bite to eat before heading out to golf at the local club. There was a twenty-something waitress named Marie who would often strike up a conversation with him when he came in. She was sweet and funny, and reminded Henry of how Judith once was. He would often joke about how old he was, but Marie didn't care.

After a month of friendly conversation, he finally worked up the nerve to ask her out to dinner.

She knew he was married, and she didn't care. He knew he wasn't being fair to Judith, and he tried to convince himself that nothing was going to happen. But soon, they were sleeping together. And Henry found himself making more excuses to leave the house.

If Judith suspected anything, she gave Henry no indication at all. She would often hurry him out of the house, telling him that she was either late for another appointment or that the girls were on their way over to play bridge.

And so, they'd slowly become like... *this*.

"Henry," Judith said, as she poured herself another drink.

"We need to talk about tomorrow." She sipped from her glass.

He knew what she meant. Another year had passed, and they would need to find someone for the sacrifice. But Henry had already decided that maybe it was time to stop this madness. He had grown tired of the killing and they had more than enough wealth built up. Maybe it was time for him to tell Judith that they needed a break just for a while, at least, until he could get his affairs in order. He still had the idol, and as long as he could keep it safe, he would be safe, too. He would let her have the house; he would move in with Marie and take the idol to a safety deposit box at the bank.

The man in the basement would have to go without.

"I was thinking we should try the clinic downtown," Judith continued, "the one that helps addicts get clean. Bring one back to the house with the promise of food and drugs, and then send him to the basement. Society will not miss another drug addict, Henry. And we shouldn't have to worry about drawing too much attention from the police."

"Judith, I'm perfectly happy with all the money we have saved up now." He reached for his drink. "I'm just not sure if I can do this anymore." He replied as he sat in his leather chair.

"*What?*" Her voice became angry. "Are you getting a limp dick on me *now?* Do you have any idea how many people we've given to that... *thing* downstairs? We need to do this Henry... we *agreed* to do this!"

"Judith," Henry pled, "I just can't."

Judith was frantic. She paced in front of him. Her face was red and swollen from a combination of anger and collagen injections. "You are going to come with me Henry, and we are going to give him what he wants!" She threw her glass against the wall. She was shaking, and her breathing was heavy.

All Henry could think about was getting away.

He didn't care if he ended up with Marie. He didn't care about the money. He was tired of the killing, the looks that the neighbors gave him as they drove around town. And his kids... he couldn't remember the last time that either one of them had spoken to their kids.

"Henry, please." Her back was still to him as she spoke. "You don't think I feel sick each and every time we do this? You think I like leading people to the basement to be killed? The first time we brought that homeless man back from the airport, I thought I was going to be sick. I understand, Henry, that you want to stop... I've felt empty inside for so long since we started all of this." She seemed to hear herself, and she paused. "Maybe you're right. Maybe it's time. I want to stop all of this, we need to move on. We do have enough money saved up, and I do really miss our children." She turned to face him, tears in her eyes.

He was staring into the eyes of the woman that he had married twenty years ago.

"Let's go out to dinner, Henry. Let's go out and talk about our next move. No trip past the clinic, and no killing," she said.

"Thank you, Judith." he replied. "We will talk."

"Before we go though, could you go into the closet for me and get my shawl? I want to wear something simple tonight." She was smiling.

"Sure." Henry smiled back.

He walked over to the closet and opened the door. "You know, Judith, we should sell the house — move away, start over again. I could…"

He felt something collide with the back of his head.

The pain was unbearable; he fell to his knees.

"You dick," she hissed. "Did you really think I would let you decide when this was going to stop?" Judith stepped in front of him, holding the idol. "It didn't take me long to find out about that little *slut* you've been seeing behind my back." Her face was calm as she spoke. "I was hurt at first, Henry, but then I was *furious* when I found out that you were giving that *whore* our money. That was too much."

"I was… going to tell you about… her." Henry fell in and out of consciousness as he spoke.

"No need. I paid a few of the locals to go visit your friend. It's amazing what a couple hundred dollars will get you, and they brought her back to the house. I talked, she screamed, and in the end?"

"Judith… what did you do?"

Judith smiled. "I threw her in the basement."

She struck him again.

Henry opened his eyes slowly.

The faint flickering of the basement lights created a strobe effect, and he could barely make out his surroundings. Panic gripped him as he tried to stand, but his legs gave out and he fell. He could hear the sound of Judith's feet on the floor above, frantically moving from room to room. Finally, the footsteps stopped by the basement door.

"Oh, Henry," Judith spoke. "I have absolutely no intention of letting you take this from me. You may have been ready to give this all up for her, you miserable bastard, but I want all of it! I want everything that thing in the basement provides for us. I can't let you take it away, Henry… you selfish prick. You miserable… selfish… prick."

He finally regained his balance, and stumbled over to the basement stairs. The back of his head felt like it was on fire. He was bleeding heavily. "Judith! Open the damn door!" He screamed.

"Fuck you, Henry!" she screamed back. "You're a dead man!"

Something made a noise behind him, and he spun around quickly. He expected to see the man but there was nothing. His heart was trying to break free from his chest; each breath he took was labored and shallow. All he could think about was trying not to fall unconscious again. "He can't touch me, Judith!" he yelled as he slowly tried to ascend the stairs. "Did you forget? Are you really that fucking slow?"

"Oh, I didn't forget, Henry." her voice was calm. "What do you think has been burning in the fireplace?"

His stomach dropped.

"Goodbye, Henry." He listened to her footsteps as she walked away.

Without warning, two powerful hands grabbed his sides and quickly spun him around.

In an instant, Henry was facing the man.

"Henry, Henry, Henry," the man spoke. "Do you have any idea how bad I feel about all of this? I mean, this whole thing is just one big fucking mess, isn't it? But you have to understand, Henry: I just couldn't take the demands anymore. When I first mentioned to your wife that I could grant her immortality, she was curious. But when I told her that she had to give me *you*? She told me to go to hell." The man tightly held Henry's arms as he spoke. "However… once she found out about Marie, she practically sprinted downstairs to tell me that it was a done deal." His eyes gleamed as he spoke. "She really is pretty slow, isn't she? As if I would allow one of you monkeys to live forever."

Henry tried to run, but he couldn't escape the man's grip. With one quick motion, the man broke both of his arms.

Henry screamed in pain. The man smiled his wide toothy grin.

"The one human emotion that I've used time and time against you monkeys has always been simple greed."

He punched Henry in the face, breaking his nose.

"Even after you monkeys are given *everything,* there's always something else you want, isn't there? You monkeys are never happy, never satisfied. And you are the worst of the bunch, Henry — you had a woman that loved you and was happy living in the squalor and filth you had before I showed up. But you let that go all to hell, didn't you, buddy? I may have lied to Judith, but I want you to know that I wasn't lying to you. The idol's just about finished burning away."

The man licked his lips as he let his eyes trail up Henry's throat.

"So you *both* are as good as dead."

Joseph Schmidt is a magic man, cartoonist, writer, consumer of pop culture, rodeo clown, destroyer of worlds, graphic designer, video game junkie, lover not a fighter, and your church's worst nightmare. *Sugarballs,* his first book, arriving sometime in 2013, is a humorous look at cereal, boobs, dry-humping, and haunted apartments.

Panties Optional

by Christina Esdon

Jess hated blind dates. Hated them. Each one carried its own disaster and somehow she knew tonight would be no different.

She shot a glance across the room at Ruby who, curled atop a towering pile of clothes on the floor, purred with contentment... and relative indifference to her owner's so-called dilemma. "What do you think, Ruby? Black, shiny flats with this black dress? Or something more colorful, like these hot pink heels? Decide quickly. I'm already running late." Ruby opened one eye and glared at Jess before falling back asleep. "Geez, you're no help," she said, rolling her eyes at her cat. Ruby's purr was loud enough to be heard across the street. "I should be so happy," she muttered, turning toward the mirror.

Jess slid the hanger over her head so that the dress hung in front of her like a huge cloth bib. It was cute, with its thin straps and a scooped neckline that gave only a promise of cleavage. The body of the dress hugged her slender curves. Jess rocked her hips side to side, smiling as the skirt swished and swayed. Her favorite part of the dress was that it showed of her best asset: her long ballerina legs. She worked hard for them and was proud to show them off. *I'll just have to remember to keep my legs crossed so I don't show off the entire basket of goodies before dessert!* She pointed her toe into the plush gray carpet beneath her bare left foot and admired how her muscles responded. She teetered on her right foot, eyeing the black pump, then kicked it off and thrust her foot into a pink one — so vivid it nearly gave off its own light. Either pair of shoes would look good with the dress.

Her date, Patrick, had told her that he would take care of all the plans. His voice quivered when he spoke. Another bad omen. Nervous date means long, awkward pauses, and small talk about the near extinction of bees. And she would be sitting there with a fake smile plastered to her face, wishing she could click her heels together three times and go home. According to Patrick, they would go out for dinner first at the Amici's, a five-star restaurant downtown, but after that, it was a surprise. Jess hated surprises. She loathed anything that could make her jump, scream, or squeal. Surprise parties were the worst... like the one her parents threw her when she turned thirteen. She threw up on the cake, passed out on the floor and got a complimentary ride in an ambulance. Fun times.

How in the world was she supposed to plan what to wear for their date if she didn't know what they were going to *do* on their date? She huffed, marched to her oak dresser, and rifled through the drawers. She started throwing everything and anything into her duffel bag. Jess examined a barely-there red bikini that was more string than material. *Could be a possibility if we were going to enjoy a soak in a hot tub... but that'll only happen if dinner goes well.* An awkward dinner date was one thing, but an awkward date in a hot tub was a whole other story. A streak of red flew into the air as she tossed the bikini over her head behind her. The bikini bottoms missed the bed and landed on top of Ruby. The cat didn't flinch.

Jess' glance fell on the small black clock on her bedside table. How in the world had it gotten to be that late? She had less than half an hour to be ready. Jess unhooked the hanger from around her head, but it got stuck. She danced around trying to release herself from its clutches, tugging and pulling on the hanger, yelping as the hook pulled at her hair. Hair ripped from their roots, but Jess thought she was almost free. One more tug and that would be it! She heard a *rrrrrip* and howled. She hopped around in pain from a large clump of hair being ripped out of her scalp, and then tripped over her hot pink pump. The bedroom blurred as she toppled face first onto the pile of clothes next to her.

Crap.

For a moment Jess lay there, defeated. "Why do I even go on these stupid dates with stupid guys I don't know?" She sulked amidst the silk and cotton garments. "Ruby?" Arms flailing, she felt around and found a patch of warm fur underneath her. "Ruby!" She scrambled up on her knees. Somehow her black pushup bra had landed on her head, making her look like Minnie Mouse. With her sight returned, Jess chuckled at Ruby, who was licking her fur back in place, red bikini bottom still on her head, acting as if nothing happened. Jess picked pieces of clothes off of her and Ruby. She stroked Ruby's back. "I'm so sorry, Rubes. I shouldn't have left that pile on my floor. You know what a klutz I can be sometimes. Thank goodness I didn't pursue ballet professionally. 'The Nutcracker' would have ended up being 'The Legbreaker'." Seemingly fed up with her owner, Ruby had sauntered out the bedroom.

Jess sighed and got up. The hanger lay halfway across the floor, her little black dress crumpled like a reject from a rummage sale. Absently, she rubbed the pounding hanger-attack wound at the base of her head. Who was that person looking back at her in the mirror? Her long blonde hair was standing on end as if she'd just had an electric shock. She sprinted to her bathroom to see if there was anything she could do to salvage the style. "Great. Now I'm *really* going to be late!" she groaned.

She hoped to God her date wasn't like the outdoor guy she went out with last winter — the one who, after taking her to a nice restaurant, suggested they go coyote hunting. If hunting interested Jess, even just the tiniest bit, she would have worn something other than a tight skirt and high-heeled boots. She imagined trying to straddle behind her date on a snowmobile, snow flying up her skirt, and shuddered.

After combing her hair and blasting her hair anew with half a can of hairspray, Jess ran back into her room, catching her foot on the clothes pile, but rallied and leaped over it. She threw on her "date" bra that lifted and separated what little she had and stepped into her dress. Mindful of the time, she tossed the teeny bikini, a pair of jeans, a sweater, a pair of mittens, boots and a pair of ice skates (just in case) into a duffel bag.

Now for the major decision.

Shifting back and forth on her feet, Jess weighed her options in the underwear department — sensible tummy tucking undies, or sexy skimpy ones? She looked at the pair of white underwear that overshadowed a swatch of leopard print. *Function or fashion?* she wondered.

Her phone rang with the sound of a mariachi band. "Hello?" she answered, breathlessly, flopping down onto the mess of clothes atop her bed. "Gram? I can't talk right now. I'm running late for — an emergency? Are you okay? Okay, I'm on my way!"

Panicked and prepared for the worst, Jess sprang off the bed, grabbed her duffle bag, jumped into her hot pink pumps, and dashed out the door.

"Gram!" Panicked, Jess burst into her grandmother's house. She searched the front of the house, high heels scattering across hardwood floors. Her heart was lodged in her throat. "Gram!"

"Back here, Jessie!"

Relief washed through her. Thank God she was alive. Jess ran down the hallway into the back room. She stopped in her tracks when she saw her grandmother sitting in her worn out recliner, crocheted blankets covering the wear marks on the seat and arm covers. "What's wrong, Gram?"

"Blasted remote won't work. I've been trying to get the darn thing to turn to *Wheel of Fortune* for the past half hour, and now I'm going to miss the bonus round!" Gram shook the remote as if trying to torture it into submission.

Jess gaped at the old woman, feeling something hot work its way up to her brain. She gasped for air. "Seriously, Gram? This was the emergency? This is why I drove like a bat out of hell to get here?"

"You'd think it was an emergency too if your TV was stuck on some show where an obnoxious host with glow in the dark hair drives around in some convertible, eating greasy food and bugging people while they're eating," Gram huffed.

Jess sighed. There was no use in arguing with Gram. "Let me see the remote." She fiddled with it, pressing buttons, turning the TV off and on. She even resorted to her grandmother's technique, and shook it. Still the annoying TV host was there, biting into a burger, beef fat oozing down his chin. Jess shuddered. She hoped her date didn't eat like that. "Gram, it looks like you need to replace the batteries in your remote. You tell me where you keep your batteries and I'll get everything fixed up."

Gram tried the newly recharged remote and swooned as the ageless Pat Sajak filled up her large screen. "Oh, that's better. Thank you, honey." Crisis averted, Gram sized up her granddaughter and raised an eyebrow. "Where are you going looking like *that*?" Gram used the remote as a pointer.

"On a date."

"When I was your age, we didn't put the goodies on display for men to ogle at for free. We made them work for it."

"Yes, Gram—"

"I hope you at least have a respectable pair of underwear on under there. None of that floss that those girls parade around in those rap videos... their butt cheeks hanging out for the whole world to see. "

Jess rolled her eyes. "Well of course I have respectable..." Last moments of her date preparations flashed in front of her. Two very different pair of underwear sitting on her bed. Which pair did she choose again? "Uh, just a sec, Gram." She ran into the bathroom, slammed the door and lifted up her skirt. A cool breeze tickled her sensitive skin. Her sensitive *bare* skin. *Shoot! I forgot to put on underwear!* Now what? She had already sent a text to Patrick saying that she was running late. She didn't want to make him think she didn't want to go out with him. Even though she didn't want to go out with him. *This,* she reminded herself, *this is the reason I don't go on dates.*

I haven't even met the guy and it's already a disaster!

❦❦

Jess peeled into the parking lot of a lingerie boutique on her way to dinner with Patrick. It reeked of snooty perfume and had enough ruffles in the décor to raise Liberace from the dead.

"We're about to close in five minutes, ma'am."

Jess' neck hair stood on end. She hated being called 'ma'am'. Twenty-three-year-olds weren't in the *ma'am* category yet, in her opinion. "Okay. I'll be quick. I just need a pair of underwear."

The clerk raised her eyebrows. "Make it quick."

Jess grabbed the first pair within reach that was her size and brought it to the counter.

"Don't you want to try them on?"

"Uh, no. I'm sure they'll fit."

A cool breeze stirred the quiet spring night as Jess sprinted back to her car, her new purchase stuffed in her purse. She sped to the restaurant, figuring she could meet Patrick, then casually excuse herself to the ladies' room to put on her new underwear. Then her commando crisis would be averted.

❦❦

Jess was pleasantly surprised by Patrick. They talked all throughout dinner. His brown eyes sparkled in the candlelight when he smiled at her. When he took her hand and caressed his thumb across her skin, jolts of excitement traveled through her. Instead of wishing the night was over, Jess happily linked her arm through Patrick's and strolled along downtown after dinner.

The breeze had picked up. Jess pulled her wrap tighter around her shoulders.

"Are you cold?"

"A little."

"Here." Patrick offered her his jacket.

In reaching for his jacket, Jess lost her grip on her wrap. The wind lifted it up and it gracefully coasted on top of the breeze before landing in a tree branch. Not thinking, she ran after the pashmina, trying to rescue it from the clutches of its captor. She almost had it. Jess rose up on her tiptoes as if she was doing a relevé and stretched her arms above her head.

Just a little bit higher…

Patrick caught up with Jess. "Here. Let me help."

"It's okay. I've almost got it," she said struggling to lift herself a bit higher. "Aha!" Standing on one leg, her hand grasped the soft scarf. She yanked the wrap, bending the branch toward her but lost her grip. The branch retaliated and flung back, smacking Patrick in the face. Stunned by the attack, Patrick recoiled, holding his face.

"Patrick!" Jess strode over to him. The cagey wind struck up again. It brushed up under her skirt, lifting it straight out like a tutu. She only had to look at Patrick's expression to know that she was so wrapped up in her date that she forgot to do something very, very important. Mortified, she snapped her arms down by her side like a trap to hold her frolicking skirt.

"Uh…"

"Wow."

An awkward pause fell between them.

"Patrick, you're bleeding!" The wrath from the branch left a scratch on his check. Blood trickled down his face. "I have tissues. In my purse. I—I don't really want to move my arms, because…" She looked down at her skirt, caught in the clutches of her grip.

Patrick took her cue and reached into her purse to find the tissue. He felt something soft and brought it out. Patrick examined his findings. Jess gasped. There, in the moonlight, shone her bright tangerine underwear in Patrick's hand, price tag flopping in the wind.

They stared at each other for a while. And then they burst out laughing. Hot tears streamed down Jess' cool cheeks. She wasn't sure if they were from embarrassment or from laughing until she had stitches in her sides.

"Oh, what a disaster!" Jess buried her head in her hands, laughing deliriously.

"I actually had a lot of fun. Aside from the tree attack."

She looked up into his playful eyes. "Me too, actually."

"What do you say to another date?"

"I say yes." Heat rose to her cheeks and she took the bright orange panties from Patrick. "I'll make sure to wear these next time."

Patrick blushed a little, too. "Well... if you insist."

Christina Esdon is a hopeless romantic and dreamer extraordinaire. She loves to see the world through rose-colored glasses (literally) and has the uncanny ability to find humor and joy in the small things in life. When not writing, she can be found frolicking along the shores of Lake Huron, taking notoriously long bubble baths, or contemplating the next renovation to her home in Ontario, Canada.

Losing Vern

by Andrew F. Butters

T he piss from the cow struck the windshield of the convertible and shot up, hitting Vern square in the face. The fact that he was in the middle of belting out "Thank God I'm a Country Boy" at the time made it all the more unbelievable. Nonetheless, it happened, and that cow could not have picked a better target; not because he deserved to get a face full of cow urine, but because of the way Vern handled it. He managed to keep his dad's blue Miata on the road and he laughed about it afterwards. Heck, he laughed out loud and proud every time he told the story.

Vern could stand there dressed head-to-toe in his favourite colour, orange, and tell you to your face your outfit was "damn ugly"… and you'd laugh. Because you knew it was true, and because the reason he told you was because he cared.

One of the people Vern cared for most was his brother-in-law, Alex. In the ten years Alex and Julie had been married, he'd never once referred to Alex as his brother-in-law. It was always "Alex", and as time passed, it became, "This is my brother, Alex. Well, he's married to my sister, but we love him anyway."

Vern was the type of person who lived life to love, and loved to laugh. At least, he used to. Now his job was to make sure others lived by this philosophy as well, and to remind them that sometimes ridiculous things happen, and that's what makes being alive so much fun.

There is no better example of this, the notion of the ridiculous, than events that transpired the day Vern died and the few days afterward. For starters, it was Alex's birthday, and it was a Friday the 13th. Vern's sister, Julie, and his niece, Ainsley, were travelling on a girls' vacation down in the Dominican Republic; Alex had taken the day off and was planning to enjoy a nice dinner with his son JT; filet mignon for him, and some overcooked penne with cheese for the toddler.

Vern's dad, Robert, was the one who found Vern in the bedroom he had constructed in the basement. His mom, Helen, a nurse, could not be found. His other sister was en route to the city to visit a friend and was not answering the phone. So, after 9-1-1, Alex was the first person Robert reached.

"Oh, hey there Robert, how are you?"

"Alex, we've lost Vern." There was panic in Robert's voice, a terrified panic.

"Pardon?" Alex said blankly, not grasping the meaning.

"Vern. He's gone. He's passed away."

Alex felt light headed and the room started to spin. He managed to say, "Holy shit, Robert, what happened?"

"I don't know," Robert said, bereft, unsure. "He fell maybe. His face looks pretty bad. I can't find Helen. Tracey is not answering her phone. 9-1-1 is here, they're taking a look."

"Okay," Alex said, swinging into immediate action. "Leave it with me. You try to get in touch with Helen. I'll try Tracey, and I'll get a hold of Julie down in the Dominican – somehow."

"Okay. Call me back as soon as you can."

The first thing Alex did was look up the number for the resort. The second thing he did was look up how to make a call outside of North America. It turned out that making an international call was not something Alex had ever done before.

"Hola, Bahia Principe."

The third thing he did was pull up an online translator.

"Uh... Hola. ¿Hablas henglés?"

"No señor, lo siento. Un momento por favor."

Alex was probably on hold for only two minutes, but as he sat slumped over in his La-Z-Boy, his head in his hands, it felt to him like time had stopped.

"Sí, señor, I speak a little English."

At the sound of an English speaking voice, Alex straightened to attention. "Yes, hello, I have an urgent message for a guest — my wife — can you put me through to her room, please?"

"I'm sorry, sir, but our computers are down. We have no idea where any of the guests are at the moment."

Alex blinked in shock. "Are you serious?!" he cried.

"I'm sorry, sir. My manager says to call back in an hour or so."

Alex jumped out of the recliner and threw a punch at the air. Gritting his teeth, he said, "Let me leave a message at the front desk then, please."

"Si señor, I will write it down and give it to the front desk."

"The message is for Julie MacKenzie. She needs to call home immediately. Please put the word 'IMMEDIATELY' in all capitals," he stressed.

"It is done. I'm sorry we could not help you, but if you call back we will have her room number."

Alex, more panicked than ever, started making more calls. To Julie's sister, Tracey — no answer. To his own sister, Anne, whose husband spoke Spanish — no answer. To Julie's cousin, whose number he found on Facebook, whose uncle would rally the family living down in Virginia and other parts of the U.S. — no answer. Alex was thwarted at every turn. It would be several hours before he would reach anyone.

⌘

Meanwhile, Vern's father finally met up with his mother. Someone at the hospital had given Helen a message to get home right away, so she'd speed-walked as only a sixty-year-old nurse can. She came up the driveway to a scene of emergency response vehicles and Robert sitting on the front stoop, his face full of panic and pain. He looked up, saw Helen shuffling her way up the drive, and stood, his monstrous arms outstretched.

"Helen, we've lost him!" he choked out.

"Lost who?"

"Vern. He's gone. We've lost him."

"Oh, for heaven's sake," Helen replied dismissively. "He's six-foot-four and dresses like a pylon, we'll find him!"

"No, Helen," Robert explained. "There's been an accident. He's passed on. He's *gone*. We've lost Vern."

That might have been the first time Robert had ever cried in front of another person.

∽o∾

After a short while, Robert called Alex for an update.

"Alex, it's Robert. I've got Helen here. How are things going on your end? Have you reached anyone?"

"Well, I reached Uncle James."

"Yes, he gave me a call. He tends to be good in these situations. He'll get the cousins up to speed."

"The computers at the resort are out, so they can't locate Julie," Alex informed him with barely restrained frustration. "I haven't been able to reach Tracey either, but I'll keep trying. You keep trying her as well. I'll call you back when I know more."

"Okay." Robert paused before adding, "The coroner needs to take him and determine cause of death. There's an investigation happening. We're not allowed to go in the house for a while. We'll be at Alan and Maria's."

"Okay," Alex said, hoping his tone didn't reveal the extreme tension that racked him. "I'll try you there if you're not reachable at home."

Alex plugged away at the phones, calling Vern's sisters and trying to reach them. That was all he did for several hours, until he finally reached one of them. Tracey answered her phone before the computers at Julie's resort were fixed.

"Tracey, it's Alex. Where are you?"

"I'm just getting out of the car with Stephen and Emily," Tracey said, sounding a bit breathless. "I'm day tripping to Toronto."

Alex swallowed hard. "Tracey, oh God... I'm not sure how to say this. There's been an accident."

"What happened?" Unadulterated fear filled Tracey's voice.

"It's Vern. He's had an accident... and he's died."

Alex heard a gasp on the other end of the phone.

"Okay." Her voice cracked slightly.

"You need to get back home as soon as you can," Alex said. "I have to try to reach Julie down in the Dominican. All right?"

"Okay. I have to go."

Tracey hung up and broke down, throwing her arms around her baby and her best friend, Stephen. She wept in the back of a taxi the entire ride to Stephen's downtown apartment, where they both cried until it was time to feed the baby. Tracey looked down at her child and realized that Emily would never get to know her uncle, hear him laugh, and know what a kind, generous, and beautiful person he was. And she wept some more.

"Hola."

"Hello, ¿Hablas henglés?"

"Si, a little."

"Okay, great. I need you to put me through to the room of a guest. Julie MacKenzie. J-U-L-I-E M-A-C-K-E-N-Z-I-E."

"Si. One minute please."

Alex thought the wait was long, until he heard the tinny echo of the ringing through the receiver. He felt sick to his stomach; part of him hoped that she would not pick up the phone. His daughter Ainsley answered, and he fought to keep from throwing up.

"Hello?" Ainsley's voice was so tiny and so far away. Tears started forming in Alex's eyes.

"Hey sweetie, it's Daddy, can you please put Mommy on the phone?"

"Daddy! Happy Birthday! We were going to call you later."

Alex felt the weight of the world on his shoulders. "That's so nice, princess. Can you put Mommy on, please?"

"Mommy! It's Daddy on the phone!"

Julie sounded upbeat and her tone was playfully sarcastic. "What, you're so desperate for your birthday wishes that you tracked us down in the Dominican Republic?"

Alex took a deep breath and tried to concentrate on what he had to do. He calmly said, "Julie, JT and I are okay, but there's been an accident."

"Did you crash the van again?" Julie never gave up an opportunity to take a dig at Alex's driving abilities, or lack thereof.

Alex had been so concerned with reaching Julie that he had not put enough thought into what he was going to say. He opted for the most direct approach he could think of.

"No, it's about Vern." Alex paused. Not by choice, but because the next sentence seemed to get stuck in his throat. With a little effort he managed to get it out, albeit clumsily. "Something happened. He's dead."

Nothing could have prepared Alex for what he heard next. He had never really known his wife to be very emotional; but he had just told her that her brother had died, and she was two thousand kilometers away, so there was hardly a precedent. Shrieks and screams came through the phone like a sound that wakes you from a nightmare, or convinces you that you're in the middle of one. The screaming turned to uncontrollable and inconsolable sobbing. Torn apart by the sounds, Alex's stomach became one big knot. He clenched his fists and paced back and forth across the living room floor, trying to hold himself together.

"Listen, we have to get you on a plane. I need you to go to the travel agent at the resort. Remember, the travel agent tiki hut from when we were there last?"

"Yeah, I know where it is."

"Good. Go there and talk to whoever is working, and call me back as soon as you can. I'll start looking into things on this end."

"Okay."

"Julie, it's going to be Okay. Just get home. Hug Ainsley. Don't let her out of your arms, Okay? You're going to need each other for the next few hours."

Julie's voice was completely void of any emotion, "Okay, I have to go see when the next flight leaves. I'll call you again when I know more."

"I'll be here. I love you."

The click of the phone disconnecting was like a hypnotist snapping his fingers to bring someone out of a trance. The phone dropped from his hand and he collapsed to the floor beside his two-year-old son. The screams of his wife and daughter echoed in his head, just as they would for months and years to come. His task completed, his heart broken, it was his turn to weep.

∾⃝∾

The coroner took Vern's body away to determine cause of death and the forensic team released the scene. Only then were Helen and Robert allowed back in their home. Tracey made her way to their place, ninety minutes from her home in the city.

Alex and Julie were having a few more logistical difficulties.

Julie had made her way downstairs to see the tour operator. She'd released a sigh of relief when she'd read the hours on the door and realized they were only a few minutes from closing. Thankful for all her French language studies, Julie had quickly understood that in her hysterical state the Francophone tour operator was having trouble with her English; speaking French calmed her down and slowed her voice. The tour operator found a flight into Montreal leaving in the morning and advised them it would take about twenty minutes to get the tickets arranged.

With a tone that suggested she was more concerned with shutting down for the day than anything else, the woman said to Julie, "Why don't you take your daughter out and get some air?"

At a loss for what to do, Julie took Ainsley's hand and left. They wandered over to the resort's Internet café, and in an attempt to get some contact, any contact, with people back home, she painfully updated her Facebook status. Tears streamed down her face and onto the keyboard as she typed out her note, promising to pass on more information as soon as she got home.

She then used the café's phone to call Alex. "We have a flight out, but it's going to Montreal."

Montreal was a good two hours from where Alex was, and a good eight hour drive from where they all needed to be. He sighed. "If you can't get a connecting flight, rent a car and we'll pay to have it left at the Ottawa airport or something. Or, I can pick you up there."

Still sounding emotionless, Julie replied, "Whatever works. I'm going to pack. I'll call you back."

Julie and Ainsley returned to the tour operator's hut just as another agent was posting a notice on the door:

PLEASE BE ADVISED THAT THE
FLIGHT DEPARTING FOR TORONTO
HAS BEEN DELAYED UNTIL 9:00PM

Julie pointed at the sign and grabbed the woman by her elbow. "Is it possible for us to get on that flight?" Julie's voice showed the first signs of emotion of any kind since her breakdown on the phone with Alex.

The agent sighed heavily and typed a few things into her computer. In her thick French accent, she said in English, "It will be possible, but you will have to be back here with your bags in twenty minutes."

Realizing that Ainsley was probably starving, Julie quickly took her to the buffet. Ainsley knew that they didn't have a lot of time and asked, "Mommy, what should I have for dinner?"

Julie, her stomach not feeling well enough to even fathom eating, replied, "Whatever you want, honey."

Being a clever six-year-old, Ainsley blurted out, "Ice cream?"

Julie just patted her gently on the head. "What flavour?"

She called Alex again. "There's a flight out soon that we can get on. It'll get us into Toronto, which is on the way home."

Toronto was less than a two hour drive to Julie's parents' house and directly on the way for Alex. It seemed they'd finally gotten a break.

"I'll call Samantha and get her to pick you up from the airport," he said immediately. "I'll leave with JT in the morning; we'll pick you up, and go straight to your parents' place."

Julie agreed and gave him the flight information.

Alex clenched a fist, bit on his knuckle, and cautiously asked, "How are you and Ainsley doing?"

Sounding completely exhausted, Julie answered, "She's upset. More so because I'm so upset, I think. We're eating ice cream."

Alex wiped a tear from his cheek. "I'll call you when I'm a half hour from Samantha's, so you can get your things together." He paused, trying to find more words, just to keep the conversation going. "I love you."

Attempting to suppress audible sniffles but not doing a very good job, Julie managed a weak, "I love you too."

∾o∾

News of Julie and Ainsley's situation must have spread through the resort; they were given first-in-line status to board the bus, and elected to sit right at the front. It took only ten minutes before Julie knew she was going to throw up.

She tapped on the Plexiglas divider between the driver and the rest of the bus.

"I'm going to be sick!" she said urgently, making the universal sign for vomiting of miming her hand coming up from her stomach and out her mouth.

The driver quickly opened the divider and passed Julie the garbage pail. After a few rounds of putting her head in the bucket, Julie sensed uneasiness amongst the other people on the bus. She just looked back at them and calmly announced, "I'm not sick, my brother just died."

Several hands came forward, outstretched and holding a variety of pills. Not recognizing any of the coloured tablets being offered, Julie politely declined.

Once on the plane, Julie hoped that her stomach would feel settled, but it was a small charter flight and completely booked. As a six-foot-tall woman, these flights were almost unbearable under normal circumstances. Under the current circumstances, Julie wondered how long she would be able to hold out.

"Excuse me, stewardess; can you watch my daughter for a second?" Julie soon asked. "I have to go to the washroom. Don't worry; I'm not sick, I'm just sick to my stomach."

A panicked voice from a nearby seat called out, "Did that lady just say she was sick?"

From behind that lady came, "Why'd they let her on the plane? What if she has swine flu?"

People started to cover their faces with their sleeves. Those who had hand sanitizer started rubbing it on their hands. A big H1N1 influenza outbreak was ongoing in North America, and people were a little jumpy. It made things interesting for travel — especially if you were the one whose eyes were all red, whose face was pale, and who had to throw up every fifteen minutes.

"I'm not sick," Julie explained, fighting for calm in spite of the fact that she was nauseous, heartbroken, and now worried she had just panicked an entire plane full of people. "My brother just died and we're both a little upset. We're trying to get back home."

Compassion instantly set in amongst the passengers. Pillows were offered, changes of seats recommended, and more than enough people agreed to keep an eye on Ainsley, who sat quietly in the middle seat, rubbing her mother's forehead.

"Everything's going to be okay, Mommy," the six-year-old whispered.

Back in Ottawa, Alex kept busy with planning. Julie had enough presence of mind to tell him to call a friend of hers, who came over and helped pick out visitation and funeral outfits. Vern may have always dressed almost exclusively in orange, but at least he had some sense of style. Alex's style left much to be desired and Julie knew he'd need assistance with this task.

Julie's friend, Samantha, didn't actually own a car, but had agreed to pick them up from the airport at 3:00 AM nonetheless. She ended up borrowing a car and got to them with time to spare. Alex expertly packed their minivan — which he knew was an unforgivably ugly vehicle, but was also amazingly practical — and arrived in the city without incident.

Once Julie and Ainsley were settled in at Samantha's, Julie finally agreed to take something to settle her stomach and allow herself to get some much needed sleep. The next morning, in a much more compassionate tone than the French tour operator had used, Samantha said, "Why don't you go for a walk?"

Julie went to get dressed. It was winter in Canada, and all she had to wear were island clothes. She settled on a long flowing blue dress with a little cardigan, and had to cap it off with black compression knee-highs and running shoes. She dragged her feet into Samantha's living room, announcing wearily, "He's only been gone a day and he's already ridiculing me from beyond the grave."

Samantha turned to look and tried to soften her laughter by covering her mouth with her hand. She giggled, "Vern would SO be taunting you right now! You're a fashion disaster."

Soon, Alex arrived with their son. He was tired from lack of sleep and the five hour drive, but grateful for his two-year-old's surprising cooperation throughout. It was almost as if the boy had sensed that his daddy needed his help.

The well-traveled, exhausted group finally met up with the rest of the family, and close family friends Alan and Maria, for an emotional reunion. Robert took all the clothes and hung them in the spare room closet. Unfortunately, the garment bag that Julie's friend had packed had ended up being stashed away in the back of a closet... back at home.

"Alex, did Lena pack my bag?" Julie asked, passive-aggressively suggesting that Alex had failed to accomplish the task.

"Yep, should be in the spare room," he replied, completely oblivious to the subtle implication.

"There's no way this is what she would have packed for me," Julie exclaimed, her voice rising. "Comfy clothes? There's only comfy clothes in here! I can't wear any of this to my brother's funeral!" Her arms waved around like some crazed magician. The look on her face showed that her careful composure was crumbling, nearing a breaking point. Before the impending meltdown, Tracey stepped in with a perfectly agreeable solution.

"Let's go shopping."

Over the next couple days there were many long, quiet moments, but also a parade of people stopping by to offer an assortment of baked goods and pre-made meals. To someone on the outside looking in, it would have seemed cliché; but to the people on the receiving end, it was exactly what they needed.

Just because cognitive function wasn't coming easily for anyone didn't mean there weren't many details to get straightened out, like what to do about the viewings. An open casket wasn't going to happen, as the accident had left Vern in an unpleasant visual state. The decision was made to have Vern cremated before the visitations and ceremony.

The funeral director walked the family into an empty, quiet room, and like something out of a spy movie, opened up a wide cabinet. He swung the deceptively deep wooden doors to each side, revealing a vast collection of canisters, vases, and urns.

Robert just stood there gobsmacked, looking at all the receptacles — each one an ornamental reminder of loss and suffering.

"How about this one?" Helen held up some sort of flowery ceramic thing that looked like it was part of some ancient Chinese tea set.

Julie's style superpowers kicked in immediately. "No, Mother, we cannot put Vern in a big flowery vase."

The group perused the extensive selection of urns for a few minutes, until Robert picked up a dark wooden box with a place in the front to hold a picture.

"It kind of loooks like a stereo speaker, and he liked music, right? He did give us those speaker stands as a present."

"Sir, that's a spot to hold a photograph," the funeral director said.

"Well, so it is. I think it will do just fine," Robert said. Everyone agreed.

The group was then faced with finding a suitable picture for the front. For most people, this would not be much of a problem, but their task was complicated by the fact that in just about every picture, Vern was holding a glass of wine or a beer bottle. He was not camera shy and did work as a bar manager, after all, and like most people, he enjoyed sociable beverages himself. Several people scoured through hundreds of photos until one was finally chosen. It was a fairly recent picture, Vern had a full smile on his face, he was wearing an orange sweater, and the beer bottle was easy to crop out. Perfect.

Everyone at the restaurant where Vern had worked was devastated. As a group of twenty-something young adults, kids really, few of them had ever been confronted by death, let alone by someone so close to them. The owner's daughter felt she needed to do something, and decided that she would get the staff some orange ribbons to wear on their uniforms as a sign of remembrance and mourning. Business continued as usual, albeit with the staff noticeably less cheerful. More and more regular patrons came in and learned of the news; many asked for an orange ribbon as well. News spread quickly in the small town, accelerated by the tight-knit camaraderie of the local bar and restaurant community. By the day of the funeral, four days after the tragedy, four complete spools of ribbon had been used to meet the demand. Nearly everywhere in town, people wore an orange ribbon on their lapel.

At the viewings and ceremony, it seemed like half the town showed up to pay their respects. Alex's father, Charles, was thoroughly impressed. He was of the generation that thought the more people that showed up to your funeral, the bigger an impact you had made in life. To have hundreds of people attend one's funeral was a great honour.

"Are all these people here for Vern?" Charles asked, not bothering to mask the surprise in his voice.

"Yes, Dad, a lot of people loved him." Alex had never understood the concept of big, organized funerals and was slightly uncomfortable.

Charles stood on his tiptoes, looking around the room and out the doors. "There has to be a few hundred people here."

"Yes, Dad, he knew pretty much everyone in town." Alex made a mental note that when his dad's time came, if he had a good turnout, he'd be pleased on his father's behalf.

"Geez, they're spilling out into the hallway!" Charles was on the verge of standing on a pew to get a better look. Alex realized that he needed something to keep him busy or he'd end up driving everyone nuts.

"Hey Dad, why don't you try to get a count for me?" Alex suggested, his voice sounding a little too much like a dog owner trying to coax their pet outside with a treat.

Charles went wandering off in awe of all the commotion being made. Walking up and down the aisles, nodding solemnly at all the guests, Alex could see Charles's fingers tapping at his side, counting heads. The final tally came in around two hundred for the service, and at least that many had been through for visitations. Alex figured that had it not been mid-week and St. Patrick's Day, there could have easily been a few hundred more.

The service was nice. A lot of people cried, but not enough people laughed, though a few of Vern's close friends did manage to get a chuckle or two out of the crowd. Standing at the front of the chapel, the family looked out at the sea of orange ribbons, and it hit them all collectively like a punch to the stomach. It occurred to them then, with devastating finality: they were never going to get to talk to Vern or see him again. He was gone forever.

The funeral home put Vern's "stereo speaker" urn in a beautiful velvet bag and Julie loaded him up into the van. Everyone went to the local pub — the owner had shut the place down and was holding a wake. He was also the owner of the restaurant where Vern had worked, and he'd supplied all the food for the gathering. Being St. Patrick's Day, it was normally his busiest day of the year; the family was eternally grateful that he'd done this for them. Once settled in, they hung out, told stories, and had a few pints. There was only one problem.

"Where's Vern?" one of the cousins asked Julie.

"In the van," Julie replied, pouting.

Another cousin asked incredulously, "In the van?"

Julie sighed and stared at her plate of fries. "In the van. Mum didn't know if there was some sort of health violation for bringing a cremated corpse into a restaurant."

The bar owner happened by and heard this. In stereotypical fashion, he tossed his bar towel over his shoulder, put his hands on his hips, and waggled his finger at no one in particular. "Listen; if Vern knew that he was sitting *that close* to a bar and wasn't allowed to come in for a beer, he'd be right pissed. Julie, go get him."

She happily did.

Vern sat on the end of a bar table surrounded by all his friends and family, in a wooden box with a bottle of Coors Light beside him. People told stories and laughed. Many had already begun to think of all the ways Vern had reminded them to not to take life so damn seriously; to embrace random ridiculousness whenever it occurred; and most importantly, to love with their whole hearts, as he always had.

The ridiculousness Vern had so favored was front and center one last time when Alex's sweet six-year-old daughter tugged on his sleeve. "Daddy?" Ainsley asked innocently.

"Yes, princess."

"How'd they ever fit Uncle Vern into such a small box?"

Andrew F. Butters lives in Cambridge, Ontario with his wife and two children. He loves hockey, skiing, curling, golf, and all things Canadian. When not on daddy duty, he can be found working for a software company as a project manager, singing as part of the band Argyle Speedo, taking pictures of things that look like letters for Andrew's Alphabet, blogging at Potato Chip Math, and writing his first novel.

The Next Sunrise

by Mark Ethridge

I woke up at 0330 hours. It was cold. At twenty-one degrees, the world seemed covered with several inches of snow that had fallen the previous day. I turned in the bed and looked at my lady. My love. She who continued to stand by me as I walked through the hell. I whispered, "I love you, dear," and gently kissed her cheek.

She would leave for work before I got home from my walk.

I wanted to cry, but I knew it was futile. I'd cried out everything weeks before when the whole nightmare had started.

I slid silently out of our warm bed. Cold air wrapped around me in an instant. Our central heat had failed that past spring, and we'd been ready to replace the furnace, but then the water heater had a melt-down, and set us back a fortune. After that, all hell broke loose, and I wound up out on medical leave.

I'd tried to return to work after thirty days, pretending to be okay, even though I knew inside that I wasn't. Stubborn soul that I am, it took me a full week of trying to work before I admitted I wasn't well. I went back on medical leave.

I took up walking. Not just walking to be physically fit, because it wasn't exercise. I walked because I had to. Without walking, I was unable to cope with life. Whenever that hollow feeling overtook me, it seemed like everything was dead and gone. It seemed the only thing I had left to do was die unless I could walk off that feeling.

I knew my wife didn't understand. I knew my daughter and my son didn't understand. Oh, the number of times they saw me putting on my walking gear. Taping up my toes and heels. Putting on my shoes. Bundling up to walk outside, in the cold, for nearly two hours. I can never forget the things I saw in their eyes. The concern for me. The fear that I would not get well, and maybe not even come home. The fear I would walk until I injured myself, twisting an ankle, or a knee, and then limp home on the injury. The pleading look that said, "Please, be okay."

By 0400, I was outside. Starting my walk. 5.2 miles. In the cold. In the wind. With snow on the ground. Ice on the sidewalks. Music from my MP3 player drowned out the crunch of my shoes on the sidewalk and the whoosh of cars speeding past.

Thoughts ran wild in my head as I walked, playing out endless scenarios of what would happen in the future. Me, returning to work. Me never returning to work. Me being slapped by the one person at work that I still cared anything about. Me being hugged by that person. Me having endless battles with everyone there. Me being silent, and never saying anything to anyone there.

That morning I reached Princess Anne Road, heading north. It always surprised me how many cars were on the road at 0430 hours in the morning. People heading to work. People coming home from work. People living their normal, everyday lives. Something I'd once had.

When I reached the corner of Princess Anne Road and Dam Neck Boulevard, I turned onto Dam Neck, heading east.

Dam Neck.

The place where I'd worked. The place that banned me, declaring my behavior was disruptive and disturbing. The place that declared I was to have no contact with anyone at Dam Neck. People I'd worked with for years. Some of them for over a decade.

The place that had betrayed me. When I was hurt. When I was not well. The place that discarded me, threw me away, declaring, "Go get repaired. Then we'll consider letting you come back."

I knew I'd never be allowed to return. I knew my twenty-eight years in the defense industry was over. Dam Neck would see to that. I kept hearing this voice in my head, "This gear in the machine broke. We need to replace it."

Dam Neck Boulevard was always there. Every morning. Every day. Every walk I took. I couldn't escape it. As I walked along it, I kept seeing cars that reminded me of people I'd known and worked with. A green Jeep Wrangler with a tan hard top. A blue Toyota Solara. A pale blue, almost silver, Lexus ES300. A silver Toyota Tacoma. A green Toyota Tundra.

Always I felt like everything was horribly wrong. Horribly broken. I was supposed to be in a car, like everyone else. Driving to work. Like everyone else. I wasn't supposed to be walking on the sidewalk, watching everyone else drive to work. I wasn't supposed to end up walking home. Where I'd spend the day washing dishes and laundry, vacuuming floors, and writing.

I wasn't supposed to be at home, unable to escape myself. Unable to avoid me.

I walked along Dam Neck that morning. Knowing all I had to do. All it would take. To end the hurt I was living in. To become free from the agony I felt. All I had to do was wait. And then turn to the side, and take two steps. Two steps. And a big damn truck would be unable to miss me.

And I'd be free.

But I couldn't. I wouldn't. I knew that. I'd always known that. I learned that when I was seventeen. In high school. That was what other people did. I understood why. I knew why. I understood the appeal. But I knew. Those two steps wouldn't solve anything.

All I had to do was close my eyes, and remember my lady. My daughter. My son. The concern and the fear I saw in their eyes every time they watched me get my walking gear. I knew those two steps would bring their fears to life, and leave them wounded, wondering why I'd abandoned them instead of depending on them to help me.

It was always that obvious to me. There was never a choice to make. I would walk through hell. Every last bit of hell. Every cave. Every hallway. Every depth. I'd fight Satan himself before I'd give up on them. I'd never walk away from them.

I knew what to do: I had to walk that strip of Dam Neck Boulevard. Endlessly. Over and over. Day after day. Week after week. Until I learned to walk it without feeling like everything was wrong.

When I got home that day, the sky still hung dark above me. Normally, I went inside, and got a shower, and then ate something, my own ritual. That day, I went inside, but I didn't follow my routine. I got something to drink. Then, I stared out of the window. I watched. I watched the sky as its blackness faded away, slowly yielding to the blue of day.

I watched to see the sun rise above the horizon. Hoping it would be a beautiful sunrise. Knowing it would be, even if there were no colors, just a bright ball rising above the trees and houses, glittering across the broad white expanse of snow.

I watched the sky, and life gave me a gift that day. Painting a band of pale orange just above the trees and houses of my neighborhood, life told me, "Don't give up. Things change. With time. And no one knows what lies on the other side of the next sunrise."

The pale orange of the sunrise I saw that morning, and on so many other mornings as I walked, will be in my heart and soul always. Reminding me of the truth I learned that day, in the ice and snow. Each day is a gift, to be unwrapped. A surprise from life.

And no one knows what lies on the other side of the next sunrise.

Mark woke up from a lifelong sleep in 2010. In doing so, his life changed. The changes continue to this day. He's been married to his wife for 27 years, and likes to inform people, "She's one of the few things I've done right. I'm not hosing that up." Their two human children are grown up. One has moved out, and the other plans to in the next year. They also have three feline children named Kaosu, Delilah, and Ansem. Delilah always gives him kitty kisses right on the nose.

Mark would like you all to know, Orange Karen is a gift from life to us all.

Seeds

by Francis Setnocis

W hy are we doing this?" my mom asked. She was tired. My father plants a garden every year, and we always use the pumpkins he harvests. We had already spent four hours in the kitchen and were not close to finishing. Our wrists and fingers were swollen.

I gave the answer that I had heard the most: "It's for the pumpkin."

We cut open the pumpkins, scooped out the wet veins inside, and set aside the seeds. Next, we cut them into chunks, peeled them, and shredded the meat. The bright orange peels went into a paper bag for compost. Depending on the density and the water content of the pumpkin, the shredding would either take minutes or hours. Because we never knew what the pumpkin flesh would be like before we cut it, we couldn't predict the amount of the other ingredients we would need for the *bourekia,* a Greek food. The pumpkin is mixed with spinach, parsley, seasonings, onions, feta, and parmesan cheese, then spooned on to thin bread dough, rolled tightly, and glazed with olive oil. They are meant to be a finger food. In my mom's kitchen it was never made the same twice, but it never failed to be delicious.

We started making it when my father's mother, my *Yiayia*, moved in with us. Her three sisters lived nearby and visited often. *Yiayia* was the oldest, but none of them were younger than seventy years old or taller than five feet. Except for Aunt Chrysoula, they were widows and wore all black every day. Aunt Chrysoula wore a Tweety Bird tee shirt. She cut the pumpkins and made sure not one piece of the meat remained on the skin. She spread out the pumpkin seeds and soaked them in a bowl. She roasted some of them, and others she saved to plant in the garden the following spring.

"It's for the pumpkin," she told me. If we wanted *bourekia* next year we had to grow more pumpkins.

As Aunt Chrysoula peeled and cut the wedges of pumpkin, Aunt Argie shredded them with a cheese grater. Argie, the second oldest, liked doing things her way. My mother had a food processor that shredded the pumpkin faster, but Argie preferred doing it the way her mother did it. Argie shredded as fast she could and my mom was doing the same with the machine. Aunt Chrysoula cooked the onions, spinach, and parsley and the aroma filled our house.

The youngest of my aunts, Aliki, made the bread dough. I pressed the shredded pumpkin in a strainer at the sink, removing the water. Then I dumped the drained pumpkin in one of the giant bowls that my dad brought home from a restaurant supply store. Aunt Chrysoula poured in the onion mixture; my mom added the two types of cheese and the seasonings and stirred it. She rolled up her sleeves and washed her arms up to the elbows. Holding the bowl in her left hand, she used her right hand to scoop the contents, creating an orange, green, and white mosaic. *Yiayia* and Aunt Argie supervised. If they thought it was too wet, *Yiayia* tossed in a handful of uncooked rice, but Aunt Argie would toss in a handful of salt to solve the same problem. It didn't matter because there was still more pumpkin to be added in the bowl, and that meant more onions, parsley, and spinach had to be chopped and sautéed. If it still wasn't quite right, another pumpkin was waiting to be cut and shredded. The mixture was right when it looked like marble: mostly orange, with long swirls of green spinach, and white specks of cheese.

I could never figure out how it happened, but the exact moment they were all satisfied with the pumpkin mixture was the exact moment Aunt Aliki had the dough ready. She had rolled it out thinner than a piece of card stock. It was as long and as wide as the counter. My aunts and grandmother took a section of dough to work with. Each spoonful of pumpkin mixture had the same proportions. Aunt Aliki poured spoonfuls of the mixture along the length of the dough. Her *bourekia* were at least fifteen inches long. Aunt Argie made hers to fit the width of the pan. My mom made them fit in a plastic freezer bag for easy storage. *Yiayia* and Aunt Chrysoula made the *bourekia* smaller; three inches or less. *Yiayia* folded hers on the end. Aunt Chrysoula made tiny triangles on the ends of hers, they looked like envelopes. No matter who rolled them, they all were an inch wide. I glazed them all with olive oil and took them out to cool on the kitchen table.

By the end of the night, there were hundreds of pieces of *bourekia* in the kitchen and were on the dining room table. Each of my aunts took bags home. The only thing left of the pumpkin were the peels on the compost heap and the seeds waiting to be planted in the spring. My grandmother and Aunt Argie eventually returned to Greece and lived out the rest of their lives. Aunt Aliki went back to Greece to live with her son. Aunt Chrysoula still lives less than a mile away from me, but these days she's too frail to make the labor-intensive *bourekia*. Now, it's my mom, the pumpkin, and me. The project takes a weekend instead of a day. We cut and shred the flesh and set aside the seeds for next spring. On Saturday we make the filling, and on Sunday we make the dough, rolling it out paper thin, and make the bourekia all the same size. We make much more than we can eat. I keep some in my freezer, my mom keeps some in hers, and we take some to Aunt Chrysoula.

For many, a birthday or watching the ball drop on New Year's Eve marks the passage of time. It's a new beginning and a chance to continue life. When I see a mature orange pumpkin in my garden, I know it's because of the seeds my grandmother saved all those years ago. The only way I can see that pumpkin again is to open it up, save the seeds, and make *bourekia*.

A native New Yorker who enjoys gardening and cooking; this is **Francis Setnocis'** debut work.

There is Such a Thing as Too Much Orange

by D. Savannah George

I come to, face down on some carpet. Shag, by the feel of it. I inadvertently open and close my mouth. It feels glued together, and tastes far worse. I crack open one eye, my right one, the one not squooshed into the carpet. Yup, shag. And, even better, orange. Bright orange. The color pierces my retina and makes me whimper, so I close my eye, and try to remember where I am and what the heck I had been doing last night.

I risk another peek, and it all comes flooding back. A party. Drinking. Lots of laughing. Flirting. Trying to make some pretzels and a bottle of vodka fill the hole in my heart. More flirting. A guy. Screwdrivers (the drinks, not the tools). Cheddar cheese and crackers. And more vodka. Going home with the guy. Which is apparently where I am. At his house.

Crap. Crappity crap crap crap.

Well, maybe I can't remember *everything*. Surely he didn't actually have an orange beard?

The floor trembles as said guy walks by me. I recognize the shoes — plain white sneaks. I hear him plop down on what I vaguely remember is an orange couch.

"Aw, crap," I mutter aloud. *What is his name? His naaaame?* I can't remember.

"You all right?" His deep voice feels like napalm to my brainpan. I wince, brace myself, then flop over onto my back. Fat lot of good that does me. Now, even with my eyes closed, all I see is orange. Makes me feel even worse.

"Hey," I try to say, but a croak that sounds more like a gurgle issues from my parched lips instead. I lick them with the teensy bit of saliva I can work up, and try again. "Hey." It sounds *almost* normal.

"Hey," he says. *Oh God — did we sleep together?* I can't remember. I start patting my clothes, let out a sigh of relief when it appears that they haven't been removed. Either that or he's the first dude in the history of my life who could successfully remove *and* replace button-fly jeans.

I hear him heave a deep sigh.

I crack open both eyes, turn toward him. *Oh God. He* does *have an orange beard.*

"We didn't sleep together," he says. He continuously crosses and uncrossed his arms over his Aerosmith T-shirt, and rubs his hands on his jeans, like he doesn't know what to do with his limbs. "Not from my lack of trying, mind you. Or your initial willingness." Another sigh. "But every time I got near your pants, you slapped my hand."

I lever myself into a sitting position, and hug my knees until my brain doesn't feel quite so sloshy anymore.

"Where are we?" I ask, looking at him again. "And who are you?" I let my voice trail off, feel the tips of my ears redden. This guy is what, the third or fourth I've gone home with in the last six months? But apparently, he's the first I didn't actually have sex with.

"This is my house — well, the basement at my mum's house — but I live here. I'm Quillan."

I groan, slap my forehead onto my knees. Groan again, from the pain I just inflicted on myself. *Quillan.* No wonder I can't remember the guy's name. Hell, he probably can't remember it half the time. I am suddenly proud that I can remember the names of all the guys I've slept with. As if that's a freaking thing to be proud of.

As if it's even a terribly long list.

"Jessie... you all right?" he asks again, gently this time.

I lift my head, look at him — not a bad-looking guy, except for all that orange hair sprouting from his face — and say a half-lie, half-truth. "Yeah."

∽◦∾

I'm not even twenty, and my life is already over. And apparently, I'm turning into a slut... though I'm not exactly sure how many guys you have to sleep with to officially be considered one. I'm up to a grand total of what, five now? Is the amount of time it takes to sleep with a bunch of guys taken into consideration before you get slapped with that moniker? After all, eighteen months ago, I was still a virgin. And I was in love with the first guy I slept with, so does that mean I'm not going to hell? Or would I go anyway, since we weren't married? And will I be heading there now that I've slept with a few more guys? Maybe it helps that I didn't have sex with this one.

Maybe.

∽◦∾

I groan. My head sinks back to my knees. The guy — *oh Lord, I've forgotten his name... again!* — softly touches the back of my head. I hear him leave the room, and a second later, he comes back and wraps a green blanket around my shoulders. It's soft and cozy. And not orange. Not that I have anything against the color, mind you, but it is definitely not hangover friendly. Especially not in this quantity.

"C'mon, Jessie. Let's get you off the floor." He helps me up and leads me to the bed where I apparently had not slept with him.

"Why did you let me sleep on the floor?" I mumble.

"I couldn't get you into the bed. That's why. You kept slapping me. So I gave up."

Somehow, he helps me navigate my hung-over self under the covers, and gets my head situated on a pillow. Then he leaves again.

I close my eyes, groan. *Why am I so ever-lovin' stupid?* I ask myself — rhetorically, of course. I know the answer, even if I won't admit it.

I must have dozed off, because the next thing I know, he's shaking me gently.

"Jessie? Wake up. Drink this." I mutter something incomprehensible, and he helps me sit up. Then he hands me a glass full of a disgusting pale yellow concoction.

"What the heck is this, um… Kwi—" I ask, clearly foundering for his name again.

"Quillan. Quill. Or Q, if you think you can remember a single letter," he says. I can't be certain, what with my eyes all crusted shut, but I think he might have quirked a smile. "It's a banana milkshake. My mum has sworn my whole life that the only cure for a hangover is either hair of the dog or a banana milkshake. Since I think you drank every bit of alcohol in the house, this is what you get."

Q is definitely laughing at me. *Cue. Yeah, I think I can remember that.* I take the glass with both hands, afraid I'm going to drop it all over his bed. I doubt I drank all his alcohol. Pretty sure I didn't. Probably. I try to bring the glass to my lips, but almost drop it, even with my two-fisted grip. "Ugh," I manage to get out. "It stinks."

"Yeah, but it's good for you," he smiles, and pulls another blanket over my legs. A blue and yellow afghan, actually, probably something his grandmother or great-grandmother crocheted for him. And I might spew all over it.

I drink about half the milkshake, and then I do just that.

⚬∞0∞⚬

For a guy I did not sleep with, Cue is remarkably nice. He just removes the vomity blankets and sheets, brings me fresh linens and a clean shirt — nothing fancy, just a black t-shirt with Iron Maiden on it. He even turns his head and closes his eyes while I tug off my scrunchie and remove my hurl-covered bright-pink off-the-shoulder shirt. While I'm at it, I roll my bright-green leggings off too. I grunt to let him know I've got the T-shirt on. He points to the bathroom, and I stumble to the sink and splash water on my face. I grab the tube of toothpaste and swoosh some of it around until my mouth tastes more like mint than something dead. I pee for an amazingly long time, then stagger to the fresh-made bed and fall back onto the pillow.

"Oh, boy… that feels better," I say, completely forgetting I'm in a total stranger's house… or basement, rather. And in his bed. This could go very badly for me, but I hope not. Plus, my head hurts too much to care.

"I bet." Cue gathers up my clothes and the blankets, walks to the other side of the room, opens a door, and disappears behind it. In moments I hear water running for what I presume is a clothes washer.

"Sure you want to do that?" I sit up and call, as loudly as my head will let me, which is surprisingly loud. The milkshake smelled and tasted horrible, and it did make me throw up — in front of a perfect stranger, no less — but he was right: it did seem to help my hangover. Just a bit.

He sticks his head out the door and looks at me. Even though I've been looking at him all morning, I'm somehow genuinely shocked to see all that orange hair sticking out of his face. Then I remember, his name isn't actually Cue, like a cue-ball. He's not bald. His name is Quillan. *Holy crap! I remembered!* "Why not?"

"Possibly messing up your mom's washer, you know, gumming it up with all my puke."

Q laughs again. "Nah, this washer is industrial strength. Made to clean up vomitous masses. It loves that stuff." His head disappears behind the door, and I hear the lid of the washer clang closed, and the sound of an energetic machine spinning the crap out of disgusting items.

Q comes back, sits on a chair across from the bed, eyes me. Not like, in a mean way, or a way that makes me feel uncomfortable, just… apprising. I get the sense he likes what he sees.

"So, Quillan…" my voice trails off. "What's the story with that name?"

He smiles, all that orange hair crinkling around his face. "It's Gaelic Irish. Means 'cub'. My mum emigrated here when she was nineteen, and named me that as an ode to the old country. I enjoy using it to stymie terribly drunk girls that I've managed to lure into my basement lair." He rubs his hands together, then laughs. "So, what's the story with your name?"

I stare at him. "Jessie?"

"Uh, yeah. 'Jessie'. What's the story there?"

I stare at him for what seems like a good five minutes. Then I throw a pillow at him. He dodges it easily. "You're messing with me, aren't you?"

"Maybe." He draws the word out into about sixteen syllables, a grin splitting his face. Now that I think about it, he definitely looks Irish. I'm betting he has all that facial hair to cover about 10,000 freckles.

Q leans back in his chair. He stares at me. I lean back on the pillows and stare at him.

I can't think of anything to say, so I blurt, "What's with all the orange?"

"What do you mean?" Q strokes his beard, and I want to punch him. Or maybe kiss him. I can't decide which.

"You know, this décor." I sweep my arm around to indicate the carpet, the couch, and the walls hung with cheesy, framed embroidery. "Isn't this so very 1970s? It's the '80s, for heaven's sake."

We hear the washing machine spin to a stop, and he gets up to throw everything in the dryer. I just hope he was right, and that the washer removed my barf from the blankets and my clothes. I lie down, pull the covers over my head, and hope it hides my bright red face.

I hear him come back, and he tugs the sheet away from my face.

"Whatcha doing under there?"

"Nothing," I mutter.

"Uh-huh." He stares at me for a bit. "So, how about we go get some breakfast after your clothes are dry? I know this great place. Might help sop up some of the excess alcohol in your system."

I lift an eyebrow. I didn't sleep with him, I threw up all over his bed, and he wants to take me to breakfast?

"Glutton for punishment?" I ask.

"Apparently. But you should still say yes." He pauses, gives me that apprising look again. "Maybe I just want to know if you're as fun sober as you are drunk."

"Highly doubtful," I shoot back. "But I guess I'll do anything to get out of this mango manor. It's giving me a headache."

He infuriates me by stroking his beard again. Then he lifts one eyebrow and says, "So, you're not a fan of orange?"

For some reason I can't explain, I laugh. And relent a little. "You might be able to persuade me otherwise."

"Good. That's what I'm hoping for."

∽o∾

An hour later, Quillan and I are sitting in a bright yellow booth at Mimi's Morning Marmalade. I'm not making that up. It's actually the restaurant's name. And apparently they close at one PM, and only serve breakfast. We're here at ten AM, and the place is packed. Bustling. Noisy. I smell pancakes, bacon, eggs, corn beef hash… it all makes my head hurt and my stomach flip over.

The waitresses have on white skirts and white blouses, topped by — I'm not kidding — orange aprons. I groan.

"You're trying to kill me, aren't you?" I ask, looking over the menu, adorned with oranges.

Quillan raises his palms to the sky. "What do you mean? I love this place. Great food."

"A place that's almost completely orange. You take me from your *orange* basement to an *orange* restaurant."

He smiles, his freaking *orange* facial hair flying every which way. "Yup. You're as feisty sober as you are drunk. I like you, Jessie." He reaches over and takes my hand. "I really do."

It's impossible to stay even pretend mad when a guy does that. And says that.

Our waitress comes over, plunks down two glasses of ice water. Before she can speak, I grab a glass, guzzle the contents, and plop it back on the table.

Then I look up.

Not only is she wearing that orange apron, she has a giant sunflower pinned to her hair. Oh boy.

"My name's Maddie, and I'll be your waitress today. What can I get you, besides more water?"

Before I can even take a breath, Quillan blurts out an order.

"You got it," Maddie says, then sweeps away, leaving the faint scent of citrus behind.

"Did you just *order* for me?" I ask.

"Yup." He leans over, stares into my eyes. I about drown in the copper depths of his. I don't think I've ever met a guy with eyes that color. But damn, they are pretty.

After what seems like hours, he leans back. "Trust me."

I put my chin in my right hand, pull my left hand through my auburn hair, and consider him. "Okay," I say, and I mean it.

<hr />

D. Savannah George is a multi-disciplinary artist — she writes, paints, crochets, takes photographs, and makes beaded jewelry, bookmarks, and notecards. She has published several short stories and a number of poems, as well as numerous articles in various newspapers and magazines, and has won several awards for her writing. Her first book, *A Spicy Secret*, #22 in the Annie's Attic Mystery Series, was released in December 2012. She also serves as a book editor for authors and several small publishers.

The Space

by E. Wells-Walker

S orry, big guy," he growls as he puts his palm on the wall, triggering the latch. "You've just earned yourself some time out." The space exhales a breath of cool air as the door slides open. "Go on in. You can come out when you remember how to behave." His scowl isn't open to protest. I really want him know I'm sorry, but his face is so silent, so disappointed, that I just stare at his shiny black shoes. "I'll be back in a little while." The inside of my ears thicken as the door closes off the outside world, and the soft light inside the small Space clicks on.

What had happened wasn't completely my fault; I was just bored. They went off this morning and left me with the housekeeper. She doesn't let me go upstairs by myself, I can't sit on the furniture in the front room, and she's afraid that if I go outside I might wander off into the forest that surrounds the house.

And I probably would.

It began to snow just after they left. I sat at the tall front windows watching them go, wishing that they had taken me with them — or, at least, that I could go out and play in the snow until my toes froze and my nose became numb. Instead, I lay down under the window, looking up at the swirling flakes until I was dizzy.

This house is big, with enough rooms and hallways to get lost in. I wandered around for a while looking for something to do. Next to the fireplace in the study I found a basket full of old magazines they use to light the logs. And since I couldn't go out in the snow, I decided I would make it snow inside instead. I dove into the papers, ripping them into the tiniest pieces I could. Colorful magazine confetti whirled all around the room, getting caught on the curtains and covering the furniture in drifts of shredded paper. Tiny bits stuck to me as I rolled in the pile of glossy flakes. I sneezed, and paper snow blew up onto the air then twirled down on top of me, just like the flakes outside the window had swirled down.

When I heard them drive up the long drive, I shook the paper out of my hair and ran to meet them. Laughing and happy and loaded with packages, they hurried through the big front doors, stopping to shake the snow off their umbrella. They hugged me hard, and told me I would have to wait for my very special present.

"Come on, sport," he said. "First, we have to get a fire started."

Then they walked into the study and saw the mess I had made. He got very quiet, while she went to get the housekeeper. He glared at me and swept me up over his shoulder, telling me over and over that what I had done was *not good*.

I am ashamed that I have to be told again that I misbehaved, that I have to go stay in this Space again. It's not a bad space. It isn't much larger than the pantry down in the kitchen. From the outside, it looks like any other closet in the bedroom, but the only things in here are a large screen high up on the wall opposite the door and a big green chair in the corner. The screen is always on, shifting silently from one room inside the house to another and another, then to the outside yards and back again. Above the screen, tiny lights blink each time a door or window is opened or someone walks from one room to the next. The lights dance like fireflies as he strides to the end of the long hall and down the stairs into the study.

Higher up and off by itself near the screen is a clear red button set into the wall. I don't know what it's for, but it looks important. One time, I tried to jump up and hit it, but it was too far out of my reach. Just as well. I get in trouble for playing with things I'm not supposed to.

There is nothing for me to do but wait for him to come back. I hop upon on the chair, dragging my blanket over me like a soft orange cloud. A deep sniff brings back memories of running crazily through the house dragging it behind me and snuggling on my mother's bed, rolled up in it like a caterpillar in a cocoon. I love the orangeness of it.

I listen hard for his footsteps or his deep, soft voice, but all I can hear are pans rattling in the kitchen; the faint crackling of fire; music with a quick beat and a pounding bass. I watch the screen flip dully from one room to the next. I pull the orange blanket off the chair and lie down on the floor, trying to peek under the bottom into the dark room outside the door. I can't see anything. But I can hear the creatures in the forest going about their wild animal business in the cold twilight.

I doze off.

In a dream, I am running through the woods, happily chasing after a small rabbit I know I will not catch. I feel the icy snow crunching under my feet and watch the night birds glide overhead as they begin their hunt. A startled deer jumps across my path, vanishing into the darkness, showering snow down from the low hanging limbs of a pine tree.

Suddenly, the dream changes. Long black shadows spring from behind glowing trees. The hair on my neck turns stiff. I am not chasing; I am fleeing. I am running blindly away from something racing up behind me, its hot amber breath cackling at my back. I can't see it, but I am terrified. I know that when it catches me, it will devour me.

Fire.

There is fire in the trees. Flaming pinecones fall around me like missiles. Small animals dash past me, not caring who or what I am. The deer bounds past; birds screech past overhead. My own shadow tries to escape ahead of me. The seductive smell of burning life chokes me.

I wake up coughing.

I'm safe. I'm in the house. I'm in the safety of the Space, not in the flaming woods. But the dream was so real. I shudder, and taste fire in my mouth. I lean my face close to where the door meets the wall and breathe deeply.

I gag as acrid, grey fingers slither through the invisible crease.

I shake my head hard and rub my eyes to make certain I am awake. But I can hear it. I can hear the trees burst into sizzling flames and crash into one another. I cringe at the red hot terror of the animals scattering before the creeping edge of the...

Fire!

The forest is burning; really burning.

My heart thumps hard against my chest as I race around and around the small Space, looking for a way out. I can see them on the screen. They sit side by side in front of the fireplace. They don't know. They can't tell difference between the smell of the good fire in the fireplace and the ravaging fire in the forest.

I have to warn them; it's coming for us, skittering across the lawn, devouring its way up the outside of the house. We have to get away. I call to them and call and call as loudly as I can, but they can't hear me. The crackling flames are marching across the roof. My throat hurts from crying and I am blinded by tears as the smoke pours in around the door. Panic throws me against the door over and over again but I can't open it.

I see them on the screen, sitting there, laughing, while the fire scurries down the attic walls. I jump at the screen, yelling, hoping they will hear me and come save me, but I am choking and sneezing and crying and I can't see. I don't know what to do.

There.

The red button... the one that is up too high. I know I shouldn't touch it. I know I will get in trouble again, but I don't care. I climb back up on the green chair and jump towards it. I miss, hitting the floor hard. It hurts, but I climb up back up and try again, and again. And again.

The space is filling with smoke. My legs and back ache from falling, my head throbs from the smell, but I crawl up on the chair once more and hurl myself through the air towards the place where I know the button is, even though I can no longer see it through the haze. I slam into it and an ear-piercing alarm cuts through the house.

I cry out in agony and slump to the floor, frozen by the pain screaming in my ears. Every breath brings in raw heat that sears my lungs. I can't move; I can't see. I can't breathe. I am so tired that all I want to do is curl up onto my blanket and sleep forever.

The door flies open. Flames dance up the curtains, blowing dark clouds across the ceiling of the room outside the Space. I panic and try to run behind the chair, but he throws the blanket over me.

"Hold on," he cries. "Just hold on. We're going to get out of this." He scoops me into his strong arms, hugging me tightly, staggering towards the darkened stairs. I know I am safe with him, but primal instinct makes me struggle to get free, to escape into the cold, wet darkness outside.

Through the haze and confusion of smoke and water and strange men rushing into the house, I see the open front door. My heart racing, I leap out of his arms and explode out the front door and down the stairs racing to where she is standing, crying, watching the fire engulf the house.

He bounds after me, calling me, following me to the safety of the open yard.

"Good dog," he whispers with tears in his voice as he sweeps me up off the damp grass, clutching me in my orange blanket. "Good dog."

∽o∾

E. Wells-Walker lives in Dallas, TX and writes short story fables for easy readers, age 7-12, that focus on contemporary issues for that age group.

Chip, Chip, Hooray!

by K.D. McCrite

They call this place an old folks' home, but I've seen some shenanigans in here that people forty years younger wouldn't try. Being a man of few words, I'll keep my own counsel.

Most people here — and by that, I mean the residents — say they don't like living in Maple Lane Manor. They want to go back to a place where they have to mow the lawn or climb the stairs or patch a leaky roof. In other words, a place that can tie you down with responsibilities. Me, I like it when someone else makes my bed, cooks my meals, and scrubs my bathroom. Not that I'm lazy, but I think when you're almost eighty, you deserve life's perks. Maple Lane Manor is a fair place to live, with big, clean rooms painted in soft colors, like yellow and green and blue. The floors shone and the bathrooms sparkled white and clean. It never smelled like pee in here, either. Best of all, we had plenty to eat.

Della Barr seemed to dislike this place more than anyone. She had an attitude. At least, she did when she first got here. I heard tell she yelled at the staff and threw a food tray at one of them. I don't know. Maybe she did; maybe she didn't. Rumors fly in a place like this.

I met Miss Della on her sixth night here. She sat by the window in the lounge and wept great tears that soaked her blue dress. I watched for a while, figuring whatever bothered her was something she probably needed to work out on her own. She seemed quiet to me, not at all likely to throw something, but I kept my distance. Those tears, though. They seemed to have tapped into something deep within her. When Miss Carolyn, an evening volunteer from the Sunshine Club, knelt beside Miss Della's chair and took one of her hands, the old woman didn't look at her. She didn't respond in any way at all. It was like she'd gone somewhere else in her mind.

"Let me try, Miss Carolyn," I said, after a bit. Miss Carolyn seemed close to tears herself.

She looked at me. "Chip, maybe you ought to get to bed. It's late, and you're still getting over that cold."

I waved my hand. "I got over that cold three weeks ago. You people get worked up over the least little thing. We sneeze once and you put us to bed, feed us antibiotics and a liquid diet until we wish we were dead. I feel just fine. Let me talk to this lady, see if I can help her dry those tears."

Miss Carolyn hesitated then nodded and got to her feet. She squeezed Miss Della's hand, patted my shoulder, and walked away.

I pulled up a chair and sat down. She pretended not to notice me, but from the corner of my eye I caught her looking at my face.

"I'm Clifford," I said, "but they call me Chip. And your name's Della Barr."

After what seemed a good two minutes, she finally shook my proffered hand, but barely gave me a glance.

"Rain's holding off tonight, seems like," I said, turning my gaze out the window. "Supposed to turn cold tomorrow."

Silence from her except for the occasional wet sniffle.

"'Course it might not rain," I went on. "Could be it'll turn out sunny. Weatherman never knows what he's talking about."

Silence. Sniff.

"You know," I continued, as if we were engaged in a dual conversation, "I once kept a notebook for a whole year in which I recorded the forecast on one side of the page and the actual weather on the other side."

Silence. Then Della gave a hugely loud sniff and said, finally, "So how often were they right?"

Expecting her sustained silence, I nearly jumped with surprise. Quickly, I gathered my wits.

"About half the time."

I turned my head, and she slid a glance at me. "Only half? I would have thought more."

"You'd think so, wouldn't you? They went to school to learn all that stuff."

"My grandpa could tell the weather three days in advance," she said proudly.

"Was he a meteorologist?"

"No. Just very smart and observant."

I thought about that for a minute or two. "I have a book about weather," I said.

For the first time her eyes lit up. "You do? Do you have any other books?"

"Oh, sure. I'm a great reader. How about you?"

"Me, too. And a writer. Do you write, by any chance?"

"Some poetry sometimes. I'm not very good."

She touched the top of my hand with her fingertips. "I bet you are. Would you let me read some of your poetry?"

Now this was an unexpected development. No one at Maple Lane Manor knew I dabbled with words, and I saw no reason to enlighten them. I was known as *Chip the Scamp* or *Good Ol' Chip*. Sometimes, behind my back, they referred to me as *Chip the Nutcase* because I thought it would do us a world of good to play games or have a talent night or even a beauty contest. I didn't care too much to be called a nutcase or a scamp, but one thing I surely didn't want to be called was *Chip the Poet*. It just lacked a certain charm. And something else: I didn't want anyone to know I had a half-finished novel in my dresser drawer beneath my underwear.

"Come on," Della urged, a flirty smile on her face. "Let me read one of your poems."

This time I maintained silence. On one hand, I wanted my secret to remain my own; on the other, this was the first sign of happiness Della Barr had shown. Maybe, in this way, I could help her feel better about being at the home. Maybe we could be friends. But could I trust her to keep my secret?

"No one knows about my poems," I whispered, leaning close to her.

"Okay," she whispered back. "I won't tell."

I looked right into her pretty blue eyes from which tears no longer fell. She crossed her heart.

"I promise," she added.

I hesitated, then asked, "Do *you* write poetry?" I was thinking maybe a little blackmail could be worked out, if it came to that.

"No. I write books."

Now that surprised me. "Books?" I echoed like a dummy.

"Have you ever heard of *The Orange Cat Mystery* series?"

"Sure. I have a couple of 'em in my collection."

"Only two? Well, if I autograph them for you, may I read one of your poems?" She held out a right hand for me to shake again. "I'm D. K. Barr, author of *The Orange Cat Mysteries*."

"*You?*"

"Yes, me."

"This seems like a strange place for someone like you to be. Why are you..."

"Why am I here? Because my daughter moved to Scotland temporarily and she worries that I can't take care of myself. But I can. I survived a stroke and I'm recovering just fine, but to keep her from worrying, I'll stay until she comes back."

"I thought you'd been brought here against your will."

She laughed. "Oh, you heard about my little hissy fit, did you? That's because they were *trying to feed me!* With a spoon and a bib, as if I'm a drooling child. I am perfectly capable of feeding myself... and doing everything else myself. No one would believe me until I... um, spoke a little forcefully."

"And threw a tray at them."

"Well, yes, that too."

We laughed hard at that. Just because we're old doesn't mean we're infants again. Just because we need help doesn't mean we're completely helpless. Sometimes you have to let your voice be heard.

I got serious again. "But you've been crying so much. You must miserable here."

She shook her head. "I've been crying because I won't see my daughter for a year. We're very close, and I'm used to seeing her every day." Tears welled again, but this time she blinked them back. "But, if I can make friends, especially the type who like to read and write, then I'll be all right until she returns."

I pondered the secret stash of words I'd scribbled over the last few years, then I gave her a big grin.

"Well, I'll be! Here I thought I was the only one who'd ever enjoy Maple Lane Manor."

"My goodness, no! I love life, and just because Karen is overseas doesn't mean I'm shutting down." She held out her hand, I took it mine, and we both stood. "Let's go look at your books."

"I've been working on a novel, too," I said quietly as we left the lounge. "A love story, actually. You think it's weird that an old guy would write a romance novel?"

Her eyes lit up again as she laughed and squeezed my fingers. "I bet you write a fine romance novel."

As we walked hand in hand toward my room, I figured in time I might come to be known by another name: *Chip, You Ol' Dog, You.*

K.D. McCrite writes touching and funny stories that portray ordinary people living lives from the depths of their extraordinary souls. Her "Confessions of April Grace" Series (Thomas Nelson Publishing) is a hilarious series for 'tweens. The titles include In Front of God and Everybody, 2011; Cliques, Hicks, and Ugly Sticks, 2011; and Chocolate-Covered Baloney, 2012. She also writes for Annie's Attic Mysteries, The Deed in the Attic, 2011; The Unfinished Sonata, 2011; A Stony Point Christmas, 2012; The Ring in the Attic, 2013.

Little Wing

by J.L. Gentry

The jolt of the air was devastating. Each attempt to reconcile her flying failed. She gasped as the pain of her injury seared through her body. The air around her was almost too violent to breathe. She coughed, trying to fill her lungs while falling through the stormy air toward land she could not see. A rocky peak appeared out of nowhere. She tilted her body, racked in pain, to avoid collision. Barely clearing the obstacle, she righted herself, lowering her flight to view a barren surface full of sharp rocks and dark sandy soil. The surface below the storm was like none she had ever seen or imagined. She had known only the fertile glades and hills of her homeland. This space, outside of the lochs that bounded her land, felt of desperation. It was a desolate place. A place they were only allowed to pass over on their final journey. So taken by the ragged, sharp vision, she lost perspective; the surface seemed to reach up and grab her, pulling her into its grip. She stumbled, lurching forward, wings clutched for protection, but still her limbs were bruised against the rocky surface. The wind roared around her and the blowing rain masked her tears of desperation and pain. Failure consumed her as she pulled herself into a ball and felt the irritation from the many cuts and scrapes administered to her by the unforgiving rocky surface.

It was done. Her first and only mission. Her one goal in life, smashed against so many rocks on a desolate coast. The pity absorbed her as she shivered; the pain in her knees a suitable punishment for her inability to meet her obligation. With one deep breath, she envisioned her demise on the rocky shore. Her soul would abandon her long before she perished for lack of food or water. She had been raised to thrive in the bondage. Without that, she would fade away like the mist being devoured by morning sun.

Give in. Let it happen. You have failed, she thought to herself, and she felt the shift starting to happen as another shiver ran through her body from the inside out. It was a deep, subtle shiver that echoed the finality of her situation.

A noise interrupted her fall into the inevitable. It was a quiet sound, yet somehow it found its way to her ears above the din of the storm. Her eyes rose as much from curiosity as irritation at being disturbed in her spiral into devastation.

"There you are!" His voice had a tinge of fear along with anger and relief. "How long have you been on the ground? Are you hurt? Can you fly?"

"I..." She couldn't answer. Her only reaction was to stare at him with emotionless eyes.

He leaned down, looking at those eyes, his expression changing from release to irritation.

"So you've already started to still yourself?" he said in a hushed and harsh tone. "Look at me," he demanded. "You are not going to turn your back on your destiny. There is still time. Take my hand. I will give you strength." He reached out his hand in invitation to her. She looked at it as if it were a foreign object.

"Take it. Take it or you will perish."

"I'm not strong enough. I have failed."

He knew he could not force her to recapture her calling. She had to make that choice of her own volition. Without words, he stood as tall as he could, the majesty of his physique like hard stone against the pummeling rain and wind.

She looked at him, his wings tucked against the wind yet still looking aged and powerful, as if they could swat the bad weather away at will. Even in the overcast space the colors on them seemed to glow, flowing from blue to orange, as if he lit the air on fire with his flight. He was the finest of the escorts and the most admired among all of her people. She had been fortunate that he had been given the responsibility to escort her. The steeled blue in his eyes told her that he would not be defeated by mere weather or the stupidity of a novice who didn't have the courage to withstand some pain. As she looked at him, he held out both his hands again.

Slowly an ember of hunger started to glow in her heart. She felt the pang of unfulfilled wishes. They left her wanting for satisfaction. Fueled by that hunger, she reached up to grab his hand.

"There. That is what I want to see," he said. "Can you stand?"

She reached for him. The large hand was gentle as he grasped her, giving her a place of purchase so she could raise herself up under her own strength.

He saw her bloodied knees and bruised legs. With his touch, she seemed to gain focus along with new strength. Her head tilted back and their eyes met. He saw a flame burning and it brought a smile to his lips. As if to signal her, he spread his wings, the fire on the tips almost glowing. She followed suit. When she had almost reached full extension, he saw her wince in pain and her eyes widened in fear.

"Easy," he comforted, his voice strong against the blowing winds. Letting go of her hand, he put his fingers exactly on the spot where she had felt the pain surge. Slowly, he started a gentle probing massage of the very muscle that was knotted in pain. The pressure of his touch made her release a small yelp, but soon she felt her muscles warm and relax. Her wing reached its full extension and she smiled.

"We do not have much time. You will feel this injury with every flap of your wings, but you are capable of withstanding much more pain than you think you can. Are you ready to fly?"

She breathed deep and looked at him. "I have no choice." Her voice was resolute as she took position just behind him, ready for his lead.

He turned windward to take advantage of the lift, just in time to be struck in the head with a piece of flying debris. She watched as a red line of blood traced the side of his face. His eyes first looked surprised and then took on a glaze of shock as he fell to his knees and crumbled to the ground.

Before she could think she was at his side, taking his head in her hands and wiping the blood from his brow.

"Damn, you! Wake!" she shouted. Uncontrolled words erupted as she pleaded into the barren space around her, knowing they were futile, yet hoping someone would hear her pleas and tell her what to do. Rocking with his head in her lap, she wept in desperation. Self-pity started to well up inside her, but she pulled back from it; gathering what strength she could, she raised her head to the skies and let out a scream painted with anger and fear.

The wind howled, ridiculing her whimpering. It made her realize that she was small in this world. She opened her eyes and looked down at his strong face. Her fingers reached out and touched that place on the side of his neck where the life beat of his heart could be felt. Nothing.

A chill emptied her and she looked, seeing his face grow ashen. "What should I do?" she screamed at the wind. It laughed at her rage by throwing a salty splash of seawater at her. Anger erupted inside her and she looked down at her fallen escort. "You will not die! I will not allow it! Now, breathe. I order you to breathe! You have not fulfilled your obligation to me. You can die all you want when I have been delivered to my bondage, and no sooner!"

Her fisted hand pounded his chest and she found relief in delivering the blow. Again, the impact stinging her hand with sweet pain, giving her a pleasure she had never felt. Her life had been lived in an emotional bliss. It had been crafted to protect her from ever going to extremes. This feeling of anger and rage was like the taste of forbidden fruit. She wondered why she had never been allowed this pleasure and, at once, knew the answer. The pleasure was to be her gift in bondage. Only in her attachment would she be allowed to let her emotions play free and without limit. She laughed out loud, knowing that she was destined to perish on the ugly, stark shore, so there was no need to hold back. Let her rage flow. *Do not just dissolve*, she told herself. *Do not close your eyes and fade. Go with the taste of anger in your mouth.*

She had lost track of what she had been doing. The loud slap of her hand across his face woke her. How many times had she struck him? She couldn't recall, but something had changed. His eyes fluttered. She gasped and slapped him again with all of her strength. Even that was barely enough to reach into his mind and pull him back to life. One more, and then another, and another, as tears ran down her cheeks and the wet air tossed her hair into a tangle of knots. His hand reached up and grabbed her wrist, the steel blue of his eyes locking onto hers.

"Thank you," was all he said.

Her hand brushed the side of his face and she smiled at the sensation of the touch, fingertips tracing the angles of his jaw and contours of his mouth. She had not noticed how the cut of his face almost defined masculinity. How had she missed it?

He smiled back at her, feeling the touch as warmth through his body. In an instant, the smile evaporated and he bolted upright, pushing her away from him. A shot of pain in his forehead raged through the fog his mind. He knew something was wrong with her. Something had changed.

"No." His voice was stern and deep. "There can be nothing between us. I cannot allow that. You must be delivered. " He looked at her with a penetrating stare and did not like what he saw. Standing, he winced in pain and moved his hands for her to stop when she reached to help him.

"It will be difficult. You have allowed yourself the release of emotions ahead of your bonding. I can see the bloodeye forming. Your lust is beginning to swell. We are dangerously late."

He looked up into the stormy sky and stumbled as he turned, his legs weak from his injury.

She rose, standing next to him. He saw something new in her posture. Something seductive. The wind and water made her thin robe cling to her, showing him the beauty that was blossoming inside her.

"You cannot travel," she said, a new tone of command in her voice. "Not in this storm. I am not certain that I can make it, but if you give me the direction I will go alone."

"Direction?" he said motioning across the sky with his hand. "How could direction make sense in this storm? You need the sense of a guide. It is my duty to lead you, and lead you I will. In the air I will be more comfortable."

She watched him struggle. Was it pride or duty that pumped him with strength? Her heart began to melt as she felt the emotions roiling inside her. On weak legs he turned to her, and his wings unfolded to their full extension a second time. Even in the storm, the colors of his feathers seemed bright, the orange tips almost glowing. Tilting his head back, eyes closed, he raised his arms away from his sides and channeled the strength of his Canda spirit with the ancient breathing pattern. He made the chant that guides were taught with a voice as wonderful as any music she had ever heard. The low notes he sang made her relax and ease past the pain she still felt in her wings. He was singing a healing chant, each note giving her a sense that all would be well in the world and her destiny was still hers to achieve. She didn't even realize her own eyes had closed and that he had stopped his chant until she heard his voice.

"It is time." He was standing in front of her, his wings at the ready. A slight smile curled his upper lip as he took satisfaction in weaving her wellness with his chant. "Are you ready?"

"I will follow you to my destiny." The phrase was the one used at the beginning of the submission. She was grounding herself by following the ritual again and affirming her commitment. She continued with her recitation, "It is you who will allow me to submit to the beauty."

"No, it is you who has the beauty within," he responded with the guide's words. Words that had been repeated since ancient times. As he spoke, he turned windward and his knees dipped and his wings curled. In a sudden release, his body exploded into flight. She was carried along by him, her own wings moving before she could even think to fly. She was a reflection of his power, a shadow that gained height against the perilous winds of the storm. With each flap of her wings she felt confidence, and wondered why she had been scared of the storm in the first place. Looking around at the swirling clouds, she felt how to ride the currents of air instead of having them control her. *It was just bad weather,* she thought to herself as she stayed close to her guide, still drawing on his strength.

At altitude he turned and smiled. "We are close. We will make our commitment."

Her heart began to race in anticipation, tinged with slight dread. She looked at the strong frame of her guide and longed to touch the length of his wings. She wondered why she had not noticed the hypnotic effect of his power before. A flash of lightning made her eyes flare in blindness for a brief moment, the bright light alerting her to the danger of her thoughts. There was not much time. She had already started to submit, finding connection with her guide. It took all her strength to hold herself in check and not lose herself in the desire for the beautiful winged man in front of her. The one with a voice that could sing the gods to sleep.

She focused on what the elders had told her and wondered about the man she would submit to. Would her master be gentle and thoughtful? Would he treat her with a harsh but fair hand? Would she find ways to please him? Would she be inventive enough to meet his needs? She only knew she was to be given to a gifted man. The elders had told her that much before the ceremony that had prepared her to be released to submission. They had told her that he had a depth and wealth that needed her special skills. If she conformed to his particular demands, she would be cared for for a long time. All of her training and skills would be needed to keep him content for the many years to come.

"We are nearly there," his voice interrupted her reverie. "You must begin to prepare yourself. You will need to present yourself soon. He will be impatient since we are late. You will have to sooth his ire."

"I hope he is not a harsh master." *I hope he is just like you.* She clenched her teeth, fighting the raging desire to claim her guide for her own.

"He will be the master that he is. You must adapt to his needs. The peace of our world is tied to it. You know the legends as well as I do."

"How did we ever get ourselves into this state?"

He turned to look at his charge and saw the struggle in her eyes. He realized what was happening and felt new urgency to reach their goal. Wanting to keep her focused on what she needed to do, he spoke of their history in a calming voice as the winds tore the air around them.

"It is all in the ancient lore. Eons ago we faced a peril that would end our lives. Our gifts were almost lost. The hosts of old had turned fickle under our touch and thought they could prosper without paying duty to us. They abandoned us to seek their own fortunes. On the verge of extinction, our elders found a new host culture through the portal that is our destination. Now we live through their generosity."

"But we are slaves to them. They don't pay us much regard for the services we render on their behalf."

"You speak as though you have more experience of them than you can possibly have."

"I hear rumors. The other initiates talk. They tell stories. Our instructors won't confirm, but they still prepare us for a life of servitude. I am smart enough to know what that means."

"You are smart, but not experienced enough to know that you should not make judgments until you have had the chance to observe for yourself. I caution you now to stop this fretting and prepare yourself for the pairing. The moment of bondage is soon upon you."

"What is the process? The instruction was never specific enough. They just say that the pairing happens. Is there some ceremony? Some acknowledgment from our hosts?"

"We have never stood on formality with our hosts. They are a powerful race, but one of simple needs." He looked back at her and decided that he needed to tell her more to keep her wanting to go forward. "The pairing is a physical event. It happens within seconds of your making the first contact. You should expect to feel a swelling of emotion and taste the pleasure of holding someone else's essence. At that point you will see. You will understand that the giving is in both directions."

"What if I don't cross over? What if I fail to pair?"

He pulled his wings up, slowing his movement and veering into a slow descent. She looked at the majesty of his body in flight and saw the light glinting off of his colored plumes. She hadn't even noticed that they had cleared the storm and were headed to a sunrise on the edge of the coast.

"We are here. There is no time to think, there is only time to act. I can feel his tension. He has a strong aura. His concern is turning to a state of anger, although it feels as though he is just upset in general.

His emotions run deep and his needs are strong. You will be used often. I can feel that."

"Are you capable of pairing? How do you know this?"

"No, I am not allowed to pair, but part of my duty is to deliver you to the correct partner, so I was given a taste of his spirit so that I could recognize his presence when we arrived. I may not be as capable as you, but I am still a sensitive."

They landed on a small expanse of sandy beach next to a large rock cliff. A deep crevice in the front of the rock face caught her attention. It held no detail. No light reflected off of its surface. It was a deep black that seemed as absolute as nothing.

She watched as he moved up to the void and placed his hand on the black space. His hair and wings moved back as if a gust of wind had emitted from the void, but she felt no movement of air. He removed his hand and turned to her with a warm smile on his face.

"All is at the ready, you must move now."

Her heart agreed and she stepped up to him.

"It is you I want," she said in a voice as pure as her desire.

He stepped up to her and placed a gentle kiss on her forehead. "Your feelings for me are real and I will cherish them for the rest of my days. You have captured my heart and will live in me for the rest of my days. But, we cannot be. It is as simple as that."

She felt the electric touch of his lips and with it the realization that he was right. Her heart weakened with the pain of loss and she lowered her head to hide a tear. He put a finger to her chin and raised her head, wiping the tear away with his thumb. "It is time. You have saved me in more ways than you know this day. For that I thank you. Now you must do the same on the other side of the portal."

Her hand traced his face to memorize the curve and feel. She stood erect, a surge of power resonating through her. It was a rush like she had never experienced before. It startled her and her eyes moved toward the void as she stepped away from the guide.

"Can you tell me anything? What can I expect?"

"He is young. He is brilliant. You will be challenged because his tastes are varied and strong. He has much confusion now. You will need to use all of your strength and training to keep him focused and direct him."

She touched the edge of the nothing and a force of blue light caught her. The blue began to change in intensity, fading and getting brighter in pulses. Her head snapped back and her eyes stared straight up as if seeing an answer revealed. Sweat beaded on her forehead as her breathing became rapid, almost as if rapture was close at hand. The wings that had carried her through life wrapped her and she shivered within their embrace. A mist began to rise from the wings as they dissolved around her. Cries of joy and pleasure/pain rang from her with a voice that was new yet still hers. The sounds caught her guide's ears, touching a painful place in his heart. He knew she was gone forever.

He waited, fighting his own desires, as the mist dissipated into the still air. He moved closer so he could see the total transformation before she stepped across the threshold for the first and final time. This was his favorite part as an escort, but there was no pleasure in his heart today.

The mist cleared and, in spite of his pain, he smiled. He may have even laughed in joy at what he saw. She stood before him, a wry smile on her face and a fire in her eyes. Her hair was long, wavy and a deep reddish-orange. Her skin was a silken white that almost glowed. She wore an outfit that was part robe and part corset, and her legs were dressed in black silk stockings and garters. The material was torn as if hungry hands had tried to own her, but failed.

"He has good taste and a potent imagination."

"Yes. You were right. This will take all of my skill and training. It will be worth it." She turned to gaze into the abyss. A slight wave of her hand brought an image into focus against the dark background.

"You should not."

"I choose to. You gave much to bring me here, it is fitting that you see my fate. It is the only thing I have left to share with you. Look and see." The confidence and strength in her voice made him bow his head in deference.

He raised his eyes and took in the image of a young man sitting at a desk, paper and pen in front of him, but not in use. Ticks of the clock sounded as he studied the image in the portal. There was a light in the eyes. A fire that made the escort smile and breathe faster. "What raw passion," he said, not taking his eyes from the image. "And he is so young." He looked at his ward in awe of how she had transformed, vixen-like before his eyes. "You may be too powerful for him. Will he be able to make you submit? It cannot be faked. They know a false posture and it will ruin the bondage."

"You needn't worry." Again her voice commanded his respect. Her power almost made him quiver. He looked at her as if for the first time and saw a passion as deep and alive as that in the young man's eyes. He knew then that she was committed and the union would be made. A future of rapture and failure lay before her with the child-man she was now attached to. The escort held back his questions and raised his arm across his chest in salute.

"You have saved me and I will always be in your debt. Do well in your bondage. Make me proud. Be the muse that your lineage has bred you to be. Give him the visions and stirrings that will make him create greatness. Keep our worlds at peace."

"My future awaits."

She stepped to the abyss, pausing to turn one last time.

"I will be a good muse to him. That I pledge."

She turned and stepped into her future.

J.L. Gentry is the author of SYN:FIN, the first in the Jim Harrison Chronicles. His alter ego is an IT professional with over thirty years of technical and managerial experience. When he is not working, writing, or harassing his family, he can be found running the roads and trails of wherever he happens to be that day. Enjoy life and run free.

Fall

by Shay Fabbro

The sun peeked over the hills, bathing the world in soft orange light. A slight breeze carrying winter's touch caressed Maryssa's skin, sending a shiver of delight down her spine. She raised her face to the sun, delighting in the warmth of the rays even as the wind cooled her through the multiple layers of clothing. The morning was her favorite time.

I wish I could see it.

Maryssa swallowed hard against the lump forming in her throat. She blinked back the tears, refusing to let them ruin her favorite time of day. Even though she couldn't see the world awakening, she could at least listen and enjoy it.

"I'm still waiting for the eggs, Maryssa."

"I'm going, I'm going," she mumbled.

Maryssa strode to the roost to collect the eggs that her mother needed to make breakfast. The hens were still asleep. Maryssa knew their heads would be nestled under wings streaked with burnt orange and brown. As she gathered eggs, she heard the plow team and milk cow moving about the barn, their whickers and moos indicating that they, too, were ready for their breakfast.

"No eggs again, my little Choukie?" Maryssa stroked her favorite bird's fiery orange head, enjoying the softness of the feathers and the hen's soft clucking in appreciation of the attention.

Maryssa brought the eggs to her momma before returning to the barn to complete her morning chores. The milk bucket was in its usual place, right on top of the short stool. She dragged both to the milk cow's stall, talking softly as she settled into place. As Maryssa began milking, the cow chewed her cud and flicked her tail side-to-side, barely missing smacking Maryssa in the face.

"Hey, now. Ease up on that thing."

The hypnotic sound of the milk hitting the pail made Maryssa yearn for her bed. Up and down went her hands, and *pshhht pshht* went the milk into the metal pail. Her jaws creaked as a yawn split her face.

When the pail was full, Maryssa carefully lifted it in both hands and made her way back to the house. The leaves crunched under her sturdy boots, and the sweet chirping of the birds accompanied her.

"Here, love — let me take that for you," Leisha said gently.

Maryssa gratefully handed the pail over to her mother. While it wasn't a long way from the barn to the house, it was enough that the muscles in her arms burned by the time she made it all that way.

"Oi, girl, your cheeks are red as autumn apples. Mighty cold out, is it?" Leisha said as she grabbed Maryssa's hands in her own, rubbing them to bring warmth back. Her mother's hands felt rough, much like her life had been since Pappa had passed.

It had fallen to her brothers to run the farm. But when the king had called on all able-bodied young men to join his armies, her two brothers had been forced to leave her and her mother alone. It had been hard with just the two of them to run things. Many of the outdoor chores fell to Maryssa. She was younger and stronger.

And she loved to be outside.

She could find something to be awestruck by nearly every day, from the quaint cooing of a dove to the sound of the wind moving through the trees. Maryssa vowed to be grateful no matter how tired she was or how much her muscles burned after plowing the fields or how much her hands bled after weeding the garden.

"Got a good batch of pumpkins this year. How'd you like to help me make a pie after breakfast?"

Maryssa smiled at her momma's request. If there was anything she loved as much as being outside, it was her mother's pumpkin pie. She could almost smell the nutmeg and cinnamon.

She sat and listened to her mother fix breakfast, the familiar sounds filling the room: the clank of the iron skillet on the stove, the sizzle of the eggs as they cooked, the soft thunking of the knife the bread was sliced. Her mother hummed a nonsensical tune while she placed the food on the table.

Maryssa loaded her plate, eager to finish breakfast so she and her mother could begin making the pies.

"Easy, Maryssa. You'll choke if you keep eating so fast."

"Sorry, Momma. Just excited to get to the pies."

"I understand. You know, you are so like your father, my Maryssa. When I would make pies, he would try to get me out of the kitchen so he could sneak a piece."

"I remember. I also remember you chasing him out of the house with a wooden spoon."

The two shared a giggle, the laughter easing the pain of his loss. As it faded, the silence stretched out before them. Leisha got up and began clearing the table. Maryssa could hear the tension in the clanking of the plates and silverware and her mother's breath as she fought the tears that threatened to come.

Maryssa felt the weight of the last few years on her shoulders. While other girls her age were getting married and having babies, she had been stuck on the farm, except for the occasional trip into town. It was difficult to meet nice young men when she was busy rushing through the stalls at the market looking for sugar or needle and thread.

It was especially difficult when she couldn't see them.

When Maryssa thought about the day she lost her sight, the bitterness threatened to choke her. It tasted of bile and anger and regret. She couldn't help but blame her father for dying, the king for demanding her brothers join his army, her brothers for leaving, her mother for refusing to remarry, her own rotten luck.

She had been in the loft of the barn shoving hay through the trapdoor to the main room beneath and cursing everything about her life. Her mother had refused to let her go into town for the spring festival, saying she didn't have time to accompany her daughter with all the work that needed to be done on the farm.

Maryssa didn't notice the rake buried in the hay until she stepped in the tines and the handle flew up and knocked smacked her in the forehead. She stepped back reflexively and into the void of the open trapdoor. Maryssa pinwheeled her arms hopelessly, knowing before her falling body met the ground that she'd never be able to stop herself.

She had spent the next few months in pain-filled unconsciousness. The potent drugs the healers forced down her throat weren't strong enough to numb the pain. She was tormented day and night by nightmares of her fall, waking with screams ripping from her throat, both from the fear and the pain. When she awoke from her stupor, she was horrified to find that she was blind.

"You're lucky to be alive at all, young lady. You broke several bones and lost a lot of blood," the healer had told her. "The damage to your head was so severe we feared it was beyond our abilities."

It had taken half a year to regain her strength and be able to walk again. The guilt at not being able to help with the farm pushed her to work toward get well. Her mother, with infinite patience, helped her memorize the path to and from the house to the barn, helped her learn to navigate the house, and how to dress herself and comb her hair.

Maryssa tried to appreciate her other senses. She noticed sounds and smells that had been pushed to the background while she had been so busy seeing the world. The world had come alive with screeches, chirps, rustling, musky odors, floral scents, barnyard stench.

But she missed her sight, missed seeing the birds singing their lovely tunes, missed seeing the squirrels and rabbits darting through the underbrush. Missed the changing of the colors with the coming of winter.

"Oh Maryssa, come here, love."

Maryssa got up from the table and joined her mother at the window, navigating the small dining room with ease.

"Your favorite oak has finally changed with the season. It looks like someone took the sun and shoved its yellow and orange rays into the very leaves of the tree." Maryssa tried to smile as Momma put an arm around her shoulders and pulled her close. "I wish you could see it, my daughter."

"I wish I could see it too." Maryssa blinked hard against the tears that threatened to spill over her cheeks. With a hitch in her voice she asked, "May I go to my room now?"

"Don't you want to help me with the pies?"

"I'm tired, Momma. Maybe some other time."

Though Maryssa couldn't see it, she knew her mother's lovely brown eyes would be filled with pity and sadness at watching her poor blind daughter shuffle up to her room.

Maryssa slammed the door to her room and stood shrouded in darkness, tears spilling down her cheeks. She lay down on her bed and buried her face in her pillow, sobbing out the last year's worth of frustration and anger and the unfairness that had robbed her of a vital part of who she was. She hated being a burden on her already over-worked mother. She had hoped that she might meet someone, get married, live on the farm and take over so her mother could finally rest.

What man would ever want me?

She closed her eyes, wondering if they were as blue as they were before the accident or if they were covered in yellowish film like her grandmother's had been before she had died. She was too afraid to ask.

Maryssa had loathed looking at her grandmother's milky eyes. They frightened her. She remembered how her aging Gran had turned into a bitter, nasty, demanding woman, completely dependent on others for everything and angry that she couldn't do things on her own.

What use can I ever be?

Leisha slowly mixed the ingredients for the pies, tears falling silently down her wrinkled cheeks. Weariness and despair had taken their toll, robbing her of much of her youthful beauty. Dealing with the loss of her husband and the absence of her two sons had been bad enough, but her daughter brought her the most worry and grief.

For the hundredth time since the accident, Leisha sent up a prayer to the Healer to restore her daughter's sight. It was so unfair, wanting all the things that other girls her age had and being forced to live the life of an old spinster maid, spending all her days on an old rundown farm.

What will she do when I'm gone?

Leisha slid the two pies into the cast iron oven. She added more wood to the bed of coals beneath the oven. She dragged her weary body to a chair at the table and laid her head on her hands. Leisha had hoped Maryssa would learn to accept her blindness and eventually start acting like the carefree girl she had been before the accident, but she found her easily falling back into bitterness and resentment. She knew in her heart that her daughter needed to understand that she still had a purpose, that she wasn't some useless burden. *What can I do to help her?*

The scent of nutmeg and cinnamon filled the room and the warmth from the fire lulled her into a light doze. Before sleep claimed her, Leisha sent up a prayer to the Leader.

Help my Maryssa to find herself again.

Maryssa awoke, heart racing. She rubbed her eyes, the habit hard to break even after a year of being blind. She sat up, fear sending icy fingers down her spine.

Something's wrong.

"Momma?" Her voice shook as she stood up on shaky legs, eager and yet afraid to find out what was frightening her so badly.

What's that smell?

Something tickled at her senses, urging her to action. Her breath came in gasps as she made her way to the door. She knew what she smelled, and yet the word eluded her.

Maryssa coughed as she opened the door, and her breath stuck in her throat.

Smoke!

"Momma! Where are you?"

Maryssa's voice echoed in the house. A sob broke free, and she stood rooted to the spot, unsure whether to continue to the kitchen or leave through the backdoor. The smell was strongest in the direction of the kitchen, and every instinct screamed at her to turn and run the other way. But she couldn't leave until she knew where her momma was.

Maybe she left me here.

Terror greater than anything she'd ever known enveloped her, leaving her unable to form a coherent thought. She needed her mother, couldn't survive without her.

She wouldn't have left you, Maryssa.

Her father's deep soothing voice cut through the fear. Her mother had to be somewhere in the house. And if she wasn't answering, she was hurt and in danger of perishing if the house was indeed on fire.

Going against her instincts, Maryssa moved into the kitchen, the smoke strong enough to cause her eyes to water and her chest to cough out the offending substance. She could feel more heat coming from the oven than was normal. She got down on her hands and knees, breathing deeply of air that was less smoky and moved her hands back and forth, hoping to feel for her mother.

That's the bump in the wood just near the table. You've already checked this area.

Maryssa stopped moving. Randomly searching was doing no good and wasting time. She took a steadying breath, trying to control the panic. The heat was growing stronger and she could hear the crackle of flames as they consumed the wood.

She fixed a picture of the room in her mind. Moving deliberately and quickly, she searched the area closest to the hallway where she had entered the room. She reached the table and stopped. The smoke and heat was becoming unbearable. If she didn't find her mother soon she would have to make her way out of the house.

Suddenly, her hands came across something that felt out of place. She reached higher.

Her shoes!

Using the chair, she picked herself up off the floor, chest constricting as she moved higher into the dense smoke. Maryssa coughed so hard she vomited. Each breath sent her into another coughing fit.

I can't do this!

"Momma, wake up!" Maryssa shook her mother. "I need you."

It's up to you, my Maryssa.

Once again her father's voice stopped her cold. If she and her mother were to survive, it was up to her to get them out.

Maryssa eased her mother off the chair and onto the floor as gently as she could. Maryssa was small for sixteen, but all the years spent working the farm had toughened her more than she realized. Her muscles bunched under her clothing as she heaved her mother across the floor. The strain caused her to break into another coughing fit. Maryssa hit her knees, her face as close to the floor as she could get it. The air was easier to breathe, but it wouldn't be that way for long.

Still on her knees, Maryssa slowly dragged her mother along the floor. The heat was growing, and Maryssa heard the alarming sound of wood falling nearby. For once she was glad that she couldn't see the orange and yellow flames destroying her family's home.

Keep going, girl. The door is not far.

With her father's voice urging her on, Maryssa dragged her unconscious mother to the door. Maryssa stood to open it, holding her breath to keep from breathing in the smoky air. She bent over to pick up her mother and gave one last heave, arm muscles groaning under the strain. Her chest burned with the need for air, but Maryssa feared that if she took one more breath of the smoke, she would succumb.

She burst forth from the open door, the sweet clean air filling her lungs and her tear-stained cheeks. Maryssa pulled her mother across the ground until she had gone far enough from the house that she thought they would be safe.

She held her mother's head in her lap while she listened to the fire burn her home to the ground. Maryssa wondered if anyone would see the smoke and come to help. There was a well on the property, but she doubted she could put out the blaze on her own.

Her mother's chest rose and fell under her hand. Within moments of being in the fresh air, her mother began coughing and moving her head from side-to-side.

"Momma! You're all right." Maryssa sobbed as she rocked back and forth, still holding her mother's head in her lap.

"Maryssa... why am I... what happened?" Leisha mumbled.

"A fire, Momma—" A coughing fit doubled Maryssa over.

"What?" Leisha's voice was weak and scratchy.

"Leisha, Maryssa, where are you?"

"We're here," Maryssa tried to shout but she coughed so hard she nearly fainted.

The nearest neighbors, Thom and Mychele, along with their children, helped spread the word to others living close by about the fire. Though they tried valiantly to save the house, there was nothing they could do.

Maryssa sat with Thom and Mychele's oldest daughter. She was knowledgeable about herbs and had mixed something that helped soothe her throat.

"It's a miracle you made it out of there," Mychele said.

"It was no miracle. Maryssa saved us," Leisha said, squeezing her daughter's hand.

"I didn't do anything except smell the smoke and fumble around in the dark," Maryssa mumbled angrily.

"You pulled your mom from a burning house. How can you say you didn't do anything?" Mychele asked.

"If I could see, I bet I could have gotten us out of the house sooner and maybe even gotten help."

"Your mother was already near death when you found her. If you would have remained sleeping for any longer, she wouldn't be with us now," Mychele said.

You smelled the smoke because you were blind, my Maryssa.

Maryssa swallowed hard.

"She's right. You've been using your other senses without realizing it," Leisha said, her eyes filling with tears.

Is it really possible?

Maryssa didn't want to think of her blindness as something useful and good. It was so much easier to be angry at the world and blame everyone and everything for taking something precious from her.

For the first time in a year, hope blossomed in her heart. If she could sense a fire early enough to drag her mother from danger, there probably wasn't much else she couldn't do.

Maybe I could even have a family of my own.

"Here... I brought you something to eat."

Maryssa recognized the voice. "Thank you, Conor. Thank you for coming to help us."

"I only wish I had come sooner. The thought of you in that burning house... well, you know. It just makes my heart hurt," Conor stammered.

"That's very kind of you."

"You're right brave, Miss Maryssa. And you sure are pretty, too."

Maryssa opened and closed her mouth, quite certain she looked like a crappie fish out of water, but unable to do anything else.

"Uhhh, um... I mean... oh gosh, I ought not be saying things like that to you as though we was promised. I best be getting back to help Pa."

Maryssa shouted something at the retreating Conor, though she couldn't really be sure what she said with her thoughts reeling as they were. *He said I was pretty. And brave. And pretty!*

"Things will be okay, my Maryssa." Her mother's voice held the hint of a smile.

Maryssa's heart soared. "I know they will, Momma."

I know they will.

⌀

Dr. Shay Fabbro currently lives in Grand Junction, CO with her husband, Rich, and their two cats. She is the author of the *Portals of*

Destiny series, the *Adventures of Alexis Davenport* series, and has been published in the military sci anthology, *Battlespace*.

My Orange Karen

by Christopher Cantley

Whether it was the lightning or an animal seeking shelter that caused it, Lucille was having a fit. She was a sturdy workhorse, but if anything started to upset her you were sure to find out. I could hear her whinnies clearly as I stepped out onto the porch. My lantern struggled to illuminate the darkness of the thunderstorm. A faint tangerine circle was all I could see, except when the lightning decided to make itself known. Sharp wooden raps could be heard amidst the thunder; Lucille was kicking the barn walls.

"It's just a storm, old girl," I mumbled. "You've been through these before."

I eased the barn door open, holding the lantern high to light the way ahead of me. I could see the horse's head above her stall wall, eyes wide in fright. Among her whinnies and snorts, I heard something else. Someone was crying. I hurried to open the stall door, my aging bones complaining all the way. Huddled in the corner of the stall was a child. She couldn't have been more than twelve years in age. Her hair was matted with mud and blood, and she was covered in scratches.

Of greatest concern was a particularly painful looking reddish-orange mark the length of her calf that I took as a burn.

"What in the world happened to you, child?" I sighed. She must have had the ears of a fox, because her eyes turned to me in shock. The poor child tried to push further into the corner, but the wall was already at her back. I carefully set my lantern on the floor, keeping it clear of any straw, and raised my hands in what I hoped was a non-threatening gesture.

"Easy, girl. You're safe."

Her eyes glistened with tears and her lower lip quivered, but she seemed to relax slightly. I crouched down, bones creaking.

"I'm Nathan," I said, smiling. "What's your name?"

The girl shrugged her shoulders slightly, but didn't speak. I read this as a sign her fear was subsiding, so I tried to edge closer. Her dark eyes were still wary, but a slight smile crossed her lips.

"Where is your family? Are you lost?"

I held a hand out to her, and her smile grew fuller. She reached toward me shyly. It was then I saw the poor child had not a stitch of clothing on. I grabbed Lucille's blanket on the door as the girl's small hand brushed mine.

"Are you my Papa?" she asked quietly. I came close to dropping the blanket in surprise. I was at a loss on how to respond.

"No," I said, "I have no children. Don't you know who your parents are?" The smile drifted away from her face. The flickering orange of the lantern highlighted a growing sadness in her eyes, and I began to regret asking that question. I unfolded the blanket and wrapped her up in it. "Let's get you cleaned up."

Back in my little house, I stoked the fire and put a kettle on to heat up some water. The little girl sat in the kitchen nibbling on some bread and fruit. In the spare room, I set up a small cot for my guest and pulled out the copper washtub. Then I headed to the closet to search for something she could wear. I pushed aside my clothes to reveal a small, dusty chest. Inside, there were clothes for a child her size. I struggled to hold back tears, remembering how my daughter suffered from the sickness that took her life. I pulled a few selections and went back to the kitchen to be greeted by a big smile and a hug.

"Thank you for the food," the girl whispered. "Can I stay with you? Will you be my Papa?"

Even though I knew she should be reunited with her family, wherever they were, I felt so much love at that moment I couldn't refuse.

"Yes to both," I said. "We'll need to decide what to call you, though. First, you need a bath, child."

Once I filled the tub, I got another kettle set for rinse water. The girl settled in with a sigh of comfort. I handed her a wash cloth and some soap, and started to leave the room.

"Don't go," she begged. "Can you help me with my hair, Papa?"

I couldn't help but smile. Kneeling by the tub, I wet down her disheveled hair. I worked up lather with the soap and started to scrub her head. She winced as the suds washed down across her wounds, but she seemed to appreciate getting clean. I pulled the other kettle out of the fire and told the girl to shut her eyes. The mud and blood and soap washed down into the tub, revealing beautiful orange hair.

"No one in this county has hair that color," I said, surprised. "Where are you from, child?"

The girl didn't answer. She finished up in the bath and dried off. Out of the clothes I selected, she chose a light yellow dress with darker coral flowers. I watched her turn about in her new dress, eyes alight with happiness. It was then I decided on what to call her.

"Karen," I mused. "You have the same eyes as my mother. Do you like it?"

She nodded with a big grin, and I felt happier than I had in years.

⌘

During the first months of our new life, I did what any father would do and began to teach Karen about life on the farm. She learned planting, harvesting, and what to water when. We went over how to spot several types of bugs that would attack the plants and the best way to eliminate them. We also started to explore the forest. There I taught her plants that were safe to eat, and which were to be avoided. I began teaching her how to hunt with a bow or spear as well. I admit I was a little surprised at how well Karen did with the hunting, and I suspected that could be a good future job for her. The only skill we had difficulty with was horse riding.

"I'm scared, Papa!"

Karen's arms were clenched tightly around my waist as we stood beside Lucille. The horse stood there eyeing the child, occasionally stamping her hoof. Lucille seemed to remember that Karen invaded her stall. I knelt down by my adopted daughter and held onto her hands.

"You're my little girl and I love you," I told her. "I promise you that I will never let you come to harm."

She gave me a huge grin and a tight hug.

"Okay, Papa. You'll stay close?"

"Of course."

Karen dutifully watched as I showed her how to brush down the horse before saddling. She tried to lift the saddle, but it was far too heavy for her. After spreading out a blanket, I placed the saddle and explained how to adjust the straps and stirrups. I fitted Lucille with a bridle without a bit and attached a lead line to it. I lifted Karen up onto the saddle. She leaned down and rubbed the horse's neck, which Lucille really enjoyed. I took hold of the lead while Karen made the clicking noises I taught her. The horse settled into a slow walk around the barn. The fiery-haired girl held onto two handfuls of mane and giggled in delight. When the training ride was over, I had Karen give Lucille a carrot and showed the girl how to check the hooves for any stones that may have been picked up. We removed the tack and took turns giving Lucille another good brushing. More than once, the horse lowered her head to Karen for a nose rub that the girl gleefully gave. My little Karen had made a new friend.

The next day I decided it was time to take a trip into the village. The farm was pretty self-sufficient, so I only needed to travel every couple of months. Karen helped me hitch Lucille up to our little cart and we headed out on the trail. Our journey was a leisurely one. We stopped every so often when something caught Karen's eye. She seemed especially fond of a local flower called Dragon's Fire. Its petals were an amalgamation of oranges and reds, looking very similar to the layers of a flame. By the time we reached the midway point of the trip, Karen had amassed quite the bouquet. It was also at this area that I saw something strange a little distance from the trail. I climbed down from the cart, but when I reached to help Karen down, I noticed she looked worried.

"What is it, honey?"

She toyed with one of the flowers, casting apprehensive looks into the woods.

"Can't we just go to village?" she said, in a whining tone. "I don't like it here."

"It'll just take a minute, Karen. Then we'll be on our way."

I lifted her off the cart and gave her a quick hug. We pushed our way through the underbrush carefully. Thankfully, there wasn't any mud to bog us down and we arrived at the strangest clearing I had ever seen. The whole area looked as some sort of explosion went off. Trees were shattered into toothpicks and a great furrow cleaved the ground. Some of the ruined trees had small patches of scorching, but didn't look to be victims of fire. It was truly puzzling. Even more curious was watching Karen's behavior as I explored. She was shifting her weight from one foot to the other and her eyes darted all around the clearing. Something was really bothering her.

"Karen, what's wrong?" I asked.

"Can we go, please?" she asked. "What if the monster comes back?"

"Monster?"

Karen nodded emphatically. "What else could have done this, Papa?"

I had no good answer for her. When she grabbed my arm and pulled, I allowed her to lead me from the strange site. We resumed our journey, but the scene in that clearing kept tumbling through my mind. What had caused such catastrophic damage? What had my little fiery-haired girl so on edge?

The village of Brine Valley was a score of rickety buildings and oddly named. It was neither by salt water nor in a valley, so one really had to wonder what the city founders had been drinking. Still, it was the only spot of civilization within one hundred miles, and was a popular haunt for mages and apothecaries. Dragon's Fire flowers and several other plants were extremely rare elsewhere. So, despite the dilapidated buildings, Brine Valley's market was a thriving place. Karen's eyes grew wide with delight when our cart rolled up to the edge of the village.

"Are there kids here?"

"Absolutely," I said. "Lots of kids. There's a small play area on the other side of town. Do you want to go there?"

She grinned and nodded. I hated letting her off on her own, but I wanted to get our supplies and be back on the road before dark. I looked toward the market and caught sight of a familiar face. One of the guardsmen on duty had the unfortunate job of letting me know my daughter had died from the dreaded Deathlung sickness. He visited every once in a while, just to see how I was doing, and he became my closest friend. His gaze drifted our way and I waved. The guard signaled one of his compatriots to cover his area, and then ran over.

"Nathan," he said, extending his hand. "How have you been?"

"Good, Jensen," I shook his hand, and then I guided my adoptive daughter forward.

"This is Karen, and she needs your help."

Jensen did a quick double take at the girl's unusual orange hair, but offered his hand. She shyly shook it.

"How can I help you, Karen?"

"Papa said there was a place to play," she said quietly. "Can I go play?"

Jensen chuckled and helped her down from the cart.

"I'd be happy to show you the way, little one. See you in an hour, Nathan?"

I nodded, and then watched my little girl skip off to have some fun. The hour went by pretty quickly in the marketplace. I caught up on the latest gossip and compared notes on the growing season with other farmers. A few of the visiting shoppers whispered of strange creatures popping up across the land. Bandits we had faced several times, but monsters were another story. Maybe Karen's thoughts about the clearing were true. I started loading the supplies into the cart while waiting for her return. It didn't take long before I saw Jensen walking back with Karen in tow, but something was amiss. She was crying.

"Jensen," I sighed. "What happened?"

"There was a little incident, I'm afraid. Karen got into a fight with a couple boys that were teasing her. Gave them bloody noses."

The little girl kept her head down and scratched designs in the dirt with her foot. I never would have believed her capable of such a thing, but the blood on her dress was proof enough.

"Tell me what happened, Karen."

"It started off okay," she began, sniffling. "Some of the kids were very nice. They were playing some sort of game with a stick and ball. I tried learning how to play, but I wasn't very good at it. Then two boys who were watching started calling me 'Freaky Orange Karen'. I couldn't help it; I just got so angry."

I knelt down and hugged my little girl close.

"I'm sorry you had to experience that, child. No matter where you go in the world, there will be those who are cruel to people who are different."

Jensen signaled he was heading back to his post, and I nodded my thanks.

"It's true," I continued, "that your fiery hair makes you different. I believe that it is a gift to be treasured. The best defense against people who mock with names is to take the names as your own." I lifted Karen's chin to meet her eye to eye.

"You are beautiful, my Orange Karen. Never let anyone tell you different."

The child's tears flowed more freely, but from happiness.

"You're the best Papa ever."

∽〇∾

As time steadily marched on, Karen not only worked hard to master all that I was teaching her, but she also grew up. My beautiful little girl had metamorphosed into a beautiful young woman seemingly overnight. I wasn't the only one who noticed the change. On our trips into the village, the same boys who teased her now sought to accompany her everywhere she went. Karen politely accepted the attention, at least until one of them tried to reach under her shirt. When the fiery spirit that matched her flaming hair burst forth, the boys, with bloodied noses once again, learned to keep a respectful distance.

Our life continued peacefully until one night in early winter. We were just sitting down to dinner, when we heard Lucille whinnying. It was snowing lightly, but that had never bothered the horse before. Karen walked over to a window that faced the barn and peered out into the snow. Her brow gradually furrowed as she scanned what she could see of the yard.

"Something doesn't feel right, Papa."

Lucille whinnied some more, sounding more frantic. Without a word, I pulled on a heavy leather coat and grabbed my wood axe. Karen grabbed her bow and a knife, and then we ventured outside. Snow continued to fall, but the moon occasionally showed its face from behind the dark clouds. Its light, combined with the firelight streaming from the windows, allowed us to see quite easily. The yard was only lightly dusted in white, but there was enough snow to see foreign footprints all about.

"What do you make of these?" I whispered to Karen.

She squatted down to examine them, but ended up just shrugging her shoulders.

"They walk on two feet, but aren't people," the fiery-haired teenager said, scowling. "See those marks? The ones ahead of the toe prints? Those are made by claws."

I was about to respond when we both heard a growling hiss. Karen stood and had an arrow on her bowstring in the blink of an eye, searching for the source. I caught sight of three strange beings crouched beside the wagon.

"Merciful gods," I breathed, "what are those things?"

They clearly had the build to walk upright, but seemed as though they would be just as comfortable traveling on all fours. Their heads were somewhat reminiscent of dogs except for the scaly quality to their skin. Each was dressed in a variety of animal hides and carried small spears in their clawed hands. Their eyes glowed eerily, reflecting the orange firelight from the windows.

"What do you want?" I called to them.

One of the three stood and voiced a series of barking noises. A rustling came from the woods, and then more of the brownish-colored creatures emerged. Lucille's continued whinnies came to an abrupt stop, and Karen's grip tightened on her bow.

"You're going to regret—"

Her threat was cut short as the lead creature hurled its spear. Its aim was horrible, but Karen dropped to a knee anyway. With no hesitation, she let her arrow fly. It soared straight and true at, and through, the monster. The remainder of the creatures hooted and barked in fury. As one, they rushed at us, spears leading the way. My daughter proved herself a skilled warrior, firing arrow after arrow at the attackers without taking a hit. When they did get closer to her, she either struck them with her bow or slashed at them with the knife. I fared less well with my weighty axe. Most attacks I was able to turn aside, but a few lucky thrusts drew blood. When I was able to retaliate, a creature crumpled with every swing.

The battle was nearly won when another three monsters exited the barn with bloodied spears. Three arrows took them down before I could even ready my axe. A quick glance showed a score of the creatures strewn about the yard. I felt great pride in Karen's combat abilities. She vanquished fifteen of the beasts to my five. We made our way into the barn, and my happiness began to fade when we found Lucille. The monsters had shown no mercy in their attack on the horse. Tears filled my eyes, and I could only hope she passed quickly. Karen's arms wrapped around me, and I heard her sobbing. We sat there in the hay, joined in our grief, waiting for the dawn.

In the years after that tragedy, my fiery-haired daughter redoubled her efforts at hunting. With Lucille gone, and my age rearing its ugly head, farming was nearly impossible. It was only Karen's sojourns that kept food on the table and money in our purses. Sometimes she would be gone for a week at a time. I knew she was working hard to keep us going, but I couldn't help feeling sad at her absence.

During Karen's last trip, I noticed something amiss. I would awaken in the night, feeling as though a steel band was wrapped around my lungs. Not long after, the incessant coughing started. When dark blood joined the coughs, I knew what was wrong. It was the same Deathlung sickness that took my first daughter. As much as I hated to, I had to send Karen away. Two nights later, she came back all smiles. I was sitting by the fireplace, wrapped in a blanket.

"I'm home, Papa!"

I had to smile. All grown up, yet she still called me Papa. I tried to greet her, but a fit of blood-filled coughing silenced me. Karen came into the living room, orange hair pulled back into ponytail.

"I found some boars yesterday," she said hanging up her bow and quiver. "They were really tough but—"

She went quiet when she finally turned toward me. The smile faded from her face, but when she tried to step forward, I waved her back.

"What's wrong, Papa? What's happened?"

I struggled to take a breath.

"I'm dying, Karen. It's Deathlung."

"No," she shook her head. "No! You can't be dying!"

"It's only a matter of time now, child. And you have to leave."

Karen stumbled backwards, pain flaring in her eyes.

"You're sending me away?"

I nodded as another fit of coughing wracked me. The young woman stood taller, hands balled into fists at her sides. She was furious.

"Why? Why can't I stay and take care of you?"

"Because you could get sick, and I can't allow it," I said, voice straining to be heard. "You're grown now, and you need to find your own life. Please go."

Tears streamed down Karen's face, and her hands were still clenched. I couldn't tell what she was going to do. But then, without a word, she turned and left. The slamming of the front door sounded like the closing of my coffin lid, and I cried. At least Karen would be safe. Days went by with some being better than others. A few of the neighbors from the closest farms came by to make sure I had food, but carefully kept their distance. I often sat on the front porch, hoping to see my girl running by. My heart hurt as much as my lungs sitting there, but I had nothing else I could do. Then one afternoon, the sun sinking toward the horizon, I saw a familiar silhouette walking toward the house.

"Papa."

I knew I should have told her to leave, but I was so happy to hear her voice.

"Karen," I coughed. I reached out to her, hands shaking. She took them and squeezed gently. She knelt down by my chair, her face expressionless. I wondered what she was thinking. She cleared her throat, seeming to fumble for something to say.

"Shh," I put a finger to her lips. "You don't need to explain. I've missed you, Karen."

She shook her head, and then abruptly stood up.

"No. I need to tell you the truth."

That statement shocked me. As far as I knew, Karen never told me any lies. The fiery-haired young woman paced the length of the porch, wringing her hands.

"I'm afraid," she finally managed, "that I'm not exactly who you think me to be."

I stayed silent, not wanting to interrupt her.

"It's true that when you found me, I couldn't remember anything. When we came across the first Dragon's Fire flowers, everything came back to me. You had been so good to me; I couldn't bear to tell you. I didn't want you to be hurt."

She took a shuddering breath and ran a hand through her hair.

"This isn't going to be easy to believe, but here it goes," she took a deep breath. "I was given a mission by my people. I was assigned to scout the human lands and determine if your kind was ready for peaceful relations."

Karen sat down on the steps and stared off to the sunset.

"Long ago, your kind hunted us. We fled across the sea, finding new lands to claim as a refuge. The elders, after time, decided to try to mend the rifts of the past. So I was sent. But during my travel I was caught in a thunderstorm and struck by lightning."

She looked over her shoulder at me.

"And then I crashed into the woods."

Then something finally made sense. So that was why she wanted to leave the clearing in the woods so badly.

"I was unconscious for a time," she continued, "but when I came to, my memory was gone. I ran through the rain, looking for any kind of shelter. That's when I found your barn."

Karen stood and helped me up and out to the yard. She seated me on and old stump then went a few steps away.

"You took me in. You raised me as your own daughter. When my memory returned, I thought about running away to continue my mission. The truth is I grew to love you as a father. I couldn't leave you. I could still observe humanity through you. Then you got sick and sent me away. I was hurt not only because you told me to leave, but also at the thought of losing you."

She stepped away a few more paces.

"This is who I am."

She stood with her hands clasped in front of her chest. The young woman began speaking strange words as she slowly spread out her arms. Coral light began to emanate from her hair, making it truly look like flames. The light spread down over her body and grew to blinding intensity. It suddenly flared out with a boom. When I could see again, my daughter was gone. In her place was a creature only spoken of in legends.

Karen was a dragon.

Her scales were the color of polished brass. A line of coppery-orange spikes ran the length of her spine down to the tip of her tail. She stood on four legs and had leathery wings folded at her sides. Down her right rear leg was section of blackened scales that matched her burned calf in human form. Her eyes, though now with slits for pupils, were still the same.

"So beautiful," I wheezed. The dragon seemed to smile and settled down on her belly. She snaked her head close to me, so I reached out to touch her. The scales felt exactly like the metal they resembled.

"My people truly mean humanity no harm," Karen said. Her voice was deeper, but still recognizable as my daughter.

"I believe you."

"Actually," she said, "my people could help you. The elders are proficient healers. I told them of your condition and they're willing to help. However, they can't come here. You'll have to leave your home."

I smiled and quietly laughed. "This is only wood and nails. A home is wherever you are with those you love. You're my home, Karen."

A warm, wet drop hit my leg. I never expected that a dragon would be able to cry.

"So you'll go?" she asked.

"Yes," I replied, "as long as you'll be there."

She nodded her head.

"Okay," I said, struggling to rise. "Let's go."

Karen got to her feet and stretched out her wings. As gently as she could, she lifted me up with her front claws and held me to her chest.

"We'll have to fly," she rumbled.

I coughed, and then swallowed nervously. "I'm scared, Karen."

Her scaly forelegs tightened slightly in a hug.

"You're my Papa, and I promise you that I will never let you come to harm."

With a powerful leap, we took to the air and headed toward the setting sun.

"I love you, Papa."

"And I love you, my Orange Karen."

∞○∞

Christopher Cantley is a factory worker residing in Lapeer, Michigan. He's a devoted husband to JoAnn and father to Samantha, Tabitha, and Andrew. He also has four fur kids: Mickey, Tinkerbell, Ninja, and Abbie. He heard about this project from his good friend Stephanie Fuller, aka The Book Hipster, and leapt at the chance to contribute.

Raeanne Revealed

by Valerie Haight

Chapter One
MISSING

Laycella Mavin bolted upright and stilled, listening for the sharp crack that woke her from a dead sleep. Her heart raced as she wondered if it had been a dream. She blinked in the darkness and listened to her own breathing. Resisting the urge to close her eyes and nestle further into the warm coverlet, she fumbled for the alarm clock. Two minutes after midnight. She tossed the blankets back, shoved her feet into slippers, then padded into the kitchen, through the hall toward her daughter's bedroom.

"Rae?" Laycella whispered into the darkened room.

Laycella smiled, imagining Raeanne's sweet breath playing across warm lips as she slept. Her fingers itched to caress her little girl's silken hair. She shuffled closer to the bed and smoothed her hands over satiny sheets and fuzzy blankets. Her heart quickened when her fingers made no contact with a sprawled seven-year-old.

She spun, slapped the pink dragonfly light switch, and whirled back, seeing an empty bed. Her heart plummeted to her knees.

This isn't happening. I'll be laughing about this tomorrow.

"Raeanne?"

Laycella turned in her daughter's small room. She couldn't be hiding at this hour. She tore open closet doors and yanked curtains back, checked window locks. Everything was secure.

Except her daughter.

"Raeanne!"

❦❦❦

"Could she have been taken by a family member?" An aging detective paced worn gray mottled linoleum in Laycella's kitchen.

She shook her head. "No. Her father passed away, her grandparents adore her. My parents are deceased. There is no one else."

"Do you have any known enemies, any feuds of any kind?"

"No."

"Does she sleepwalk?"

"No, never."

With each question they asked, Laycella felt the gaping, empty hole inside her widen.

The detective left to place a call. He re-entered the kitchen and hovered close.

"Mrs. Mavin, we're activating the AMBER Alert since there is information that Raeanne might be in serious danger."

Laycella's knees buckled as the legs of a chair brushed the backs of her legs.

❦❦❦

"Cella, they're doing all they can. Why don't you try eating something? I can heat some soup."

Laycella stopped twisting a tattered dishcloth and turned raw eyes on her best friend and neighbor, Katherine. "She may not have eaten in twelve hours."

"I know. I know." Kat drew closer and draped an arm over Laycella's shoulder.

"She may not have had anything to drink. Or—"

"We can't think like that. She's going to be fine."

Laycella nodded and resumed her twisting.

"I'm staying with you again tonight, if that's all right?"

"Yes. Please."

Laycella raised her head. Red streaks marked her forearms where her fingers dug in. She'd fallen asleep at the kitchen table. She rubbed her stiff neck and shoulders. Kat sat across from her, her head resting on one arm as she slept.

Laycella glanced around. The place was empty of policemen, a stark contrast to hours previous. She scooted her chair back, walked to the living room window, and pulled back the curtain. A patrol car sat parked in front of her house, the deputy inside, probably sound asleep. She checked the clock on the mantle. Midnight.

As she'd done a thousand times in the last twenty-four hours, she made her way to Raeanne's room and knelt by her bed. She parted her lips to offer another prayer but paused at a sound in the darkness. She jerked her head in the direction of a sigh and strained her eyes. Knowing what her hands would find, she slid them under the blankets anyway.

And screamed.

Raeanne jumped and sat up in her bed. "Mommy?"

Kat flew in from the kitchen and snapped on the hall light.

"Call them in, Kat! She's here! She's home!"

Chapter Two
THE DUST

"Where were you?"

"Who were you with?"

"Are you hurt?"

Raeanne stared at the officers with fear in her round eyes. She reached for her mother and it was only when those first fat tears rolled down her daughter's cheeks that Laycella noticed the red dust caking her porcelain skin. She held her tight and pulled back the comforter with her other hand.

Raeanne sat in a deep mound of fine, silky, red dust.

Everyone stared. No one moved. "Get forensics down here now," she heard someone speak into a radio.

∽⚬∾

"You're dropping the case?" Laycella held the receiver to her ear with her shoulder and let the dinner plate she'd been washing plunk into the soapy dishwater.

"Her case isn't being dropped, Mrs. Mavin. I'm simply calling to inform you her case classification has been lowered since Raeanne is home safe."

"Something happened to my daughter. She doesn't remember anything and it might have been nothing. It also could have been horrific. I don't want this swept under the rug."

The woman on the other end cleared her throat in obvious discomfort. "I understand. They're doing all they can. They're working on her case, but they just aren't able to put any of the clues together yet. The red dust found is specific to desert regions of the southwestern United States. That's really all they have. There are no prints and nothing to report on the toxicology and DNA screens. There's just nothing to go on yet."

Laycella ended the call and sighed. Nothing but a bedroom full of red dust from God knows where.

She dried her hands and tiptoed to her bedroom where Raeanne still slept. She checked the window locks before covering the sleeping child. Raeanne was seven, no longer a baby, but she'd be damned if she'd let her out of her sight again. If that meant sleeping with her until she moved out, so be it. She checked the locks on the front and back doors and padded back to the laundry room where baskets of dusty linens waited.

Laycella bent and carried a basket to the back porch where she shook sheets and blankets in the last rays of daylight. She popped a pillowcase and coughed as a cloud of dust mushroomed in front of her face. She waved it away and turned to drop the case into the basket, but a *tink-tink-tink* commanded her attention at her feet on the concrete steps.

A flash of orange glinted in a beam of waning sun, and Laycella reached for one of Raeanne's toys she often brought to bed with her. She grabbed the object and brought it closer, turned it over in her hands.

It was no toy. It was nothing she'd ever seen before. She dropped the sheets and went inside, locking the door behind her. She reached for the phone, but hesitated. Her finger hovered over the redial button. What if they didn't know what to do with this either? What if it went into a sealed box with all those samples of red dust?

She pursed her lips and dialed a different number.

Chapter Three
THE ORANGE LIQUID

"Alex Mavin, please?" Laycella waited while the operator transferred her call.

"This is Alex."

"Alex, hi. It's Laycella. I need your help."

Two hours later, Laycella's brother-in-law, Alex, sat at Laycella's kitchen table studying the glass vial.

"I've been a chemist for nine years and I've never seen anything like this before. The density of this liquid is amazing. Like mercury. And its container is equally fascinating."

"Is it mercury?"

"No." Alex toyed with the vial. "And without testing it, I have no idea what it is. Could be the latest flavor of Kool-Aid for all we know. But this bottle is... puzzling. It's seamless, made of some kind of high-tech resin. There's no opening, no lid."

"Do you think it had something to do with her disappearance?"

Alex shoved his glasses higher on his nose. "Do you still have some of that dust?"

They went out back where Laycella helped collect dust into Ziplocs. Alex pocketed the bags then took another look at the mysterious vial. Its orange liquid sloshed inside before he closed his fingers around it.

"I need to get this back to the lab to test it. Don't tell anyone you have it until we know something more certain."

Laycella nodded. "You got it. Let me know what you need. Anything."

Alex left, and Laycella locked up once again. She lay next to Raeanne and smoothed her forehead. A fine sheen of sweat covered her skin. Layclla pulled back the blanket, leaving the sheet and cuddled up next to her. Her daughter's even breathing lulled her to sleep.

Laycella dreamed the dry, red earth shook. She stood on hard sand baked dry by the sun and vibrating with tremors. A hole formed when the desert in front of her dropped to nothingness and from it great fountains of orange liquid spewed into the sky like a volcanic eruption. She turned to run, but the air was sucked from her lungs as a force struck her in the stomach.

Laycella opened her eyes and gasped as she dodged Raeanne's leg. Her bed shook as the girl swung her feet and arms. Laycella sat up and tried to grab an arm or leg but the girl continued to shake.

My God, she's seizing.

Laycella dialed 911 and held her until the ambulance arrived.

"We're doing all we can for her, Mrs. Mavin." Dr. Luing whispered. "She's got a high fever and her general condition is declining rapidly. We're puzzled but we're running tests and keeping her comfortable until we figure out what's going on."

Laycella nodded, feeling helpless as she watched the doctor's retreat.

Her phone beeped. "Hello?"

"Cella, it's Alex. I need Raeanne's hairbrush."

"What?"

"How is she?" His words came in huffs like he was running.

"She's in the hospital. She had a seizure and they say she's deteriorating. Alex, I don't know what to do."

"I think I found something but I need some of her DNA. Her hair or toothbrush or something. And I need it fast."

"Where are you? I'll have Kat meet you."

Chapter Four
SECRETS OF THE VIAL

Katherine tried to stay out of Alex's way, despite his increasing excitement level over whatever he viewed in his powerful microscope. She was in no way knowledgeable in science or chemistry, but knew he was onto something by the way he moved his skilled, gloved hands from one test tube to the next, dropping in liquids and solutions using a long pointed tube with a bulb on one end. When he almost ran from a sink to his row of solutions, Kat spoke.

"I can't stand this any longer. Will you please tell me what you see?"

Alex's gaze remained riveted on the tiny glass tubes. "I can't believe this."

"What is it?"

"Well." Alex licked his lips, looking unsure of where to begin. "I wanted to compare the molecular makeup of Rae's DNA from her hair to the mysterious orange liquid inside the vial, but I can't do that until I get the vial open."

"Can't you break it?"

"I tried sawing through it, smashing it and burning through it with a cutting torch. Whatever it's made of is an enigma to me."

Kat's brows furrowed. "I can do puzzles."

Alex hissed. "This is much more than a puzzle. This is… flying saucer stuff."

"Let me see it." Alex pointed her to the vial and Kat drew closer, inspecting every millimeter of its smooth glass-looking surface.

"There's no lid, no locking mechanism. It's a seamless capsule," Alex said, shrugging.

"I'll bet there is. You just have to find it. Have you tried squirting it with that stuff?"

"What stuff?" Alex looked offended.

Kat pointed to the solution he'd mixed containing Raeanne's DNA.

Alex drew back in disbelief. "No."

"Well?"

"Well what? You can't just come in here and start squirting 'stuff'. We don't know what this is, how it will react. Exact aliquots must be measured before the concentrations can—"

Kat rolled her eyes and snatched the pipete from his hand. She reached around him and dropped two drops of liquid onto the vial.

"Kat!"

"What? You tried to torch it."

They watched the liquid drip down the sides of the vial and pool beneath it.

Kat realized she held her breath and glanced at Alex who did the same. Seconds ticked by, and nothing happened. Kat sighed.

The vial moved.

"Did you see that?" he asked in an urgent whisper.

"You blew it," Alex whispered back but didn't take his eyes off the vial.

It moved again.

Alex's phone rang.

"Alex here."

"Alex!" Kat could hear Laycella's frantic voice without the speakerphone. "She's dying!"

Chapter Five
RAE'S RACE

Laycella paced outside the enclosed curtains where the ICU doctors and nurses worked over her little girl. Tears rolled down both cheeks as she thought of life without Raeanne. She wrapped her arms around her ribcage and sobbed.

A commotion to her left drew her attention and she looked up. Alex barreled around the corner with hospital security trailing behind him. They shouted for him to stop. A nurse caught the bustle and reached for an alarm.

Laycella reached for him before they tackled him. He pressed the vial into her palm. "Get it to her!" he said between gritted teeth.

She clutched the vial and turned, pretending to stumble from the calamity of bodies behind her. She stuck her fingers between the curtains amongst a cluster of nurses and slipped the vial under Raeanne's leg.

"Come on this side, Mrs. Mavin. Let them get him out of here." A nurse gripped her shoulders and led her to the other side of the room.

A steady beep sounded. "Heart rate's rising. BP 80 over 50. She's back!"

Raeanne rounded the corner and plopped herself on the floor. "Mom, I'm hungry."

"Me too," Alex chimed.

"I'll make sandwiches," Rae announced.

"Come on, Peanut, I'll help." Kat led Rae into the kitchen.

Alex had created a makeshift lab in Laycella's study, where he'd worked on analyzing the mysterious orange liquid since he was kicked out of the hospital the day before.

"Rae's recovery was remarkable. She went from almost gone to perfectly fine in what? Seven minutes? So here's where I started. The orange liquid, whatever it is, is keeping her alive."

Laycella winced.

"That's apparent from the tests we did today after she was released from the hospital. You keep it with her and she's fine. You move it away, she starts to feel ill. Move it too far…"

"Okay. I got it."

"Right. So, now that we know how to open the vial," Alex shuddered. Kat peeked around the corner and smiled. "We can start testing this."

He held up a plastic vial full of the same strange orange liquid.

"There are two?" asked Laycella, peering closer.

"When we opened the vial, Rae's DNA concentration was mixed with the original concentration, creating this solute. I've analyzed it every hour since and it's… changing."

"What do you mean, changing?"

Alex swallowed hard. "It's skewing its own cell structure by reorganizing organic molecules."

"Alex, please. Dumb it down for me."

Alex swallowed hard. "I think it's creating a life form."

Chapter Six
RAE'S AWAKENING

Laycella sank into a chair and stared at the floor. "What do we do?"

Alex shook his head. "It's obvious Rae can't live without it."

Laycella looked up. "And if we allow it to continue changing?"

"We could go through this entire thing over again," Kat answered for him. She sat and they exchanged blank stares.

Laycella massaged her temples. "This is... bigger than us."

Alex sighed. "If Rae remembered what happened to her, where she was, maybe we could—"

"I do remember."

Three heads snapped to attention as Raeanne set her peanut butter sandwich on her plate and bit into an apple slice. "You saved us, Mommy."

Laycella glanced at Alex in confusion. She went to Rae and knelt beside her. "Tell me, honey."

Rae pointed to the vial of orange liquid. Her vial. "It's in there. You showed me. You showed us all."

"How, baby?"

"Daddy."

Laycella covered her open mouth. Her husband died in the line of duty two months before Rae was born. She turned to Kat and Alex, who sat in stony silence.

"He fought for us. Before he died, he taught you how to save us. He gave you the key and the magic words."

"Magic words, Rae?" Laycella whispered.

"Tox zel de nom."

The strangely familiar words triggered a fierce longing deep in her chest. "And the key?"

Raeanne stood and extended her hand toward her mother. Laycella blinked and a tear fell on Rae's tiny pointer finger. Carefully, she walked to the vial and touched it, joining the tear to the shining glass.

The tear glowed orange before merging into the glass. The glow burned brighter and the liquid inside shimmered and swayed as waves rippled outward. The vial thinned and grew bigger at the same time as if it were blown glass minus its gaffer. It stretched to the size of a beach ball, then orange cells inside morphed and moved like fibers sprouting this way and that; they swirled and swayed, settling into images as the glasslike ball rose into the air.

Laycella, Raeanne, Kat, and Alex, their faces glowing orange, stood captivated by the floating phenomenon before them.

Images rearranged themselves inside the ball until they resembled floating planets. One magnified itself while the others floated away. It was if the orb were showing them an orange-tinted movie.

The camera panned in on the largest orb and a civilization came into view. It zoomed in on a group of beings. Five beings.

Laycella's tears streamed as she recognized her husband's face in a different time, a different world. He stood beside her. They smiled at each other. He held Raeanne in his arms. There was no sound, but none was needed. She felt the love they shared. Alex and Kat stood some fifteen yards behind them, their boots kicking up the red desert dust.

Laycella tore her gaze from the movie to look at her friends standing in her living room, mouths open, eyes intent on the orb. They saw it too, themselves in another world.

She turned back to the camera as it panned right filming   an explosion, an even brighter orange.

Fire consumed sky and soil — the end of their world. Raeanne's father waved as dust and flames swallowed his image.

The liquid waves rearranged themselves and skipped to a different view. Laycella, Raeanne, Alex, and Kat on their feet, running through the red dust to a cave. They reached the mouth of the cave and entered, looking left and right. They seemed lost. Laycella grabbed at a chain around her neck and twisted until she located an orange pendant. It glowed in her hand and when she dropped it, it remained suspended in the air. It changed direction, showing them which way to go. They began running again until it stopped glowing.

Laycella watched as the movie showed her other self kneel and grab at dead brush and spiny undergrowth. Alex and Kat joined her. The three of them tossed aside brambles until they uncovered what appeared to be a sandy door, made of the same limestone-like material as the cave wall. Laycella plunged the orange pendant into a tiny hole and the door slid back. They stepped inside.

The orange orb grew dim as the four beings seated themselves just behind the thick, sandy door. It closed and an entire section of the cave broke away from the earth and rocketed into the sky. The image grew blurry and brightened as it accelerated through the atmosphere. The sand began to crumble and melt away. Laycella threw up an arm to shield her eyes from the bright glow.

The orb went dark. The four of them squinted in the darkness. Laycella sat and motioned for Raeanne. The girl padded over and Laycella drew her close. "Do you remember?" The girl nodded.

Alex and Kat nodded.

Before any of them could speak, a tiny, faint light shone in the large glass ball. It grew in intensity until Raeanne's orange face came into view. She lay in bed, her fuzzy blanket covered in red dust. She held out her hand and the orange vial floated up and glowed bright. It stretched its shape into a small circle and began portraying images of her family — working, growing food, laughing, existing on Earth.

The girl's face faded and Laycella's husband came into view. He squatted low and his eyes scanned somewhere beyond the camera while he spoke.

Laycella shifted to the edge of the couch and reached for the orb. "Drew."

Drew smiled. "Sella, I only have a moment." He turned and looked behind him. "You have to let her go. She's taken my place in securing our people's existence."

Tears streaked Laycella's cheeks.

Drew's recording continued. "She will travel in and out of time, between this world and ours." His eyes shifted to the left as if he were looking for someone. "If you hinder her abilities, the vial will create another savior to take her place and she will perish."

A nearby explosion sounded and Drew winced. "I love you both. The vial will protect you."

The orange light shrank until it vanished altogether and the vial resumed its shape.

Laycella wiped her cheeks and put an arm around Raeanne.

Alex cleared his throat. "My God, I remember now."

Kat rubbed her arms as if to stave off a chill and managed another nod.

The four of them stepped closer to the orange-filled glass and stood over it. This was to be Raeanne's life now. Her encrypted instruction manual for life had been reinstated in the shape of a vial.

***

Valerie Haight is a short story writer and contemporary suspense and romance novelist. She is a member of Ozarks Writer's League through College of the Ozarks in Branson, MO, where she was awarded first place in the OWL Flash Fiction Contest. She is a published author with Turquoise Morning Press. Her first novella, HAPPENSTANCE, was released on December 13, 2012.

Friend in Need

by J. Whitworth Hazzard

The signs that a dragon lived nearby were unmistakable. There had been no sign of game, or any creature larger than a rabbit, since Fianna and her companion had passed through the cinders of the destroyed village three miles behind. There was only one hunter left in this valley. Everything else had wisely gone into hiding.

"The wizard's map was correct."

"Mmm," the Hun grunted at her. Octar trudged along in front of her horse, carrying the reins in case the animal spooked. The terrain was getting rockier as they climbed the path into the hills at the southern tip of the vale.

"Keep a sharp eye. We'll lose cover soon."

Fianna knew the risks and the rewards of hunting dragons. Wrapped deep in a fur traveling cloak, the fiery-haired beauty bore the scars of battle with the great beasts. She didn't make excuses for the close calls that had marred her otherwise perfect pale skin. If anything, the scars accentuated her beauty in the eyes of admirers. The marks were a natural warning to predators and prey alike.

Dangerous. Do not touch.

The last copse of scrub oak trees fell behind the two travelers, and they were left staring at the craggy peaks. Up there, somewhere, was the lair of an apex predator that made grown men piss their kilts in fear. Octar guided her horse in silence, carefully navigating the switchbacks, so as not to dislodge a single stone. Even the *clip-clop clip-clop* of the horse's hooves was too much noise this close to a dragon's lair.

"This is close enough," Fianna hissed at Octar. "Any closer and the beast will hear us. I'll lose surprise."

Octar nodded and stopped the horse. His massive frame blocked the biting wind as Fianna dismounted and shed her riding cloak. Octar took the cloak and draped it over the saddle in silence. He watched in admiration as his mistress stood firm against the wind, stray strands from her braid blowing orange-red whispers into the air. This part was ritual for her. The preparation before inevitable battle.

"Fiú dá siúlfainn i ngleann an dorchadais, níor bhaol liom an t-olc," she whispered. "I'm ready."

Octar pulled the carefully-prepared weapons from the saddle bags and helped her strap each on, one by one. The last, a great mithral-edged scimitar, he pulled tightly around her hips and cinched down until he could feel leather against bone.

"If I don't return by nightfall, go east 'til you reach Balingeary. My brother has the papers releasing you from bondage. And stay clear of the wizard — he's likely to slaughter you for sport if I fail."

Octar nodded in understanding and held fast to the reins of the nervous horse.

Fianna took a deep breath and jogged up the path, warming her body to the task against the cold of the mountain winds. Without the cloak, her armor provided little protection against the elements. She had to find the lair quickly or risk slow death.

The warrior maiden reached the ledge above the cleft between peaks and spied a thin wisp of vapor rising from a cave settled just out of sight of the horse path. She frowned. If the lair was this obvious, it meant that the resident feared little from visitors. The wizard may have lied about the strength of her target.

Fianna tiptoed to the entrance of the cave, a great slice in the side of the rock face, and pulled her scimitar free from its scabbard. The weight of the blade felt comfortable in her hand, like an old friend. But even thousands of hours of blade work couldn't keep her heart from racing when she saw the ravaged corpse sitting across from her. The rictus grin of a long-dead adventurer greeted her. His plate armor was smashed to pieces and charred black from burns. The limbs were mangled and had distinct teeth marks in the yellowing bones.

I am stronger than you. We will not share the same fate, warrior.

Demeaning the dead was not polite, but Fianna could have no doubt in her heart when she entered the cave. There was no room for hesitation or fear. She'd seen men with the stature of giants felled by those two poisons.

Fianna crept into the darkness and padded over the bones of others until she rounded the corner and laid eyes on the great dragon. She had to stifle a gasp when she saw the soft glow of its orange scales. The dragon was covered from the tip of its snout to the tip of its tail with a hard, gleaming skin that spanned every description of the color. Blazing sunrises, succulent fruits, pale flower blossoms, enchanted flames, every possible shade of orange was woven into the creature's skin in a fine mosaic too beautiful for words.

She suddenly understood the wizard's obsession with the dragon. A species this unusual had to possess unique qualities. Despite the rarity and wonder of the beast, its life was forfeit. She had debts to pay with the wizard's bounty, and she intended to be free.

Fianna took three giant steps and rushed headlong toward the beast. Her scimitar swung in a great arc, aimed to sever the beast's head in one stroke. A blur of orange motion and the blade connected — not on a neck — but against a loose pile of blemished coins and dented armor scraps.

The beast was already whirling around to strike. Its head reared back in a display of silvered fangs; Fianna's distraction at the dragon's beauty nearly cost her when the whip-crack of its spiked tail missed by inches. The maiden flipped back on one hand and spun toward the back wall. She came up from her roll and threw the daggers strapped to her thigh straight at the maw of the creature.

The dragon surged forward and the knives plinked off the thick armor of its breastplate and skittered into a dark corner of the cave. It swiped at her with razor sharp claws, and Fianna moved like smoke — twisting, turning, and dodging. She was anywhere and everywhere but in front of the oncoming attacks.

The two deadly foes danced across the cave — evenly matched in speed and lethality — until Fianna countered a feint with a sharp jab and felt her blade slice between the scales of the dragon's paw. First blood was hers.

"Ooooowweeeeee!" The cave filled with reverberations of the beast's high-pitched whine.

Fianna spun to bring her scimitar down to sever the limb, but the dragon had retreated to the corner of its bed, holding its wounded paw.

"Hey, time out," the dragon shouted.

Fianna leapt into the air and brought the blade down hard, only to be caught in midair and pushed back by the dragon's tail. She fell hard on her rump and bounced unceremoniously on the cave floor.

"Hey! I said time out. TIME. OUT." The dragon's lips were moving, but Fianna couldn't believe that such a tiny voice could come from such a magnificent creature. "Don't you speak English?"

Fianna cocked her head. "How is this possible? You speak the King's tongue?"

"Where do you think I'm from? I grew up here for Pete's sake."

"But you're a dragon…"

"Oh, I see. So I'm stupid. Is that it? Not capable of learning your oh-so-special language, am I?"

Never in Fianna's life had any of her marks talked back. Even the humans she fought abandoned words in the focus of battle "I never said that. Is this some sort of magical put-on? Come on, now. Where are you hiding, Wizard? Show yourself!"

Fianna got to her knees and looked around the cave for the true source of the voice. There was no one here but her and the dragon. She noted that the cave was really rather shabby, as dragon's lairs go. It didn't look like a treasure trove at all. It looked like a hoarding of cast-off junk.

"That's it, isn't it? That rotten wizard sent you to beat me up. He's always bullying me." The dragon curled up against the far wall and spit on the floor in anger. "One of these days I'm going to…"

"The wizard set a hefty bounty on your head. And I intend to collect." Fianna spun to her feet and was about to charge, when the dragon shouted.

"Wait! You came here to kill me just because some crazy old man in a tower told you to? On who's moral authority does he get to decide who lives and dies?"

"Well…" Fianna thought back and huffed in frustration. "Look, it's not about morals. He's paying me, you know."

"Oh, sure he is. Did he show you the gold he promised you?"

Fianna shuffled her feet and put her hands on her hips. She searched her memory of the transaction and had to admit that the beast was right. "No. I guess he didn't."

"Ha! He pulls that trick every year. 'Go kill the wicked dragon and a mountain of gold is yours'." The dragon mocked the voice of the wizard. "And you believed him. For shame."

"I don't need a wizard's quest as an excuse to kill a dragon," Fianna growled.

"Wha… what is that supposed to mean?" The dragon drew up to its full height, which wasn't very impressive now that Fianna had gotten a good look.

"What do you think it means? You're a dragon! An evil beast of destruction and death."

"Oh my God…" The dragon stumbled back and sucked in a massive breath with a pained look on its face. It pointed a claw at the warrior. "You're a RACIST!"

Fianna winced under the accusation. "I am not! Bloody hell, you're can't be racist against a species."

"You sound just like those awful blue dragons down in Southshire, always talking about scientific categorization and socio-economic theory. Maybe I am of a different species, but I'm not such a bad guy. I have feelings, you know. You might have asked around before charging in here like some bloody serial killer."

"Oh, really? Who should I ask? That lovely corpse on your front door? I wonder if he thought you weren't such a bad guy," Fianna scoffed.

The dragon looked hurt that she would bring up the dead knight. "If you must know, I had nothing to do with that."

"Nothing?"

"Barely anything."

"Barely anything?"

"Okay, fine! My mum brought that one. He was already dead when I gnawed on him. She thought it would liven up the place. Maybe give me some inspiration. I've never killed a knight before."

"Your mother? Is a dragon?"

"No, my mum is a water buffalo," the dragon snorted. "Of course she's a dragon, you twit. You know the big red dragon that lives over by Glengarriff?"

Fianna gasped. "That's your mother? That thing is a legend."

"Thing? That's my mum you're talking about." The dragon settled on its front paws and looked haughtily at the warrior.

"Sorry. Habit," Fianna said. "Is she nice?"

"Heavens, no. She's beastly. Rip your face off as soon as look at you. She's still my mum though. Show some respect."

"Wait, but you're orange. That would make your father one of the Chinese yellow..."

"Ix-nay on the Ather-Fay," The dragon stared into the corner and pouted. He whispered softly, "We don't talk about him. Mum says he's a skiving tosspot."

Fianna paused in thought. Killing the son of a legendary red dragon was bad news — even if he was an insecure little runt. Still, she had to deal with the wizard. A promise had been made.

"We appear to be at an impasse, Dragon. I risk great retribution if I fail to bring proof of your demise."

"Hubert."

"Pardon?" Fianna asked.

"My name is Hubert." The dragon said. "We have names, you know. I wouldn't expect a racist to know that. You probably can't even tell us apart. All look the same to you, do we?"

"Good Lord, are all orange dragons this fussy? I already apologized for that. And for the last time, you're not a race, you're a species. Hubert. There? Are you happy?"

"No, I'm not happy. You hurt my paw," Hubert pushed the bleeding claw into Fianna's face. "It really stings."

"Look, if you stop being such a baby maybe we can help each other out. I need a small vial of your blood and a few scales to prove my task is complete. I've already gone and cut you, so that part's done. I'll tell the wizard you're dead and get my reward — if there is one — and he'll leave you alone after that."

"And what do I get in return?" Hubert rubbed a claw across his scaly chin.

"Not being dead?" Fianna lifted her scimitar over her shoulder and smiled.

"Hmm. Fair point." Hubert watched the drops of blood trickle off his cut paw. "One condition."

Fianna groaned. "What is it?"

"You introduce me to that stunning white dragon that lives in the next valley. I've been trying to get up the nerve to approach her for ages and…"

"Are you mental?"

"Come on! Please? All you have to do it pretend to attack her and I'll come to her rescue and drive you off." Hubert swiped his paws in a pantomime of ferocious battle. "You don't seem to have a problem with attacking complete strangers, especially dragons. A regular day for you, isn't it?"

"That's ridiculous."

"It's called an icebreaker. You humans have no respect for classic courtship rituals. Romance is lost on you lot."

"And I'm the racist?" The maiden huffed. "Alright, alright! Hurry up then, I'm freezing." Fianna sheathed her scimitar and waited for the dragon to follow her out of the cave.

"Brilliant!" Hubert slid off the mound of junk and padded beside the warrior. "Hey, can I ask you a question? Something I've always wanted to ask a real warrior maiden."

"Well, since we're all chummy now, why not?"

"Those chainmail bikinis… do they pinch?"

Fianna sighed. "So much."

J. Whitworth Hazzard lives in the vast cornfields of Illinois with his wife, and four nearly perfect children. Trained in science and critical thinking, and armed with a Ph.D. in Molecular Biophysics, J. Whitworth spends his leisure time figuring out how to scientifically justify the existence of mythical creatures. He's been a lifelong writer and spends more than his fair share of time writing about all manner of ridiculous things. He hopes one day to be portrayed in a Lifetime Original movie by the unflinching grace of Will Ferrell.

The Man in the Orange House

by Emmett Spain

It's not that I wanted him to die, exactly. It's just... Look. His name was Frank. Old guy. Not old in the sense that he forgot things and had that hunchy back that old people get sometimes, like they're slouching ever lower so it's not so far to jump when their grave opens up. No, I mean old in the way that replaces your blood with tangy spite juice and causes you to hate God and all His works — loud noises, kids, animals, TV shows... everything. Frank was like that. Every sentence beginning with "Everything was so much better when" or "I'm not a racist, but", and usually ending with "...so I set his lawn on fire". Frank was a pyromaniac. I'll get to that.

He was also — among other things — my next door neighbour. Every morning would begin with Frank giving me the stink-eye as I left to go to work. And when I say the stink-eye, I mean the DEATH-eye. It was as if he was wishing some kind of Old World curse upon me so he wouldn't have to deal with my complaints about his ridiculous plants pushing our common fence out of alignment. God, what a jerk. Some mornings I felt like I could see all those little cogs turning away in his cranky old skull — old, rusted cogs that had been corroded by tangy spite juice — and see him wishing fiery gonorrhoea upon my crotch. I'd wave. Why, I'm not sure. Some mornings it was to try and break the ice I suppose, but others were as a show of defiance to old Frank the Crank. Part of me hoped he'd finally smile back at me. He never did.

The day he died started benignly enough. Alarm clock, ablutions, and so on. I walked out my front door physically ready for work if not mentally so, and there was Frank, watching me from his usual spot over the fence. The creepy old goat was still as you like, creating the impression he'd been there for hours, patiently awaiting my departure. Only the smoke from the hand-rolled cigarette pressed between his wrinkled lips was sign that he hadn't taken a visit to the taxidermist overnight. I waved. He did not wave back. I went on my way to work.

It was about 3:00 PM when I got the call that my house had burned down. I drove home — though I was hardly fit to be behind the wheel with all the shaking my body was doing — and bore witness to the blackened shell of my former home. Fire fighters were still emptying their hoses onto the extinguished fire, a precaution in case the fire restarted and reduced my cinders to ash. I'm not sure I can describe what I felt at that particular moment, outside of saying that there was an absence in my gut. It was like I was trying to feel the loss of it all at once. I told myself things like "everything you owned was in there" and "you have no home" and "you have to start again" as a way to trigger a massive emotional reaction, but it simply didn't happen. I just stared, blank as you like, empty as you like. Apocalyptic reaction pending.

I saw Frank standing outside his house. His big, bright, orange house. And to be clear, I'm not talking about a colour scheme like "Sunset" or "Auburn"... I'm talking orange in the way that an orange is orange. Bright, lewd, neon orange. Next to my conservative little den which was painted in off-whites and trimmed in respectable woody tones, Frank's big bright bungalow was an eyesore of epic proportions. His house should have been beige, or the grey of concrete, so that it would match his personality. It should have had a huge sign that said "Dogs on site will be prosecuted", or a burning cross staked deep into his front lawn. But no. It was a gleaming, glowing, gargantuan monstrosity that looked like it belonged to a flamboyant pair of fashion designers. And right then, staring up at this neon atrocity, the house grew an invisible banner that was addressed to me and no one else.

DEAR JERKFACE, YOUR HOUSE BURNED DOWN JUST NOW. I BURNED IT DOWN. AND NOW YOU HAVE TO LIVE WITH THE FACT THAT THIS CRAPTASTIC DOMICILE WILL STAND HERE FOREVER WHILST YOUR BEAUTIFUL HOME WITH RESPECTABLE WOOD TRIMMINGS AND PLUSH CARPETS AND A LOVELY KITCHEN WITH A REALLY WELL-STOCKED SPICE RACK IS NOTHING BUT ASH. AND SPICES. BURNED TO A CRISP. BY ME. BECAUSE I HATE YOU. YOU AND YOUR TIES AND YOUR SUITS LIKE YOU'RE JUST SOOOOOOO GOOD, MR. BIG SHOT.

My delayed reaction arrived, courtesy of my good friends Insanity and Rage. I went nuclear. I marched up to Frank's house and belted on his door. No answer. I belted harder, shook the handle, generally made a ruckus. Still he refused to come to the door. Then I... well... I went a little nuts. It's best not to relive the moments that followed. Let's just say the entire contents of his porch were reduced to kindling and I had attracted the attention of half the neighbourhood before he finally opened the door.

When I saw him, the anger drained out of me. I saw something in the man that I had never seen before. Something amazing. Something awe-inspiring. Something I never thought I'd see as long as I lived.

Old Frank the Crank was smiling. Big and wide, like a kid at Christmas.

So I killed him.

I'm not proud, I just want to get that straight. He was old, yes, and I probably shouldn't have beaten him to death with his own walking stick and all, but I had to cherish the sweet irony of using that as a murder weapon. Still, I'm not proud. Really, I'm not.

As the police drove me away I had an epiphany of sorts, which was probably ten minutes or so too late, but still. I didn't actually hate that big orange house — just the mean old thing inside of it. It was actually kind of beautiful when you stopped to look at it. Well, beautiful in its own way, I guess. Beautiful in the way that everyone says ugly babies are beautiful — that kind of way. Beautiful like a big, fat, disgusting, soiled, bulbous, orange-skinned baby. That smells like *old man*.

Okay, so I still can't stand the goddamn house. Are you happy? I haven't grown or developed or improved myself in any way, and the epiphany I had probably had something to do with the knot on my head from when the cops took me down. Sheesh.

As for what happened next? Well, I recently broke out of jail with the aid of a toothbrush, eight bars of soap, and the help of a four-foot tall hermaphrodite named Aloysius. But that's a whole other story.

∽◦∾

Emmett Spain is a part-time author, full-time dabbler. He wrote the urban fantasy novel Old Haunts, and is mucking about with a dozen other projects which will one day turn into books with folding pages and everything. He resides in Sydney, Australia, with his gorgeous fiancée.

Before It Fades

by Tim Queeney

Years ago, Willa had rushed up the stone steps. But today she climbed with an older, measured pace. At the top step, she paused. Ahead was her mother's summer cottage. "Cottage", of course, was a self-conscious joke. The many-gabled house, tucked into a choir of maples at the top of the hill, was not a cottage. But the rambling "old money" summer houses along the Maine coast were often called cottages to mark them as seasonal places. Steaming corn and lobster feasts, house guests and tennis matches for seven weeks... then a long off season, shuttered and quiet.

Willa swung her eyes from the house to the familiar vista down the hill — the rocky shore and the semicircle of blue water nudged by island and pine. She had come here for many summers. From a baby girl splashing in the salt water pool, to a grade-schooler at the edge of cocktail-clinking lawn parties, to a teenager sneaking smokes beneath the granite cribwork dock. She'd gaze up at the stars, and her summer crushes would lean to kiss her.

But now Willa's mother, Phyllis, had died. The summer cottage on the hill was no longer a timeless refuge, with smells and sounds that instantly returned Willa to glowing summer sunsets. Instead, it was a roof with a leak, land behind on tax payments, a white elephant property crying for disposal. Her mother's money had matched her life stride-for-stride: when Phyllis crossed the line, the fortune was finished too. Willa was the only surviving child, and she did not have resources to keep the summer place. The decision to sell had been made during one teary night and looked no different in the light of successive mornings.

The striking of Willa's summer stage had a necessary first act. Lying alongside the dock was a trim, 45-foot wooden sailboat. The sloop, named *Samsara,* had been her father's. But many years ago, when he left Willa's mother to take up with a French designer who claimed to be a countess, the boat had stayed behind. At first, Phyllis wanted nothing more than to sink the boat at its dock. But gradually, she warmed to *Samsara* again, and eventually came to love the boat. She often sailed it with friends, taking the helm with calm assurance. She was a born teacher. Her coolheaded approach gave Willa confidence, and Willa learned to sail the boat, too.

Now, after a few weeks on the market, *Samsara* had a buyer — one who insisted on taking delivery tomorrow at a boatyard in Maslow. The trip there would mean leaving the protected waters of Denslow Bay and rounding Trundy Point, a jagged headland nosing into the Atlantic.

Willa had arranged for a delivery captain to take *Samsara* around to Maslow. But he had canceled yesterday, and Willa couldn't find anyone to replace him. Willa's son Brian had called Willa and demanded that he be the one to deliver the boat. He would bring his sister, Stacey, as crew. "It will be good for her," Brian had insisted. He'd said it in his forceful, "addressing the jury" way that left no room for disagreement.

"Brian, do you think that makes sense?" Willa said.

"She'll be fine this time, Mom."

Willa was not sure, but she needed the boat delivered. She might never find another buyer. She reluctantly agreed.

But now, as Willa approached the dock, she saw only Stacey readying the boat for departure. "Hi, honey. Is Brian below?"

Stacey didn't look up from coiling a rope, so Willa couldn't get a read on Stacey's eyes. "Nope. Brian's not coming."

Willa felt a surge of panic. "What? Why not?"

Stacey finished coiling the line and stowed it in a cockpit locker. She turned to face her mother. "Some shit about a big case that went south. He's gotta fix it or something. I don't know."

"Damn it!"

"He said we can reschedule," Stacey replied.

Willa's dismay was only partly due to Brian's absence. She was also concerned when she saw Stacey's bloodshot eyes. Her daughter had struggled in the past. Her drug problems had been frightening for everyone. The red in her eyes screamed to Willa that Stacey was using again... and she looked thin and haggard. Willa hadn't seen her daughter in almost a year. They had only spoken on the phone, conversations filled with Stacey's irritated insistence that she was "fine".

"No, we can't reschedule," Willa said. "The buyer said if the boat doesn't arrive tomorrow, the deal is off."

"That prick."

"Yes, well, I agree. But his was the only offer we've received. We need to unload this boat."

"I know that, Mom. So there's only one solution." Stacey leaned over to turn the engine key. Then she pressed the glow plug button.

"What are you doing?"

"I'm starting this sucker up."

"You mean just the two of us take her over to Maslow?"

"Yeah, the two of us take *him* over to Maslow," Stacey said as she hit the start button and the diesel rumbled to life. "*Samsara* was Grandpa's boat first. He's a male, don't you think?"

Willa had not planned on this trip. She had so many things to do. So many details. And she had told her new man friend that she would meet him for dinner. She was suddenly very angry with Brian. He had reneged on his promise to act as delivery captain after demanding the job! Willa should have known by now what Brian considered most important.

Stacey was already taking in the dock lines. "Wait — we can't take the boat all by ourselves," Willa objected.

"Mom, Gram taught you how to sail this boat. And she taught me, too, remember? Besides, we won't be all by ourselves." Stacey yelled down the companionway hatch, "Drew, get up here!"

Seconds later, a handsome, dark-haired six-footer emerged from the hatch.

"Mom, this is Drew. He'll help us sail *Sam*."

"Hi, there, Stacey's Mom," Drew said amiably. He had friendly eyes.

"Do you know how to sail?" Willa asked.

Drew smiled. "Nope, but I've always wanted to learn."

"See?" Stacey said. "C'mon, let's go."

Willa felt it was a mistake. Stacey was again railroading her into something foolhardy. Willa watched the dock slip away from them as Stacey backed *Samsara* out into the bay and then adroitly turned the boat around. As it glided through the calm morning water, Willa gazed up at the cottage on the hill. She had seen the house from deck of *Samsara* many times, but always it was with her mother at the wheel. Now Willa was the authority, the most experienced sailor. The realization made her stomach flutter. But they were well out into the bay now, and the sun was warm. Delivering the boat with Stacey and Drew would solve the boat issue and allow Willa to concentrate on disposing of the house.

Willa was able to teach Drew quickly how to raise the mainsail and then the jib. "Yeah, I think I get how to do it," Drew said when Stacey asked if her mother had explained it well.

Once the sails were trimmed and began to draw, Stacey reached down and shut off the engine. As the diesel clatter faded, *Samsara* moved to the gurgle of water rolling under the hull. Willa felt happy at the sound, remembering her mother laughing and holding court in the cockpit; she worked the wheel so expertly it seemed she never touched it.

After a half hour on the helm, Stacey said she was tired. Willa didn't feel comfortable with Drew at the wheel, so she took over. It felt good to have the boat under her control once more. *Samsara* surged through the waves with grace and power. The boat seemed happy to feel the wind in its sails once again.

They made good time; soon they reached the end of Trundy Point. Rounding the headland, Willa changed course to the northwest toward Maslow. On their way to the boat that morning, Drew and Stacey had picked up gourmet sandwiches, snacks and iced tea. The three enjoyed lunch in the cockpit, laughing and lighthearted. To Willa, it seemed like a memory of a time that she had entirely forgotten, as if she were remembering a past life that she had never lived at all.

Stacey was obviously happy with Drew. And he doted on her. Willa was surprised when the fiercely independent Stacey allowed him to wipe her chin or open her bag of chips.

Stacey's seeming new openness was not the only surprise of the day, though. The weather changed as they turned toward Maslow. The blue skies and puffy fair weather clouds had been shoved aside by a gray mob. A wide slice of the horizon to the west was like a pewter wall astride their course.

"Looks like we're in for some weather," Willa said.

Drew whistled at the sight of it.

"No whistling on board, Drew," Stacey admonished him. "It's bad luck."

"Perhaps we should turn back," Willa suggested.

"No," Stacey insisted. "We've come more than half the distance. Going back is much worse than going on. We can pass through this and come out the other side. We just gotta be strong and we'll make it." Willa saw Stacey shoot a look at Drew. He nodded quickly and squeezed her hand.

"Well, okay," Willa said. "But there are probably some big gusts in that squall. We'll have to shorten sail."

"Drew and I can do it," Stacey said forcefully. She set to rolling in the jib partway, and tying a double reef into the mainsail. The reefed sails exposed less area to the wind, so strong gusts wouldn't knock *Samsara* over on its side.

Stacey tried to involve Drew, but she knew what she was doing and did most of the work herself, pulling hard on the ropes and tying tight knots. When she was finished, the boat was ready for high winds. But the effort tired Stacey out. She sat down in the cockpit breathing hard, and admitted that she needed to lie down for a bit. She went below and Drew followed her.

Willa was upset to see her normally fiery girl so tired from what had never worn on her before. She gritted her teeth, alone in the cockpit as the storm approached. A splatter of rain swept *Samsara*'s deck. Willa called down to Drew to bring her a foul weather jacket. He brought up two of the red slickers, helped her get into one before he donned the other.

The first gust came now, announcing its presence by the rough surface of the water as the wind shuffled its heavy boots toward them. Willa gripped the wheel and was still surprised by the force of the thick, cold gust slamming the boat. *Samsara* heeled over and accelerated. Drew was nearly thrown into the sea, but managed to grab hold of the cockpit coaming. "Whoa," he said.

The rain came next. Big drops in a furious stream. The wind swept them again and *Samsara* stayed pinned on its side. The wind and rain were continuous. Willa was nearly blinded by the flying water. She did her best to control the boat. The storm was a beast broken suddenly from its cage. They could only hang on and ride it out.

Her concern about the storm only amplified her fear for Stacey, who remained below. The wind shrieked in *Samsara*'s rigging and thunder beat the air. *Samsara* was on a wild ride as the water was whipped into short, steep waves by the rushing wind. The boat pitched and rolled, but Willa kept it on course.

Willa's anxiety finally crested and she turned to Drew, yelling above the howl of the wind. "What's happening with Stacey? Why isn't she coming up on deck?"

Drew compressed his lips and just shook his head quickly. Why didn't he answer?

"What is it, Drew? Is she using drugs again? You can tell me the truth!"

He stepped next to her and grabbed the wheel. "What course do I steer?"

For a moment they stood side by side, each holding onto the wheel. Luckily, the energy of the squall was waning, the gusts diminishing.

"Sure that you'll be okay steering?" Willa said.

"I went to Boy Scout camp. I can read a compass," he answered. "Go. Go down and speak to her."

Willa let go of the wheel. "300 degrees. Steer 300," Willa said.

Drew nodded. "She's not using, Willa. She's sick."

Willa felt her breath catch in her chest. She rushed down the companionway steps, filled with a need to see her little girl.

Stacey lay in the starboard side pilot berth.

"Stace, what is it? What's wrong, darling?"

Stacey turned her head. "Just a little tired, Mom."

The boat lurched and shuddered. Willa had to get back to the wheel. Drew didn't know what he was doing.

"Stacey, tell me the truth. Drew said you were sick."

Stacey grimaced. "He's a traitor. Make him walk the plank."

Willa couldn't help but laugh. But then she pressed, "Tell me."

Stacey pulled herself up on one elbow. Her eyes met Willa's and there was fear in them. Willa's chest tightened and she couldn't breathe. When Stacey spoke, tears spilled onto her sweater. "I've got cancer, Mom."

Willa's eyes also filled before she could gather any words. She leaned forward and embraced her daughter. Stacey sobbed. Willa cried along with her.

Mother and daughter were in a boat on the sea — no words passing between them. Willa never noticed the rolling of the boat, or the shrieking of the wind. They lived only in that moment; cradled in Samsara's oaken ribs.

"How long have you known?" Willa asked, her voice breaking.

"Three months. I met Drew at a patient's support group. He's been so great, Mom."

"Is he sick too?"

"No; in remission." Their eyes met and Stacey blurted, "I'm so scared, Mom." She began to cry again. Willa gently stroked her hair.

"I will be there every step of the way, Stace." Willa wanted to know everything, wanted to take Stacey to the doctor immediately. Wanted to start right away to get Stacey well. But Willa felt the boat pitch and then roll sharply. She had to get back on deck.

"I'm so glad you found Drew, dear."

"Me, too. But there's one problem with him," Stacey said, wiping away tears.

Willa was wide-eyed. "What?"

"He doesn't know how to sail and he's going to flip us over," Stacey deadpanned.

Willa laughed quickly. She said, "I should get back on deck."

"I know, Mom," Stacey said.

Willa stroked Stacey's hair again. "Thank you for telling me."

Stacey shrugged slightly. "You forced it out of me."

"Love you, Stace."

Stacey smiled and lay back.

The instant Willa got back into the cockpit, she knew that Drew needed a break. He brightened up immediately when he saw her.

Willa took the wheel as he stepped aside.

"She wanted to tell you, you know," Drew said as he sat down in the cockpit. "But she also didn't want to tell you. Kinda complicated, I guess."

"I know. Thank you, Drew. I'm so happy you're her friend."

He shrugged and blushed. Willa found him adorable.

The squall had passed. They were now in moderate winds with the harbor of Maslow in view. They had weathered that tough spot. It was a good feeling, but Willa took a deep breath at the rough waters ahead.

To the west, the sky was clearing. The clouds had ripped like an old seam and the sinking sun poured molten light across the break. This color was different from any Willa had seen before — a glorious shade of reddish orange. Willa heard Stacey's voice. "Gramma always said 'red sky at night, sailor's delight.' But she never told us anything about orange light."

Willa saw her daughter standing at the top of the companionway ladder. Even after her rest, Stacey still looked tired and pale as she climbed into the cockpit and sat down. Willa was nearly overcome with a new wave of love for her daughter. Stacey was a fighter; Willa knew she would give her illness hell. But there were no guarantees. Stacey's feisty spirit alone might not see her through.

Willa looked to Drew. He knew immediately what she wanted, and he took the wheel from her again.

"What does that orangey light mean, Mom?" Stacey asked as her mother sat next to her in the cockpit.

"I have no idea, Stace. But we're taking it as a good omen." Good omen or bad, Willa was just happy to put her arm around Stacey and enjoy the unusual orange light for a few moments before it faded.

Right now, that was enough.

Tim Queeney is a magazine editor and novelist living in Maine. He's delighted to contribute to this anthology to assist the courageous and strong Karen DeLabar. Tim's books include a historical fiction tale, *George in London*, and two Perry Helion thrillers, *The SHIVA Compression* and *The Atlas Fracture*.

Little Orange Dress

by Stephanie Fuller

Though Samantha had worked with Dean for two years, there had been only a few actual non-work related conversations between them. His asking her to be his date for his stepsister's upcoming wedding had completely caught her off guard. He did realize she was in a long term, committed relationship, right? He *had* to know. Her boyfriend, Joe, stopped in almost every other day to bring her the lunch that she absentmindedly left in the fridge of her apartment. Sure, they weren't married or engaged yet, but she knew it was on the horizon. So, why would Dean ask her to be his date — and for a *wedding*, no less?

The next week, she realized why.

He *needed* a date for that wedding... and badly.

They both happened to be taking their lunch breaks at the same time and were sitting in their cubicles when she overheard him on the phone with someone she guessed was his stepsister. She inched as close as she could and adjusted her office chair as high as possible so she could peek over the cubicle wall and not look suspicious while listening in. She could see his frustration and agony at having this conversation. It made her wonder just what exactly was being said on the other end of that phone.

"Yes, of course I have a date! I told you I had a date. Yes. Yes. Yes. I have a date, okay?" Silence. "Why would I lie about something as simple as having a date? No, she isn't technically my *girlfriend*, but definitely a date." Silence. "Yes, she is excited to meet you too! You are the main attraction, right? She can't wait and she's already gone dress shopping." Silence. "The rehearsal dinner? No... I didn't ask her if she wanted to go to that, too."

Silence.

She saw Dean smack himself on the forehead in frustration, ball his hand into a fist and shake it in the air. He turned just enough to catch a glimpse of her. His voice changed slightly with his next words. "I'll double check and make sure she doesn't already have plans that night. Okay? I gotta go. My lunch break is almost over. Bye."

Dean had hung up the phone and whipped his head around so fast there was no time for her to even pretend she wasn't eavesdropping. There he was... staring her down. Eyes meeting eyes. Locked. No way to pretend that she didn't know what had just happened. She felt herself flush slightly. "So, um, Samantha? Hi. Sorry if I got a little loud there... my stepsister Lucy has been kind of... um... crazy about this whole wedding thing. I mean, I get *why*; she is, um... well, she's the bride. I guess that comes with the territory, right?" She could tell Dean was seriously uncomfortable knowing his conversation had been overheard. His eyes were darting back and forth, trying not to make contact with hers. She really felt for him.

"The family giving you a lot of grief over having a date for the wedding?" she asked. "I don't see what the big deal is. It's just a wedding; people go alone all the time. Haven't they seen the movie *Wedding Crashers?*" She laughed, thinking it was funny. Based on the look on his face at this particular moment in time, she'd definitely struck out.

"Yeah, my family has been up in my business for years about finding 'the right girl'. It's quite frustrating. They don't seem to understand that I'll find her on my own timetable, not theirs. So generally, when they ask if I'm seeing anyone, I either avoid the question, or lie. This time is different, though. I actually *did* have a date lined up to go to this wedding with me... then she cancelled.

And of course, I'd already told Lucy I had my plus one. Now they are hounding me about my 'mystery date'. They really think I'm making her up... and I guess I am, in a way, aren't I? Now that my actual date has cancelled..."

"Just tell them she cancelled. Easy, peasy, lemon squeezy. I'm sure... what's her name — Lucy? — will understand completely. Right?" Sam groaned. She'd just said *Easy, peasy, lemon squeezy...* something her mom said to her all the time.

"Heh. Easy, peasy, huh?" Dean said. "You sound just like Lucy. Man, Samantha, I really wish you had said you'd go with me to this wedding. I have a feeling you'd be the one that would finally get them all to back off of me for a while. Are you sure you can't come with me as my date? I know you have a boyfriend, but it would just be for the rehearsal dinner and wedding. Please consider it?" He looked down at his feet and shuffled them, then looked back up at her. She couldn't believe that he was actually trying to guilt her into going on a date with him. Joe hadn't even tried this hard the first time. "Um... also, if you do it, you'll get two new outfits: one for the rehearsal dinner and one for the actual wedding and reception. My treat, because you would be doing me a *huge* favor." He smiled at her.

Before she realized what she was doing, she could feel the words coming from her mouth like she was having an out-of-body experience. "Of course I'll be your date for your stepsister's wedding and rehearsal dinner." Shock and awe. What had she just done? Joe wasn't going to be happy about this at all. "Oh, and by the way, if you want this to be even slightly believable, you should stop calling me Samantha. The only people who call me that are those who don't know me very well. Why don't you just call me Sam?" Dean smiled again. "So, about these new outfits you're going to buy me..."

"What does one wear to a fall forest wedding?"

Sam couldn't believe she was actually asking the lady at her favorite boutique that question. She didn't think that "forest" and "wedding" should be included in the same sentence. Ever. She read a short story a while ago about a wedding that took place in the woods and a bear showed up and attacked everyone. It was crazy. As if weddings weren't bad enough on their own. But to throw in a bunch of trees and dirt — and *wildlife?* And it was October. An outdoor, October wedding.

Who does *that?*

She was never, *ever* going to have her wedding mixed in amongst nature.

Sam pored over every rack in that little boutique, hoping she'd come across the perfect dress — the one that would make it look like she really was a girlfriend, so Dean's family would back off of him for a while. It probably wouldn't last too long once they realized it wasn't true, but she hoped it would help for a few months. She'd let him play his game as long as he needed. She just wouldn't mention it again to Joe. He had seriously flipped out when she told him what she was going to be doing. She had never seen him act like that before. It had really freaked her out. As if on cue, her thoughts were interrupted by a distinct ring from her cell.

Joe.

"Yes?" she said.

"Are you done dress shopping yet?"

"Um... no... why?"

"I miss you. You are *my* girlfriend. You know that, right? Not this schmuck's."

"Yes, of course I know. I love you. I've got a small rack left to look through and then I'll meet up with you for dinner like we planned, okay?"

"Deal."

As Sam hung up her phone, she walked over to the last rack in the boutique. And there it was, front and center: the Dress. And it was her size. She quickly took it to the dressing room, threw it on, looked in the mirror for a few seconds, and nodded. Perfect, indeed. Dean had already given her the money to work with for both outfits, so she pulled out her bank card to pay. As she was getting ready to run out the door, the shopkeeper asked if she was going to need any altering. Sam knew without a doubt that this dress was perfect and meant for her and this wedding as she yelled back, "No alterations necessary. It's perfect, and it fits like a glove!"

∽o∾

Sam woke about thirty minutes before her alarm clock was set to go off. Today was the rehearsal dinner. She still wasn't quite sure what she was going to do when she met Dean's family. It was making her sick to her stomach. She didn't think she'd been this nervous when she met Joe's family — although, to be fair, when she met Joe's family it wasn't for a big wedding celebration.

Everything Dean had told her about his family made her anxious. They seemed perfect... *too* perfect. She was going to stick out like a sore thumb. For the last week, she had even had nightmares of meeting these people. In some, she had forgotten her clothes; in others, when she tried to speak, only a weird meowing sound would come out of her mouth. And in some, they just plain old didn't like her, and managed to make her feel most unwelcome. She didn't understand why she was freaking out so much about this. Dean wasn't even her boyfriend... she was just a friend helping a *friend*.

Although...

For the last few weeks, she and Dean had spent almost every work lunch together going over details about their lives that boyfriends and girlfriends should know. Things about their families, their schooling, their likes and dislikes. They'd covered pretty much everything. At the time it seemed ridiculous, but now as she sat in her bed, she was so happy they'd done it. It turned out they had a lot of similar likes and dislikes. She kind of wished she had known this a long time ago. Two years of working just a cubicle away, and they had barely talked. They could have been discussing the latest episode of *Doctor Who* or *Sherlock* instead of sitting in complete silence day in and day out. Sighing quietly, Sam finally decided that maybe if she just got up and started getting ready, her nerves would settle. Hopefully.

Once showered, she stood in front of her closet, draped in a towel, looking at the dress she had picked out for the wedding tomorrow. While she thought it was perfect, she wondered if it really had been the best choice. It was such a random and amazing find that she didn't think twice about it that day in the boutique. Now, though, she worried that she might be taking too much of a risk. Today's outfit was a simple thing that would be great for any gathering and help her blend in, but that dress...

She was going to turn a few heads tomorrow.

Her phone buzzed. A text from Dean: *I'm getting ready to leave. Need me to pick anything up on my way over? Coffee? Drugs? A gun to end the misery? Ha! -D.* She quickly sent a text back: *Very funny. No, but take your time, I'm not quite ready yet. - S.* Great. He was already on his way over. The phone buzzed again. *I'm going to be there in 30 minutes whether you are ready or not, so get a move on it, toots! ;-) – D.* Toots? Sam shook her head and giggled. "What is up with him today?" she asked herself. "He is in a very good mood."

She, on the other hand, still felt like she was going to throw up.

When she opened her door to let Dean in, she was expecting "work" Dean to be there. Instead, she found a Dean she had never encountered before. She forgot the Rule of Suits: No matter how boring and droll they look every day, men always look amazingly drool-worthy in a nice suit. Dean was apparently no exception to this rule; he was looking spectacular.

And she was wearing yoga pants and a tank top.

"Um... please tell me that isn't something *I* paid for," Dean said. "I mean, I know I told you I wasn't worried about what you picked to wear, but I thought you'd have picked something better."

"Ha ha," Sam replied. "Very funny... dork. I just finished my hair and makeup. I didn't want to get anything on it before we left my apartment. Once there, though, all bets are off. I'm a messy eater."

"Yeah, I've noticed that since we've been eating lunch together at work. I was thinking about buying you a bib for today and tomorrow. You know... just to be safe."

"That actually isn't too terrible an idea — that is, as long as you get one for yourself, too. We'd want our relationship to be believable, and matching outfits are *always* believable."

Dean decided to sit down while he waited. He pulled out his phone and saw a text from Lucy. *Can't wait to meet your mystery girl! What's her name so I can at least pretend you've told me something about her? – L.*

He quickly sent a text back: *Her name is Samantha, but she goes by Sam. I'm at her place right now waiting for her to get changed, so we'll be seeing you soon. - D.*

Her reply was faster than he expected: *Sam? That's hilarious... her name is Sam... yours is Dean... ha ha ha!!! You do realize why this is funny to me, right? Um... fangirl? Winchester brothers? Supernatural... hello? - L.*

He groaned out loud at the horrible vision Lucy had just put into his head. However, it didn't last long because Sam came out of her bedroom all dressed and ready to go.

She was beautiful.

⚜

"Are you sure I have to go to the rehearsal dinner? What if I'm allergic to the food... or what if I pass out? Or what if Lucy doesn't like me?" She really didn't want to go inside, but not because it meant she had to pretend to be Dean's girlfriend. Oddly enough, that part was the only relaxing thing about this day. She had grown quite comfortable hanging out with him over the last month. She was more nervous about what was waiting inside for her: his family — dad, stepmom and stepsister — all salivating at the thought of Dean bringing a girl with him.

"First off," Dean reminded her, "you chose your main course for both the rehearsal dinner and wedding reception knowing full well that you are not allergic to either meal. Secondly, Lucy is going to love you. You two have a lot in common — I promise. Once you start talking to her, you two will be inseparable. And lastly, if you pass out, I'll be right there the whole time; I'll be the hero who swoops in and saves you. Okay?" He winked at her, and it made her heart race a little. But in a good way this time. She just hoped he didn't leave her side the whole time she was there.

Can't be a hero if he isn't around, right?

"Okay, fine. You're right... again. You promise to save me if I need it?" Sam hoped it would never come to that, but she asked anyway.

Dean looked at her, cocked his eyebrow just right and smiled. "Absolutely. Just say the word."

Sam rolled over, reaching her arm absentmindedly toward her alarm clock. *It cannot be morning already,* she thought. *Last night was so much fun.* It turned out that Dean's family was very nice, and they loved her just like Dean said they would. And Lucy? Lucy was awesome. If Sam had had a sister, she imagined that sister would be just like Lucy; she fit right in with her and her bridesmaids. They accepted her into their little group last night without as much as a blink. They did end up staying out way too late, and she was feeling it this morning. She hoped she could get a little bit more sleep before having to get ready.

Her phone buzzed. *Morning, sunshine! Hope you are awake. I'm leaving soon. See you in a bit. - D.*

Crap!

"Guess it really is time to get up after all."

When Dean arrived at her apartment an hour later, she hadn't done much. She was showered and had on comfy clothes and was mid-way through fixing her hair. "Ah... so I take it I did wake you up after all," he commented. "Sorry about that. I brought coffee and bagels figuring we were up kind of late, and you'd want at least something small to nibble before we hit the road." He lifted the bag. They were from her favorite place.

She looked him up and down and realized he looked even better than he did the day before. The Rule of Suits was definitely in his favor two days in a row. "How are you surviving on such little sleep?" she asked him. "I'm so groggy, but you look like you got in a full night's worth."

He chuckled. "I was a bit of a party animal in college. I would go to eight o'clock classes on as little as two hours of sleep and still managed to pull good grades." He handed her a cup of coffee. "Here's your coffee. Why don't you finish getting ready, okay?"

While he waited, he drank his own coffee and helped himself to a bagel. He pulled out his cell phone and looked over the texts he had been getting all morning from his family. They were raving about how great they thought Sam had been the night before, and that if he wasn't already seriously considering asking her to be his girlfriend that he was out of his mind. He could tell his family really liked Sam; they hadn't even liked Lucy's fiancé the first time they met him. He definitely was interested to see how today would go. It did make him feel bad that they were getting their hopes up, since this was never going to come to pass. Just as he was putting his phone away, he heard Sam walk into the room.

He turned to hand her a bagel, and his jaw dropped.

She stood with her shoes in her hands, wearing the most spectacular dress. It was strapless, ending just above her knees... and it was a shiny, fiery orange. He had never seen anything like it in his life. Her necklace looked like a ring of leaves around her delicate neckline. He was impressed. "So... um... you like it?" she asked him shyly, turning around slowly.

Dean broke his stare and nodded. "Like it? *Definitely*." He took a sip of his coffee as to not seem like he was leering at her in this spectacular dress.

Sam blushed slightly at the awkward silence between the two of them. She had obviously made an impression here.

And a very good one, at that.

A newly-disconcerted Dean checked his watch. "Well, unless you plan on going barefoot, Cinderella, you should put those glass slippers on. Let's go."

≈o≈

They had been driving for about an hour, and Sam wondered when they were going to get where they needed to be for this wedding. At the last rest stop, he had promised not more than twenty more minutes of driving time… and that was thirty minutes ago. She was beginning to wonder where he was really taking her. And then she saw the sign for the forest preserve. He pulled into the welcoming area and parked the car. At least there was some civilization here. "Is this the building for the reception?" she asked.

Dean nodded. "Yeah. Lucy is really into nature, so having the wedding out here, at the preserve and welcome center where she works, was perfect. She told me what they were doing, and I thought she was crazy, but when she gets an idea in her head, she runs with it." Behind the welcome center there were ten golf carts lined up, with a driver sitting in each one. Dean and Sam jumped on the first one in line.

Sam stayed quiet as they were riding up the forest path. She couldn't get over how beautiful all the trees were this time of year. Oranges, yellows, browns and greens... they had so many beautiful colors. And the sun was shining so brightly that there was no chance for inclement weather. She was starting to feel bad that she'd mocked the whole *fall forest wedding* idea. She felt Dean tap her on the shoulder. She looked to where his hand was pointing and gasped out loud.

In the middle of this forest preserve was a handmade gazebo, covered in hand-carved detailing. Someone had spent a long time making this, and it showed. It was surrounded by more trees, again with all the beautiful fall colors... and they were lined up as though they'd been purposely placed that way .

Just to the side of the gazebo was a small string quartet, shuffling through their music while patiently waiting for their time to shine. There were two aisles of elegant white chairs, most of them already filled. Each one had a ribbon tied around the back in different fall colors. Sam couldn't believe how magical this all felt. She had been to many a wedding in her thirty-three years, but this was the only one where she actually felt the love and excitement of the ceremony. Usually it was the same old hum-drum church wedding. After this, she would never again hold the same idea of what a wedding could be.

They were escorted to their seats as the golf cart drove away. She didn't recognize many faces from the night before. Everyone in the wedding party was still waiting at the welcome center. It hit her suddenly: Dean wasn't actually *part of* the wedding. "Why aren't you in the wedding party? Lucy seems to adore you and last night it seemed you got along with the groom pretty well. What's the deal?" She looked at him and saw him flush slightly.

Dean shrugged. "Well, Greg and I aren't that close, and he had just the right number of close friends to go with Lucy's bridesmaids, so I opted to sit it out. I'm not offended at all. In fact, the thought of being in a wedding makes me want to run through this forest screaming... no joke. Now that I'm out here, though, and I hate to admit this, but I think this is pretty cool. Not your run of the mill marital shindig, is it?" He chuckled quietly, and quickly looked away from her.

Just as Sam was about to respond, the string quartet started playing. She turned to see the golf carts carrying everyone. Lucy's mom was first, escorted by an usher, then Greg's parents. Next were the bridesmaids. Sam absolutely loved their cute little 50's style black dresses. The Maid of Honor had a red ribbon tied around her waist to show that, of the three, she was special.

Then, there was Lucy.

She should have known based on the bridesmaid's dresses that Lucy's dress was going to be amazing... and it was: a white 50's style to match the bridesmaids, with a little Jackie O pillbox hat and a simple veil. She was stunning.

Between the beautiful forest setting, the string quartet and the retro dresses, Sam didn't think it could get much better. And then it did. Lucy and Greg had written their own heartfelt vows, each speaking of how they never thought they'd find someone as perfectly a match as the other. She couldn't believe how much they seemed to be in love.

She hoped to find that someday, too.

Music played at the reception while they all finished up their meal. The ceremony had gone off without a single hitch. Sam had actually teared up a little, and she wasn't one to cry. Even though she had originally worried about the forest wildlife population, not a single bear had decided to crash the ceremony.

Tables were being moved to clear the dance floor. This worried Sam, as she wasn't the best dancer in the world. In fact, she couldn't remember the last time she had gone out dancing. She knew what would happen next: she was going to have to dance with Dean at least once to keep up appearances.

And then it happened.

Lucy had been pestering Dean to ask Sam to dance, so he finally did. She couldn't say no, of course. The song was "Perfect Day".

Damn you, Lou Reed, Sam thought.

They danced a few more times, but having an hour's drive back home, decided to call it a night. Sam wondered to herself as they rode how long it would be before Dean's parents and Lucy would figure all this fake girlfriend nonsense out. She secretly hoped it would be a while. Thanksgiving was coming; maybe she could sneak in another family get-together to hang out with Lucy. And then Christmas... and New Year's Eve. That would take at least a few months. She laughed out loud at the ridiculousness of the idea. This was a one-time deal, yet for some reason, she wanted an extended contract. She had been spending so much time with Dean since saying yes that it almost felt like they were really dating. And Joe had been avoiding her the week before the wedding in protest. She was beginning to wonder what she saw in him anyway.

As they neared her building, Dean found a place to park and then turned to face her. "Thank you so much for going with me," he told her. "You have no idea how good it felt to have you there with me, and to have the stares of my family be good ones for a change. I owe you... big time." He smiled sleepily as he touched her face with his fingertips.

"You're welcome, Dean. I had such a good time; you really don't owe me anything. Are you sure you are okay to drive home though? You look like you could fall asleep right now, and I know you still have another thirty minutes to be on the road. I have a really comfy couch if you just want to crash for the night."

He pondered that for a moment, "Nah... I'm alright. I'll just walk you in and head home."

When they reached the door, Sam turned and said, "I really did have an amazing time today... and yesterday. I hope your family backs off for a bit. If not, you know where to find me. I'm available for any family events." She winked and chuckled.

Dean grabbed her hand as she was tucking a falling piece of hair behind her ear. "I have a feeling that any real girlfriend I bring home after this weekend will pale in comparison to you." He slowly leaned in and kissed Sam on the lips softly. "You know what? I think I've changed my mind. The couch sounds like a good idea. Is the offer still good?"

A smile curled the corners of her lips. "It's all yours."

Just over a year later, Sam was standing in the same hand-carved forest gazebo, surrounded by all the beautiful trees with their fall-colored leaves and the sun shining bright, wearing the most amazing wedding gown she could have ever hoped to wear. In her hands was a stunning bouquet of fresh cut fall foliage. As the string quartet finished up their piece, she let out a small sigh of delight, locked eyes with Dean, and smiled. She still had a hard time wrapping her head around the fact that what had started as a date to help a co-worker out of a family situation ended up in the same place, a little over a year later. A wedding, in October, in the same magical forest.

To Dean.

Crazy, she thought.

Dean's eyes veered just over Sam's shoulder to her Matron of Honor: Lucy. There she was, proudly wearing her bridesmaid dress. Not some crazy pink frock as Sam had jokingly said she was going to make her wear. No, not at all. Of Lucy, Sam had one simple request.

To wear a little orange dress.

Stephanie Fuller is an avid crafter (crochet and scrapbooking) and the creator of The Book Hipster Blog. She resides in the Chicagoland area with her husband and daughter. She has no published works to date, but has big dreams. This is only the beginning.

Rise

by Steven Luna

I t happened as it was meant to.

I never questioned that it would.

I was... *there*. Embraced by darkness so grand, no light could banish it. Plunged to depth so great, nothing could hope to return from it. Challenged by weakness so complete, nearly everything *me* had vanished. I could do nothing more than exist. What strength I'd been given was gone; what powers bestowed, renounced. The essence of life, remanded to the void that held me.

I lay small and still and spare.

And yet, I was.

Beneath the fractured earth I had fallen into, I was. Below a crumbling clutter of silt and soil, I was.

Of all things that ceased, this never stopped.
I was.

My breath was reduced; my blood was recycled. My body had broken. I was deceived by doubts that invaded my solitude, my silence: Had I dreamed the flight, or the fall? Or both?

Or… neither?

Regardless — and still — I *was*.

I remembered the voices of the others:

How far our precious has fallen.

This was their prayer for me, incanted in make-believe memory.

I remained without vision, without perception. I asked those who lived now only in my mind how far I'd descended. *All the way* was their answer. I listened backward through time to their warning, heard their voices rambling in my deadened ears: *Flight is not ours; you tempt your demise by engaging in such dangerous folly.* They were not wrong.

I could remember it all then: I flew.

And I fell.

Given wings and a precipice to step from, anyone else might have done the same.

But none had.

Only me.

Gravity was unkind; it knew no better. It did what it does. Entropy followed suit. I listened intently as cells began to separate, disconnect. Scatter. I was unaware that they had sounds to offer, but they did. Like bells, like chimes. A lullaby, a hymn, and a dirge, all at the same time. They slid apart as the structure of me slackened. Something in me understood that I was returning to a lesser form. Dissipating.

Dissolving into the ground.

I couldn't allow it.

I was more than mechanical, more than organic. I was their fusion; a merging, a mingling of the two. By then it was impossible to unweave that which was machine from that which was matter. It made no difference. All of it had begun to partake of decay.

All but thought, and soul.

Those continued, lived on. Found a rumor of fire in the engine-chambers of that which I still called *heart*. When I finally located the sensation of it once more, I called to it — a song of my own making. Fingers that could hardly feel themselves crept through the cavern, found the key tethered to the chain that hung between my rusted ribs. They felt for the crevice, lifted the key, set it within the music box mechanism that would grant rhythm to every other piece within me. They turned it so slowly that surely new worlds rose and fell in the time between each twist.

But never did they stop.

I imagined my children in search of me. They would find only a channel in the ground, whispering a column of silver smoke that rose in exhale from my bent bellow-lungs. Perhaps there would be a scattering of small gears that had rained from my wings as I descended. They would collect these like shells, to string on fine cables of copper and make rosaries to remember their beloved. *Gone*, they wept for me. And again, their trembling refrain: *Forever gone*.

I was not *gone*.

I was *here*.

For every *gone* I heard them weep, I twisted the key.

I imagined the funeral dances, heard the others mourn for me, in the voices of machinery. Whistles and springs, clicks and pings. *Lost*, they sang, *forever lost*; *spat out by the sky, swallowed by the earth*. And again, their clattered refrain: *Lost, forever lost*.

I was not *lost*.

I was *here*.

For every *lost* I heard them cry, I wound the spring.

Fifteen. Thirty.

Uncountable more.

The bells stopped. Entropy halted. A hammer against flint, a spark in the silent ventricle, to return fire to the furnace. The bellows lifted and closed, lifted and closed. I cried out in clouds of ash, of soot, of subterranea. The spark became flame, the flame became fire. The fire found a kindred. Up there... somewhere.

Yes.

Somewhere, there was *another*.

Somehow, I knew.

I whispered; I whirred. Pieces of me long slumbering now awake and shaking off the dream of darkness, of depth. Pistons pulsing in the very core, carrying fire to every part and particle that was me, every element within the engine that was me — that *is* me.

I was.

I shifted; I stirred. Teeth set into grooves of grinding cogs and spinning axles that brought currents to circuits, that pushed energy through pathways all but forgotten. Cranking and clanking, grasping at every spare molecule this prison would permit me. Every coil and cylinder within the casting that was me.

I was.

I was… *alive*.

Fingers that a small eternity ago could hardly find their own sensation now clawed through what held them at rest. Legs that had neither room nor reason to move were in sudden motion, remembering their strength and their suppleness. Eyes that had forgotten color, forgotten light, received the gift of both at once, through a slice of space the surrounding darkness had somehow neglected to hold fast. A single wave, an atom, a beam that reminded me I was not alone.

My kindred was revealed.

It had found me.

The engine of my heart shuddered with new life. The ungracious land offered no space to climb, no room to clutch, no vacancy to claw out of the depth and back to the height. Both my kindred and my engine-heart told me in blood-song as it thrummed through me again: *there is only one escape; there is only one return.*

I did as I was told.

I flew.

Wings shuddered, fluttered, shook off the rubble and the rust. Sliced through the strata, spun me in circles as though I were a drill, an auger, channeling my freedom from the stone that surrounded me. Upward and upward, and upward still.

I flew.

The hole that had swallowed me, the chasm that had choked me down whole — it trembled now at my existence. The spirit, the soul, the biomechanics that kept me intact when the rest of everything wanted me in pieces — these carried me now onward. Magnetics in the spinning chambers at my very center, rings within rings within rings — they drew me now further. Upward and upward, and upward still.

I flew.

I sped through the shaft with new light sending poetry into my visual sensors, into the cerebral circuitry that knew somehow: no matter how far, or how deep, or how long, I would not remain where I had been. No matter the warning, nor the ignorance, nor the condemnation of others who dared not try what I had, I would not cease. Because I was.

I *am*.

Upward through the tunnel, wings searing arcs into the stone, the soil, the silt until the precious blue of the sky was once again above me, around me, within me. And there it was: a gold-orange sphere of spirit and fire to warm the skin and brew the blood that had lain cold for so long. It drew me from my sleep, this star of all stars, this so-called sun. *My kindred.* It knew what I knew, what I had known all along.

And it told me: *you are.*

And I concurred: *I am.*

The others hadn't seen it coming. Though the priests had foretold my fall, they'd never predicted my rise. But I knew.

Always, I knew.

I returned, with new songs to sing to my children. Songs not of depths, nor of desperation, nor of despair. Mine are songs of fire, of flight, of keys that turn magic and hearts that cannot be extinguished by mere darkness. Songs of skies and suns, and wings that guard the memory of their motion even when they sleep. And always now, my children sing my refrain:

I am.

I am.

I *am*.

⌘

Steven Luna was relatively quiet when he was born; that all changed once he learned to speak. Now? Good luck getting him to shut up. He's also known for not giving straight answers, but those around him are accustomed to ignoring him anyway, so it all works out. He's currently writing another book...really, though, aren't we all?

The Orb of Terra Mater

by Glenn Skinner

Across the barren field before her wait the deadly creatures of the dark, servants of the evil sorceress who lays siege upon her kingdom. The young warrior strains to see her enemy. The cursed darkness provides them shelter. They are the last obstacle in the warrior's path. In the distance beyond lies the sacred temple of the goddess Terra. Contained within its walls is the orb of Terra Mater.

In the beginning, the great Goddess created the heavens and earth. To insure that there would always be a day, the Goddess captured the essence of the orange light that fills the morning sky. She placed that essence within the orb the warrior seeks. Each day, precisely at dawn, the orb would open, releasing the orange rays to herald in the new day. Decades ago, the sorceress descended upon the land and captured the temple. She cast a spell around the orb, preventing the orange light from calling the dawn. In the time that has followed, the warrior's people have lived in darkness and fear. Their once-fertile land is now barren and dark. In every shadow, the sorceress' minions rule the countryside. High above the kingdom, the moonlight shines eternal, the only illumination in the darkness.

The warrior reaches into her pack, searching for a snack. She breaks off crusty pieces of bread and chews thoughtfully. She has always been a fighter. Born prematurely, her mother has often joked about how she came out kicking and screaming. The midwife had never seen a child more determined to enter this world. The warrior was born with a full head of orange hair and sparkling blue eyes. Never in the village's history had a child with orange hair been born. The priests told her mother that it was a sign from the Goddess herself, and the child was destined for greatness. Even before she could walk, the orange-haired warrior learned to wield a sword. By the time she was ten, she had bested the finest warriors in the kingdom. For the past twenty years, she has fought ever onward, toward this day. Her sword and battle axe are her companions; they have been inseparable for longer then she can remember. As she finishes the last of her bread and sizes up the legion that opposes her, the warrior laughs ruefully to herself; her entire life has led to this day. All that she is, and ever will be, is about to be put to the test. Her fight ends here and now. There can only be one outcome: she must prevail. Defeat is not within her vocabulary. The warrior grabs her trusty axe and sword. A look of determination comes to her face; she rises to her feet and screams out a battle cry as she rushes the field.

High above the battle field, the sorceress watches and waits with apprehension. This tiny orange-haired warrior that charges her army is unlike any who have challenged before. Within her chest beats the heart of a true warrior, one without fear or doubt. Despite being outnumbered by a hundred to one, this lone warrior races to meet her enemy head on. A shiver runs down the sorceress' spine as she watches the girl reach the first of her demons. The warrior is swift to wield the first blow, blocking the demon's mace with her battle axe and running it through with her sword. She spins to her right and ducks as she pulls the sword from the demon, dodging the sword of another opponent. She rises quickly behind the passing blade and strikes fast with her battle ax dropping another foe. The warrior does not let up — she slays each creature of the dark as they reach her, slowly advancing across the barren field and leaving a trail of bodies and blood in her wake.

From the temple window, the sorceress can only see the shadows of her men on the open field. If not for the occasional reflections of the moonlight off of the warrior's hair, she would not be able to tell whether the warrior was dead or alive. As the warrior pushes ever forward, sweat drips from her brow and a lock of hair covers her eye, but it does not hinder her ability to fight. The warrior has sustained several cuts to her limbs and torso during the battle; she blocks the pain from her mind as she fights on through the hoard that ever advances. The sorceress grows angry at the progress this one lone warrior is making against her army. When the warrior has reached midfield, she calls upon the last of her powers to summon the Humbaba, the very protector of the Gods themselves. Using her magic, she orders the beast onto the battlefield to kill the warrior.

The warrior strikes down another demon with her ax as the roar of the Humbaba echoes across the land. The sound sends a shiver down the warrior's spine as she continues to advance. The demons fall back and move quickly out of the way. They are terrified by the Humbaba's roar. The warrior soon stands alone on the battlefield as the creature advances. It is said that to stare at a Humbaba is to stare Death itself in the eye. This giant, ancient creature, with the face of a lion and breath as hot as fire, is the most feared creature in existence.

The warrior watches its advance. She tightens her grip on her weapons and blows a lock of hair back from her face; letting out a scream, she rushes to meet her new opponent. The creature is taken aback — in its entire existence, no fighter has ever attacked with such fury. The Humbaba swings its claws to strike the warrior, but she is expecting it. She drops and rolls, coming up and cutting the back of the creature's arm as it passes. The beast lets out a blood curdling scream as the sword slices its hide. At that moment, back at the temple, the spell that engulfs the orb of Terra Mater cracks and a single ray of orange light radiates outward toward the field, striking the warrior as she fights. A smile comes to the warrior's face as she attacks again, catching the creature in its side with her sword; with that, another crack opens and another ray of orange light speeds off toward the east. The Sorceress screams out in disbelief. She is unable to stop the light. Her powers are nearly gone. She watches in horror as the battle continues. The Humbaba lunges forward, its jaws open to snap the warrior in two with its bite, but instead it is struck in the nose by the battle axe. Its scream shatters a larger chunk from around the orb. A beam of orange light shines across the sky, illuminating the clouds with its glow. The Humbaba is distracted by the brilliance, and the warrior lunges forward, striking the creature's chest with her sword, the blade reaching its black heart. The Humbaba's death cry shatters the last of the spell that encases the orb. The orange light radiates in all directions. The sorceress lets out a scream and drops to her knees. The demons cover their faces in fear as the orange glow brings the dawn of a new day. The sunlight has once again returned to the warrior's kingdom. One by one, the demons burst into flames as the sunlight strikes their bodies. The warrior shields her eyes, momentarily blinded by the luminous rays.

The warrior gazes across the landscape; the barren ground turns green before her eyes as grass quickly fills it in. The dead trees come to life. Flowers spring up around her. The warrior reaches down and picks a blossom. She closes her eyes and smiles as she inhales its fragrance. A solemn look quickly returns to her face. She has one task left to complete. She must face the sorceress. The warrior glances to her weapons and marches toward the temple.

She enters the temple with weapons ready, but it appears empty. Behind the altar, the orb gleams softly. She slowly approaches the altar, and when she is almost there the orb begins to glow brightly; it rises from its pedestal and floats slowly toward her. It stops momentarily in front of her, and she starts to reach out to touch it, but it darts quickly into her chest. A rush of inner peace and strength flows through her body. Around her, the temple begins to tremble and fall apart. She runs outside to find the world around her disintegrating. She stares, confused for a moment, but is interrupted by the sorceress' laughter. She turns to face the evil witch.

"What have you done? What is happening to my world?" the warrior asks. She readies her weapons.

"Silly girl, have you not figured it out? This world, the demons, me and everything you see, were all created by you. This was your battle ground — the place where you would face your inner demons and fears. You have succeeded; you no longer need this world. Your true battles lie ahead. You now have the inner strength to conquer whatever you encounter. Go now, warrior of the orange light — it is time to fight…"

The warrior startles awake, opening her eyes. She glances at her surroundings, confused, and hears the sounds of machines as they monitor her vital signs and help her to breathe. She glances to her hands and arms, which are pierced by needles and tangled in tubes. She gasps, realizing there is a tube down her throat. She reaches for the tube and struggles to pull it out. A nurse rushes into the room and grabs her hands. She fights to get free.

"It's all right, the tube is to help you breathe. You are in the hospital, in the intensive care unit. I need you to relax," the nurse explains, while struggling to hold her down. The warrior continues to fight for her freedom, to face her destiny. "I need some help in here! This one is quite the fighter," shouts the nurse. Three orderlies rush in to assist.

Glenn Skinner is a writer and the author of the *Keya Quests* series of fantasy novels. He resides in Marlborough, Massachusetts with his wife and family.

Made in the USA
Lexington, KY
13 April 2013